Books by Dianne Pugh

Cold Call
Slow Squeeze
Fast Friends
Foolproof

Published by POCKET BOOKS

FOOLPROOF

FOOLPROOF

AN IRIS THORNE MYSTERY

Dianne Pugh

POCKET BOOKS
New York London Toronto Sydney Tokyo Singapore

This book is a work of fiction. Names, characters, places and incidents are products of the author's imagination or are used fictitiously. Any resemblance to actual events or locales or persons living or dead is entirely coincidental.

POCKET BOOKS, a division of Simon & Schuster Inc.
1230 Avenue of the Americas, New York, NY 10020

Pugh, Dianne G.
Foolproof : an Iris Thorne mystery / Dianne Pugh.
p. cm.
ISBN 0-671-01424-2
I. Title.
PS3566.U33F66 1998
813'54—dc21 97-52306
CIP

First Pocket Books hardcover printing April 1998

10 9 8 7 6 5 4 3 2 1

Printed in the U.S.A.

For Charlie

Acknowledgments

Special thanks to Linda Marrow and Amy Pierpont at Pocket Books, Anne Williams at Headline, Nicholas Ellison, Rowland Barber, Gerald Petievich, and Lee Gruenfeld.

For letting me pick their brains, my gratitude to Genie Bakale, Karen Bizzini, Ann Escue, Michelle LaPoint, Jeff McLellan, and Jennifer Urick.

And three twirls to Laury Bird, who appreciates the magic inherent in a staircase.

Prologue

"What makes you so sure he *wouldn't* try to kill you?"

"Alexa," Bridget Cross chided her friend. "Kip's not like that."

"Desperate people sometimes do desperate things."

"I've been married to Kip a long time. There are no surprises left."

"You've never seen him like this, with his back against the wall."

Shaking her head with amusement, Bridget gazed at her five-year-old daughter, who was leading the family German shepherd by a leash far enough ahead on the packed-dirt path to be out of earshot.

"Stetson, fetch!" Brianna threw a stick and the dog ran after it, his leash dragging on the ground. He picked up the stick but playfully dodged away whenever the child tried to take it from him.

Alexa added, "You never thought he'd cheat on you."

Bridget stopped smiling.

"The *nerve* of him, screwing around right under your nose

with that Toni person at the office. Of course, you're the last to find out." Apparently oblivious to her friend's uneasiness, Alexa went on. "You think she was the only one? Did you ask him?"

"I would prefer not talking about it."

Coldwater Canyon Park was almost deserted in the middle of a weekday afternoon. It was January in Los Angeles and hot, sunny, and windy thanks to a Santa Ana that had kicked up the day before, blowing dry desert air westward to the ocean. The women and child were bare-armed, the dog was panting, and the sky was as blue and brittle as glacier ice.

A gust of wind ruffled the dog's fur and blew Brianna Cross's long, dark hair, the crown gathered at the back of her head with a bright ribbon, over her shoulder and into her face. She decorously scraped it from her cheeks and patted it back into place while her mother watched, touched by the young child's newly grown-up demeanor.

"When are you going to tell him?" Alexa Platt asked.

Bridget sighed, almost with despair. "I don't know. I keep thinking we can work it out."

"You could, if he were willing. Seems he's made it clear he's not."

"The last thing I wanted was my daughter to be the product of a broken home, but I'm at my wit's end." Bridget grew pensive as she watched her daughter instruct the dog to sit and shake hands. "Maybe it'd be easier if Brianna and I moved out."

"No way! He's the one who should move out!" Alexa flicked back her long, blonde hair and planted her hands on her slender hips. "Why are you acting like such a wuss?" she complained. "You *are* afraid of him, aren't you?"

Bridget suddenly put out a warning hand for her friend to stop talking. She turned and frowned at the empty lane behind them.

The child, oblivious, continued playing and chatting to herself and the dog several yards away. Stetson, however, was looking in the same direction as Bridget, his ears pricked.

"What's wrong?" Alexa peered down the path but didn't see anyone.

The dog cocked his head and began to whimper at the sound of heavy footsteps on the sandy dirt.

A man with stringy, shoulder-length hair dressed in a khaki uniform rounded the curve.

"It's that groundskeeper guy," Alexa remarked under her breath.

Bridget exhaled with relief. "Afternoon."

He mumbled a greeting as he passed, not meeting their eyes. They watched as he disappeared around the bend in the path ahead of them.

"Ugh," Alexa commented. "He was staring at me when I was waiting for you in the parking lot. Gives me the creeps."

Bridget shook her head and resumed walking.

"What?" Alexa stroked her friend's arm. "Is there something you're not telling me?"

Bridget paused, as if debating whether to respond. "Lately, I've felt like someone's been following me. Watching me."

Alexa frowned with concern. "When?"

"Last week, in the parking lot at the office. Then, a few days later, at home outside the French doors."

"On the patio? Did you see anyone?"

"No. Just movement, a shape silhouetted by the pool light. The dog started barking, so I know I wasn't imagining it."

"Was Kip home?"

"He was at Pandora, working late on the new release . . . he claimed."

"You think it could have been him?"

"Why would Kip spy on me?"

"Maybe it was one of Kip's scorned lovers," Alexa said excitedly. "Maybe Toni."

Bridget raked her hand through her close-cropped hair. "The noise in the parking lot was probably my imagination. On the patio, it was probably a coyote, maybe the same one who jumped the fence and got our cat. Anyway, let's not talk about Kip's . . ." She looked askance.

"Keep the alarm on."

"I do now."

"You and Kip still have that gun?"

"I don't know how to use it."

"That wasn't what I was thinking."

"*Alexa,*" Bridget scolded.

A strong gust of warm wind blew, sending dry leaves and loose dirt scuttling down the path, pushing the women and the child to take a few quick steps. The dog, more surefooted and lower to the ground, was not affected.

"You have to admit that Kip has changed a lot in the past few years." Alexa blinked at a speck of dirt that had flown into her eye. "One minute, he's a . . ." She searched for the appropriate word.

"Geek?"

Alexa laughed. "I was going to say loner. But, okay, a geek. The next minute, he has groupies. I went through that 'you may kiss my ring' thing with Jim. But Kip's forgotten one thing—you made him what he is."

Bridget dismissed the comment with a shrug.

"C'mon, B, everyone knows it."

"We built the company together."

"You said you didn't want to talk about it, but," Alexa persisted, "I think Kip slept with Toni to punish you for taking the company in a direction he doesn't want it to go."

"That's occurred to me. But I can't worry about Kip's need for control." Bridget's tone was determined. "I have my daughter's welfare to consider. I'm not going to throw away her financial security just because her father doesn't want to answer to stockholders."

"Bottom line, it doesn't matter what Kip wants," Alexa added. "He gave you control of Pandora Software. He couldn't be bothered with all that icky, business stuff. He wants to spend his time being Mr. Creative Genius."

"I never thought it would matter unless push came to shove."

"It has. No wonder you're looking over your shoulder."

After admiring Alexa's new Jaguar convertible, the women said good-bye in the gravel parking lot near the park entrance. Bridget and Brianna pulled out first, rushing to avoid being late for the little girl's ballet class. Alexa, holding her car keys, waved until Bridget's Volvo had turned down the hill and slipped out of sight.

When Alexa had not returned home by 1 A.M., her husband called the police.

Chapter 1

When the shiny black BMW sped up and cut in front of Iris Thorne, she knew why. It was one of those tit-for-tat freeway things. All she had done was change lanes, angling her 1972 give-me-a-ticket-red Triumph TR6 into position to make the connection from the eastbound 10 to the northbound 110. That was all. Nothing personal, but the situation looked as if it was going to take a dive down that slippery slope. Before she jumped, she had to ask herself one thing: Did she feel lucky?

"Well, do you, lady?" she asked aloud.

Her actions answered without hesitation. She floored the Triumph, its tractor engine squealing with delight, and sped within inches of the Beemer's bumper. The male driver—darkly tanned with a bald spot—was casually smoking a cigarette, dangling his arm out the window as if he were without a care in the world. Iris knew better. She bore down on him, getting so close she made herself gasp. Then she swung left into lane one, the fast lane, and flew past the Beemer, taking full advantage of the spotty traffic. The Triumph's top was down and her blonde hair whipped in the wind. She knew she cut quite a picture. When she was many car lengths ahead, she eased back in front of him and copped his casual attitude, sans cigarette and with more hair. When he attempted a counteroffensive, she sped up, not letting him pass.

There they were. Total strangers duking it out with tons of high-priced metal, jeopardizing themselves, their vehicles, their comprehensive and collision insurance coverage—and for what? It was just another sunny day in LA. A slow car in Iris's path gave the Beemer an opportunity to regain his position in front of the Triumph. The driver did so for no other reason than to exert this final power play, since he had reached his exit. He made a beeline for the off-ramp, flipping Iris off in farewell. She blew him a kiss. Who loves ya, baby?

A large truck was next to her in the now slowing traffic. She quickly tugged at the hem of her short skirt which had crept dangerously high as it tended to do when she was driving the TR. But today the usually PG-rated show in the TR's driver seat was an inch from an X rating. She was bottomless underneath the miniskirt. No panties. No panty hose. Nothing but skin.

Maybe it was her atypical dishabille that was making her feel reckless. Maybe it was the Santa Ana winds that had been blowing hot and dry, casting a spell over the Southland, turning the second week of January into summer on steroids. Maybe it was the excitement of having picked up from the escrow office the keys to the new house she could barely afford. Or maybe she was in love.

She adjusted her sunglasses, picked up her cellular phone from the passenger seat, and punched in a number. "Garland Hughes's room, please." She hummed tunelessly while she was being connected, taking her left hand off the steering wheel and driving with her knees as she raised her hips and gave the stubborn skirt a hard tug. "Hello there," she cooed.

"Well, hello yourself."

"I was hoping you hadn't left for the airport yet."

"I was lingering, having another cup of coffee and thinking about this morning and how nice it was and about you and how nice you are and how especially nice you were this morning."

"You were pretty nice yourself."

"I was?"

"You were . . . delicious."

They both giggled. They were in that silly, giddy first stage of romance. Touches burned, kisses were dizzying, love songs on the radio were magical and Iris had moments of silliness that surprised her.

She pictured Garland as she had left him that morning: wearing the hotel's thick, white terry cloth bathrobe and a smile, morning stubble on his rugged chin, short auburn hair rumpled, well-toned chest and legs peeking from underneath the bathrobe, sitting by the window reading the *Wall Street Journal.* She found the combination of male energy and high finance aphrodisiacal. She had just stepped out of the shower and had to have one more full-body hug before he flew home to Manhattan and away from her arms. Just one more hug, one more kiss, then, well, there was another hug. Before long, one thing led to another and she was forty-five minutes behind schedule. She didn't care.

Garland made it to the West Coast at least once a month on business, sometimes more. She wondered if the fleeting nature of their encounters was what made them so exciting, but she hoped it was more than that. She hoped it was the real thing.

"Did you find my panty hose?"

"No, I've looked everywhere."

"It's made my commute somewhat erotic."

"Oooh. The thought is giving me a . . . reaction."

"I won't see you for two weeks," she moaned.

"These partings are getting more and more difficult."

"The next time you come out, I'll be in my new house. I'm so excited! A whole house and it's all mine!"

"You got the keys? Congratulations, honey."

"Thanks. I know it's over my budget, but it was love. As long as my sales team keeps production up, I should be okay."

"The bull market still has some steam left in it."

"I was promoted to branch manager just over five months ago. I should have waited longer to make sure my promotion is going to stick before I jumped into a new house."

"You're doing great. I had lunch last week with some of the guys I used to work with at McKinney Alitzer, and they were talking about the terrific things you've already accomplished in the LA branch."

"They didn't ask whether you promoted me because we slept together?"

"That's nothing but a nasty rumor that no one would even give credibility to by repeating. We're having a relationship now, but six months ago, before I left the firm, there was nothing going on between us beyond some innocent flirting. Bottom line, it doesn't matter what people think. The honchos in New York don't care what you do as long as the LA branch is producing and you don't murder somebody or run afoul of the Securities and Exchange Commission."

"The fact that the rumor's not true hasn't stopped Sam-I-Am from repeating it." Iris made room for a woman to merge in front of her. The woman waved. LA drivers were either waving or trying to run each other off the road. "It bugs me, knowing my regional manager is actively sabotaging my career."

Iris heard a rustling noise and she imagined Garland standing, as he tended to do while talking on the telephone.

"Sam has to get over the fact that I went over his head to promote you. Sam's not on the fast track. He's too small-minded to see that your success only reflects on him. Iris, please stop fretting about what Sam thinks of you. You know by now that if you're going to be successful in this industry, you're bound to step on people's toes."

"I already have, with three-inch stiletto heels."

"Mmmm." He seemed to savor the image. "Now that's a thought—you in black, patent-leather high heels . . ."

"And what else?"

"A string of pearls."

They both giggled again.

He sighed. "You're really getting me into a state, here. I have to get on an airplane soon."

"When did you say the limo was picking you up to go to the airport?"

"There is a later flight . . ."

"I can't." She winced. "Don't tempt me. Don't say another single thing to tempt me. I have to stop by my crummy apartment to change before I go to the office. I can't show up barelegged and wearing the same suit I had on yesterday. I'm late as it is."

"You're right. I'd shoot a hole in my schedule if I postponed my flight."

"We'll see each other in two weeks."

"It'll be here before you know it." He paused. "Do you have pearls?"

"Sure."

"And you definitely have black heels."

"Taking inventory?"

"Absolutely. I'll call you tonight."

She almost told him she loved him. She felt it. She thought he felt it too. But she was heading north on the Harbor Freeway and he was about to leave for LAX, and to be truthful, she didn't want to be the first to say it. They'd been dating for five months, starting right after he'd left McKinney Alitzer to start a venture capital firm with some partners. The geographical distance between them had forced her to be thoughtful and to take things slowly. She was glad. She'd charged headfirst into new relationships too many times in the past. What if he didn't feel the way she did? Best to sit back, relax, and play it cool. Then if things led nowhere, she'd quietly limp away, but at least her pride would be intact.

"Bye," he said.

"Bye." She suddenly felt melancholy.

As she approached her exit, the phone rang again. Her heart soared. "Hi, stud muffin."

"Sorry, dear. It's not stud muffin." It was Louise, Iris's assistant.

Iris blushed. She was glad Louise couldn't see her. "Hi, Louise." To disguise her embarrassment, she tried not to miss a beat. "What's up?"

"How soon can you get to the office?"

"I'm going to stop by my apartment first. I have to . . . I need to pick something up. I have an appointment with Bridget Cross. She should be there in" —Iris looked at her watch—"ten minutes. She's a friend of mine. She and her husband, Kip, own a computer-games company and I'm helping them get things together to take it public. There's a manila folder on my desk labeled *Pandora*. When she gets there, please give it to her and say I'll be with her as soon as I can."

"Iris, I suggest you get to the office now. Sam Eastman's waiting for you and he's mad as can be."

"What?"

"He said you had a nine o'clock employee compensation meeting with him."

"What?"

"I looked on your schedule and didn't see anything for nine o'clock and told him so. He insists he set this up with you last week."

"What?" Iris couldn't squeeze out anything else. She sped through the yellow light at the end of the off-ramp and found her voice. "I don't have a meeting with him. I told him my escrow was closing today and I was going to Casa Marina before I came in to sign papers."

"He says New York needs your planned compensation figures for next year by three o'clock their time today. He says he told you about this weeks ago."

"He did not!"

"I called New York to verify and they said the figures do have to be in today. It's the regional manager's job to coordinate with their branches. I covered for you and told him you had everything worked out. I took the spreadsheet from last year, added and deleted employees as needed, and added six percent to everyone's salary. Tell him it's just a guideline."

"Louise, you're a lifesaver."

"Just get here as soon as you can."

"I'll be there in ten minutes." The low-slung Triumph hit the asphalt with a clank when Iris didn't slow down going over a low spot in the road. "But I need a favor. Can you meet me in the eleventh-floor women's rest room with the makeup bag I keep in my lower right-hand drawer?"

"Sure."

"Another favor—could you go to the little shop in the lobby and pick up a pair of panty hose for me, size B, Barely Beige?"

Louise's response was a little slower this time. "Of course."

"Thanks." Iris knew Louise wouldn't comment. Louise had been the assistant to the branch manager for over twenty years and had seen and heard just about everything. "I didn't go home last night." Iris knew Louise would figure it out anyway as soon as she saw her.

"You wore that green suit yesterday. It's rather memorable." Leave it to Louise to immediately size up the problem.

"Lime green polyester is back and it costs fifty times what I paid for it as a teenager. Who knew? Is this my punishment for being a fashion victim?"

"If anyone notices you've got on the same suit, just tell them you've packed everything."

"What would I do without you?"

Iris hung up and made a hard right into the parking garage of the black granite office tower. She screeched to a stop at the gate, jammed her parking card in the slot, and floored it when the gate opened. The Triumph's squat tires squealed against the smooth cement as she drove forward, circled down to the next level, accelerated again, then circled down again, passing parked cars at a dangerous speed. Woe to the hapless pedestrian who crossed her path.

Just then, a man carrying a long-handled dustpan and broom stepped from behind a pillar, almost in front of her speeding car.

"Get out of the way!" Iris yelled.

He stood frozen, like a deer caught in headlights, clutching his tools and gaping at Iris.

She arced around him in the narrow garage, shouting back, "You have a death wish or something?"

She pulled into her reserved spot and cut the engine. The Triumph was almost buried between a large Mercedes and a Lexus driven by executives from other firms who had the spots on either side of her. She looked to make sure no one was around before she stepped from the Triumph, an ungraceful action under the best of circumstances, but downright embarrassing today. She grabbed her briefcase from the shelf behind the two passenger seats, looked at the Triumph, and reluctantly decided to leave it as it was, not wanting to invest the time in putting up its ragtop and pulling on its canvas cover. She'd return to it once she got rid of Sam.

She quickly walked to the elevator, unzipped her purse, pulled out her brush, and tried to drag it through her hopelessly tangled hair. She punched the call button as she swatted her hair with the brush. Her cellular phone rang again. She fished it from her cluttered handbag.

"Hello?"

"Iris, it's Kip."

"Hi, Kip. What's up?"

"Isn't Bridget supposed to meet with you this morning?"

"She might already be waiting for me in my office. You want me to have her call you?"

Kip sighed.

Iris didn't have the time to drag information out of Kip Cross. She had known Kip and Bridget since they were in college together and had long grown accustomed to Kip's laconic personality, which was in stark contrast with his wife Bridget's high-energy warmth. They were a case study in how opposites not only attract but sometimes complement each other's shortcomings, creating a whole that's stronger than the sum of its parts.

Recently, Bridget, who was usually private about her personal life, had hinted that her and Kip's twelve-year marriage was unraveling. Iris had already inserted herself in the middle of the hornets' nest that was the Crosses' business affairs. She sensed it wasn't going to end there.

"Something wrong, Kip?" The elevator doors opened but Iris let them close without getting on. She again punched the call button.

"I screwed up, Iris. I really screwed up. Last night, Bridget caught me with Summer."

Kip didn't have to elaborate on what he and the nanny were doing, but Iris asked anyway. "Caught you?"

"It was completely stupid. One thing led to another and . . ."

Iris quietly stewed.

"Bridget wants a divorce."

Iris was stunned. She knew Bridget considered divorce to be a last resort. She felt a wave of foreboding. Kip was already angry at Bridget for taking their computer-games company, Pandora Software, public against his wishes. Now she was going to break up the family too.

Kip expressed what Iris was thinking. "She wants to destroy everything, Iris. Everything that means anything to me."

The elevator doors opened again. Iris got in this time, hoping the line would break up. She was not prepared to have this conversation. The elevator doors closed and the line crackled. "I'm in an elevator. I'm losing you."

"I mean it, Iris. I won't let her—"

There was a rush of static and the line went dead.

Chapter 2

Within ten minutes, Iris had met Louise, fixed her hair and makeup, struggled into the panty hose Louise had bought and was exiting the elevator on the twelfth floor. Holding her briefcase securely in her left hand, she opened the heavy glass doors that were labeled in raised brass letters: MCKINNEY ALITZER FINANCIAL SERVICES. After the clatter her pumps had made on the garage's concrete and the lobby's granite, her footsteps on the suite's plush carpeting sounded unnervingly quiet. It also made the clatter of her thoughts that much louder. Bridget wanted a divorce and Sam Eastman was impatiently tapping his foot in her office. After such a delightful start, it was shaping up to be one hell of a bad day.

Iris turned left into the sales department and put on her game face—smiling and sporting a confident attitude. It was easy for her now. She'd been doing this a long time. A long-strided, hip-swinging gait was part of the package, but today she took small steps that made her feel like a geisha. Apart from her other concerns, she had a more immediate problem. The panty hose Louise had bought were too small. They had inched down around her hips and, Iris feared, were heading for her knees.

She walked past the bullpen—the cluster of open cubicles where the younger and lower-producing brokers and the sales assistants worked—waving and making eye contact with everyone. She passed the offices along the northern wall, home to the top brokers. She waved at Kyle Tucker and Amber Ambrose, who were at their desks there. She had walked past just about everyone and was almost home, delighted that no one was paying much attention to her, her tired lime green suit, or windblown hair. They seemed too busy. Every single one of them was on the phone, talking animatedly into their headsets. Her delight turned to concern when she sensed that no one appeared to be having a good time. Brokers were happy when they were selling. But no one seemed happy.

Iris reached Louise's desk in a windowed alcove at the end of the suite. Next to it was Iris's corner office. Louise peered at her over the top of her half-glasses and underneath her well-sculpted eyebrows. "Good morning, Iris. You're looking well." She grabbed a pencil from where it had been jammed into a mound of her grayish blonde hair that she always styled into a French roll. She used the pencil as a pointer as she checked a list of numbers.

"And a wonderful good morning to *you,* Louise." Iris spun into her office.

Sam Eastman was sitting in one of the two damask-covered, Queen Anne–style chairs that faced Iris's cherrywood desk. Iris had redecorated her office shortly after her promotion was announced. Out went the previous occupant's masculine forest greens, plaids, heavy mahogany and dark leather. In went colors of peach, mint green, and cream, fabrics of damask and tapestry, cherrywood furniture, and lamps in crystal and brass. Her prize purchase was her desk chair of soft, cream-colored leather studded with brass grommets.

Sam was frowning and didn't greet her before he started speaking. "I'm curious why you chose a six percent across-the-board increase."

Sam was only in his mid fifties, but he hadn't aged well. He was a lank-haired, thin-skinned, WASPy kind of guy who had probably been good-looking in his early years. Now, his straight hair barely covered his pinkish scalp, his lusterless gray eyes were always rimmed with dark circles, and his belly and hips had gone soft. He smiled easily, like any good salesman, but it was never reflected in his eyes. He told jokes with the best of them and talked the talk and walked the walk, but to Iris, he seemed to chafe inside his own skin. There was an edge of discontent to him that none of the smiles or jokes could hide, at least from her.

Something about Sam's edginess compelled Iris to act impossibly cheerful around him. It was both her antidote to his subtly dour countenance and her revenge, as if to tell him, "Look at me, you SOB. You tried to stomp me down but I'm happy, happy, *happy!*" She was not above an occasional petty mind game.

"Good morning, Sam!" she sang. "Nice to see you!" She quickly dumped her briefcase and purse on her desk and grabbed her BUDGETS ARE FOR WIMPS mug from the top, just where she had left it the previous night.

Sam indicated the mug's slogan. "I thought that was just a joke, but now I think it actually reflects your philosophy."

She threw her head back and laughed as if it were the funniest thing she'd heard all week. "Be back in a flash. Just need a fresh cuppa Joe." She winked at him and strode out of her office.

Outside her door, Louise looked up at her. Iris bared both rows of her teeth in a violent grimace. She quickly put her professional face back on before anyone else saw her and took mincing steps to Liz Martini's office which was directly opposite hers in the suite's northwest corner.

Liz was talking into her telephone headset. "Look, sweetheart, you know I wouldn't steer you wrong. This is Liz talking! Okay, kisses to the kids." She made kissing noises into the phone. "And love to Susan. I mean, Debbie. Denise! Bye, bye." After hanging up, she said to Iris or perhaps to herself, "If he didn't keep trading in his wives for newer models, I'd be able to keep track of them."

Without a word, Iris came inside, closed the door, and ducked behind it, out of view of the miniblind-covered window that overlooked the suite. She set her empty mug on the corner of Liz's desk.

Liz crossed herself and said, "Oy, what a day!" Her father

was Italian Catholic and her mother was Russian Jewish and Liz found it expedient to claim both religions. She looked curiously at Iris, who had hiked up her skirt and was struggling to pull up her panty hose.

Iris precluded any comments. "Don't ask."

Liz opened an aerosol container and, with a sweeping gesture, sprayed the contents on her face. Several gold and diamond bracelets sparkled on her tiny wrist. She was in her middle forties but looked younger. She was five foot eight and slender—downright skinny if the truth be known. Liz adhered to the Duchess of Windsor's philosophy that one could never be too rich or too thin. She'd denied ever having had plastic surgery, although the office scuttlebutt had it that she'd at least had breast implants. It was hard to reconcile her C-cup-sized breasts with her size 3 hips.

Her hair was long and dark brown. Today, she wore it mounded on top of her head with tendrils dangling here and there. She had big brown eyes and full lips on an impish face. She always dressed in the latest fashions and as flashily as her clientele. Liz was married to Hollywood super agent, Ozzie Levinson. Ozzie managed his A-list clients' careers while Liz managed their money. They got them coming and going.

Iris, struggling with the tight nylon, slithered too close to Liz, who sprayed her face. Iris blinked wildly. "Wha . . . ?"

"Sweetheart, it's just mineral spray. You've got to rehydrate your skin or those Santa Ana winds will turn you into a prune in no time. It's got amino acids or collagen or something. Whatever it is, it's *fabulous.*" She spoke in a low, confidential tone, darting a bright red, manicured fingernail at Iris and frowning with concern as if she really cared about Iris becoming wrinkled. Maybe she did and maybe she didn't. Liz treated everyone and every issue as if it were of the utmost importance. It was a style that helped her produce over $25 million a year in sales. She kept almost a million of it in commissions. She was Iris's prize pony. And the best part was, Liz and Iris had been friends for years before Iris recruited her from a competing firm.

"Plus one of my clients sells this spray." Liz shrugged. Her phone rang. She gave the device a fatigued look and didn't answer it.

"What's going on?" Iris wondered.

"Market's down five hundred and ten points."

Iris's jaw dropped.

"It was down eight hundred. It's rebounded a bit. The phone's been ringing off the hook. I've spent all morning telling my clients not to worry, to hold tight, let's not panic sell, it's just the correction the analysts predicted . . ."

"Let's hope so," Iris said. "You want to have lunch today?"

"Sure!" Liz exclaimed enthusiastically as if she'd never heard a better idea.

"I have to get back to my office." Iris started to leave, then remembered the excuse she'd used to get away from Sam. She retrieved the coffee mug and opened the door.

"Isn't that your friend and her little girl?" Liz got up from her desk and stood in the doorway. "Isn't she precious? Hi, sweetheart!" She opened and closed her hand at Brianna. "What a cutie."

Brianna ran across the suite, dangling her rumpled Pocahontas doll upside down, and flung herself onto Iris's legs. "Hi, Aunt Iris!"

"Hi, sweetie. I'm so glad I got to see you today."

"I'm going to Grandma's house." Brianna was dressed in a pink cotton dress covered with white, stenciled stars.

"How nice!" Iris exclaimed.

"Honey, leave Aunt Iris alone. She's working." Bridget Cross had been chatting with Sam Eastman in Iris's office and now stood in the doorway. She was wearing a light gray wool, gabardine pantsuit and a silk satin blouse. It was about the most formal attire she owned, and she hated getting even that dressed up, preferring to conduct business on the tennis court or golf course. She was busy, with little time for frills. And she was practical.

Iris noticed that the years of sun were starting to take their toll on Bridget's skin. Under the fluorescent lights, it looked prematurely wrinkled.

"You've met Sam," Iris said as she greeted Bridget with a hug. Bridget was the only person Iris knew who had more energy than she did. Today however, she looked tired and worn. Iris assumed it was because of her problems with Kip. Her concern must have shown in her face because Bridget offered an explanation, although not the one she expected.

"Alexa Platt's missing. I've been beside myself with worry."

"What happened?"

Bridget twisted her hands one inside the other as she relayed the events of the previous afternoon. She and Brianna were the last people who had seen Alexa before her disappearance. "I should have waited until she got safely under way. I would have, except Brianna and I were late."

"Don't blame yourself."

"You're talking about that movie director's wife, Alexa Platt?" Sam interjected, hating to be left out. "I heard about it on the news coming over here. You're friends with her?"

"Alexa did some graphic artwork for Pandora early on," Bridget responded. "Then Jim Platt hired her as art director on one of his movies. They married shortly thereafter."

"I wouldn't worry," Iris offered. "You know Alexa. She probably dashed off to Two Bunch Palms on the spur of the moment for an aromatherapy massage, completely oblivious to the chaos she's created."

"Iris, you know the Platts as well?" Sam eagerly asked.

Bridget, consumed by her own concern, inadvertently ignored him. "And not tell Jim?"

"I know Alexa casually," Iris vaguely explained to Sam, reluctant to reveal anything, however innocuous, about her private life to her boss. Any tidbit of information was a potential weapon. Returning her attention to Bridget, she said, "Alexa probably did tell Jim. He's going in a million directions these days. He probably forgot."

"Alexa didn't mention anything yesterday. But," Bridget added ruefully, "I sort of monopolized the conversation." She grew thoughtful. "There was this weird groundskeeper guy in the park who was giving us funny looks. You know how certain people can give you the creeps?"

"I'm certain he was harmless," Iris said reassuringly. "People who work alone like that tend to be a bit odd anyway."

"I suppose you're right."

"I'm sure Alexa will turn up." Iris was trying to be optimistic but realized her comment seemed to imply Alexa wouldn't be walking out from wherever she was under her own steam. It was, if she was honest with herself, what she secretly felt.

"And I'm surprised to find out you're also friends with the Crosses, Iris." Sam surged ahead with his own agenda.

"Since college," Iris tersely answered.

"I read an article about Pandora Software in *Time* the other day," Sam said to Bridget. "And you and your husband are on the cover of *Wired* magazine this month."

"The information age has elevated computer programmers to the ranks of rock stars," Bridget said. "Kip and I even get fan mail. Who would have thought?"

Iris put her hand on Bridget's arm. "She's being modest."

Bridget stroked her daughter's hair and frowned as if she'd lost her train of thought. "I picked up the material you prepared, Iris. I'll read it at home. I've got to get Brianna to her grandma and myself to the office. We're releasing the first two levels of Slade Slayer's newest adventure tonight on the Internet."

"It's called *Suckers Finish Last,* right?" Sam laughed.

Bridget nodded wryly. "Our core audience is males, thirteen to twenty-two."

"Is Pandora still privately held?" Sam asked.

"Not for much longer, I hope. Iris is helping me set up the initial public offering. She's been in contact with your firm's investment banking division about underwriting it."

"You have?" Sam smiled at Iris with surprise, but he didn't look happy.

Iris nervously raked her hair with her fingers. She didn't think she needed to tell Sam about every deal she was into, but that was apparently what he expected. "I've talked to some people in IB about it. It's just in the planning stages at the moment. Be quite a coup for us to bring an initial public offering into this branch."

"When were you planning on bringing me into the loop on this?" Sam was still smiling.

"Sam, there isn't anything to talk about yet."

"We've really just started the process," Bridget interjected, sensing she'd got her friend into trouble. "We have a meeting with our investor tomorrow."

"You've got some venture capital invested in Pandora?" Sam asked. "Whose?"

"USA Assets. It's a group headed by T. Duke Sawyer," Bridget responded.

"T. Duke Sawyer?" Sam exclaimed. "You don't mean T. Duke the Liquidator?"

"He doesn't like to be reminded of that nickname," Bridget advised.

Sam seemed impressed by the company Bridget kept. "He's in the high-tech arena now? He was one of the big corporate raiders of the eighties. I remember when he did a hostile takeover of that food conglomerate, Consolidated Products International." He smiled dreamily at the recollection. "He dismantled CPI, sold off the pieces to the highest bidder, threw thousands out of their jobs and made a fortune. Of course, CPI was his most ambitious takeover. There were dozens of mom-and-pop outfits he gobbled up. He was worth *millions,*" Sam said with awe.

"Until the indictments came in," Iris said. "He was found guilty of tax evasion and securities fraud."

"Aaah," Sam said. "Typical T. Duke—he struck a deal, paid some fines, served a few months in one of those country club prisons, and did some community service, ladling soup at a homeless kitchen or something." Sam shook his head with amazement. "T. Duke the Liquidator . . . I'll be damned. How in the world did you get hooked up with him?"

Bridget looked amused. "Many times I've asked myself that same question. Actually, he approached us. He'd read about Pandora and essentially brought us a check."

"I'd love to meet him. We get this IPO going and I imagine I will." Sam glanced at his watch, slipped Iris's salary figures into a manila envelope, and handed the folder to Louise. "These are fine, Iris. Louise, would you be kind enough to FedEx these to New York, please? I've got to run." He shook hands with Bridget and quickly left, patting Brianna on the head as she played with her doll on the carpet outside Iris's door.

Bridget turned to Iris. "So that was the boss from hell?"

"That was Sam-I-Am." Iris grimaced. "I can see this one coming. I land the Pandora IPO for the firm's investment banking division, all of Pandora's initial stock offering will be sold through my branch office, and Sam Eastman's going to take credit for it."

"I'm sorry if I blew it for you by mentioning it."

Iris shrugged. "Doesn't matter. He would have found a way to get his claws into it somehow."

"Guess I'm finished here." Bridget slipped the thick envelope she'd picked up from Iris into her leather backpack, one strap of which she slung over her shoulder. "I'll meet you at T. Duke's office in Somis at ten o'clock tomorrow."

Iris glanced outside the door where Brianna was happily singing to herself and ignoring the rest of the world. "Kip called me. He told me about the big D."

Bridget frowned and angrily looked across the room.

"You caught him with Summer?"

Bridget flicked her hands as if feeling frustrated and powerless. "That was the last straw, Iris. Finding him with the nanny's not the half of it."

She responded to Iris's shocked expression. "Oh, yeah. There's been more than Summer. And that's not even mentioning our money problems. Spends it like there's no tomorrow. He keeps saying we're rich. I tell him, we're only rich on paper. Everything we get I plow back into the firm to expand operations and hire new people. That's why I accepted T. Duke Sawyer's offer of five million in venture capital. Kip fought me on that because he didn't want an outsider involved in Pandora. But then what does he do with the money? Spends close to three million on that Ferrari and that mansion and on chasing around. I fudged the financials I prepared for T. Duke's group to try and hide it. Everyone's telling him he's God and he's believing it."

Iris sat in one of the Queen Anne chairs. "He's still furious that you want to take the firm public."

"I can't get him to see that we need the money to build the firm. Plus we paid our employees in stock options. They're ready to realize the investment they made in coming to work for us." Bridget raised her hands. "But Kip sees himself losing control over Pandora. Other than me and Brianna, Pandora is the most important thing in his life. Sometimes I think it's *the* most important. But I own sixty percent, Kip owns twenty, and USA Assets now owns twenty. Bottom line, it doesn't matter what he wants."

"I still can't believe you had to force him to put even twenty percent of the company in his name."

"He wanted me to own all of it. Typical Kip. Naive. Trusting, I guess. Well, I never thought we'd get divorced either."

Iris remained quiet for a long time. She had tears in her eyes when she looked up at Bridget. "I'm so sorry. I really am."

Brianna came into the office. "Are we going?" She noticed Iris. "Why are you crying, Aunt Iris?"

Iris, still sitting, held the child tight. "Just thinking about something sad. You're getting so big. You get bigger every time I see you." She looked past Brianna at Bridget. "I forgot to tell you. I picked up the keys to my house."

"Wonderful, Iris! I'm so happy for you. I knew it was the perfect house for you the first time I saw it."

Iris held Brianna away from her. "And this little girl can come see me all the time and maybe even spend the night."

"I want to!" Brianna exclaimed.

"We have to go," Bridget said.

"Keep your chin up, kiddo. See you tomorrow." Iris looked curiously at Liz on the other side of the suite.

Liz was clutching the door of her office as if she needed it for support. When she caught Iris's eye, she began walking slowly across the suite toward her. After a few steps, she leaned against one of the bullpen cubicles and began sobbing.

Iris ran over to her. "What is it?"

Between sobs, Liz said, "I just heard about Alexa. Jim Platt's people called Ozzie."

"She's missing," Iris ventured.

"They found her—"

Bridget silently approached them.

"—in a ravine in Coldwater Canyon Park. Her head was bashed in."

Chapter 3

"Meet Miss Cherry Divine."

"She's awesome."

"Totally gorgeous. But can you kill her?"

"Of course," Today Rhea responded without hesitation.

Wearing a red, low-cut evening gown, the woman was leaning seductively against a wall midway down the street, one high-heel-clad foot pressed against it. Her tousled blonde hair fell past her shoulders, a come-hither look heated her eyes. A double barreled shotgun was aimed at her torso.

"But do you want to?" Today asked.

"Do I?"

"Let's find out."

Cherry Divine turned and slowly started walking down the street, her hips rolling from side to side. She looked back over her shoulder and cooed, "What are you waiting for? You afraid or something?"

A multitude of oversized monitors scattered across a spacious conference table provided the only light in the computer lab. Images created by screen savers floated across the monitors: tropical fish, zoo animals, the Simpsons, spaceships. Also on the table and around the perimeter of the lab were a maze of keyboards, mice, mouse pads, stereo speakers, joysticks, cables, electrical cords, power strips, CD-ROM writers, external hard drives, Jaz drives, cartridges, laptops, and CPUs—both whole and in pieces. Along one side of the room was a graveyard of computer components. Diskettes and CD-ROMs were scattered like cupcake sprinkles. In a chair sat Tickle Me Elmo with a cigar jammed in its mouth. Inside a CPU that had its cover removed was G.I. Joe in a compromising position with both Busy Gal Barbie and Christmas Barbie. A huge stuffed gorilla sat on the floor in a corner with a cardinal-and-gold USC Trojans cap jauntily perched on its fuzzy head. A sheet of paper scrawled with the message USC SUCKS was stuck to its chest with a steak knife.

It was called the War Room. In it, Pandora's core team was reviewing the final touches on their latest game—*Slade Slayer's Suckers Finish Last*—which was about to be released to the public.

Mick Ha stood to one side of Today. "Is that Bridget's voice? It's perfect!"

Kip Cross was seated to Today's left, his chair pulled out a few feet so that he was with the group yet slightly apart from it. His arms were crossed over his broad chest, and his long legs were stretched in front of him and crossed at the ankles. He was shod in rubber, dime-store flip-flops, which were the only shoes he ever wore, rain or shine, other than running shoes when he jogged. He'd started wearing flip-flops when he was poor. They'd since become part of his image.

Kip had a strong nose and jaw and deep-set, dark eyes. He wore his prematurely gray hair in a short buzz cut. The style accentuated his prominent facial features and made him look erratic, even slightly mad.

Kip was Pandora's system developer, the programming genius behind the graphics engines that made Pandora's games unique. The engine creates the illusion that images on a two-dimensional computer monitor exist in three-dimensional space. Walls have density, tunnels look claustrophobic, creatures have substance. The players feel as if they're speeding through virtual worlds.

Slade Slayer was Kip's creation. Pandora's team of artists and game designers put flesh on Slade and devised the thin plots of his adventures—kill or be killed, using an arsenal of real and fantasy weapons in an ultraviolent world—but Slade was Kip's baby. Everyone considered the unhesitating, direct, macho Slade Slayer to be Kip's alter ego, a theory that he consistently rebuffed.

Kip smiled at Toni Burton. "Toni and I listened to all the actresses she tested and both of us thought Bridget's voice had the right combination of sweetness and danger." His own voice was deep but the volume soft.

Toni Burton widened her lively blue eyes and playfully wrinkled her pug nose at Kip. She was cute and willingly played the role. Twenty-six years old, she had worked at Pandora for five years, starting as Bridget's secretary after dropping out of college. When she noticed Bridget observing the exchange between her and Kip, she hastily returned her gaze to the monitor.

"Why did we bother doing tests with all those actresses if you were going to use my voice all along?" Bridget Cross asked her husband. "We wasted three weeks."

The game's heavy-metal sound track droned in the background along with reports from the weapons Today fired and the screams of the vanquished.

"I wasn't sure I wanted your voice," Kip replied. "Toni convinced me it was right."

Toni smiled tentatively at Bridget. "I hope you're not mad, B. Kip and I thought it would be a nice surprise for you to be sort of immortalized as the voice of Cherry Divine."

Bridget set her lips in a line. "I'm mad about the time we lost. Every computer-game company in the world is trying to be the next Pandora. We command the market now, but if we lose market share, we'll never get it back."

"Just wait until they sample the shareware version of *Suckers Finish Last*," Today said with confidence. He mashed a keyboard key, and the image on the screen, a 3-D representation of a darkened city street, quickly turned as if the player had spun to look behind. Today pressed the key again and the image swirled forward.

"Whoa! And we thought we had a lot of complaints about motion sickness before," Mick Ha said, shifting his attention between the computer monitor and his tennis shoe, which he grasped in his hand. The top of his white Converse sneaker was almost covered with a black pen drawing of a snarling dog.

Mick was Pandora's lead graphic artist, who drew and converted to computer images the Slade Slayer games' sleek yet decayed postindustrial environment of streets, sewers, high- and low-tech structures, and their dizzying population of aliens, ghouls, zombies, rabid dogs, and deadly vixens. Mick's black hair was shaved close around the sides and back and cut long on top. He wore thick, rimless glasses. He had an easy smile, was the most consistently amiable of the mercurial Pandora group, and had been with Kip and Bridget almost from the beginning.

Today, sitting ramrod straight in the chair, furiously tapped one foot as his fingers madly traveled the keyboard. He shook his head with awe. "This game sucks like a vacuum." It was high praise.

"It's totally immersive," Toni enthused.

"It's great," Bridget said. "I was impressed by the bits and pieces I saw, but the finished product is beyond belief."

"It's your best work, Kip," Toni said, smiling broadly at her boss and, until last week, her lover.

Kip smirked with self-satisfaction at the images on the monitor, then said, almost as an afterthought, "It was a team effort."

"That's right," Today said as he worked the keyboard. "A freaking team effort." He shot a glance at Kip. "That's why Bridget is correct to take the firm public."

Kip's face darkened.

"Huh, buddy?" Today verbally prodded.

In response to Today's keyboard commands, Cherry Divine sauntered down the street. She paused at a corner then disappeared around it.

"Cherchez la femme," Slade Slayer intoned in a deep, male voice through the speakers.

Mick looked up from drawing on his tennis shoe, his index finger covered with black ink. "I can't wait to see how the final level looks."

"You don't know?" Toni asked.

"I did a bunch of work on it but Kip patched it together."

"Really?" Bridget said.

"Same here," Today added. "Our man Cross was intent on keeping the solution a secret."

"So only Kip knows how to win?" Toni grinned at Kip. "That's so cool!"

"Why, Kip?" Bridget asked.

Kip shrugged. "Someone's always leaking the solution. And I wanted you guys to have fun figuring it out too."

Bridget folded her arms across her chest. "That was a lot of extra work for you, Kip. You could have spent that time working on the engine for the next game."

"Bridget," Kip said in a clipped voice, "I did it for fun. If this ever stops being fun for me, I'm out. You can tell that to your investment bankers."

The room grew quiet except for the game's relentless music and the rat-a-tat, ka-pows, and death wails of the battlefield.

"What's this?" Today rapidly clicked some keys. "It's random. Totally random. Dammit, a bug. Arrgh! I'll fix it later. It's not material."

Bridget put her hand on her hip and pointed at the screen. "I'm not wild about this cyber-bimbo. My idea was to give Slade a girlfriend, to build more of a plot into the game—"

"A *girlfriend?*" Today bellowed. "Slade Slayer doesn't *have* a girlfriend!"

"Not a cyber-bimbo," Kip said. "Not nearly."

"Slade's going to blow her away, isn't he?" Bridget said.

"Not necessarily," Kip said cryptically.

"She has my voice, I think she looks slightly like me, and Slade's going to blow her away."

"Not necessarily," Kip insisted.

"You didn't make her the boss monster?" Mick asked with disbelief.

Kip smiled broadly with his lips closed.

"Arrghh!" Today yelled. There was a barrage of gunfire as he spastically tapped a key with his thumb.

"I hate when that happens," Slade Slayer's voice said as the screen image shifted to look as if the player were lying on the street. Blood flowed across the asphalt.

"I'm dead," Today announced, flinging his hands up. "A Morph Drone under the manhole cover."

Today Rhea was Pandora's lead designer, providing the loose plot of the games which was presented to the player in a series of levels, like chapters in a book. The games consisted of ten levels composed of discrete virtual locations, each with a distinctive physical style. The player had to accomplish specific tasks at each level before moving on. Adversaries became increasingly clever and harder to kill with each higher level. To win the game, the player had to prevail at the highest level and kill the game's most formidable adversary, who only appeared at the very end—the boss monster.

Today restarted the game and typed commands to spin the screen image backward and down, revealing an armor-encased, reptilelike creature climbing from a manhole cover in the street. "Die!" With a flurry of keyboard commands, a Molotov cocktail appeared in Slade Slayer's hand at the bottom of the screen. There was the scratch of a match being struck then the snap of fire as the fuse was lit. The hand heaved the cocktail into the manhole cover as the creature snarled and growled. There was an explosion. Bloody pieces of the Morph Drone flew from the manhole and were scattered across the street. Today's knees bounced agitatedly as his fingers frenetically worked the keyboard.

"Awright! Turning out to be my kind of day," Slade Slayer said.

"Drive on," Today pronounced.

"You got him," Toni said, laughing.

"I always get 'em, one way or another." A blue cotton kerchief was tied pirate-style around Today's head over his brown hair, which fell in curls past his shoulders. He was all-American good-looking and was wearing Top-Siders without socks, black sweatpants cut off at the knees, and an oversized T-shirt printed with a picture of the grunge band Alice in Chains. He had two earrings in his left ear: a small gold ring and a peace symbol dangling from a chain. He was twenty-six.

"I think you're ready for a deathmatch, buddy," Mick Ha taunted.

"You think so, little man?" Today was a bundle of nervous energy in constant motion. "Are you ready for a man-beating?"

"Let's do a three-way game," Kip said.

"Oh-ho. Cross the boss picks up the gauntlet," Today said.

"Remember the time." Bridget looked at her watch. "It's eleven-fifteen. At midnight we transfer the file."

Today advanced the screen image around the corner where Cherry Divine could be seen sashaying up a long set of stone steps. A stone castle loomed at the top of the staircase.

"Wait a minute," Bridget protested. "Those look like the steps next to our house, Kip."

"Bridget, those steps are just way too creepy," Mick explained. "I *had* to use them."

"I'm not liking this," she said.

At the top of the steps, Cherry went into the castle through a massive door that stood open. She poked her head back out and breathed, "What are you waiting for?"

"I don't like this at all, Kip," Bridget complained.

"What are you talking about?" Kip said.

"You know damn well what I'm talking about. Slade Slayer's going to blow her away, isn't he?"

"Chill out, Bridget," Today said, scowling.

"What's wrong, B?" Mick asked.

Bridget rubbed her forehead with her fingertips. "I'm not keen on seeing a woman murdered, even a digital woman, after I spent half the afternoon talking to the police about Alexa."

The room again grew quiet except for the sound of the game's kinetic music, special effects, and Today's bursts of clicking on the keyboard.

"Do they have any idea what happened to her?" Toni asked.

Bridget shrugged sadly. "Someone bashed in the back of her head with a large rock and she tumbled into a ravine. She was found inside the park, a long way from where I left her. It had to have been someone she knew or wasn't afraid of."

"Maybe someone forced her," Toni suggested.

Bridget shivered.

"Check out the castle!" Today exclaimed, oblivious to the tone of the conversation. "It's gloomy, it's damp. I love it." The fingers of his right hand twitched against the keys as his left hand restlessly tapped the side of the keyboard, his thumb never far from the vital key that fired his weapons. "Where'd she go? There she is! Should I shoot?"

"Go for it!" Mick yelled.

"Hey! What's goin' on? She's like sending rays or something from her eyes. Doesn't look good. Baby's going bye-bye." Today mashed his weapon key. "What?"

"A slingshot!" Mick exclaimed. "Now I get it." He beamed at Kip. *"That's* why you wanted the slingshot."

Today impatiently pounded his weapon key and moaned, "You turned my shotgun into a freakin' slingshot."

"She put a spell on you," Kip explained, leaning forward with his elbows on his knees, still looking at the monitor.

"Akkk! Look!" Mick cried.

"She's the boss monster, isn't she?" Today cried. "Kip, you maniac!"

Cherry Divine's beautiful face had turned into Slade Slayer's, still topped by her perfect blonde coiffure. From the bodice of her low-cut evening gown, she pulled out a handgun and blew Slade Slayer away. "Sorry, sucker," she hissed as his blood spread across the stone floor.

"I didn't see that coming," Bridget admitted.

Today slapped the keyboard. It slammed into the monitor with a brittle retort. "This is dark, Kip. This is way dark."

"What's it mean?" Toni asked. "The boss monster is Slade Slayer?"

"Slade's worst enemy is himself?" Mick suggested. "It's very mental, Kip."

"I get it, I get it." Today frenetically bounced his feet on his toes. "He has to kill himself to win. Or kill the dark side of himself."

"And the dark side is a woman?" Toni tried.

Bridget listened to their discussion without comment.

Kip tried to suppress a smile. "You guys are reading too much into this. I just thought it was graphically interesting."

Everyone looked at Kip as if they didn't believe him.

"Really!" Kip insisted.

Toni crossed her legs, grasped her knee with one hand, and examined the pedicure on her sandal-clad foot. "What time is it?"

"Ten till," Bridget said.

"Kip, give me the cheat codes," Today demanded. "You changed them on the tenth level, didn't you!" His fingers pounded the keyboard. "Prick!"

Kip laughed.

"Give 'em up! I've tried everything. Cherry's killed me every time. Wait . . . I know what you did." Today's fingers flew. Then he again shoved the keyboard against the monitor. "Kip, you bastard!"

Kip watched Today's struggle with amusement. "Cherry Divine has a heart of pure malice. But you can beat her."

"I give up." Today flung himself back into his chair, picked up a ballpoint pen, and started rapidly clicking the top. "Tomorrow, I'll figure it out in ten minutes."

"Tough talk, cowboy," Toni said.

"What time is it now?" Today asked.

"Six till," Mick said.

Today nervously clicked the pen. "So when do we cash in on this deal?"

Bridget hoisted herself onto the table, first sliding a keyboard out of the way. "I'm taking steps to initiate a Pandora IPO right now. Kip and I are meeting with T. Duke Sawyer tomorrow."

"We're going to be rich!" Mick exclaimed.

"Nothing has been decided yet," Kip said.

"Yes, it has," Bridget responded.

Kip glared at his wife. She met his stare.

Today continued madly clicking the pen. "C'mon, Kip. I left bug-fix and ship-cycle hell at Microsoft to come here for less money and more stock options. That was the whole point. Go with a small start-up firm, build the company, go public, cash in. It's high time. I've got a family now."

"I've got stock options too," Toni said.

Mick looked at his watch. "Two minutes!"

Using a mouse, Today accessed the communications software, instructed the modem to dial, and logged onto the Internet. He dragged and dropped into place the .ZIP file that contained the programs.

Bridget started counting down. "Five, four, three, two, one."

Today clicked on OK, uploading the shareware version of

Suckers Finish Last—consisting of the first two levels of the game—onto Pandora's FTP site on the Internet.

The group silently watched as the files copied.

"Done!" Kip solemnly pronounced when the upload was complete.

"Within minutes, *Suckers* will be mirrored to dozens of other sites and after that, users around the world will be downloading it and playing," Toni said.

"Then they'll get hooked and send us fifty bucks for the rest of the game." Today rubbed his palms together.

"I'll get the champagne." Bridget hopped off the table and left the room. Outside, she walked on a catwalk past offices, reached a roughhewn staircase, and descended to the ground floor. She crossed the massive airplane hangar and walked to the large lunchroom that occupied one end of the structure. Inside, she opened the refrigerator and retrieved the bottle of French champagne she had put there earlier that day. From a cabinet, she gathered plastic flutes. She gasped when someone touched her shoulder.

"You scared me," she said to her husband.

"Why are you doing this, Bridget? We're going to get revenue from the release of the new game. We can pay T. Duke back. Pandora will be ours again. You promised you'd think about it."

"I have." Bridget looked at her husband with dismay. "Kip, things can't stay the way they are. You heard them upstairs. We promised them this. We can't stay a small computer-games company forever."

"Why not?" Kip's posture grew rigid and red blotches appeared on his cheeks.

Bridget had long grown accustomed to the way anger transformed her husband. She responded calmly. To do otherwise would only inflame him further. "I have to think about Brianna's future."

"Bull. You're more concerned about *your* future. About building your empire, your name." His face was now bright red. He menacingly leaned toward her, his fists tightly clasped by his sides. "All I ever wanted was to develop games with no one bothering me. Now I'm going to have to worry about someone's grandma losing money because she bought Pandora stock. You're going to change our whole way of life."

She did not move away. She imagined she felt heat radiating from him. "Like you haven't done anything to change our way of life? And you're the last one to talk about keeping promises. I saw the way you and Toni looked at each other. You said you'd ended it with her."

"I have."

"To free up time to ball the nanny?"

Kip's bluster left. He suddenly seemed to run out of things to say.

She touched his chin and ran her thumb against the cleft there. Her eyes grew glassy. "Where did we go wrong?"

"I made mistakes, Bridget. I want to make it up to you."

She smiled sadly. "Things can't be the way they were. Not for us, not for Pandora."

"Let's try again, B." He reached for her and she stepped back. He beseechingly held his hands toward her.

A tear rolled down her cheek but her voice was firm. "Tonight, I'm firing Summer. Tomorrow, I want you to fire Toni."

"Sure. Anything you say."

"And I want you to move out."

"All right. Okay. We'll separate for a while. Give ourselves some space. Then you'll call off your investment bankers and we'll pay T. Duke his money back."

She moved her head almost imperceptibly, but the message was clear.

Kip stared at her the way he'd stare at code he'd written that wasn't running right. But this problem couldn't be fixed by analytically putting zeros and ones in the right order. He drew back his fist and slugged his wife in the face.

She let out a muffled cry and went down, banging against the counter before sliding to the floor. She looked at Kip with horror.

He loomed over her, appearing even taller than he was. His fists were balled by his sides, his face still scarlet. He made a shuffling movement toward her and she cowered against the cabinets.

"You're not going to destroy my life." Struggling to regain his composure, Kip ran his hands across his bristly hair and left the room without looking back.

Chapter 4

Traffic was moving and this was good. This was always good. It had been a happy time for California drivers ever since the state had raised the speed limit. The price of gasoline crept up a short time thereafter, which made drivers cranky all over again. Eventually, the prices had slowly come back down. All was again well in the kingdom.

Iris had negotiated the downtown maze of freeway overpasses known as the 4-level and was traveling westbound on the 10 at a fast clip. She was driving with the Triumph's top up in an attempt to save her hairstyle, but the Santa Ana winds still found ways inside. There was a gap in the rear of the ragtop where a fastener had broken, and a space above the driver's-side window where it didn't make a clean line with the top of the frame. Errant strands of her shoulder-length blonde hair flew into her mouth and eyes. She sang along with a melancholy Bruce Springsteen ballad on the radio as she picked at her lips, trying to dislodge hair stuck to her lipstick. The ballad was about loss and seemed appropriate. Before she'd left the office, she'd been interviewed over the telephone by a police detective regarding Alexa Platt.

She didn't have much to tell him. She hadn't seen or spoken to Alexa for several weeks. The last time was when Iris and her group of women friends had got together for what they called "girls' margarita night out." The conversation consisted of their usual round-robin dishing and bitching. Alexa was the same as always: pretty, stylish, funny, bold. She had talked to Iris about a creative dispute she was having with her husband over the movie they were making, but it wasn't anything over which Jim Platt would have murdered his wife. From what Alexa said, she and Jim were always arguing over something. That was their style.

"Do you know Jim Platt?" the detective asked her.

"I met him once at a charity function. I doubt if he'd remember me. Alexa had promised to host a *Melrose Place* party at their new house in Calabasas for the girls." Iris attempted to confirm some information gleaned by Liz Martini's well-connected husband, Ozzie. "I heard there's not much evidence at the crime scene. No skin under Alexa's fingernails, no fibers . . . just a large, bloodstained rock."

"That's correct."

"Is the groundskeeper a suspect? Bridget Cross told me he gave her and Alexa the creeps."

"We've talked to him," he cryptically responded.

"Hmmm. He's still walking the streets so I assume you don't have enough evidence against him."

"That's correct."

"Sounds like the perfect crime."

"Either someone was very smart or very lucky."

The interview with the detective had put Iris behind schedule. She was in serious danger of being late to meet Bridget and Kip Cross at T. Duke Sawyer's office—a facility that he called San Somis. Iris wasn't certain whether San Somis was a homage to or a rip-off of William Randolph Hearst and his oceanside castle, San Simeon. Clearly, T. Duke viewed himself in the same league. She had heard and read a lot about him and was eager to finally meet the man.

Iris drove the 10 across the city to the west side. There she took the 405 north and drove almost to the end of the San

Fernando Valley where she caught the 118, the Ronald Reagan Freeway. Driving west, she passed the Reagan Library and neighborhood after neighborhood of neat, tile-roofed, mission-style houses in earth tones of putty and ocher hunkered right up against the freeway. An occasional mini-mall or school broke up the landscape.

After ten miles, the houses became sparse and shoddy, the landscape again grew flat, and ragged industrial parks sprouted. In Somis, the 118 ended. Iris traveled past rows of vegetable crops and groves of citrus trees. Acres of cultivated flowers created a patchwork of purple, green, orange, and yellow. Produce stands dotted the street corners. Farmworkers stooped in the fields.

There was a stoplight at Division Street, and Iris turned left. She looked for something resembling a castle or mansion but saw nothing but low, drab industrial buildings landscaped with straggly boxwoods, overgrown clumps of bird-of-paradise, and dirt. The wind had free rein here. Dust devils twirled. A tumbleweed rolled down the street.

After deciding she must have made a wrong turn, Iris saw a building faced in black marble. There were no identifying markings or insignia other than the street address in small brass letters next to a glass door. The building was surrounded by a large manicured lawn and neat flowerbeds, the brilliant colors appearing extravagant in the plain surroundings. Clumps of trees with cement benches under them dotted the lawn. Curiously, no one sat there even though it was lunchtime. Iris concluded that no one wanted dirt blown onto their bologna sandwiches. It still seemed odd to her that there was nothing human to detract from the ominous black building that reflected the surroundings in its shiny surface.

Iris parked the Triumph on the street and was glad to see Kip's butter yellow Ferrari nearby. There were no other cars. A long, gently rising staircase led from the sidewalk to the front door. She ascended the stairs which were arranged in a pattern of three steps followed by a long flat walk, then another three steps. On each side of the stairs was a shallow reflecting pool surfaced with small, irregularly cut mosaic tiles in bright shades of blue, gold, and green. The sunlight shimmered on the water, which was dotted with leaves and debris scattered by the wind. Where the three steps ascended, the pools were elevated as well. The water babbled as it ran down. Birds, which seemed to have abandoned the rest of the bleak neighborhood, sang from the trees.

At the building's entrance, Iris tried to pull open the heavy glass door and found it locked. She noticed a button set in a brass plaque to the left of the door and pressed it. She didn't hear any response to the buzzer, but momentarily, something in the door metallically clicked. She again pulled the door. It opened.

She walked into a large room that was several stories tall with pearl gray marble floors and brilliantly white walls. A ramp carpeted in pale blue extended around each wall and slowly rose three stories until it reached closed double doors of dark wood. Lit display cases were set in the walls along the ramp. They appeared to be full of objects, but Iris didn't pay too much attention to them. She was mesmerized by the antique cars. The entire ground floor was covered with spit-and-polish-perfect cars. There was no one around.

Iris wandered among the cars, ogling the Lamborghinis, Rolls Royces, Cadillacs, and Bugattis. There was a collection of small sports cars with Alfa Romeos, Austin Healeys and even an early Triumph.

"Ma'am?"

She hadn't seen the tall, good-looking, twenty-something man enter the area. Perhaps he'd been standing there the entire time watching her. She was glad she hadn't touched anything.

"Miss Thorne?"

She walked purposefully toward him, her pump heels resounding sharply and, she hoped, authoritatively. "Yes, I'm Iris Thorne." She extended her hand. "And you are . . . ?"

He hesitated momentarily before taking it, as if surprised that she had initiated physical contact. He shook her hand firmly but briefly. "Baines."

Something in his bearing and the formality of his speech suggested a military background. He wore a navy blue suit, a crisp white shirt woven with fine blue lines, highly polished black shoes, and a small enameled pin of the U.S. flag in his lapel.

He was clean-cut, with a closely shaved jaw and fair hair cut so short, his scalp showed through. His pale eyebrows and eyelashes were almost invisible. He had a squat nose and a small mouth that was fixed in an expressionless line. Everything about him was unremarkable, except for his eyes. These were deeply set and a clear, icy blue.

"The Crosses have arrived. T. Duke is completing some business and will be with you shortly." His voice echoed in the large room. "The elevator is this way." He gestured at the far side of the building. He was wearing a large signet ring on his right hand. Affiliations seemed important to him.

"Can I go up the ramp?"

He seemed dismayed that she had suggested an alternative. "Of course." He extended his hand in the direction of the carpeted ramp and waited for Iris to begin walking. Once she did, he followed a few paces behind.

She looked back at him as she walked on the plush blue carpet, finding his formality amusing. "Is Baines your first or last name?"

"I prefer to be known as just Baines."

"Are you a bodyguard or something?"

"I'm T. Duke's driver."

"Just Baines is just the driver? You seem like a capable guy. I bet you do more for T. Duke than just drive." She smiled broadly at him. It had no effect. "A man like T. Duke must have made a few enemies."

"I drive, ma'am."

"I bet you used to be a police officer. A Secret Service agent, maybe?"

"No, ma'am."

Iris walked a few more steps then again turned. "You an Army man, Baines?"

"Marines, ma'am."

She'd suspected that Baines would refuse to be misidentified.

"Look at this stuff!" Iris arrived at the first display case which was full of brightly painted porcelain miniatures of ladies' shoes. There were fancy slippers, high-buttoned boots, and high heels, all daubed with gold paint. Three other cases contained more of the same.

Beyond the shoes were several cases of porcelain carriages, each with a driver holding reins of fine gauge chain, leading a team of porcelain horses. After that, there were cases of delicate china plates, cups, and saucers. Then there were teapots. Then dolls with fragile glass faces and real hair dressed in period costumes. Then toby jugs of all sizes.

After that, came the Disney memorabilia. Dozens of Mickey Mouse figures crowded several cases. Also on display were Donald Duck, Goofy, Snow White, and so on. After that, there was Coca-Cola memorabilia, followed by case after case of Depression glassware, followed by cheerful cookie jars and salt shakers of the 1940s and 1950s. There were pillboxes, makeup compacts, and antique toys. It was an entire museum—too much to absorb.

Iris and Baines had walked up two stories in silence. She finally spoke. "Must be nice to be rich, huh?"

"I wouldn't know, ma'am."

"This is a side of T. Duke I didn't expect. Teapots and porcelain slippers. Very interesting."

Baines didn't respond.

They'd almost reached the top of the landing and the set of heavy wood doors. As she went up, Iris trailed her hand against the steel railing that bounded the ramp, looked down at the antique cars three stories beneath them, and glanced at the examples of conspicuous consumption packed inside the display cases lining the walls.

"I understand why someone might want an Aladdin-style teapot manufactured by Hall for their collection," Iris continued, playing it through. "I can even see owning one in each color they were made in, but buying every single one in existence is another game altogether. My impression is that T. Duke Sawyer isn't content to have some of something, he has to have it all."

There was silence behind her.

Iris didn't really think he'd respond. To herself Iris considered how T. Duke's acquisitiveness was reflected in his attitude regarding Pandora. Bridget had told her T. Duke had been extraordinarily intrusive in Pandora's affairs, acting as if he owned much more than 20 percent of the firm. She'd confessed to Iris that she now regretted having taken USA Assets' money—even though she'd never let Kip know that.

This meeting today was a courtesy call to inform T. Duke of Bridget's plans to take Pandora public. Of course, she could take the firm public without Kip or T. Duke's blessing. She owned 60 percent of the stock. Kip and USA Assets owned 20 percent each. Bridget expected T. Duke to support her plan. Why wouldn't he? It meant a nice return on USA Assets' money.

One of the double doors at the top of the stairs opened unexpectedly, startling Iris. Through it walked a tall, leggy, pretty woman with long, blonde hair. She was wearing a well-made pink suit that was suggestively short and snug; a hint of ample cleavage was visible between the lapels. Her makeup was model-perfect and dramatic for the middle of the day. Oddly, her lips were unadorned, without lipstick.

She walked in her high-heeled, do-me shoes to the wood-paneled elevator near the double doors, pressed the button, then turned to look at Iris and Baines. She slightly parted her lips, reached out her tongue, and touched the depression above her top lip. The gesture was frankly sexual. Her eyes were smug.

Iris glanced at Baines, who was still two paces behind her. His face remained immobile, but his eyes sparked.

The elevator doors opened. The woman got in, faced front and bit her bottom lip. The elevator doors silently closed.

"T. Duke's secretary?" Iris ventured, although she doubted the woman's skills had anything to do with word processing.

He ignored her question and held open one of the double doors.

"Thank you for the tour." Iris stepped through the doorway. "Tell me, what kind of a guy is T. Duke to work with?"

Baines's eyes shone. "He's an inspiration. It's an honor to work for him."

"I doubt Rita Free would have shared your opinion."

Baines stared hard at her.

"You must know who Rita Free is." Iris didn't wait for a response. "I read all about her and T. Duke in a *Business Week* article I found on the Internet. About six years ago, T. Duke was having a little party in a Las Vegas hotel suite. Before the night was over, Ms. Free, who made her living as a prostitute, ended up flying off a seventeenth-floor balcony. She didn't have a soft landing. T. Duke's twenty-three-year-old son, Randall, was convicted of manslaughter."

Baines's voice was even but tinged with anger. "Randall Sawyer was a drug addict and alcoholic. He was stoned out of his mind that night. That girl made some comment he didn't like and over she went."

Iris continued, "Randall Sawyer later claimed he took the fall for his old man. He had a lot less to lose by the scandal than T. Duke did. Randall wasn't expected to serve more than eighteen months at the most. Ended up serving five years."

"Randall got all the time that was coming to him. His father was not about to help him get off scot-free."

"People wondered whether Randall was T. Duke's hired gun."

"T. Duke Sawyer does not have hired guns."

"You're sure about that, Baines?"

"Positive." He continued holding one of the heavy double doors open.

Iris looked at his lapel pin. It was then she noticed that instead of stars on a field of blue, there was this insignia: *1x1*.

"T. Duke is one of the finest people I've ever met."

"You're not mad at me, are you, Baines?"

"No."

"I wondered, because you stopped calling me ma'am."

"No, ma'am."

Chapter 5

Iris stepped through the doorway into a large anteroom. A competent-looking middle-aged woman dressed in a conservative suit was working at a desk in a corner. Two couches upholstered in berry and ecru stripes were against the opposite corner. A small coffee table in front of them held several thick books and the remnants of refreshments that had probably been served to Kip and Bridget: a china coffee cup and saucer, a small china plate with cookies, a cut crystal glass, and a can of Pepsi. The books were about modern art. The room's rear wall was taken up by a large window that overlooked the park-like grounds surrounding the building.

The walls were painted flat white like those in the gigantic lobby, but instead of display cases, they were hung with abstract paintings. Iris didn't recognize any of them—which didn't mean anything, given her thin knowledge of art. A carved wooden door was on one wall.

"He's just called them in." The woman at the desk made a sweeping gesture with her hand toward the door.

Baines opened it for Iris and she stepped into another office, larger than the anteroom. This room was also hung with paintings and furnished with a couch, chairs, and a coffee table covered with art books. The centerpiece was a huge desk made from a slab of polished black marble. The desk was void of everything except a multiline telephone. There wasn't even a paper clip to be found. A telephone was the only tool T. Duke needed.

Yet another door led off this room and Iris wondered where she was going next in this opulent but weird place. She felt a vague and unpleasant sensation of being imprisoned.

Baines had already crossed the room and opened that door, but Iris lingered, trying to take it all in. She noticed that the throw pillows and cushions on the couch were askew and mashed as if someone had been relaxing or napping there. On the coffee table in front of it was a crumpled tissue smeared with what appeared to be pink lipstick. Iris remembered the woman at the elevator. Now a girl only removes her lipstick to avoid smearing it on herself or someone or some*thing* else. T. Duke, you old devil you, she thought to herself.

Baines was standing impatiently with a slightly disdainful curve to his lips. Iris sauntered past him and through the doorway, restraining herself from patting his cheek to irritate him.

She spotted Bridget and breathed a sigh of relief at seeing a friendly face. Bridget and Kip were seated at a large, oval table of dark wood that was circled with armless chairs upholstered in a nubby, bright raspberry-colored fabric.

Bridget smiled at Iris. She had been idly doodling with a cheap felt-tip pen on a small, spiral-bound notebook on the table in front of her. A half-full goblet of cola and ice was also on the table. She was wearing a herringbone weave suit with slacks and a cream silk blouse. She looked attentive and alert, exuding the high energy that had always made Iris, no slug herself, feel like a slacker. But Iris detected fatigue around Bridget's eyes.

Kip, who was sitting with his back to the door, turned when Iris came in. He nodded at her, kicking his head back once and raising his eyebrows. He was wearing worn jeans, a rumpled, white dress shirt with the sleeves rolled up and the collar open, and flip-flops on bare feet. The soles of the shoes consisted of layers of bright colored rubber. An open laptop computer was in front of him.

From the head of the long table, T. Duke Sawyer animatedly waved Iris toward him as he continued talking. "So the blind man asks the bartender for another drink. Bartender makes it, puts it on the bar, blind man drinks it. After a while, just like he did before, the blind man picks up his Seeing Eye dog and swings it around by the tail. The bartender's watching this. Finally, he can't restrain himself any longer. 'Mister,' he says, 'I served you three drinks, and after each drink you pick up your dog and swing the poor thing around by the tail. I've just got to ask. What in heaven's name are you doing?' The blind guy shrugs and says, 'Just having a look around.' "

T. Duke looked pop-eyed at his guests then slapped his thigh, threw his head back, and laughed.

Iris laughed as well.

Baines, standing near the door, cracked a grin.

Bridget politely smiled, caught Iris's eye across the table and raised an eyebrow ever so slightly. Iris divined the message: "Just like I described him, isn't he?"

Kip was frowning and staring at a point in the center of the table, as if mulling over what he'd just heard.

Undaunted, T. Duke said, "See, Kip, the blind guy, the Seeing Eye dog"—T. Duke moved his arm as if swinging a lariat—"so the blind guy could have a look. Get it? Have a look. The dog could see but the guy—"

Kip puffed, "I got it. I just don't think it's funny."

"You don't think it's funny," T. Duke repeated. "Well, I guess humor's a sort of individual thing." He stood and walked around the table toward Iris. "And this must be your investment banker, Iris Thorne."

She briskly shook his hand. "Very nice to meet you, Mr. Sawyer."

"Call me T. Duke. Everyone does. From presidents and royalty down to the folks who scrub and clean for me, bless their hearts. We have no formality here. We're all in this together." He still clasped her hand and laughed heartily.

From her research, Iris knew that T. Duke was fifty-six years old and a descendant of Sam Houston, the Texas statesman who was president of the Republic of Texas, then U.S. senator and governor after Texas joined the Union. Although T. Duke had made his home in California since 1979, he remained an active and vocal participant in Texan as well as Californian politics. He'd made his first million before he was twenty-five, turning a $1,000 investment in a beat-up truck into a successful overnight package delivery company. The heady mergers and acquisitions craze during the go-go eighties were custom-made for T. Duke's skills and temperament. It all came crashing down when his ambitions got ahead of his abilities and the law.

T. Duke had a face that could either make or break a person. It was a springboard for T. Duke's trademark self-deprecating humor. His head was shaped like an angular egg with a high and broad forehead, sharply prominent cheekbones, and a narrow, square chin that had a slight dimple in the middle. His nose was large all over, as broad as it was long. A pair of pendulous ears, showcased by T. Duke's closely cropped and well-pomaded graying brown hair, hung like front-door wreaths on either side of his head.

But the most remarkable feature among the eclectic assortment on T. Duke's face was his eyes, which were small in proportion to the rest of his face and dark brown. They shone with intelligence, persistence, and right now, with humor. Iris suspected that could change in an instant to malice.

He was wearing a gray suit with a fine chalk stripe, a bright white, button-down shirt, and a red tie that was fancifully printed with tiny images of Mickey Mouse—an appropriate choice since the Sawyer Company had a large position in Disney. Iris heard he always wore handmade western boots for every occasion, the heels and soles built extra high to boost his five-foot-six-inch height. Today his boots were of black, tooled leather.

Iris said, "I'm not an investment banker. I'm branch manager of McKinney Alitzer's LA office. I'm hoping to use McKinney's IB division to underwrite Pandora's IPO."

"Pandora's IPO." T. Duke finally let go of Iris's hand. "That's why we're here, isn't it?" He looked at her. "Welcome and have a seat. Can I offer something? Soda pop? Coffee?"

"Anything diet."

Without a word, Baines left the room.

T. Duke resumed his position, leaned deeply back into his chair and propped his feet on top of the table.

Iris looked around.

The room was oval, the walls painted in Wedgwood blue with ornately carved crown and base moldings in glossy white. There were several oil paintings, all nineteenth-century landscapes that contrasted sharply with the abstract work displayed in the other rooms.

Baines returned, first placing a heavy coaster on the table in front of Iris before setting a crystal goblet filled with ice and cola on it.

T. Duke clamped his hands behind his head. "Bridget, bring me up-to-date on Pandora."

Bridget leaned her arms against the table and spread her hands in T. Duke's direction. "At midnight, we released the first two levels of *Suckers Finish Last* onto the Internet."

T. Duke nodded as he gazed at the ceiling. "A marketing method you folks pioneered that's now widely imitated. It's brilliantly simple, using the same logic that turns songs into hits by playing them over and over on the radio. You get your Net surfers hooked with a small free taste and hope they want more."

"And they do want more," Bridget interjected. "We've already had a hundred thousand orders—a twenty-five percent increase over sales of *Slade Slayer 3-D* during the same time period. *Slade Slayer 3-D* generated eighteen million in sales. I expect sales of *Suckers Finish Last* to top twenty-five million. There's already buzz in the chat rooms about how *Suckers'* three-D environment tops everything out there."

"Baines took a look at the game you sent over and you thought it was pretty good, didn't you?" T. Duke, still sitting with his hands clasped behind his head and his boots crossed on top of the table, crooked his head over his shoulder to look at Baines, then returned his attention to the ceiling.

Iris casually followed the direction of T. Duke's gaze and was surprised by what she saw there. The high ceiling was painted with a trompe l'oeil fresco of winged cherubs staring down from an expansive blue sky strewn with white clouds backlit by yellow sunlight. The painting gave the illusion that the flat ceiling was domed. The cherubs were positioned in a circle and looked as if they were peering down onto the visitors below. Their faces were oddly quirky, even ugly.

"It has some good stuff in it," Baines said.

Bridget continued, "For *Suckers,* Kip created a radically different graphics engine that produces mesmerizing three-D modeling with detail that's unprecedented in the industry. Baines, maybe you've noticed in other games that are out there and in our previous Slade Slayer releases, that a surface—like a wall or an alien character—will look solid until you get close to it. Then it disintegrates into blocks of colors—the pixels the image is built with."

Iris looked away from the ceiling and refocused her attention on the meeting, but something compelled her to take another look. She now knew why the cherubs seemed peculiar—one of them looked like T. Duke. She covertly glanced at the real-life version and again at the other one, to be sure. It was a younger image, but it was him. The cherub flying next to him had a beautiful woman's face. The two others had the faces of young girls. T. Duke had immortalized himself and his family as heavenly creatures. Iris found the gesture both pompous and touching.

Iris looked more closely at one of the clouds. It was white and puffy like the others, but was irregularly shaped and had a dark shadow behind it. T. Duke spotted Iris looking at the ceiling. She returned her attention to Baines.

Baines's eyes were bright with the most interest Iris had seen since he'd watched the prostitute get on the elevator. "I know what you mean. But in this game, you can almost get toe-to-toe with your enemies."

"Thanks to Kip's new graphics engine," Bridget enthused. "The detail is finer and closer to reality than anything out there."

Iris looked at Kip. Even though his work was the topic of conversation, he sat with his chair pushed far back from the table as was his habit at meetings. One leg was propped on top of the other, and his arms were folded across his chest with one hand stroking his eyebrow. He slowly and rhythmically rocked his upper body back and forth. His eyes were focused on a point three feet in front of him. He seemed completely detached from the scene, but Iris knew better. She had seen Kip like this before and had also seen him abruptly speak after a long period of silence, interrupting whoever had the floor, and draw the conclusion that no one else had seen or answer the question that had eluded everyone else.

"So you've got a promising new product, a stream of revenue, and you think Pandora's sexy enough to interest investors in an IPO," T. Duke said. "But even though the computer-games industry has grown twenty-five percent over the past few years, you're in the middle of an industry shakeout. There's dozens of small game companies like you out there now. In five years, they'll be consolidated into a handful of big players."

"Pandora is going to be one of those players." Bridget folded her hands in front of her on top of the table as if demonstrating the barrier she was setting around Pandora. "We're going to do it by making a major commitment to the game platform of the future today. In the early days of computer gaming, the predominant platform was dedicated, stand-alone consoles for interactive video games. Sega and Sony dominated the industry. Today, the primary platform is PC-based with groups of contestants playing over networks. Stand-alone machines offer speed and performance that most networks can't yet achieve, but the gap is closing. The Pentium opened doors for graphics acceleration development. New technologies are springing up daily, and performance is doubling about once every eighteen months."

Bridget warmed to her topic. "But games played over PC-based networks will soon be a thing of the past. The gaming platform for the future will be the Internet. Pandora already has a Web site where competitors can play each other, but the number of players is limited and the speed is not there. The race is under way to develop cyberspace arenas where literally millions of PC users separated by thousands of miles will be able to electronically locate opponents in activities ranging from flight simulators to sports competitions to hunt-or-be-hunted games like *Suckers.*"

T. Duke removed his feet from the table, scooted his chair forward, rested his elbows where his feet had been, and formed a steeple with his hands, pressing the point of it against his long nose as he listened.

Kip was still staring hard into space, rocking and stroking his eyebrow. Once or twice, Iris caught him longingly glancing at the laptop computer, like a punished child might look at his friends playing outside.

Iris listened to Bridget with admiration. Her friend was in control of her subject and the meeting. She was a natural leader and had always been calmly certain about any challenge she undertook. Iris had always envied Bridget's inbred confidence and had emulated it with mixed success, feeling sometimes as if she were folding the flimsy tabs of elegant paper doll dresses over her own, naked insecurity.

She leaned forward to get a better look at what she at first thought was a dirty smudge on Bridget's jaw. It appeared to be a bruise that Bridget had tried to conceal with makeup. Her eyes must have conveyed her concern because Bridget casually rested her fingertips against her chin, hiding it.

Bridget lost her train of thought, pausing in her presentation and frowning as she grappled for words. She recovered and now avoided Iris's eyes, focusing only on T. Duke. "There are currently several heavily financed start-up companies developing cyberspace arenas. My goal is to position Pandora at the vanguard. I've already started the process to recruit some of the top system architects in the field."

"If we build it, they will come," T. Duke declared. He moved his chair back, pushed himself up with his hands against his knees, walked to the window that formed one wall of the room, and stood there with his hands clasped behind his back. "Legions of anonymous players will be able to slaughter each other in cyberspace."

Kip finally spoke. "You say that like it's a bad thing."

T. Duke turned and focused his penetrating eyes on Kip. "I'm stating a fact." He folded his arms across his chest and looked down his big nose at them. "R and D costs money. You think you'll raise enough with your IPO. I don't think you will."

"Of course we will," Bridget insisted.

T. Duke's eyebrows shot up as if startled over being asked to put his checkbook away. "Bad timing for an IPO. The market's dropped close to a thousand points over the past two weeks. If you're faced with a bear market, Marilyn Monroe wouldn't look sexy to investors."

"I see it as an expected and long-overdue correction," Iris said hopefully. "The worst is over."

"Whatever you want to call it, there's a chill in the market. Many analysts claim that we ain't seen nothin' yet. The IPO parade has passed you by. Firms who were planning IPOs are pulling back and waiting. Investors have grown skeptical after the rash of offerings by Internet firms that still haven't turned a profit."

Iris said, "Granted, there was a lot of foam on the cappuccino with high valuations for Internet companies which had illusory profits. That's not the case with Pandora."

"If the dog's head isn't in the dish, you're not going to have any takers for your IPO," T. Duke said with finality. "Pandora's living on credit and dreams. You've got a good revenue stream, but you've overextended yourself and you haven't spent the five million in venture capital my group invested according to the plan we agreed upon."

"That's not true," Bridget protested. "We hired people, invested in equipment, moved into larger office space—"

"I guess you can call that airplane hangar with that tree house inside it offices." T. Duke laughed good-naturedly, but his eyes didn't convey warmth.

"The competition is fierce for good people," Bridget continued. "I can't afford top salaries yet so I thought the money was better invested in creating a unique, fun, and supportive working environment."

"And that's why you give away food and soft drinks and have in-house baby-sitting and a company basketball court. Does seem like a fun place to work. I see your people spending half the day playing basketball."

"My people frequently work twelve-hour days, seven days a week. They need someplace to blow off steam." Bridget glared at T. Duke. "I'm surprised about your lack of enthusiasm over an IPO. The venture capitalist's goal is to invest in a company, build it, take it public, and realize a return."

"Dear, believe me," T. Duke said, "I do want a return on my

investment, but an IPO is not the way for Pandora to go." He again sat down, leaned forward onto the table, and steepled his hands. "I've got a better mousetrap for you. I want to make Pandora a wholly owned subsidiary of the Sawyer Company. I'll either swap Sawyer stock for Pandora or pay you cash outright."

Iris and Bridget gaped at T. Duke. Kip stopped rocking. Bridget asked the question that was on all their minds. "Why?"

"The Sawyer Company owns several Internet service providers, Web publishing outfits, high-tech magazines, and games firms. My goal is a synergy among the companies I acquire. I see Pandora as a cornerstone of an Internet-based games division. Bridget, you'll head up the profit center. Kip, you'll be our resident guru. You'll be free to design systems to your heart's content on whatever projects tickle your fancy. I'm prepared to take on your entire staff and give them cash bonuses to stay on, up to a hundred grand to your top people, as well as trade their options in Pandora for Sawyer stock. You know I'm very generous with bonuses to my management. Last year, our MIS director earned a million-dollar bonus. Our head of publishing earned five hundred thousand. Both of you can do the same. You don't have to make a decision today. I'm sure you'll want to think about it."

"I warned you, Bridget," Kip said. "You gave him an inch, now he wants everything. The answer is no. Pandora is not for sale."

T. Duke smiled crookedly. "Forgive me, Kip, but your wife is the majority shareholder and is the only one who can make that decision. I'm prepared to offer seven dollars a share for Pandora. That's very generous and more than you'd expect to receive as a lay down price in an IPO in these market conditions."

"That's barely equal to the equity of the firm," Iris said.

"We'd easily get more than that from an IPO," Bridget added.

T. Duke clasped his hands behind his head. "It's typical for an entrepreneur to overestimate the value of her firm."

"You don't get it, do you?" Kip said. "None of you get it. This isn't about money. It was never about making money. Money was something that just happened. It's about vision. It's about doing what we love and having the freedom to do it."

"You'll have all the freedom you could ever want."

"Bull." Kip put both his feet on the ground. "You try to control Pandora now. If it was up to you, you'd turn the Slade Slayer games into advertising vehicles for the Sawyer Company." He imitated T. Duke's Texas accent. " 'How about a nice little ol' billboard on this street for *Computer Nation* magazine? What about embedding United Telephone's logo along this wall, sort of a subliminal suggestion to the game's players?' " Kip scowled. "You've already tried to influence our games' content." He again imitated T. Duke. " 'How about less violence, kids? Does Slade Slayer *have* to use the Lord's name in vain?' "

T. Duke jabbed his finger angrily in Kip's direction. "You don't consider embedding pentagrams into a wall pattern or having a statue of Jesus lifting his robes destructive to the youth of this nation?"

Kip sniggered. "Look how fast his folksy, corn pone act goes sour once he doesn't get what he wants."

"No—you think it's funny, just some sort of big joke. Now you've inserted even more sexual content into the game with this Cherry Divine character."

Kip looked at Baines. "So, my man Baines made it to the tenth level?" he sneered. "All *right!* But I bet you didn't kill her, did you?"

Baines ignored him.

"All this is part of what made Pandora what it is today," Bridget interjected. "We're out there, on the edge. That's what our customers want, that's what they like, that's why we're number one. You of all people ought to understand that."

"It saddens me that you had a perfect opportunity to set a good example for the young people of this nation and you chose to use your brilliant minds and talents to create something sordid."

Kip stood and began prowling back and forth. "This was a violent world before I developed my first game ten years ago. I think I'm providing a service. Kids can play one of my games, kill dozens of bad guys in cyberspace, release their aggressions, then turn off the computer and go peacefully into the world."

"T. Duke, I'm confused," Iris said. "Last year, you approached Pandora with the offer of venture capital knowing full well what the firm was all about, even though you apparently have a problem with the product. Now, instead of encouraging the firm to go public so you can see a return on your investment, you want to shell out more cash to buy it and pay its employees top dollar to stay on. None of this makes good investment sense. If I were a member of your USA Assets group, I'd be angry."

"When I see a good investment, I pounce. My sole goal in offering to buy Pandora is to own what I consider the best of Pandora—the patents on the games engines and the intellects of Kip and Bridget Cross. It's the only way I have a prayer of getting back the five million in venture capital my group invested. Five million that you two spent inappropriately."

"That's not true!" Bridget protested. "I just explained to you how it was spent."

"Yes, and you conveniently left out the cars and that hilltop mansion and all the other trappings of the good life that you and your husband felt you had to have as newly minted high-tech superstars. The only thing you bring to the table to remedy the situation is an ill-timed IPO. We're not going to make any money off that. And that's the bottom line."

Iris glanced at Bridget who seemed at a loss for words. Kip was pacing sullenly, staring at the carpet, his arms folded across his chest. T. Duke looked irritatingly self-satisfied.

Iris broke the tense silence. "T. Duke, you've done a lot of talking about making money, which is why we're here, after all."

T. Duke smiled indulgently at her.

"For all your assertions about how you need to show a return on your investments, the Sawyer Company—a hodgepodge of business interests, a few dating from your takeover days—isn't making money. Any of this so-called synergy that you were talking about not only eludes me, but Wall Street isn't getting it either. During a bull market, Sawyer stock's performed poorly. Plus, the firm's carrying a high level of debt due to these high-priced acquisitions you mentioned. Some analysts have soured on Sawyer stock, and many mutual fund managers are dumping it. If interest rates go up, you could be in a lot of trouble." She casually crossed her legs.

"Iris, I'm pleased to see you've done your homework. You're a smart lady—and beautiful too, by the way—but darlin', what's your point?"

Iris noticed Bridget stiffen at T. Duke's comment, but Iris took it in stride. "Why take on more debt to own Pandora? It doesn't make sense."

T. Duke stood and gave his trousers a hitch before he strolled across the room. "Iris, anyone who knows me understands that money is what makes T. Duke Sawyer tick. I have a long-term perspective in terms of the Sawyer Company. Being of the MTV generation, you probably don't have an appreciation for that sort of thing. As a balance, my venture capital group, USA Assets, is positioned to take advantage of near-term profits."

"So take your profits, with a Pandora IPO," Iris said with emotion. "I know the market for IPOs has cooled, but Pandora has a good track record and reputation. USA Assets would see a nice return."

T. Duke put his hands in his pockets. "Iris, we've been over this already."

"There's another thing that bothers me," Iris persisted. "I can't find any information on USA Assets. I've asked around, but no one can tell me who the other partners are. Why the secrecy?"

"Why not?" T. Duke winked at her.

"Iris is right," Bridget said, looking at her husband who was still wearing a path into the carpet at the far end of the room. "There are many things that don't make sense in relation to the Sawyer Company and USA Assets."

"Bridget, you sound as if you regret having jumped into bed with me. Fact of the matter is, we are in bed and we've got a problem."

Kip stopped pacing and faced T. Duke, his arms straight by his sides. "Enough!" he yelled. "Out! I want you out of my company! I'll buy you out. How much?"

"You don't have the ten million I'd ask for my twenty percent stake."

"Ten million? You only invested five!" Bridget said.

T. Duke shrugged. "USA Assets has entrusted me to show a return on our money."

Bridget sat erect in her chair. "I'm not interested in being a subsidiary of the Sawyer Company. I'm going to take Pandora public. You'll get your return on your investment that way."

Kip bitterly shook his head. "We can buy him out. VC firms call us all the time. We can get ten million. It would be worth it to get him out."

Bridget looked at Kip with annoyance. "We're taking the firm public."

"You're doomed to failure," T. Duke said. "In my humble opinion. I've offered you a parachute and you're about to let it slip through your fingers."

Bridget laced her fingers on the table. "T. Duke, you yourself told me that if you want to run with the big dogs, you have to lift a leg."

"I'm full of old sayings. Here's another one: There's more than one way to skin a cat."

"You're not getting my company, T. Duke," Bridget said with finality.

"So this is your company now," Kip said. "I'm the one writing code all night long and now it's your company."

"Ma'am, I always get what I want," T. Duke said. "I'd advise you to take my offer now. It will be best for you and your husband in the long run."

"Is that some sort of a threat?"

"Of course not."

Bridget stood. "You've got twenty percent of Pandora and that's all you're going to get unless you buy more stock after we go public."

"Dear heart, that's one of the great misconceptions about life. Everything's for sale. All you have to do is determine the price."

Bridget hoisted her briefcase from the floor onto the table, slipped her notebook and pen inside, and snapped the lid shut. Kip closed the personal computer and zipped its case closed.

T. Duke walked to Bridget with his hand extended. She reluctantly took it. "I so enjoyed our meeting. Thanks for stopping by. We'll be in touch."

Iris stood and took a last look at the fresco on the ceiling. She now had a better view and could see that the irregularly shaped cloud disguised the vague outline of another cherub. T. Duke had apparently had the image of someone painted over.

Chapter 6

From Pacific Coast Highway, Iris sharply turned the Triumph and ascended Casa Marina Drive. The road was steep and narrow and its asphalt was cracked and sunken in places, revealing rows of wood piles that supported it. A sign at the base of the hill warned that the streets of Casa Marina were so fragile, passage was reserved for residents and guests only.

"Thanks for taking me to pick up Brianna and giving me a lift from T. Duke's," Bridget said.

"That was a hell of a thing for Kip to do," Iris said. "Just take off and leave you standing there."

Bridget stared through the Triumph's windshield.

Iris patted her leg. "C'mon. Things are gonna get better."

Bridget gave her a wan smile.

Iris frowned sympathetically. "Poor you. Squeezed between Kip and T. Duke. Two bullheaded men."

"I felt T. Duke was making me an offer I couldn't refuse." Bridget glanced at her daughter, who was sitting on the shelf behind the TR's two seats, singing along with a song playing on the radio. "T. Duke said the Sawyer Company owns other computer-games firms. Do you know who they are?"

"I don't recall. They have such a mishmash of holdings. Wait a minute . . . What about 3-D Dimensions?" Iris squeezed the TR close to the side of the narrow road to allow an approaching car to pass. "Do they produce games?"

Bridget nodded. "I didn't know they'd been bought out by Sawyer. Kip was friendly with one of the guys who built the company. I think his name was Harry Hagopian. He was a computer geek, like Kip. A few years ago, they put out a hunt-or-be-hunted game called *Fate* that was very state-of-the-art. Kip and I were impressed."

"Have they put out anything since they were bought by Sawyer?"

"There was a second version, *Fate Two.*"

"Be interesting to talk to Hagopian and see why he decided to sell to T. Duke and how he's found the experience."

"He's dead. Flipped his car one night in the Mojave Desert near Baker, I think about a year ago." Bridget scraped her hair back with both hands and turned her face toward the sun. They were driving with the TR's top down.

The news chilled Iris. "That's weird."

Bridget looked at her friend skeptically. "You can't possibly think T. Duke had anything to do with it."

"I told you about the Las Vegas prostitute who ended up . . ." Iris glanced at Brianna. "You know."

"And his son was found guilty. C'mon, Iris, T. Duke's a businessman, not a gangster."

"Are we going home?" Brianna asked.

"We're going to see Aunt Iris's new house, then we're going home," Bridget answered.

Iris said, "I must have been nuts to buy in this neighborhood. I had every intention of buying closer to downtown. Where do I end up? Casa Marina, five miles from my old, quaked-out condo on an even more fragile piece of property. The quakes shake harder here. Streets and houses get regularly washed down the hill in floods." She maneuvered the TR around a hairpin turn constructed to circumvent a section of the hillside that had washed away. "And let's not forget all this natural vegetation the residents love that regularly goes up in flames."

"C'mon, Iris," Bridget chided. "You like living on the edge.

That's why I knew this house was perfect for you when I first saw it. Plus we can be neighbors again."

"Now I'll be literally living on the edge. The backyard has lost ten feet in the last six years to erosion. That's why I got the house as cheaply as I did. The previous owners were glad to unload it before it slid down the hill."

Bridget scoffed at her friend's concern. "You had all the geological tests done. Just have the backyard shored up and it'll be fine."

"You're ruining all my fun. I just got my mother worked up into a near frenzy over the possibility that I might perish in a mudslide."

"We'd be lucky to see any rain this year. This has been the driest winter I can remember in a long time. They're already talking water rationing."

"I wish these hot winds would stop."

Casa Marina Drive, where Iris's new house was located, was one of three streets that circled the large hill, dividing it like a wedding cake. Capri Road was the street above Casa Marina Drive, and above that was Cielo Way, which circled the crest. Two narrow, almost vertical lanes—Capri Court and Cielo Court—connected the three streets. The streets were also linked by steep cement stairways, constructed in the 1920s. At the bottom of the bluff below Casa Marina Drive was the Pacific Coast Highway. A cement bridge spanned its four, constantly busy lanes. On the other side of the bridge, a spiral staircase led down to the sand of Casa Marina Beach.

"How is your mom?" Bridget asked.

"Good," Iris curtly responded.

"She must be happy about you and Garland."

"She doesn't know about me and Garland. And she won't know until I'm reasonably certain the relationship will stick. So don't tell her."

"Does she still pester you about getting married?"

Iris looked blankly at her friend.

"Mom still needs to get a life, huh?"

"An understatement. You'd think my sister, her three teenagers, and her ongoing marital discord with my brother-in-law would keep my mom occupied. But she still finds plenty of time to butt her little nose into my affairs."

"What about Garland? Is he marriage-minded?"

"I don't know. He was only divorced two years ago. He's got two kids, one in college, the other still in high school. We haven't broached the issue yet."

"Are you?"

"I've been thinking about it."

"Will miracles never cease!"

"Shaddup."

The street wended past houses that were scattered haphazardly across the face of the bluff, wherever the land appeared sturdy enough to support a structure. In between were native sycamore trees, scrub oak, cactus, sage, bougainvillea, wild mustard and wheat. The thick chaparral was home to lizards, gophers, an occasional rattlesnake and several camps of homeless people.

Casa Marina's houses were all sizes and shapes. There were tiny wood-framed bungalows from the 1920s built well back from the street with large front lawns, neat flowerbeds, and white picket fences, alongside huge, brand-new homes in minimalist designs with glass blocks and staggered terraces that consumed all available space on their lots, their front doors almost on the street. There were a few old mansions left—most of them built in the 1930s by motion picture people. Kip and Bridget's house was one—a turquoise and white Spanish Gothic manse built in 1932 by a blonde bombshell of the era. It was the sole house on the crest of the hill.

The backyards of most of the homes were terraced down the face of the bluff. Some residents had reinforced their chunk of hill with steel and concrete supports and had bravely installed swimming pools, patios, and expensive landscaping. These same enhancements sometimes created tourist photo opportunities when the shifting earth scattered the pools and patios across the hillside, leaving the broken edges seemingly suspended in air.

Iris stopped the Triumph in the middle of the street near a clearing that gave a view of the coast. The wind-blown sky was rendered blue-white by the bright sun that speckled the calm ocean. "Wow."

"What a beautiful day."

"You can see all the way from Point Dume to Palos Verdes," Brianna piped from behind them.

"That's right, sweetheart," Bridget said. "And what's that shadow out there in the ocean?"

"Santa Catalina Island. It's thirty miles away."

Bridget turned and squeezed Brianna's leg. "That's very good."

Iris drank in the scene. "It does something for me, being able to see the horizon and the curve of the earth. Calms me. I never get tired of it."

"It makes me happy to share this with you since things in my own house are in disarray."

"What's disarray, Mommy?"

"Messy, sweetheart."

"Because Summer's leaving, we don't have anyone to clean the house?"

"Yes." Bridget winked at Iris. "But we'll find someone."

"I'm going to miss Summer," Brianna declared. "She was fun. Why does she have to go?"

"It was time for Summer to leave," Bridget said.

Iris let the clutch out too fast and stalled the Triumph. "Darn." She turned the key in the ignition. It just clicked in response. She tried it again, and again it clicked.

"What's wrong?" Bridget asked.

"The starter's been acting up." Iris tried a few more times before the engine finally turned over. She put the car into first gear and headed down the street.

"You'd better get that fixed before you get stuck somewhere."

"Yes, ma'am." Iris leaned close to Bridget and asked in a voice too low for Brianna to hear, "So it's *hasta la vista,* Summer?"

Bridget leaned close to respond. "She was moving out at a snail's pace this morning. If she's not gone by the time I get home tonight, I'm throwing the rest of her stuff on the street. You should get a load of the attitude. Hell hath no fury like a bimbo scorned. She's not the only one who's making an exit. I told Kip to fire Toni Burton."

"You're making him do it?"

"I think it's appropriate."

"Do I see a little vengeance showing?"

Bridget tweaked her lips into a sly smile.

Iris pulled into the driveway of a tiny yellow bungalow and cut the engine.

"Is this your new house, Aunt Iris?" Brianna scrambled from the TR, kicking her hard-soled shoes against the finish.

Iris gritted her teeth.

Brianna ran to the front door and pressed the doorbell. "You already have mail, Aunt Iris," she shouted as she pulled a handful of junk mail from the box. She ran to hand it to Iris, then skipped after a butterfly that was floating across the lawn.

"Thank you, honey." Iris got out of the Triumph.

Bridget also got out and arched her back. "After I finally figured out what was going on between Kip and Toni, Toni approached me about it. She was very sorry, embarrassed, et cetera."

"You believe her?"

Bridget shrugged. "She told me she did it because she admired me so much."

"Weird way of showing it."

"I thought so. Anyway, she was concerned about losing her job."

"She any good?"

"She works hard, has a lot of enthusiasm, but she's not as smart or talented as she thinks she is. I made it known that I'm recruiting a VP of marketing. She pitched herself for the job, but I had to honestly tell her I didn't think she had what it takes. Anyway, both Kip and Toni swore the affair was over. But last night, they were just too cutesy with one another, and it pissed me off. Enough is enough. But I'm putting myself in a bad position by getting rid of both Toni and Summer. I need all the hands I can get at Pandora right now, and someone has to stay with Brianna."

"And you're still going to divorce Kip?"

Bridget nodded.

Iris sighed as she watched Brianna who had caged the butterfly on the grass between her hands.

"Iris, he hit me last night. He crossed a line and there's no going back."

"You're right," Iris said with resignation. "I can't believe he'd hit you . . . that it's come to that. Maybe if you talked to someone . . ."

"You know how Kip is. I could never get him to a marriage counselor. If it's not something that can be logically laid out in black and white, he thinks it's witchcraft. Kip was never good with change. It's ironic because he loves staying on top of new developments in high technology, but in his personal life, he craves stability. I was his only girlfriend before we got married."

"I think he would have had every meal by himself his entire college career if you hadn't approached him in the dorm cafeteria." Iris watched Brianna release the butterfly into the air. "You saw a side to him that no one else did. And you were right. He was playful, funny—even a hunk in an unkempt, Tarzan kind of way. At first, the girls on the floor thought you were nuts for going out with him, then we were all jealous."

Bridget put her hands in the pockets of her slacks. "I love Kip—I always will. But I'm not in love with him anymore, if you know what I mean."

"Do you guys still own that gun?"

"It's around somewhere. Why? Afraid I'll use it on him?" Bridget said jokingly.

"I fear it might be the other way around."

"That's what Alexa was afraid of, too." Bridget closed her eyes and shook her head.

"That detective who interviewed you called me today about Alexa. Apparently, they don't have much to go on. I'm afraid they'll never find out who did it. You read about so many murders in LA going unsolved."

"It's a nightmare. And I was the one who felt I was being watched."

"You did? When?"

Bridget pursed her lips. "It was probably nothing."

"You're not going to tell me what happened?"

"It was *nothing*, really. A noise in the Pandora parking lot. A shadow on the patio. My imagination on overtime, is what it was." Bridget sighed and changed the subject. "Anyway, Jim told me that Alexa wanted to be cremated, but didn't leave any instructions about the disposition of the ashes. He and Alexa's mother are now engaged in a war. She wants the ashes interred in the family cemetery. He wants to shoot them into space, like Timothy Leary did with some of his."

Iris rolled her eyes.

"They might end up dividing the ashes between them."

"Oh, ick."

Bridget looked at her daughter, who was standing at the edge of the lawn with her hands on her hips, gazing at the hillside across from Iris's house. "What are you looking at, honey?"

"I don't like that house. It's spooky." Brianna pointed at a large, abandoned house built on Capri Road, the street above Iris's. The back door hung open from a single hinge. The walls were cracked and the chimney had fallen through the roof.

"What's the story with that house, anyway?" Iris asked.

"It was damaged in the Northridge quake, and from what I heard, the owners walked away from it. I don't know why the bank doesn't tear it down. Homeless people live in it. I'm afraid they're going to set it on fire one night." Bridget turned toward Iris's house. "Now, let's have a look around, Miss Homeowner."

The small two-bedroom, one-bath, wood-framed bungalow was built in 1922 and had been lovingly maintained. It was painted pale yellow with white trim. Half-circles carved with rays resembling sunbursts were set atop each window. A large sunburst was visible beneath the eaves of the attic.

A brick path lined with flowerbeds led to the front door which opened directly into the sun-washed living room. All the rooms except the kitchen and bathroom were floored in narrow-planked hardwood. To the right of the living room, beyond an arched entryway was the dining room. This led to the kitchen which had been updated with frosted glass-paneled cabinets, tiled counter tops and floor. Off the kitchen was a laundry room and a back door. A guest bedroom was down the narrow hallway next to the living room. The recently remodeled bathroom was next to that. At the end of the hallway was the master bedroom. A sliding glass door had been installed on the outside wall. It opened onto a hardwood deck that ran the width of the house.

"Do people live in houses this small, Mommy?"

"Brianna, our house is much bigger than what most people live in." Bridget looked apologetically at Iris. "Out of the mouths of babes."

Iris shrugged. "It is a small house. But—location, location, location."

Brianna pulled open the glass door off the master bedroom and bounced across the deck and down to the flower-trimmed yard. A short chain link fence separated the yard from the steep bluff just beyond.

Iris stood in the bedroom in the spot where she'd decided to place her bed and looked at the view. "Every morning, the first thing I see will be the ocean." She spread her arms as if to encompass it.

"This house is really cute. I'm so happy for you!"

"Thanks. I'm still a bit overwhelmed. It's going to be a killer to pay the mortgage."

"You'll do fine. You're doing great. Many good things ahead for you, Iris, and you deserve them all." Bridget hugged her friend.

They watched Brianna squat down to examine something on the lawn. "She's the best thing I've ever done. Everything else pales in comparison to her," Bridget said.

"Lately I've been thinking about having one of those myself."

"No kidding?"

"It's been on my mind, sure. I'd love to have a little girl just like her. Then I think about how it would change my life. I'm so used to only considering myself. Oh, it's all so confusing."

"Would you do it on your own?"

"*If* I do it—no, I wouldn't. I've thought a lot about it and have discovered I'm surprisingly traditional. I think a family should have a mommy and a daddy. It's not fair to the kids otherwise." She bit her lip, knowing this was tactless, but refusing to be less than honest.

"Your parents' divorce really affected you."

"I was fourteen when it happened, and it remains one of the

defining experiences of my life." Iris looked carefully at her friend. "I wouldn't want to put a child of mine through that."

Brianna was carrying whatever she had found on the lawn to the flowerbed, where she carefully deposited it. The sun on her long, dark brown hair shone red.

"Iris, what am I doing? Am I going to ruin her life?"

Iris put her arm around Bridget's shoulder. "Now that you've forced the issue, maybe Kip will come to his senses. This is none of my business, but why don't you see how things go for a few weeks? Breaking up a family is so hard on the children."

Bridget wiped a tear from her cheek. Another quickly followed. She retrieved a tissue from her purse and blew her nose. "Maybe you're right. Maybe I should try to make it work for my daughter's sake. I asked Kip to move out, but . . ."

Brianna was now pulling dandelions from the lawn, holding them by their stems in a bouquet.

"What about Pandora?" Iris asked.

"I'm still taking it public. Kip's got to get over it."

Chapter 7

Bridget Cross slipped off her oversized T-shirt, tossed it on a lounge chair next to the pool, and stood barefoot on the diving board wearing a red, one-piece, racer-back swimsuit. The elastic cut her slender hips only slightly. A gust of dry, warm wind blew, rustling her short brown hair and sending an empty aluminum can scuttling across the patio. She faced the wind, squinting against the airborne debris, then gazed at the black ocean, at the same time turning her back on Kip, who had just walked onto the patio.

The curved coastline was outlined by the Pacific Coast Highway and its endless procession of head- and taillights. The wind had thinned the air, rendering colors and shapes with a surreal clarity. Bridget looked at the sky. A crescent moon hung high and a spray of rarely visible stars shone. Another gust of dry, hot wind blew. She licked her lips and dragged her fingers through her tangled hair.

"I wonder how long it's going to blow?" She could have been talking to herself. "It makes me edgy."

"I don't know what to say to you anymore," Kip said as if he had been carrying on some other, silent conversation with his wife. He wore nothing but red jogging shorts and running shoes. The patchy reflection from the water cast him in a crazy light.

Bridget looked at him as if she had only just realized he was there. She pressed her hands together above her head and bounced on the diving board once, twice, three times, going higher with each jump, then propelled herself into the blue water with a splash.

Stetson, their German shepherd, dozed on the cool cement. He sleepily raised his big head from his paws and pricked his ears when a drop of water hit him on the back.

Kip watched Bridget swim underwater until she touched the wall on the shallow end. Without surfacing, she turned and headed back toward the deep end. Her body grew luminous as she neared the submerged pool light. He held his breath along with her, unaware he was doing so. At the wall, she turned again and forcefully pushed off, almost reaching the middle of the pool before stroking.

At the shallow end once more, she finally broke the surface, panting and smiling. She was proud of herself. "Not bad for an old broad, huh?"

Her smile warmed him. "I love you."

Still trying to catch her breath, she gracefully swam across the pool on her side, her head above the water. She admired her house as she swam. It had a sloping roof of turquoise blue tile, white stucco walls and windows fitted with shutters. The wood trim was painted turquoise blue. A wall of French doors opened onto a large room. It was designed to be a family room, but Kip had appropriated it as a work area. He had left one of the doors open and it banged in the wind. In a corner of the patio near the French doors was Stetson's doghouse. It was wooden with a pitched roof and was big enough to comfortably accommodate the large dog.

The glamorous, blonde, 1930s movie star who had built the mansion had been murdered in the garage—shot in the head. Her killer was never found. Even though the murder had happened a long time ago, Bridget didn't want to buy the house because of it, but the history made Kip love the house even more. He had always had a morbid streak. Bridget couldn't begrudge him that. It was part of the reason they had become successful.

Bridget reached the end of the pool and started swimming in the other direction, this time looking across the patio at the stars. Beyond the patio, their property dropped steeply down the hill, which was densely planted with ice plant to help keep the earth from eroding. A cinder block supporting wall was built at the edge of the property against the street below. On the other side of that street, smaller homes clustered together on the precious oceanfront land. Kip and Bridget's home was the only one on the hilltop.

"You're the love of my life," Kip told her. "You know that, don't you?"

Bridget turned and again swam in the other direction, now watching her husband. "I do."

Kip nodded as he walked around the pool to stand at the edge of the patio. The dog rose and followed him. Kip looked at the black ocean and scratched the dog's head. "I'm so sorry for hurting you."

Bridget swam to the shallow end of the pool and climbed the steps. She picked up a towel from a lounge chair and patted herself with it. "I know."

Kip dragged his hand back and forth across Stetson's back. The dog crouched with pleasure. "Now that I've come clean about everything and promised not to hurt you again, maybe you'll do the same for me."

Bridget wrapped the towel around her and walked to the flowerbed at the edge of the yard beyond the shallow end of the pool, reached down, and picked up the empty aluminum can that had rolled there. She crumpled the can in her hand and walked to the row of garbage cans on the other side of the yard, lifting a lid and dropping it in one labeled CANS AND BOTTLES. "What do you mean?"

"You want to take Pandora public to get back at me, don't you?"

Bridget gaped at him incredulously. "Kip, we've been over this time and time again."

Kip's face grew red. Still standing on the other side of the pool, he clenched his fists and leaned slightly toward her, his back rigid. "You're not destroying everything I've built!"

"We've built, Kip. *We.* And you can't keep spending money like you have been. That was embarrassing today in front of T. Duke. We have to look good for people to want to invest in us."

"Hey, I promised I'd clean up my act. Now it's your turn to fulfill your part of the bargain."

"Bargain? The only thing I committed to was giving our marriage another try for Brianna's sake. I never said anything about not taking Pandora public."

"I've *earned* the right to do what I want with Pandora, even if that means running it into the ground. *I'm* the genius behind Pandora. Anyone can manage the books." Kip waved dismissively.

"Please stop shouting before you wake Brianna."

He walked across the patio to the wooden fence in the cinder block wall and punched a series of numbers onto a keypad next to it. The light on the keypad changed from red to green, indicating the alarm was disengaged. "I'm going for a run." He opened the gate, stepped outside, glanced back at her, then bolted down the cement staircase that ran next to the house, leaving the gate ajar.

She listened to his footsteps until they faded, when she slowly closed her eyes. She opened them when the dog nudged her hand. She patted his head. "You're a good boy, aren't you?"

She pushed the gate closed. "Probably doesn't have his key. And I don't want to get out of bed to let him in." She left it unlocked.

"How about one more swim to adjust the attitude, Stetson?"

The dog cocked his head at her.

She unwrapped the towel from around her, dropped it on the ground, walked to the side of the pool, and leapt in. No fancy diving this time. She did the crawl hard and sloppily, kicking up a lot of water, expending a lot of energy. She didn't see the dog get up, take a few steps, then stand with his ears pricked as he watched the gate slowly swing open.

She swam to the shallow end of the pool, walked up the steps with her back to the gate, and bent over to pick up the towel. She frowned at the soft sound of flip-flops slapping against the cement. Stetson started barking. She quickly spun around, clutching the towel to her breasts.

A bullet whizzed in front of her, hitting the cinder block wall. She dove for the ground between the lounge chairs, but not before a second bullet hit her in the thigh. A third hit her in the side as she tried to scamper away. She made it behind the doghouse, barely avoiding a fourth bullet that tore through the structure and embedded itself in the cement patio in front of her. She crouched behind the flimsy shelter, screaming. Blood spilled across the patio and she clutched at her wounds as if she could stop the flow.

Stetson was ferociously barking and growling.

Bridget began to creep from behind the doghouse and closer to the unlatched French door that still banged in the wind. She stopped and looked with horror at a small shape that was almost hidden in the shadows inside the house.

"No!" she hoarsely whispered. "Brianna, run!"

There was a fifth gunshot. Stetson yelped, then was quiet.

A sixth shot hit Bridget in the neck. She collapsed on the patio, turning with difficulty to look at the approaching figure.

Chapter 8

They were in the frozen food section of the market, shrink-wrapped in plastic. When I pushed the cart past, their eyes started rolling around."

"Gross!" Kyle Tucker exclaimed.

Iris entered the lunchroom and caught the end of the story. "Liz, what in the world are you talking about?"

Liz Martini clenched a styrofoam cup between her long, red fingernails. She was wearing her signature white: a white leather miniskirt, a matching jacket, and a bright orange jersey top. Her long, dark hair was teased and fluffed into a big style that would have done the Grand Ole Opry proud. "My toy poodles, Thelma and Louise."

"I don't know why you take that stuff." Kyle sorted through the sections of the daily paper that were tossed on one of the tables. He held his long, rubbery lips in a diagonal line.

"Oh honey, puh-leese." Liz slapped her nonexistent belly. "I've put on ten pounds right here since—"

"Would someone please tell me what the hell you're talking about?" Iris complained.

"Redux," Liz pronounced momentously. "I just started it two

days ago. It's *fab*-ulous." She pressed her fingertips against Iris's arm. "Now the government's taken it off the market, but I have a friend who can buy you some in Tijuana" —she leaned close to Iris and whispered—"real cheap."

Iris filled her mug with black coffee. "I thought you were taking fen/phen."

Liz pursed her lips as if tasting something bitter. "Redux is much better."

"Doesn't it have side effects, like heart damage?" Kyle asked in his straightforward manner.

Liz brushed away his comment with a flick of her hair. "Some rats got sick or something. What does that have to do with me? I feel great. Know what I ate last night? A rice cake. And I couldn't even finish it. Ozzie had a fit. 'Liz,' he tells me, 'you're going to end up in the hospital at the rate you're going.' I told him, 'Ozzie, you're the one who's always looking at all the skinny tramps.' "

"So what's with Thelma and Louise?" Iris asked.

"Another side effect of Redux," Kyle explained. "Vivid dreams."

As Kyle left the lunchroom with the sports section, he held the door open for Amber Ambrose who entered and greeted everyone with a cheery, "Hi!"

Iris and Liz smiled and greeted her unenthusiastically. Iris liked Amber's sales performance and Liz admired the clientele Amber had built in her relatively short number of years in the business, but neither of them trusted the young woman farther than they could throw her. Amber was hopelessly competitive and a proven backstabber. A backstabbing bitch, according to Liz. Even worse, Amber was suspected of taking office news directly to Sam Eastman, Iris's boss. That made her a spying, backstabbing bitch.

When Amber entered the room, Iris and Liz exchanged a glance, both of them knowing what the other was thinking. Silently, both decided Liz's notorious mania for dieting didn't need any further propagation throughout the office.

Iris was about to make her departure when Louise abruptly opened the door.

"Ah, here you are," Louise said. "There are two police detectives to see you."

"Detectives?" Iris repeated. "About Alexa again?"

Iris could almost see Amber's ears prick up. Liz, on the other hand, looked concerned.

"They wouldn't tell me why they're here," Louise said.

Without another word, Iris quickly walked back to her office. Standing at the window was a small, dark-haired woman in her thirties. A fiftyish man with a fringe of black hair encircling the base of his shiny head was sitting in one of her damask chairs. He had protruding, almond-shaped eyes and stood when Iris entered.

The woman made the introductions as the man closed the door.

"I'm Detective Tiffany Stubbs and this is Detective Jess Ortiz. We're with the West LA homicide department. Casa Marina is in our jurisdiction."

Iris sat in her leather chair. She sensed it might be necessary.

The woman continued, "There was a homicide at a house there last night around ten o'clock. Has anyone told you . . . ?"

Iris slowly shook her head.

"I'm sorry to bring bad news. Bridget Cross was shot to death."

Iris stared at the woman. She was aware of the other officer dispassionately watching her from where he sat. Something in her head started to buzz. Stubbs was talking and she could barely make out what she was saying.

". . . a terrible loss. Her husband told us you're a friend of hers and saw her yesterday."

Iris swiveled her chair to look out the window behind her desk. The day was clear and she could see Catalina Island. "Where's Kip?" she blurted, thinking she was interrupting Detective Stubbs, then realizing the detective had asked her a question and was waiting for a response.

"He's been arrested for his wife's murder," Ortiz said.

"Do you have evidence?" Iris asked defiantly.

"Yes, ma'am. We do." Stubbs hooked a lock of her straight, dark brown, chin-length hair around an ear. The severe style did not complement her round face. She was wearing an inexpensive gray flannel suit with nap that had balled in spots and a white blouse with a round collar and a narrow self-tie. Her shoes were plain, low-heeled, black pumps. She had deep-set brown eyes and thin lips that barely moved when she talked. For some reason, Iris took an immediate dislike to her. Perhaps it was simply because she had delivered the bad news.

"We'd like to ask you a few questions," Stubbs said.

"I wanted her dead, Iris. I did. I'm not going to lie to you. But I didn't kill her." Kip talked to Iris from behind a window of thick, scratched plastic. He was wearing a royal blue jumpsuit. "You believe me, don't you?"

She responded with conviction, even though she had her doubts. "Yes."

"The police are after me, Iris. I heard some of the guards talking: 'Another rich guy who murdered his wife. Watch him get away with it.' "

"What do you think about Tommy Preston?"

Kip grimaced. "What a blowhard."

"He's one of the best criminal attorneys in town."

"Is that why I'm paying nine hundred and fifty dollars an hour, because he's got everyone duped into thinking he's a superstar? I saw him in the paper at some benefit standing next to Barbra Streisand. Mr. Big Celebrity," Kip sneered.

"They haven't even officially charged you yet. Preston thinks there's a good chance the DA will decide there's not enough evidence to prosecute. They'll have to let you go."

"If this thing goes to trial, I'll have to file bankruptcy. Bridget doesn't keep that kind of money in our personal accounts. She has it tied up in the firm."

He was talking about his dead wife in the present tense. Iris didn't correct him. She'd been having the same problem herself. "Pandora can pay your legal fees. You're a principal of the company."

"Why do I need an attorney when I'm innocent? The only reason I'm in here is because they're afraid I might flee. I can thank O. J. Simpson and his Bronco ride for that."

Iris looked at a guard standing in a corner who was eyeing them and lowered her voice. "Are you innocent, Kip?"

His face hardened. "You think I'm not?"

Iris persisted. "Kip, you wouldn't be in here if the police didn't think there was at least a possibility that you murdered Bridget." The words almost stuck in her throat. That was how she would always think about Bridget now. Her murdered friend. "Preston filled me in on what happened last night, but I'd like to hear it from you."

"Okay, okay." He rubbed his forehead with both hands. "Last night . . . God, it was just last night. Things were tense, but they were okay. She was swimming. I told her I loved her." His eyes grew glassy. "Then we had a fight. Not a big one, but a fight."

"About what?" Iris asked even though she thought she knew.

"I'd done what she wanted. Summer was gone."

"And Toni?"

"Didn't get around to Toni. Hell, Bridget wanted to fire everybody. Run everything. The big boss," he said loudly as his anger rose. "Just like her asshole plan for Pandora."

Iris was surprised he'd talk about his murdered wife that way. Her expression must have shown it.

He defiantly stared at her. "I didn't murder my wife, Iris."

"Go on."

"We fought about Pandora, again. Then I went jogging. All I had on were my red jogging shorts and running shoes." He looked squarely at her to emphasize the point. "I guess she didn't lock the gate after I left. I was too mad to lock it." He covered his face with his hand. After a moment, he wiped his eyes and continued. "Anyway, I ran down the staircase to Capri Road. Crossed the street, then ran down the staircase to Casa Marina Drive. Crossed that street, then took the last set of stairs that lead to the bridge. Didn't see anyone."

Iris remarked, "Preston said the police interviewed your neighbors. One of them, an elderly woman, Marge Nayton, lives in the house on the corner of the stairway and Casa Marina Drive. The house I bought is next to hers. She was watching television, an old *Dick Van Dyke Show* that had just started at ten o'clock when she heard someone run past."

"Good." Kip brightened. "The time element is everything. I crossed the bridge and ran down the stairway to the beach.

There were some kids up on the bluff, getting high. I said hello to the guy with the metal detector I see sometimes when I'm jogging."

"That was ten-seventeen," Iris said. "He was certain of the time because he'd just dug a watch out of the sand. It was still running and he'd compared its time to his own watch."

"And he saw me wearing running shoes, not flip-flops, not carrying anything, not covered in blood, and not looking particularly distraught, right?"

"Right." Iris added, "Some of your neighbors reported hearing popping noises or car backfires shortly after ten."

"By the time I saw the guy on the beach at ten-seventeen, my wife was dead and Brianna had already called nine one one. Those jerk cops made me listen to the tape. Idiots with guns and tin stars. Thought that listening to my five-year-old's call for help would jar me into a confession or something." Kip closed his eyes as if the memory was painful.

Iris had heard the recording too. The media had somehow got ahold of it that morning and had been playing it relentlessly: "My mommy's sick. Please come now."

Iris slid to the edge of the hard metal chair. "Preston told me Brianna either didn't see the murderer or doesn't remember."

"She doesn't remember anything after she went to bed. Not even calling nine one one. When the police arrived, they couldn't find her. That dyke, Detective Stubbs, finally found her, crouched in a corner of her bedroom closet." Kip's chin trembled.

Iris wanted to scream, to rage, to tear to pieces whoever had done this. "She might remember in time," she said to be encouraging.

"She doesn't remember anything!" Kip said sharply. "I don't want her dragged into this. The police are already talking about child psychologists and all that bullshit. They're not getting their hands on my daughter!"

Iris didn't know how to respond. She stuck to the facts. "Brianna made the nine one one call at ten-twelve."

Kip was still angry. "Tell me how I could have murdered my wife, left bloody footprints in flip-flops all over the patio and halfway down the stairs, disposed of the murder weapon, and be seen wearing tennis shoes and jogging shorts a half mile from home five minutes later at ten-seventeen?"

"The police acknowledge the time frame is tight. Plus they found black fibers on the bushes at the side of the steps. The murderer may have been wearing black sweats or something."

"And I have to spend time changing clothes? And why would I kill my dog? I loved that dog. Iris, someone murdered my wife and set me up. When I came back from my run and saw the lights and the cops everywhere, I knew immediately what had happened."

"T. Duke?"

"T. Duke. Or someone."

Bridget had scoffed at Iris's concerns regarding T. Duke, but business associates of T. Duke had died under mysterious circumstances before. With Bridget's murder, it seemed unlikely that all the deaths were coincidental. "Did you suggest that to the police or Tommy Preston?"

"Of course. Cops said they'd look into it," he said scornfully, "but they won't. They think they've got their man. It's always the husband, isn't it? And I played right into this person's hand. Acting like a jerk, fighting with Bridget, slapping her . . ."

You mean *slugging* her, Iris mentally corrected him.

"He seized the opportunity."

"I guess that's how he made his fortune, timing the marketplace."

Kip laughed bleakly. "And then Alexa Platt on top of it."

"Did the police ask you about that?"

"Oh yeah. Before the cops are done, they're going to be hanging Hoffa's disappearance on me. If I was going to murder Bridget, don't you think that I, of all people, could come up with a better plan? I certainly wouldn't wear the shoes that are my trademark and tramp through her blood in them."

"It seems as if the murderer deliberately left bloody footprints in size-eleven dime-store flip-flops to incriminate you," Iris said wearily. "Bridget was shot from a distance—he didn't have to step in her blood. The footprints go out the gate, down the steps, and disappear into the brush at the side where the police found the black cotton fibers on the bushes." She pulled a folded envelope from her purse and started writing on it. "I need to lay all this out. Okay, Marge Nayton heard you at ten . . ." She looked at Kip. He had folded his arms across his chest, was stroking his eyebrow and slowly rocking back and forth.

"It's my fault, Iris."

She looked at him with surprise.

"Before I cheated on Bridget, the worst thing I'd done is drive too fast or go through a yellow light too late. But after I crossed that first boundary, a process was set into motion. It has to run its course."

Iris spoke under her breath, trying to move her lips as little as possible so that the guard couldn't make out what she was saying. "Are you saying you murdered Bridget?"

"No!" He bitterly shook his head. "It's cause and effect. I crossed the first line."

"Are you talking about divine retribution?"

"Not religion!" He slammed his hand on the table. "Physics! Action and reaction."

Iris tried to take in what he was saying. She wasn't getting it.

"I've thought a lot about this since last night. I'm convinced I'm right. I have an adversary."

"T. Duke Sawyer."

"I'm not completely certain about his human form. It's the boss monster. I made my move, now he's made his. The cops kept asking me about a slingshot."

"They asked me if I knew whether you had one. What's the significance? Tommy Preston couldn't get any information from the cops on that."

"It's his trademark. I'll bet there was one left at the crime scene. He's made his move. He's trying to beat me at my own game." Kip looked at her meaningfully.

Iris not only had no clue regarding what he was talking about, but she was getting irritated. This was no time to play games. "Kip, in my heart I know you're innocent, but there are a couple of things about Bridget's murder I can't square in my mind."

Kip impatiently nodded.

"Bridget was shot with a forty-five-caliber revolver. You have a forty-five registered in your name. The police can't find it."

"Bridget fired a housekeeper for stealing. I haven't seen that gun in ages. It could have been gone for months. Next."

"You had gunshot residue on your right palm."

"It's a secondary transfer. I probably got it on my hand when I touched the gate in the same place the murderer did."

"The police claim that's impossible."

He glowered at her. "It's *not* impossible!"

She stared back at him. "Kip, you and Bridget have been two of my closest friends for years. Old friend to old friend, tell me the truth about what happened last night."

He abruptly stood. "Guard, I'm finished here."

Chapter 9

Bridget Cross, née Tyler, was raised with her three brothers in a modest neighborhood of small, neat homes in the Orange County city of Anaheim, in the shadow of Disneyland. The Tyler house was unremarkable, indistinguishable from any of the other forty-year-old, stucco, tract homes that wore twenty-year-old paint in outmoded colors of pastel pink, seafoam green, or Popsicle orange. Trees that homeowners had planted nearly half a century ago—pretty pines, clusters of palms, and matching poplars, lined up like soldiers during inspection across the front of the yard—now dwarfed the homes behind them. Many of the original owners still lived in the neighborhood where scads of children once played in the streets. Young families were once more moving in as the old people died or went to live in retirement villages.

Iris had spent many weekends at Bridget's house when they were in college. The Tylers never seemed to mind having Iris around. She enjoyed fleeing the turmoil of her own house for the Tylers' unremarkable middle-America-anywhere life of weekend barbecues, televised ball games, driveway basketball, and Chinese takeout. She also found the idea of having brothers fascinating.

Iris walked past the overgrown poplars and down the cement path crossing the Tylers' front lawn and rang the bell. Chimes dingdonged inside the house. The fifteen years that had passed since she had last rung that bell seemed to pancake. Regret washed over her. If she'd only advised Bridget to run for her life.

"Iris, I'm so glad you came." Natalie Tyler's face and eyes were puffy from extended crying. She was still slender, but now her round belly protruded from underneath her yellow and brown floral-print shirt and beige polyester pants. Her hair was Bridget's dark brown but heavily salted with gray. She wore it short and tightly curled—the work of her hairdresser whom she visited once a week for a wash, set, and comb-out. Natalie's face bore a striking similarity to her daughter's; Bridget used to observe that all she had to do to know how she would appear in twenty-five years was to look at her mother.

"Mrs. Tyler . . ." Iris dropped the bag she was carrying onto the porch and embraced Bridget's mother. For the first time since the police had told her of Bridget's murder earlier that day, she was overwhelmed with grief. She wanted less to comfort Natalie than be comforted herself. She clutched the woman tightly as tears rolled down her face. She recovered and felt embarrassed for laying her needs on this poor woman.

Iris reached into the bag on the ground and retrieved a thick paper napkin with which she wiped her face and eyes. Much of her workday makeup came off onto it. She handed Natalie the bag from the trendy grocery store that she had driven out of her way to visit and where she had shamefully overpaid for their deli department's prepared food. "Here's some lasagna. It's a little different, in a béchamel sauce, but I think Joe will still like it. And there's a Caesar salad, Italian bread, and a bottle of Barbera."

"Thank you, Iris. That's so sweet of you."

"And a lemon cheesecake." Iris felt silly. The food seemed a pitifully inadequate gesture.

"Come in." Natalie stepped away from the door and Iris walked inside. She followed Natalie through the modest, clean house that was decorated with sturdy furnishings and numerous framed photographs. They reached the rear of the house where the family room was located. It was crowded with people, some of whom Iris recognized as Bridget's brothers. Through a picture window, she saw a throng of children playing in the backyard.

"Joe, look who's here."

Joe Tyler slowly rose from a La-Z-Boy recliner. He had always been a burly man but had filled out since his retirement from the tire factory where he had worked his entire adult life. His full head of wavy hair had gone silver. He clasped Iris in a bear hug that took her breath away. It was as if he could somehow touch his daughter by clutching her friend. Grabbing both of her arms, he held her away from him and looked piercingly into her face. He didn't say a word and neither did she. His eyes were glassy with tears. It took everything Iris had to stand upright and not to collapse into his arms, irrationally feeling that surely this man with his bear hug would be able to ease her pain.

He had once, a long time ago. It was something to do with a guy, Iris couldn't even remember the details now. Joe Tyler had seen her crying and given her a hug and offered to talk to the young man. She was touched beyond words that someone had not only recognized her distress but had offered to help. She was so accustomed to toughing out life's difficulties on her own. But he couldn't help her today. He released her and trudged back to his chair.

Iris endured the introductions and reintroductions and accepted a glass of wine and half a sandwich from the dining room table which was piled high with food brought by friends who had the same notion as Iris—grief could be fed or drowned into oblivion.

"It's Monday, eleven o'clock at Pleasant Hills." Natalie was telling her the funeral plans. "The Chapel of the Good Shepherd." They were standing in the dining room. Iris nibbled on the sandwich and sipped the wine which felt pleasantly warm in her throat.

"We'd wanted the funeral sooner, of course, but the police wouldn't release her body before then. They said they'll let Kip come to the funeral." Natalie was dry-eyed as she related these details. "I guess the DA has to decide by Tuesday whether there's enough evidence to press charges."

Over Natalie's shoulder, Iris watched the children playing a game of tag with complicated rules that seemed to grow more convoluted with each round. The Tylers' two small, mixed-breed dogs had joined in and were barking and nipping at the kids' heels as they ran. Brianna was sitting in a child-sized, white resin chair away from the crowd, reading a book to her Pocahontas doll who was sitting next to her.

Iris's heart sank. "I should have brought her something."

"Honey, there's at least two dozen brand-new, beautiful dolls in there that people have brought her. Some of them were sent by total strangers who heard about it on the news. She won't touch them." Natalie sighed. "She won't play with the other kids, she won't talk to anyone. I don't know what to do. I'd like to have her talk to a professional. But, you know Kip. They're all quacks and charlatans to him."

"Kip says she doesn't remember anything."

"All she remembers is going to bed at home and waking up here. She's blocked it out. It's too painful. I'm no psychologist, but I know that much." Natalie gave Iris a bold look. "I think Kip doesn't want Brianna to remember."

"Frankly, I don't know what to think."

Natalie blinked several times as if she hadn't heard correctly. "You can't believe that Kip's innocent."

"I'm just not sure. He's the most likely suspect, but the way the murder took place doesn't seem like him. Everyone knows he has a temper. I've seen him throw things, put his fists through walls—"

"He hit my daughter."

"But that's the problem. Kip is not that complicated a guy. His temper is explosive. I can see him impulsively grabbing a gun or knife and killing out of rage, then feeling such remorse that he'd shoot himself or call the police on the spot. But Bridget's murder was premeditated. And even if Kip *did* plan it, he's a master of details. Why would he have gotten rid of the murder weapon yet left incriminating footprints? On the other hand, I've known Kip long enough to be aware that common sense is not among his strengths. His fatal flaw is thinking he's smarter than everyone else."

"As much as I hate to say it, I'm convinced Kip murdered my daughter." Natalie defiantly arched her eyebrows. "*And* I think he murdered Alexa Platt."

"Kip had no reason to murder Alexa."

"What if they were sleeping together and she threatened to tell Bridget? Maybe she *did* tell Bridget when they were in the park and Kip found out about it and killed her."

Iris thought that Bridget would have told her about an affair between Alexa and Kip. Perhaps it was too painful for Bridget to reveal that her good friend had betrayed her. Iris frowned and shook her head slightly, as if debating with herself. "I don't think so. Bridget told me what she and Alexa talked about in the park. She said Alexa encouraged her to divorce Kip." She silently tortured herself with her own advice to Bridget—stay and work it out.

"Alexa wanted Kip for herself, that's all." Natalie grew agitated as she spoke.

Iris touched her arm. "This speculation is pointless."

Natalie didn't calm down or stop. "One thing I know for sure, there's a side to Kip that none of us knew about. Or maybe it was there all the time and we just denied it."

The same thought had occurred to Iris, but she refused to give it credibility. She didn't like what it meant for Brianna. She again looked through the window at the little girl sitting with her doll. "Can I say hello to Brianna?"

Outside, Iris pulled a tiny chair next to the one that Brianna was sitting in and barely crammed half of her behind into it. "Hi, sweetheart."

Brianna's dark brown eyes were guarded. She now approached the world with fear and mistrust. It tore at Iris's heart.

"Hi, Aunt Iris." Brianna casually turned the pages of her book. "I can read this book. A lot of it, anyway."

"You're very smart, Brianna."

"Did you move into your new house?"

"Tomorrow. After I move in, you can come and spend the night with me." Iris stroked the child's long, wavy hair and swallowed hard to keep down the tears prickling in her throat. "Would you like that?"

She nodded.

Iris ran her fingers through the little girl's hair again. Brianna sat impassively, as if enduring yet more attention from adults. Iris sensed this and rose from the chair, using her hand to dislodge it from her backside. "Bye, Brianna."

Iris made a tour through the house, saying good-bye. She was glad to see that the cheesecake she'd brought had been discovered and partially devoured. Natalie insisted that Iris take food home with her and set about wrapping up selections from the dining room table in aluminum foil and salvaged Cool Whip and margarine containers.

"You must be busy packing for your move. You don't have time to cook."

"That's kind, Mrs. Tyler, but I'm not much for cooking anyway."

Natalie resolutely set her jaw as she worked. Her movements were brusque. After a long silence, she spoke on a subject that seemed constantly on her mind. "One thing I know, if Kip gets out of jail, I'm going to fight to have Brianna live with Joe and me. It's not because I don't think Kip's a good father. It's not that at all. He's always been an excellent father to Brianna, but he plans on living in that house. He told us he won't sell it. That can't be good for our granddaughter."

Iris shook her head with dismay. It was just like Kip to be stubborn about something like that.

Natalie ladled chili from a Crock-Pot into a plastic container that appeared to have been warped in the microwave. Her lips were pressed firmly together. "I hate to say it, Iris, but I have to. I'm afraid for Brianna. She *saw* the murderer."

"We don't know that."

"The murderer doesn't know that either. Whoever killed Bridget will always wonder whether what Brianna saw will come back to her one day. I don't trust Kip to properly protect her. Especially if . . ." Natalie ran her thumb around the container's lid, sealing it. "You know."

Iris remained silent.

Natalie packed the containers into the shopping bag that Iris had brought with her. "I appreciate your giving Kip the benefit of the doubt. I know Bridget would too. But damn it, if Kip didn't murder my daughter, then who did?" She held the handled bag toward Iris.

Iris took the bag from her. "The police will find out," she said with more confidence than she felt.

Chapter 10

Iris awoke from a restless sleep sometime in the middle of the night and made her way into the bathroom by the thin light that filtered through the miniblinds. There, she turned on the overhead light, which glowed harshly, making her squint. She stood over the sink and looked at her face in the mirror. "It's going to be all right," she said to the image, which was cast in hard shadows. "You were a good friend. You've always tried to do the right thing and will now." She spoke lovingly. "It will be all right. Don't worry about me. I'm fine." Iris realized she wasn't controlling what was coming out of her mouth. She tried to stop talking, but couldn't. She stared at the moving lips, barely hearing the words that went on and on in a soothing tone, the message repeated over and over like one would speak to quiet a child. "I'm fine. Worry about yourself and Brianna and Kip."

As she stared at the face and the moving lips, the image morphed into Bridget's face. "Don't be sorry," her friend murmured. "Don't feel guilty. You couldn't have stopped it." Slowly the image transformed back into Iris's own face and she was talking to herself in the mirror; she could stop when she wanted. Blinking, confused, she did.

Iris awoke at what was a late hour for her. She didn't remember the dream immediately. It suddenly came to her as she was busy making final preparations before the movers arrived. She walked to the bathroom mirror and peered into it, trying to recapture Bridget's image. She even touched the cold, silvery glass as if she could penetrate it, but her friend was gone.

It was near the end of the two-hour time window the movers had provided and they still hadn't arrived. Iris didn't have much to move. She'd never replaced the living room furniture from her condo that had been drenched by a broken water pipe during the earthquake. She'd furnished the downtown apartment she'd moved to after unloading the condo with bare necessities that she'd picked up cheap. The living room contained a plain couch, a TV sitting on a plastic crate, and a ginger-jar lamp she'd bought for $15 at Thrifty. Another plastic crate served as an end table. All her crystal and china had been destroyed in the quake, and she'd replaced them with cheap nothings. She did have a dining room set, however, bedroom furniture, and a furnished office. And she had clothes. Lots and lots of clothes.

The Bunker Hill apartment she'd lived in for the past year was just a few blocks from her office. In true LA style, she drove to work anyway. She saved many commuting hours but couldn't get used to living downtown. It was full of people during the day, but grew deserted shortly after 6 P.M. except for multitudes of street people. Downtown LA was set up for people to work, not to live. Simple tasks became a hassle since there weren't any dry cleaners or grocery stores downtown and the surrounding residential neighborhoods were shabby and unsafe. There was a terrific view from her fifteenth-floor apartment of the LA skyline. The swooping, clean lines of the Harbor Freeway, lit at night with a river of white lights in one direction and red in the other, was like a living work of art. But after a few months, the advantages of downtown life faded for her. She felt smothered by asphalt and concrete and longed to get back to the coast.

As she waited for the movers, she logged on to the Internet and accessed some of the chat rooms for computer-games aficionados. Several were devoted to Pandora, and Iris eavesdropped on a few until she found an especially lively conversation in one room.

"SUCKERS FINISH LAST is AWESOME!!! Free the Kipmeister!" GameGeek.

"Kip's a gone man. He totally immersed himself in the game life. The dude couldn't tell cyberspace from reality." Errorprone.

"WRONG! WRONG!! WRONG!!! Kip's not the man. Kip couldn't be the man. Get a clue people!!!" Arsenal.

"What about the slingshot? No one's talking about the slingshot!" MindF.

"It was the tenth-level battle played for real." GameGeek.

"The slingshot was a brilliant touch, don't you think? It was the boss monster's move in a larger game." MindF.

Iris finally typed in a comment. "What slingshot?" ITGirl.

"What slingshot?!? Stupid bitch! If you're not with the program, get lost!" Errorprone.

Iris persisted in spite of having been flamed by Errorprone. Chat room etiquette was exacting and unforgiving. Participants were expected to be well versed on all the previous conversations and not to ask obvious questions. "Someone please tell me about the slingshot." ITGirl.

"Word of mouse is the murderer put a slingshot in Bridget's hand. The police are trying to keep it out of the press. Ease up, Errorprone, you snert." GameGeek.

"Take a flying fuck." Errorprone.

"Some secret! Any Websurfer can find out about it. Cops are idiots!" MindF.

"What's the significance of the slingshot? Does it have something to do with SUCKERS?" ITGirl.

"ARRGGHHH! NO WAY!! BEGONE, ITGirl!!!" Errorprone.

"What's the significance of the slingshot? :-)" ITGirl. Iris tacked a happy face drawing onto the end of her message as a cheery response to Errorprone's relentless flaming.

"Fucking female! Do your homework, ITGirl, and stop wasting our time. Download SUCKERS FINISH LAST and play it to the end, and then and only then attempt to chat here." Errorprone.

"What's up with the tenth level? Kip Cross, you freak!" Arsenal.

"Free the Kipmeister!" MindF.

"The boss monster's made her move. Let's see if Kip can get out of this trap." GameGeek.

"Wait a minute. We're talking about real people and a real murder, not some computer game." ITGirl.

"Oh really? Duh. I didn't know that." Errorprone.

"That's why it's so much more fun. Isn't this what Kip wanted all along?" MindF.

"One thing's for certain. If Kip goes down, Pandora's going down. Kip's irreplaceable. He's the master. After him there will be no other." GameGeek.

Iris's phone rang. The movers were downstairs.

"Lily, I raised you and your sister on my own. Don't tell me how hard it is. I know," Rose Thorne said authoritatively.

"I know you know, Mom. And I appreciate your opinion, but I'm going to make my own decisions, okay?"

"It's not good to raise kids in an unhappy house. It was hard at first when I divorced your father, but I did it and you can too."

"Mom, I'm not divorcing Jack. We're having a rough spot right now and we're going to work through it."

"You don't know men, Lily. I've been around longer than you. They never change."

"Mom, you've known *one* man." Lily's voice was muffled as she spoke with her head deep inside a kitchen cupboard. She struggled with a rectangle of adhesive shelf paper and finally managed to press it flat. She withdrew her head, wiped a lock of damp hair from her forehead, and carefully moved onto the step stool from where she had been kneeling on top of the sink. "And Dad wasn't the best example of a loving husband and father." She used a tape measure to mark another length of shelf paper which she then began to cut. "And frankly, I'm not certain you and Dad couldn't have done more to work it out."

Rose Thorne was sitting on the floor straddling a drawer in which she was awkwardly laying shelf paper. She was wearing black-and-white polka-dotted pants with an ample, long-sleeved, black top that covered her once shapely figure. Her white sandals set off her pedicured toenails. Her dyed red hair was carefully styled and she wore dramatic makeup, including false eyelashes. She never allowed herself to be seen without full makeup and perfect hair, even if the circumstances, like today, warranted something more casual. She came of age during the glamour days of Hollywood and never left the style behind.

She twisted to look at her eldest daughter. "You're not trying to insinuate I did the wrong thing by divorcing your father, are you?"

"I'm just saying you made what you thought were the best decisions for your life, and I'm going to make what I think are the best ones for me and my family." Lily D'Amore was wearing blue jeans, tennis shoes, and one of her husband's navy blue, single-pocket T-shirts which came down low over her hips. Her ash blonde hair was cut in a short, layered style and had a wiry, dried-out texture from too many home dye and perm jobs.

"Mom, I feel like you're pressing me to get divorced because it would validate that you made the right decision with your life."

"That's ridiculous! I just want you to face facts. Once a marriage is gone, it's gone. Why beat a dead horse?" Rose fiercely plowed a pair of eight-inch scissors through the shelf paper. "All you and Iris talk about is how bad you had it growing up. There's lots of kids out there who had it worse. Kids will survive their parents getting divorced. You did."

"Let's see what Iris thinks," Lily chirped when her sister came into the kitchen.

"See what Iris thinks about what?" Iris said suspiciously. She rifled through some plastic shopping bags that were scattered on the floor and pulled out two rolls of blue shelf paper printed with seashells and starfish.

Rose summarized, "About whether Lily should leave Jack because he'll never change and she's still young enough to find someone else, or whether she should continue to let Jack walk all over her."

"And I think Mom's negative about marriage in general and wants to justify her own life."

Iris looked from Rose to Lily who both petulantly waited for her response, clutching the rolls of paper more tightly in her arms as if they might shield her. "I'm going to work in the bathroom."

"Coward!" Lily spat.

"She agrees with me," Rose said smugly. "She just didn't want to hurt your feelings."

"She did not!" Lily protested. "Tell her, Iris!"

"I'm trying to stay out of this!" Iris yelped.

"Well, you're in it!" Rose snapped.

"Mom, you need to get a life so you'll stop being so involved in Iris's and mine."

"I think I hear someone at the door." Iris tried to slip from the room.

"Get back in here!" Lily ordered.

"Iris doesn't accuse me of ruining her life, do you, Iris?" Rose demanded.

"No one's said you ruined our lives, Mom," Lily insisted. "You always go off the deep end. No one can tell you anything."

"Mom, it's harder to try to work something out than it is to leave," Iris finally said.

"See there!" Lily said triumphantly.

"Hellooo?"

"Neither of you girls were there." Rose was annoyed. "You can't judge me."

"We weren't *there?*" Lily said incredulously.

"Hel-*looo?*"

"Why do we have this same conversation over and over again?" Iris loudly complained. "Is there no getting past this issue?"

Lily saw the woman first. "Oh! Sorry! We didn't hear you at the door."

"*I* heard her," Iris corrected.

"I'm *so* sorry to have startled you, but I rang the doorbell. You might want to have it checked because I don't think any sound came out. The door was ajar and I heard voices and thought I'd come in. I brought you some sandwiches." The woman carried a silver platter lined with a paper doily and piled high with sandwiches cut into finger-sized rectangles with the crusts removed. "I'm Marge Nayton. I live next door. Which one of you is my new neighbor?"

Iris took the tray from her and set it on the counter. "I'm Iris Thorne." She shook the tiny hand that the woman extended. "I'm pleased to meet you at last. Unfortunately, your name came up when I was talking to the police about Bridget Cross's murder. You helped them confirm the time that Kip said he went jogging. The Crosses are . . . friends of mine."

"Ghastly business, isn't it?" Marge Nayton stood just over five feet tall and couldn't have weighed more than ninety-two pounds. She was smartly dressed in a beige suit with a hip-length, shawl-collared jacket which she wore buttoned to the neck, a slim skirt, and bone-colored, high-heeled pumps. She was delicate and blonde with a heart-shaped face. Her hair was carefully coiffed in a smooth style that was teased high and round in back and curved into a wave on one side of her face. Several jeweled rings that appeared to be the real thing glittered from her bony fingers. She might have been in her seventies.

"My condolences about Bridget. On a happier note, I'm *thrilled* to meet you, Iris, and I want to congratulate you on your new home." Marge spoke slowly, carefully enunciating each word, smiling all the while.

"Thank you," Iris said. "This is my mother, Rose Thorne, and my sister, Lily D'Amore."

"I'm *very* pleased to meet you," Marge said. "And I'm glad that this charming house has found a good owner. I always thought it was just the sweetest thing."

"I'm so proud of Iris," Rose gushed. "She's still single, but she hasn't let that stand in the way of her making a home for herself."

Iris glowered at her mother.

"We ladies need to know how to live on our own." Marge fastidiously ran a manicured finger across the wave in her hair. "Men are wonderful when you have them, but they just don't last."

"That's what my daughters and I were discussing when you came in," Rose said enthusiastically, thinking she had a reinforcement for her side. "I've been divorced for many years and my daughter's headed that way."

Lily scowled but said nothing.

"Are you married, Marge?" Rose was never one for subtlety.

Iris glared at her mother to no avail. Rose ignored her.

"Oh, *noo.*" Marge widened her eyes.

"I'm divorced too," Rose offered.

"When I said that men don't last, I meant *literally.*" Marge chuckled and pressed her fingertips against Rose's arm. "You see, I've been widowed three times. I was married to three of the most wonderful men in the world. Lost them all."

"They died?" Lily asked. "What happened?"

"Lily!" Iris was consistently mortified by her family's lack of manners and good taste.

"Oh, I don't mind, love. I married my first husband, Ely, just before the war. I helped him establish his business, Nayton Manufacturing Company. He made nuts, bolts, screws, and such. It was very prosperous during the war. I ran it while he was overseas, fighting in Europe. We built our house, the one next door to you, in '48. We had a son in '50. Shortly after that, Ely died. Dropped dead of a heart attack."

"Poor thing, left to raise a child on your own," Rose commiserated. "I know how hard that can be."

"I married Herb in '76. He died in '87. Heart attack." Marge leaned forward as if to divulge a secret. "Happened when we were having sex." She paused. "Most embarrassing. But I was glad that Herb died happy. Then I married Dub in '89. Poor soul wasn't around too long after that."

"Heart attack?" Iris ventured.

"Oh, *noo,* love. He drove his car off the bluff one night. I told him his night vision was failing, but he was too proud to admit it." With her thumb and middle finger, Marge turned a gold watch that was loose on her thin wrist so she could see the face. "I've got to beat it. I have a *million* errands to run." With a swoop of her hand, she gestured toward the platter of sandwiches, like a game show hostess. "I made an assortment of sandwiches—cucumber, watercress, egg salad. I hope there's something there for everyone."

Iris said, "Thank you, Mrs. Nayton."

Marge patted Iris's hand with long, bejeweled fingers. "Call me Marge. So nice to have met you all. Come by for cocktails. I have my martini at five and I always make a few canapés. No problem to put out a few more. Stop by anytime." She turned on her heel and left the kitchen, head held high, back straight, hips swaying not too much, but enough. "I can find my way out."

Iris, Lily, and Rose followed her out the front door. A well-preserved black-and-white 1955 Buick Roadmaster was parked in Marge's driveway next door. Marge had made it halfway down Iris's brick walk when the group of them were startled by screeching tires. A butter yellow Ferrari swung around the corner of the street and zoomed past, hanging a quick right onto Capri Court. The top was down and a woman with long blonde hair was driving. Soon they glimpsed the Ferrari tearing along Capri Road, the street above Iris's.

Marge took mincing steps back to Iris. "We've just had a close encounter of the *bimbo* kind."

"That looked like Summer Fuchs driving Kip Cross's car," Iris said.

"Oh my dear, she's not Summer Fuchs anymore," Marge said. "She's Summer *Fontaine.*" Marge angled her eyes meaningfully. "She has a modeling career and will soon be on TV. Feature films will surely follow. Just *ask* her. She's already booked appearances on talk shows."

"No!" Lily shouted with outrage.

"Yes!" Marge continued. "Due to poor Bridget Cross's misfortune, the modeling jobs have just been *flooding* in. So much that she can now afford silicone injections in her lips. She had it done today."

The women winced at the thought.

"Oh, *yes.* Summer idolizes Pamela Lee. Her goal is to remake herself to look as much like Pamela Lee as she can."

"Bridget told me Summer had her breasts redone because they weren't large enough after her first operation," Iris said.

"Well she should be very happy with them now," Marge commented. "I've never seen such large breasts in all my days. They're quite remarkable."

"What's she doing driving Kip's car?" Iris asked.

"She's caretaking the house," Marge responded. "I saw her in the market yesterday. She bragged to me that she has the full run of the place."

"Why on earth did Bridget ever hire her?" Rose asked. "She must have been out of her head to let someone like that move into her house with her husband around."

"Mom, not all men cheat on their wives," Lily said.

"All the ones I've known have."

Iris shot a withering look in their direction, mortified that they would persist in airing the family's dirty laundry in front of a stranger.

"Summer didn't look like that when the Crosses first hired her," Marge interjected.

"You know how bighearted Bridget was," Iris said. "Summer was a casual friend of Kip's cousin in Ohio. He called and asked if Summer could stay with them for a few weeks after she moved to LA to seek her fortune. A few weeks turned into a month and longer. Bridget had been thinking about hiring a live-in anyway. Summer and Brianna got along great. So . . ." Iris shrugged and gazed at the top of the hill. She could barely see the turquoise tile roof of the Cross house. "Bridget fired her the day before she was murdered. I guess Kip rehired her."

Marge again twisted the face of her watch. "I've got to *fly*. See you girls later."

Iris, Rose, and Lily wished Marge good-bye and watched her get into the classic Buick in which her head was barely visible above the steering wheel. After she had driven away, Rose and Lily turned and walked toward the house.

Iris watched as a minivan with two men in it drove past and turned on Capri Court. Soon the car passed on the street above, just as the Ferrari had.

"Iris?" Lily said.

Roused from her thoughts, Iris looked at her sister. "Oh, I . . . I'm going to put some things away in the garage so I can park the Triumph in there tonight." She made a show of walking in that direction.

After her mother and sister had gone back inside, Iris sprinted across the street and up the cement staircase. A contractor's stamp pressed into the first step indicated the stairs were built in 1927. There were many such staircases—remnants of pre-automobile-crazed LA—scattered across the hilly, older neighborhoods of Los Angeles. A group of enthusiasts mapped and walked them.

The city had not maintained the staircases. It was a credit to their original design, solid construction, and sheer luck that they were still usable. Three staircases comprised the Casa Marina stairways. A set of sixty steps led from the bridge traversing Pacific Coast Highway to Casa Marina Drive where Iris and Marge lived. Eighty steps led from Casa Marina Drive to Capri Road. Seventy steps led from Capri Road to Cielo Way, where the Cross house was located. The Casa Marina stairways were decrepit in spots but functional enough to allow Bridget Cross's murderer to escape.

As Iris ascended the steps that led to Capri Road, she passed the backyard of the abandoned house on the street above hers. She gingerly stepped over the thick brush, flowering vines, overgrown ivy, and creeping roses that grew from the house's long-untended backyard past the staircase's two parallel, round steel railings. The thorns of a bougainvillea vine caught her jeans leg. She struggled to quickly free herself, not wanting to be stuck there.

At the top of the staircase, Iris scurried across Capri Road and only paused to look back at the derelict two-story house when she was a safe distance away. Most of its window glass had been broken out. Its front door stood ominously open. The foyer beyond the open door was strewn with garbage, bricks, and broken pieces of masonry.

She climbed the next set of steps, stretching her legs to cross a section that had pulled away from the hill and was separated from the step above by a gap a foot wide. A storm drain ran along the ground in the brush and scrub oak beyond the railing. It led from the Crosses' backyard and drained rainwater from their patio. Last year, Bridget had the patio and pool installed but ran out of time to properly bury the drain before the rainy season arrived. The drain consisted of several long aluminum pipes, about twelve inches in diameter, connected by aluminum sleeves. It extended the length of the hillside all the way down to Capri Road.

Iris mentally counted the steps as she ascended. Something rustled in the brush and low trees nearby, making her jump. After hearing no other noise than her pounding heart, she continued. At the fifty-fourth step up from Capri Road, she saw rust-colored stains and carefully tiptoed around them. This was where the police said the bloody flip-flop footprints disappeared into the brush. The blood had been incompletely removed by a crew Bridget's parents had hired. The Tylers were shocked to discover that the police only took care of the bodies. The clean up was not their job.

Iris now reached the cinder block wall that enclosed the Cross property. She tried the wooden gate that led into the patio, but it was locked. She continued up until she reached Cielo Way where she turned left toward the front of the Cross house. The yellow Ferrari was parked in the long driveway, and the minivan Iris had seen go up the hill was parked behind it. Cielo Way dead-ended into the Crosses' front yard.

Iris was reaching for the doorbell button when she noticed that the massive wooden front door of the Spanish Gothic house was ajar. The door, made of broad planks held together with strips of riveted metal, was originally from an old church in Spain. It creaked appropriately when she pushed it open. She walked into the foyer, her tennis shoes silent against the ceramic tile floor.

"Summer?" she said, none too loudly. She didn't want to be accused of breaking in but had no intention of warning the woman of her visit. She crossed the foyer and descended the three steps into the family room which was separated from the foyer by an arch. The living room, dining room, and kitchen were to the left. Standing in the family room, through French doors that opened onto the patio, she saw Summer Fontaine vamping in skimpy lingerie on a patio lounge chair. One man was looking at her through a camera positioned on a tripod. The second man was holding a sheet of reflective material behind Summer's head. Photography equipment was scattered about.

Iris saw red. Without hesitation, she burst through a set of French doors. "What the hell do you think you're doing?"

Summer's swollen lips, heavily colored with two tones of pink, first parted with surprise, then curled with disgust. "You ever think of ringing the doorbell?"

The two men looked at Iris with mild interest.

"Who are you?" she demanded.

The man who had been looking through the camera answered, "We're from the *National Enquirer*. We purchased exclusive rights to photograph Summer at the murder scene."

"Rights? You can't sell rights you don't have, Summer!" Iris snarled at the men. "Get out!"

"We've paid for photographs," said the man with the camera, shrugging, "and I'm not leaving until I get them."

Summer bolted from the lounge chair. Her heavy breasts swayed beneath the sheer lingerie. "*You* get out! Kip knows all about this, okay? He doesn't care if I make a little money. This is none of your business."

"I won't have you profiting from my friend's murder."

Summer put her hands on her hips. Her abdomen was so flat it was almost concave. "Bridget's not around anymore and you don't have a damn thing to say about anything that goes on here." Summer drew back her lips, revealing bleached-white teeth. "Get out before I call the police and have you arrested for trespassing."

Without another word, Iris left by the front door and ran back down the stairs all the way to her house where her mother and sister were still arguing.

Chapter 11

On Sunday morning, Iris awoke early after her first night in her new house. At first she feared not being able to sleep, then she feared having nightmares like the one with Bridget and the mirror, but she was so exhausted, she went out once her head hit the pillow. The next thing she heard was birds singing. She opened her eyes to muted sunshine filtered through a light haze of morning fog and cool, fresh air. She sat up in bed, hugged her knees, and looked out her sliding glass door at a blue-gray ocean. The only thing that was missing was Garland.

He hadn't called the night before. She hadn't called him either, but she figured that since she was the one who was moving, he should have called her. Then it occurred to her that he might have thought that she was going to call him since she was the one in transition and probably harder to get ahold of. Then she thought that he should have at least called her to congratulate her. That was her final verdict: he should have called her and he didn't. She was alone on Saturday night and he didn't call. Maybe he was too busy to call. Maybe he wasn't alone. She didn't like that idea. She tried to put it out of her head.

She climbed out of bed, grabbed her worn terry cloth bathrobe, and padded barefoot into the kitchen, dodging boxes that were piled everywhere. The coffeemaker's familiar red light glowed gaily next to a fresh pot of coffee that had automatically brewed. She poured a mug and drank it black while she picked the gooey top off an apple-spice muffin she'd bought the night before at her new, local grocery store. A little breakfast treat on her first morning in her new house.

She slipped her cordless phone into the pocket of her robe so she wouldn't have to run inside in case Garland called, gathered the muffin and mug and Sunday paper she'd also purchased the night before, and walked outside onto her redwood deck. She reclined in the Adirondack chair that had once upon a time been crammed onto the tiny terrace of her condominium. Then she'd only had room for one chair. She now had room for two. But, she thought sadly, she was still alone, so what difference did it make? One chair was plenty. She pulled the phone from her pocket, glared at it as if willing it to ring, then slipped it back.

After finishing her muffin, retrieving a second cup of coffee, and idly looking through the newspaper, she again took out the phone. This time she dialed. It was 10 A.M. in New York. Garland would probably be relaxing, reading the Sunday papers, having his own coffee—and missing her, of course. The phone rang four times before his answering machine picked up. She hung up while the message was still playing. He wasn't sitting at home missing her but, she assured herself, he was bound to be missing her wherever he was. Or maybe he wasn't missing her at all. Maybe she was being a stupid idiot and in reality he couldn't care less about her. She got up and took a shower.

Within an hour, she was at the glass doors of Pandora's corporate offices. She cupped her hands around her eyes, pressed her face to the door, and waved at someone inside.

Shortly, Toni Burton appeared on the other side of the door and unlocked the two dead bolts. "Hi, Iris. Sorry you had to wait, but there's just been so many weirdos hanging around I didn't dare stay here by myself with the doors unlocked. We've even had death threats. Can you believe it?" She pulled the door open and hopped to the side so Iris could enter. Her bright blue eyes sparkled. Toni's boundless cheerfulness made Iris suspect she was half-witted the first time she'd met her.

"Death threats!" Iris followed Toni into the bowels of the converted airplane hangar. Iris had visited Pandora a few times with Bridget and had previously met Toni and the firm's other key employees. "Against whom?"

The high-domed walls of the hangar were dimly lit with strings of tiny, twinkling white lights that were woven through the exposed steel and wood lattice. Daylight dimly filtered through scattered rows of windows lining the walls. The loose structure of offices, meeting rooms, and common areas of raw pine and unpainted wallboard meandered across the large space, rising high against the side walls and cascading down toward the middle. The different sections of the structure were connected by a series of catwalks. The work areas were harshly lit by fluorescent bulbs. The place looked like a set of interlocking playhouses made by children with backyard junk.

Toni skipped ahead of Iris, periodically turning to walk backward as she spoke. "Oh, Ki-ip"—she gave his name two syllables—"mostly. I feel like telling these people, you know, if you, like, have the guts to do something like that you ought to have the guts to stand up and be recognized, you know? Ugh!" She made a guttural noise and wrinkled her nose. "And then, here we are trying to get over poor Bridget being shot to death and people have the nerve to send these snotty letters about how she was to blame for what happened to her. How she created an environment that, like, breeds violence or something." Toni turned to look slack-jawed at Iris who was following two steps behind. "Unreal, huh?"

"People can be amazingly cruel."

They walked past life-size figures of what looked like alien warriors. Each one stood on its own pedestal and was illuminated by spotlights. Slade Slayer was there, armed to the teeth with plastic renderings of his fantasy weapons.

"Wow!" Iris commented.

"Kip commissioned some guy to make these."

"Must have been expensive." Iris recalled T. Duke Sawyer's anger over how Kip and Bridget had spent USA Assets' money.

"For sure."

They passed a glass display case that contained T-shirts, sweatshirts, and tank tops with Slade Slayer's silk-screened image. Positioned on hat stands across the top of the case were rubber, full-head masks of Slade Slayer, complete with Stallone-esque sneer.

"I'm particularly proud of that stuff," Toni said in response to Iris's interest in the display case. "It was my idea to license Slade Slayer's image. I did all the deals myself. We do ten thousand dollars a month in sales of Slade Slayer merchandise. Next year we'll do even more once the Slade Slayer line of toy weapons goes into production. I just signed a deal with a major toy producer." Toni paused as if waiting for applause. When none was forthcoming, she continued, "We hope to have them on the shelves in time for the Christmas season."

Toni mounted a wooden staircase that led to a catwalk. They entered a large room fitted with windows against the inside and outside walls. All the blinds were closed tight. A large table was cluttered with computer equipment as was almost every other flat surface. "Of course we've received *tons* of fan mail—letters, E-mail, and faxes. Everyone's worried about what's going to happen to Pandora with Bridget gone and Kip . . . you know."

Toni waved her hand to indicate the room. "This is our computer lab. We call it the War Room. It's where we come together with our ideas, prototypes, and sketches and fight it out." The morning dampness had frizzed Toni's wavy, strawberry blonde hair, undoing her efforts with a curling iron earlier that morning. She was dressed casually in snug jeans that accentuated her well-toned hips and legs, a crisply pressed white cotton shirt, and lug-soled hiking boots.

She turned the rod to open the blinds. "Everyone likes it so dark in here. It drives me crazy. If I didn't have a window in my office, I'd go absolutely nuts out of my mind. There's a patio off the other end of the hangar that Bridget had constructed. Sometimes, when it's nice outside, I work out there." Toni looked wide-eyed at Iris and pulled her mouth into a small *O*. "I forgot to offer you something. What a terrible hostess I am!"

"I'm fine, thanks," Iris said. Toni's pug nose and tiny,

rounded mouth reminded her of a Kewpie doll. "I just had breakfast."

Toni sat in a chair in front of a computer monitor on which *Suckers Finish Last* was running. Iris sat next to her. Slade Slayer was massacring the same aliens over and over behind the opening menu as hard rock music blared from the speakers. Slade's baritone voice periodically intoned, "Die, suckers!" Toni turned a knob on one of the speakers, lowering the volume.

"After we talked, I logged on to some of the Slade Slayer chat rooms." Toni crossed her legs at the knees and again at the ankles, looking like a gawky teenager waiting to be asked to dance. She pivoted her legs back and forth on one toe. "Is that gross or what? A slingshot in Bridget's hand!"

"That's the first you heard about anything concerning a slingshot?"

"Hardly. The police came down here and were asking questions, all casual like, about slingshots, like that's something you talk about every day. Mick and Today and I are looking at each other like, what's up with this? We tell them, yeah, we have slingshots. We have them all over the place. Mick wanted one to use as a model, and Bridget ordered a box of them. Everyone in the company has one. I could hardly go anywhere without getting hit on the butt by somebody shooting me with something. Bridget drew the line at anything hard being used as a projectile. Today found these little rubber balls and bought a bunch of them. Here's one right here." She fished a red ball that was about an inch in diameter from between the jungle of cables in the center of the table and handed it to Iris. It was made of pliable rubber.

Toni continued searching among the clutter of computer equipment and components as she talked. "So Today goes, 'There's a slingshot in the new game.' Like, duh. So he shows them the tenth level with Cherry Divine and all that." She crawled underneath the table and returned with a slingshot. It had a sturdy wood base and a thick rubber pull. She handed it to Iris who used it to propel the red rubber ball across the room. Iris smiled.

"See? It's fun!" Toni exclaimed. "We need to have fun here. We work long hours and we're together all the time and we'd really kill each other otherwise. Anyway, the cops are still being all coy about why they're so interested in slingshots. They took a couple of ours with them. After they left, Today and Mick and me figured out that the murderer must have left a slingshot at the scene, like a signature or something. We got all weirded out because it's like Slade's fight with Cherry Divine."

"This Cherry Divine is one of Slade's enemies?" Iris asked.

"She's more than that. She's the boss monster. I'll show you." Toni started tapping on the keyboard with fingernails polished in hot pink.

"I'm sorry I'm so uneducated about high tech stuff. I tried to get people in the chat rooms to explain some of the terminology to me, but they weren't very pleasant."

"I know how arrogant techies can be sometimes. Bridget used to explain things to me because no one else would. Kip and Today are the absolute *worst*. Don't worry. I'll explain anything you want to know."

"To start with, what's the boss monster?"

"At the highest level of a game, there's one really bad, very powerful, totally awesome monster that the player has to kill to win the game. It's very hard to do, and ninety-nine percent of players can't do it because it's designed to be almost impossible. So they E-mail us, begging for hints or the cheat codes."

"Cheat codes?"

"They're special commands that the programmers develop so they can test the game without having to actually play it. That way, they don't waste time getting killed and starting over, over and over again. The cheat codes let you go through walls without having to find the secret buttons or let you get shot but the bullets go straight through you. Stuff like that. See, I'm using cheat codes now to go straight to the tenth level. There she is."

"What are you afraid of?" Cherry Divine asked in Bridget's voice.

A chill tickled Iris's spine. "Can you play that again?"

"Sure." Toni turned up the volume on the speakers and restarted the game from the same point. She answered Iris's unasked question. "It's Bridget's voice. We got tapes from all these actresses, but Kip and me liked her voice the best."

Iris mulled over the casual way Toni had tossed off "Kip and me."

"And Cherry's face looks a little like Bridget's," Toni added.

Iris looked more closely at the screen. "It does. Whose idea was that?"

"Kip's. Watch this." Toni let the game proceed and Cherry Divine started ascending a long stone staircase.

"Those are like the steps next to Kip and Bridget's house!"

"That was Mick's idea. He always thought those stairs were too spooky, and Kip agreed. He took Mick home with him one day so Mick could do some sketches."

"Bridget thought all this was okay?"

"No, she was pissed. Cherry Divine was her concept, but she pitched it as a love interest for Slade. Today and Kip blew that out of the water, but liked the idea of some sort of supervixen adversary for Slade. I'll show you how Cherry turns Slade's weapon into a slingshot. Here." Toni tapped keys on the keyboard. Slade's shotgun began to glow, then transformed into a slingshot. "She robs him of his big gun. Sort of like cutting off his dick, isn't it?" She emitted a tinkling laugh and pressed keys that changed the view of the game to now show Slade Slayer's shocked face as he discovered his weapon had suddenly become impotent.

"How do you kill the boss monster?"

"Only Kip knows how to win the final level."

"And Cherry turns into Slade Slayer?"

Toni widened her eyes. "That blew all of us away. Everyone knew Bridget and Kip had been fighting and knew how the boss monster looked and acted like Bridget, and we were all like, 'Whoa, Kip! What are you saying here?' "

"You think Kip murdered Bridget?"

"It makes me sick, but what other explanation is there?" Her eyes welled with tears and grew red, which made the bright blue color of her irises stand out all the more. She wiped a tear from her cheek with her hand. "You must know about Kip and me." She unwrapped her legs and leaned forward with her elbows on her knees and her head in her hands. "You probably think I'm a stupid bimbo who can't keep her knees closed. I wouldn't blame you."

Iris sighed. She felt sorry for Toni but couldn't bring herself to comfort this woman who had brought pain to her friend's life. She leaned back in the chair and contemplated Toni's frizzy blonde hair and wondered why Kip had slept with her. She couldn't imagine Kip having any real feelings for Toni. Iris believed absolutely that his heart was and always would be with Bridget. It must have been just physical for him. But she knew it wasn't as simple as that for Toni. It never is.

"Why did you do it?" Iris finally said.

Toni abruptly tossed her head back, her eyes shiny with tears. "He came on to me!"

Iris looked at her coolly.

"I know. I hate that 'I'm just a helpless victim, just floating with the flotsam and jetsam of life' thing. It makes me want to puke. But Kip started it and I jumped right in. I so admired Bridget. She saw potential and had confidence in me that I didn't have in myself. And that's the thanks I gave her."

Toni wiped her face with her hand, then leaned toward Iris on her elbows. "When I started with Kip, I'd just broken up with a guy I'd been dating and I was really vulnerable. I know this is going to sound sick but, in some twisted way, I thought that by being with Kip, I could have a piece of B's life. Now I feel like her murder was partially my fault. I was part of the reason they were fighting." Toni held up a cautionary finger. "I wasn't the *only* reason, mind you. He was banging the nanny too."

"How did you feel when you heard that?"

"I was mad and hurt. But I told myself, 'Toni, you're sleeping with a guy who's cheating on his wife. You think he's going to be loyal to you?' "

"Do you know that Bridget told Kip to fire you?"

Toni widened her already round eyes. "No!" Her face dropped. "Well, could you blame her?"

"So Kip didn't fire you?"

"Of course not. If he had, why would I still be here?"

Iris indifferently observed her.

"I didn't kill B, if that's what you're thinking. I even have an alibi. I was at the movies. They were running a special showing of the director's cut of *Retrograde in Havana* at the Nu-Art."

Iris continued to watch Toni.

"I'd been thinking about Alexa Platt all day. She was the art director of that movie and her husband gave her a bit part in it. You knew she was married to Jim Platt, the director?"

Iris nodded.

"Anyway, I'd seen the movie before, but I wanted to see Alexa. Kind of sick, huh?" Toni didn't wait for Iris to respond. "I was sorry I went. The movie's really ultraviolent and it didn't sit well with me."

"That's why I never went to see it." Iris raked her fingers across her head, stopping with hair clutched in both hands. The slight pain sharpened her thoughts. She released her hair, frowned at nothing on the floor, then looked up at Toni. "Could I see some of those threatening letters and faxes sent to Pandora?"

"The police have them."

"Do you remember who sent them?"

"Not really. Some were from lunatics, raving. Some were from these antiviolence, pro-family groups. Some were from religious groups, that right-wing stuff."

"How long have you been receiving them? Just since Bridget's murder?"

"No, all along. From when Pandora released its first game. Bridget always responded to them, sending a one-size-fits-all letter, except to the lunatics. Them she ignored." Toni crossed her arms over her chest and eyed Iris quizzically. "What's up?"

"I don't know yet. An idea popped into my head."

Toni bit her bottom lip and narrowed her eyes. "I know what you're thinking. Alexa Platt and Bridget Cross were both involved in creating violent entertainment. But Iris, you don't really think one of those right-wing groups would go *that* far, do you? And why kill just the wives? The men are just as involved, if not more so."

"I don't know what to think, but I know one thing for sure—the police aren't doing any thinking. As far as they're concerned, they've got their man. Talk about a rush to judgment."

Toni released her lower lip and it rolled out into a pout. "I wish it wasn't Kip. I really do. But he's the most likely one to have murdered Bridget."

"True, but all the evidence is circumstantial, and there's not very much of it. I think the police should do a bit more looking, for Brianna's sake. She needs to know definitively whether her father killed her mother. I can't imagine how horrible it would be to have a question like that dog you your whole life. And we need to learn the truth for Pandora's sake." Iris stood. "I'd better get home. I moved into a new house yesterday and I've hardly unpacked."

Toni stood also and walked to the computer lab door. She stopped and looked at Iris. "When you asked me to show you Cherry Divine and the final level, that wasn't the only thing you wanted to see, was it?"

"No," Iris conceded.

Toni nodded. "That's cool. I don't blame you for wanting to check me out. If I were you, I would hate my guts. I wouldn't be as nice as you are. My hair would be on the ground in clumps by now, know what I'm saying?"

Iris had to smile at the image.

"So we understand each other, yes?"

"Yes."

"Peace?" Toni extended her hand.

Iris took it. "Peace."

" 'Kay." Toni bounded out the door, down the stairs, and across the hangar.

Iris struggled to keep up.

Toni unlatched the front door and held it open.

"Aren't you leaving too?" Iris asked.

"Nah. Too much work to do. I'm the only one who had a handle on what B used to do. I'm doing my best, but I can't dictate what the next project's going to be, even though I have some great ideas. We need someone to be in charge. How can Kip run Pandora from jail?"

"Kip didn't like how Bridget was running the firm, now he can run it himself, into the ground if he wants."

"Let's do lunch."

"Sounds good."

Iris heard Toni lock the big glass door behind her and turned to wave good-bye. Through the glass she saw Toni waltzing by herself across the open floor.

* * *

Iris pulled the Triumph into her driveway and cut the engine. Her garage was still too full of boxes for her to park there. She was deep in thought and didn't notice the packages on the front porch until she was almost on top of them. Standing like a sentry among them was a black Weber kettle barbecue with a big red bow tied around it. She was searching for a card or a note when she heard her neighbor.

"You-hoo!" Marge called. "Hel-*looo!*"

Iris walked to the edge of the porch and saw Marge mincing across the lawn with Garland Hughes. Iris's heart soared.

Garland was grinning boyishly, his arm supporting Marge's bony, well-dressed hand. His cheeks were pink and his hair was askew.

Marge was patting his arm with her free hand. She was again dressed in a suit and heels. "I rescued this charming gentleman from your front porch where he was sitting all by himself, looking so forlorn waiting for his lady love."

"I didn't know you were going to be in town." Iris tried not to gush.

"I had that dinner in Denver on Saturday. I have to be in Seattle tomorrow, so I thought I'd pop by and surprise you and fly out of LA."

Iris now felt foolish as she remembered that Garland had told her about his business dinner Saturday night in Denver. She quickly sifted through her actions this morning, trying to remember whether her jealous, wretched thoughts had manifested themselves in any public and embarrassing behavior. There was the phone call . . . She silently rejoiced when she remembered hanging up without leaving a message. She was clean. She'd narrowly escaped appearing like a clinging, desperate woman. "I'm so glad you did."

"I *like* this man," Marge enthused. "I just might steal him from you."

"She makes a very dry martini," Garland commented.

"Don't forget, he likes his with a twist," Marge added.

"A twist?" Iris said as she twisted a lock of her hair.

"Instead of an olive, love," Marge said.

"I don't know how to make a martini," Iris confessed.

"A skill every good hostess should have." Marge languidly waved her hand toward Iris. "I'd be *delighted* to show you. The secret's in the vermouth—just a whisper. And they're *always* shaken." Marge swooped her index finger in an arc back toward her. "Just thought of the *perfect* housewarming gift for you." She disengaged herself from Garland. "I must take my leave. I've a million things to do." She turned and unsteadily walked across Iris's lawn in her heels without looking back. "Ta-taa!"

When they were alone, Iris looked shyly at Garland. "You brought me all these things?"

He smiled crookedly at her. "All the boxes are barbecue accessories. What's a Southern California beach house without a barbecue?"

"I don't know how to barbecue either!" Iris wailed. "Is that what you expect from me? Barbecues and martinis and home-cooked meals?"

He joined her on the front porch and put his arms around her. "One of those bags has some swordfish steaks and other groceries. I thought I'd set up your barbecue and cook you dinner. All you have to do is keep me company."

"That's all?"

"That's more than you realize."

They kissed. She opened her eyes. It thrilled her to see him this close to her. He opened his eyes and they stopped kissing.

"Something wrong?" He looked concerned.

She breathed hard twice, then three times as she tried to voice the words, but they wouldn't come. "I love you." She winced almost in fear and backed away from him, but his hands held her tight. "I just wanted to tell you before you got on another plane or I got on the freeway or someone had a gun and something happened and we never saw each other again. I just wanted to tell you." Tears popped into her eyes.

"I love you too, sweetheart." He drew her close. "Don't worry. I'm not going anywhere."

After a few seconds, she straightened and wiped her face. "Yes, you are. You're going inside to make me dinner and I'm going to keep you company."

Chapter 12

"Where are you, you little SOB?" Iris muttered to herself, slamming on the Triumph's brakes as she hit the banked ramp that spiraled down to the next parking level. She accelerated on the straightaway, swerving to avoid a car that was backing out, all the time scanning the nooks and crannies of the garage and peering behind the supporting pillars.

She could see her reserved parking space, one more turn and one more straightaway ahead, when he stepped from behind a pillar directly into the Triumph's path and began sweeping something invisible into his white, long-handled dustpan. She slammed on the brakes and screamed as he guilelessly looked up at her as if the last thing he expected to see was a car.

"You're a madman!" she yelled as she barely squeezed between him and a row of cars. "A suicidal madman!" In her rearview mirror, she saw that he hadn't budged and stood watching her holding the handle of his dustpan in one hand and his broom in the other.

Iris quickly forgot her encounter with the garage janitor when she hit the doors of McKinney Alitzer's suite, smiling and with a spring in her step. Today, she wasn't faking her high spirits. "Hello! Good morning!" she sang to everyone she passed.

Each morning, Iris's staff greeted her with a hint of trepidation as they assessed her mood. Simply because she was smiling and walking energetically didn't mean anything. The telltale signs of a bad mood could be detected by a stiffness in her lips and in deepened lines around her eyes. Careful attention to these critical barometers could save a hapless sales associate or junior broker the pain of limping from Iris's office carrying his bitten-off head underneath his arm. But when Iris's good mood was genuine, she tended to be magnanimous. It was a good time to confess a screwup or ask for the moon.

Iris waved at Kyle Tucker and Amber Ambrose who were in their offices on the other side of the suite. Liz Martini's office was still dark and the door was closed. Iris walked past the bull pen and the junior brokers and sales associates. Most of them were talking into their telephone headsets and smiling as they did so. Could this mean they were selling? There were bargains galore after the market drop the previous week. They must be selling.

Ha, Iris silently said to all the doomsayers who had predicted that last week signaled the growling of a coming bear market. *Ha, ha, ha.*

When Iris passed Rick, one of her junior brokers, he quickly switched to another window on his computer monitor, but not before she saw that he was playing *Suckers Finish Last* while talking to a client. She didn't care. As long as he was selling, he could stand on his head in his cubicle and whistle "Dixie." Besides, the Slade Slayer games were Bridget's work. Long live Slade Slayer!

"Good morning, Louise," Iris chirped as she entered her office where Louise had already unlocked the door.

Iris took off the jacket of her Anne Klein II suit, hung it behind the door, and stashed her handbag in the top drawer of a filing cabinet. Instead of sitting down in her chair, she walked to the floor-to-ceiling window that faced south. Her view was blocked by a tall office building on the other side of the street, but if she pressed her cheek against the glass, as she did now, she could glimpse the hills of northeast LA where she had grown up. She took a quick look, as was her habit at least once a week. It grounded her. She then turned to look out the other window behind her desk which faced west.

"Brought you some coffee," Louise said behind her.

"Thanks. It's hazy today. I can't see Catalina. The Santa Anas have finally stopped."

"You must have a tremendous view of Catalina from your new house."

Iris turned and picked up the mug of black coffee Louise had set on her desk and gushed, "It's wonderful. I woke up Sunday morning after spending my first night in the house and the first thing I saw was the ocean."

"You're all moved in?"

"Hardly. I have so much shopping to do. I need to buy a washer and dryer, and I never replaced my living room furniture after the earthquake."

"You poor dear. All that dreadful shopping," Louise clucked in ersatz sympathy.

Iris's eyes narrowed at the visions of superstores dancing in her head. "Yes," she said, trancelike. "The world of consumer durables is opening before me like a flower."

They both turned when they heard barking. An apricot toy poodle skirted past Louise's legs, ducked under Iris's desk, and leaped onto her chair where it trembled and yipped with excitement.

"Thelma!" Iris exclaimed.

Shortly afterward, Liz appeared in Iris's doorway, with Thelma's black counterpart, Louise, wriggling and barking in her arms.

"Iris, I'm so sorry." Liz walked around Iris's desk and retrieved the errant dog. "I was hoping to slip them into my office until lunch, then leave them at the vet's for their shots and no one would be any the wiser." She put her face close to the dogs, who licked her wildly. "But you two had different ideas, didn't you?" she baby-talked. "Mommy's little itsy-bitsy babies." Her face now covered with dog spit, Liz addressed Iris. "I promise they'll be quiet." She walked across the suite to her office, drawing the attention of everyone in the sales department.

"Sam-I-Am will have fun when he hears about this," Iris commented.

"There's no reason he should hear about it," Louise said.

"But he will. He has a little spy who has big ears and big eyes."

"The better to *hear* and *see* you with, my dear."

"There she is now, checking out the situation firsthand."

They turned to see Amber Ambrose sidle into Liz's office and coo over the dogs.

"Bottom line, as long as Liz continues producing over two million a month, she and I are untouchable," Iris said. "Money talks and BS walks. It's the law of the jungle."

Iris's phone rang and Louise reached to answer it. "Iris Thorne's office." After briefly speaking, she told Iris, "Mr. Connors is here."

Iris nodded.

"I'll come get him," Louise said into the phone.

"He's Bridget's attorney," Iris explained. "I still don't know why he wants to meet with me. Something about her estate—he wouldn't discuss it over the phone. I can't imagine she left me anything of any monetary significance."

Louise left, then returned followed by a well-dressed, squat, balding man. Behind him was Natalie Tyler, Bridget's mother, and Brianna.

"What a surprise!" Iris exclaimed as she hugged Natalie.

"Hi, Aunt Iris," Brianna said quietly.

Iris bent over to hug the little girl. "Hello, Brianna. I'm so glad to see you. Now I know it's going to be a good day." Still tightly holding Brianna around the shoulders with one hand, Iris extended her free hand to Mr. Connors. "I'm Iris Thorne. Please come in."

After Natalie and Connors were seated in the two chairs facing Iris's desk and Brianna was settled on the couch, Connors got to the purpose of his visit.

"About two months before Bridget Cross's passing, she and I revised her will. At that time, she also drew up a living trust covering some of her property. Are you familiar with living trusts?"

"Slightly. Please give me an overview."

"A living trust differs from a will in several respects. An important difference is that property subject to living trusts avoids the cost and delay of probate. Avoiding probate and potential challenges to her desired disposition of her property after her death was important to Mrs. Cross. She was especially concerned about one piece of property in particular—her block of eight thousand shares of Pandora Software Corporation preferred stock, representing a sixty percent ownership stake in the firm. This is the property she had subjected to a living trust, naming herself as trustee."

Iris nodded, becoming more curious by the moment. She had assumed, as she knew Kip did, that Bridget's shares would go to him. So why was Connors talking to her about this?

Connors went on, "Bridget Cross named Brianna Cross as successor trustee."

Iris was perplexed. Bridget had left Pandora to her daughter? "A five-year-old can't run a company."

"Mrs. Cross named you, Ms. Thorne, as administrator of the trust." Connors sat quietly as if waiting for the effect of his announcement to sink in.

"Administrator?" Iris echoed. "What does that mean?"

"It means that you're in charge of managing the property."

"Managing the property?" Iris grew more confused.

"Doing whatever Bridget did to manage the property," Connors roughly explained.

"Me? Run Pandora?" Iris looked at Natalie. "Instead of Kip?"

Natalie shrugged. "I was surprised too, Iris. I was also surprised that Bridget didn't mention anything to you." She turned and touched Brianna's legs, which the girl was wildly swinging. "Honey, please."

Omnipresent Louise was suddenly at Iris's door with a suggestion. "Brianna, would you like to draw? I have some colored pens and paper." Nothing in the office, not even the slightest ripple, got past Louise.

Brianna looked eagerly at Natalie.

"Go ahead," Natalie said. "Go with the nice lady."

"Thanks, Louise." Iris slowly exhaled. She rested her fingertips against her cheeks and looked from Connors to Natalie and back. "But I don't know the first thing about running Pandora."

"Bridget Cross was a savvy businesswoman," Connors said. "She was confident in her decision regarding Pandora and"—he shot a glance out the door, then lowered his voice—"was very clear that she did not want to turn control of the firm over to her husband."

Iris and Natalie exchanged a long look. It was unnecessary to vocalize what they were both thinking. Natalie's eyes grew glassy and Iris had to look away.

"When is this effective?" Iris asked Connors.

"Technically, it was effective at the moment of Mrs. Cross's death."

Iris swiveled her chair to look at Brianna, sprawled on the floor outside her door, coloring with felt-tipped markers. "Does Kip know?"

Connors crossed his chubby legs. "Mrs. Tyler and I decided, as a courtesy, to speak with him before our meeting with you. We went to the jail yesterday."

"How did he take it?"

Natalie raised an eyebrow and shook her head. "Not well. He was angry. He felt Bridget betrayed him. He accused you of having known about the trust the entire time and not telling him."

Iris stood and looked out the window at the hazy day. "What about T. Duke Sawyer, Pandora's other shareholder?"

"We thought we'd leave that to you," Connors said to Iris's back.

She turned again to face them. "And Pandora's employees?"

"Again, we thought it best if it came from—"

There was a piercing scream. It was followed by another and another.

Iris looked at the floor where Brianna had been playing. Only the papers and pens were there. Louise bolted past. Natalie flew from her chair, knocking it over, and ran out. Iris struggled to get past the slower-moving Connors. All the while, the screaming continued.

When Iris finally got out of her office, after it seemed a lifetime had passed, she saw Natalie on her knees, clutching Brianna. "What is it, honey? What is it?"

Brianna continued screaming as she stared with horror into Rick's cubicle. The junior broker sat as if petrified, babbling, "She just started screaming. I don't know what I did."

Gradually, Brianna started to calm down, her screams subsiding into sobs. Iris walked to Rick's cubicle where his screen displayed the office E-mail program. She pressed the ALT and then the TAB keys and changed the window. Slade Slayer's image filled the screen.

Brianna started screaming again.

Chapter 13

The sight of the open casket on display at the front of the chapel almost drained Iris of her resolve. She had planned on approaching the funeral as a business function, which it was in large measure. T. Duke Sawyer, the Pandora employees, and the press would be there, and she had to maintain her composure lest everyone think the reins of Pandora were held by a babbling, emotional wreck. Iris had told herself that she had already grieved over Bridget, both alone and with others, so any histrionics at the funeral were an unnecessary and costly indulgence.

Besides, Bridget herself had told Iris in a dream that she was okay and not to worry, and Iris had taken comfort from her message. But the sight of the casket and a glimpse of Bridget's profile inside it changed all that.

Iris had arrived slightly late to the rustic stone, hillside chapel. A few reporters were hanging around outside and several dozen lookie-loos. Bridget and Kip weren't nearly as sexy as Nicole and O.J., but the bizarre circumstances of the Cross case and the latest twist—the victim's daughter's repressed memories being jogged into consciousness by an accidental encounter with a computer game—provided a few juicy sound bites. And the Crosses did represent money and power, which the public found endlessly captivating. Then there was Summer Fontaine, suddenly omnipresent on the airwaves, who cut a profile that was intentionally hard to ignore. Iris would have found the Cross case as fascinating as the next couch potato if she weren't smack in the middle of the whole mess.

As Iris walked down the aisle between the pews, Toni spotted her and made Mick Ha and Today Rhea shove over to make room. Iris sat, grateful that Toni had found her a space so that she didn't have to take the one next to T. Duke. He was sitting a few rows closer to the front than Toni and was watching the door when Iris entered, as if he'd been waiting for her. There was an empty seat next to him, one of the few remaining in the crowded chapel, and it occurred to Iris that he had been saving it for her.

The pastor from Bridget's church was speaking. Bridget had been raised as a Presbyterian. She'd let her involvement in organized religion lapse until Brianna was two years old, when she began taking her daughter with her to church in spite of Kip's objections. In Kip Cross's world where reason and logic were revered, the existence of God occupied the fuzzy world of things that could not be proven by the rational mind and were therefore spurious.

Toni patted Iris's leg, and Iris noticed her eyes were red and swollen. Next to Toni, Mick was sketching on a small pad of drawing paper. Next to him, Today was sitting restlessly, stiffly wearing his conservative dark jeans and white shirt, crossing and recrossing his legs, and beating a rhythm against his knee with his hands. Iris cocked her head to see what Mick was drawing. It was a fine-line pencil sketch of the open casket with a hint of Bridget's profile.

The pastor recounted the events of Bridget's life, but Iris could not pay attention to him. To do so would be to go to that sad place. She even avoided looking in his direction so the casket wouldn't enter her line of vision. Instead she studied the many sprays of flowers and the mourners. She saw the wives of Bridget's brothers and their children, whom she remembered from Natalie and Joe Tyler's the day she had visited. She recognized a few friends from college. Baines was sitting stiffly next to T. Duke Sawyer. Near the back, she spotted Tiffany Stubbs and Jess Ortiz, the homicide detectives who were investigating Bridget's murder. She did not see Bridget's parents or brothers. They were probably sitting in an area, designated for close family members to the right of Bridget's casket, that was shielded from public view by a gauzy pink curtain. Brianna wasn't here. Natalie had decided it would be too much for the already distraught little girl. Kip had been released from jail to attend his wife's funeral and was probably sitting behind the pink curtain with Bridget's family.

Someone touched Iris's arm. She turned and was surprised to see her boss, Sam Eastman, standing in the aisle. He somberly nodded and proceeded into the chapel. To her knowledge, Sam had met Bridget for the first time when she had come by Iris's office the day before her murder. It was a slender reason to attend the woman's funeral.

Iris was staring holes into Sam's back when he plopped down next to T. Duke Sawyer. She didn't think too much of it—the seat was on the aisle and almost all the others were taken. She began to grow suspicious when she saw Sam shake T. Duke's hand but stopped herself from reading too much into a handshake. In the office last week, Sam had expressed his admiration for T. Duke. Sam was a bit of a social climber. Maybe he thought Bridget's funeral was a good place to meet the infamous takeover king. Now Sam and T. Duke were chatting into each other's ear, much longer than necessary to exchange banal pleasantries, especially while the service was going on. Something was definitely up.

Iris was roused from her thoughts when Toni squeezed past her to walk to the podium at the front. Iris whispered to Mick, who was now sketching Toni, "She's giving a eulogy?"

"She wanted to," he replied.

Toni cut a surprisingly sedate and mature figure as she stood at the podium. She'd traded her trendy clothes for a tailored black suit with a modest hemline. Her thick hair was tied at the base of her neck with a black ribbon. She cleared her throat and began.

"I met Bridget Cross five years ago when I applied for a job answering phones at Pandora. I had just dropped out of college after two years. My life was without direction and in many ways, without hope. I was involved with drugs—"

Iris raised her eyebrows with surprise at Mick, who sagely nodded in reply.

"—and a fast crowd, and my life was spiraling out of control. But I needed money and I saw the ad that Bridget had placed. Over the years, I'd express to Bridget and Kip my amazement that they'd hired me." Toni chuckled. "There were a few times when Bridget almost fired me, but we managed to work it out. With Bridget's help, I grew up at Pandora. She had faith in me when I didn't have it in myself. I came to admire her determination, vision, intelligence, guts, and above all, passion for the business that she and Kip built. I'm now Pandora's manager of sales and marketing. I owe my success to Bridget Cross."

Toni's voice broke. "I don't know what I'm going to do without her. Already during the past week, I've wanted to ask her advice a million times." She pulled a handkerchief from the sleeve of her jacket and dabbed at her eyes. "In addition to her busy schedule running a company, and being a wife and mother, Bridget Cross gave selflessly of her time to schoolchildren and the improvement of childhood education. My two close friends at Pandora, Today Rhea and Mick Ha, and myself want her work to continue. We're establishing the Bridget Cross Foundation, the goal of which will be to promote computer training in public grade schools. Our activities will include purchasing hardware, software, and funding teacher salaries. Bridget knew that high technology is the future and that we must do a better job of putting this powerful tool into the hands of our children if the country is to prosper in the decades to come."

Iris lost it. She snatched the wad of tissues she'd shoved into her pocket in case something like this happened. But she wasn't alone. The level of weeping escalated throughout the chapel. Iris looked at Mick, who was intently focused on his drawing, then at Today, who was quietly watching Toni. He quickly wiped away a tear that was caught in his lashes.

Toni continued, "So don't be surprised when you get a letter from us hitting you up for a donation."

There was scattered laughter. Toni made a few closing remarks, then walked back to her seat next to the weeping Iris. Toni grabbed her hand and squeezed it.

The pastor made a few more remarks. Then there were some prayers and music and more prayers. Then the time arrived to view the body.

Iris didn't want to go, but made herself. She looked down at Bridget's corpse. *Look what they did to you,* Iris said in her mind to Bridget. *You hardly ever wore makeup and they've got you painted like a Hollywood Boulevard hooker. You wore your hair carefree and loose and they've got it curled, teased, and frozen with hairspray. And that dress! All those ruffles and lace! Bridget, you wouldn't be caught dead in that getup.* Iris snickered at the irony. She imagined Bridget's response. *But, Iris, I* am *caught dead in this dress, for all eternity.* Iris laughed out loud as the people nearby paused in their weeping to look askance at her.

Get a grip, girl, Iris scolded herself. *Earlier you were afraid of what people would think if you became too emotional, now here you are laughing at the corpse. How inappropriate is that, Ms. Thorne?* But no one knew that she was sharing the joke with her friend. She then grew solemn. *I won't let you down, Bridget,* she vowed. *I promise.* She moved on and quickly left the chapel.

Outside, the weather was fine. After the Santa Anas had subsided, the temperature had dropped to a comfortable seventy degrees. The sky was slightly hazy, but there was no hint of rain. The sun reflecting off the haze made the sky bright. Iris put on her sunglasses.

Some people were getting into their cars to drive to the grave site, but many were walking up the steep hill. Iris walked along with the crowd, eavesdropping on conversations.

"Terrible when a child dies before her parents," an older woman said. "She was too young," her companion agreed. Someone else said it was a tragedy and the man behind him that it was God's will. Another mourner blamed society. Platitudes all, and all of them true. Death was, after all, the most mundane event in the world.

The high-pitched, nasal voice behind Iris grated like a needle scratching across a vinyl record album: "A priest decides to pay a visit to a nearby convent in a run-down neighborhood."

Iris glanced behind her, expecting to see Sam Eastman trailing along with T. Duke Sawyer, but instead saw T. Duke surrounded by Toni, Mick, and Today, who seemed enthralled with his story. Baines was walking a few paces behind with his hands behind his back. Iris looked around for Sam Eastman and didn't see him anywhere.

T. Duke went on, "As the priest walks down the street, several prostitutes approach and proposition him, shouting, 'Twenty bucks a trick! Twenty bucks a trick!' He's a young priest from the country—wet behind the ears—and these solicitations embarrass him. He lowers his head and hurries on until he gets to the convent. Once inside, he asks the mother superior, 'What is a trick?' She answers, 'Twenty bucks, son, just like on the street.' "

The group laughed, but Iris was appalled. She wondered why Mick, Toni, and Today were laughing so heartily, almost as if they were trying to impress T. Duke. It occurred to her that it was the same way one would attempt to impress a boss. She was still scowling when T. Duke pulled her into the group.

"There's the lady of the hour. Maybe she'll tell us her plans for Pandora."

Iris slowed her pace to match his. "I have some ideas, but I want to formalize them before I make an announcement." In reality, she knew exactly what she was going to do, but refused to be nailed on the spur of the moment by T. Duke Sawyer. She would pick her time and place.

T. Duke sucked air through his teeth. "Uh-huh. I imagine a smart girl like you would have some ideas."

Iris gritted her teeth, but let the patronizing comment pass.

He nodded slowly as if digesting the information. "We-ell," —he added a Texas twang to the end of the word—"you might like to have some information that'll help you *formalize* your ideas." He deliberately parroted her words. "Toni, Mick, and Today are quite interested in my plan to purchase Pandora. You may recall the offer I made Kip and Bridget the other day."

Iris thought, yeah, the one they dismissed because it was too low and required them to relinquish control over the company they had built from nothing.

The sunlight's harsh glare made T. Duke's exaggerated features look grotesque. It occurred to Iris that even candlelight wouldn't help his mug. He stopped walking and so did everyone else, as if on command.

Iris begrudgingly stopped as well.

"The offer's still on the table, with a few modifications, naturally, due to the recent unfortunate events."

Baines stood next to Iris. He seemed as solid as one of the cemetery's oaks. "I'd love to discuss it with you, T. Duke."

"How about tomorrow? I'll stop by your office at ten."

Baines's chest was even with Iris's eyes. "I'll look forward to it." She smiled at the group. When she turned to include Baines, she spotted his unique lapel pin with its red and white stripes, like the U.S. flag, and the tiny *1x1* on a blue background in the corner.

"Look," Toni said. "There are those two detectives."

Iris turned to see Stubbs and Ortiz unlocking the doors of a dark-colored sedan. She excused herself and quickly walked to catch them. "Detective Stubbs, Ortiz—hi! Excuse me for bothering you. I'm Iris Thorne, Bridget Cross's friend. You came to—"

"Sure." Ortiz nodded. "We know who you are."

The detectives patiently stood and waited for Iris to tell them what she wanted.

"I'm told you took possession of a file of letters and faxes sent to Bridget Cross from various individuals and groups who are critical of Pandora. Have you looked through it? Was there anything pertinent to the case?"

"I read it," Detective Stubbs said. The bright sunlight highlighted the deep pores of her skin. "The people at Pandora can have it back. I didn't see anything of interest."

"Hmmm," Iris said. "I was told that some of the letters were pretty strong."

"Some were," Stubbs said. "But there wasn't anything worth following up on."

"You're aware that Kip Cross believes he was framed for his

wife's murder." Iris soberly looked from one detective to the other.

Ortiz impatiently drummed his fingernails on the hood of the car. His expression just skirted being surly.

"Yes, ma'am, we are," Stubbs said, unsmiling.

"According to Brianna Cross, the murderer was wearing a Slade Slayer full-head mask."

"And Kip Cross couldn't have done that?" Stubbs asked.

"Why would he?"

"You don't know why a criminal would wear a disguise?" Stubbs exchanged a smirk with Ortiz.

Iris persisted. "After taking such care to disguise his face, why would Kip leave bloody footprints in the type and size of shoe he's known to wear?" She exhaled with frustration. "What about Alexa Platt's murder? Have you considered that there might be a connection?"

"There's an obvious connection. Both women knew Kip Cross."

"Look, Kip's attorney, Tommy Preston, thinks that with Brianna Cross's eyewitness testimony, the DA may let Kip go tomorrow because of lack of evidence. If that's the case, someone else murdered Bridget."

Stubbs listened with a disbelieving look on her face. "That's what Preston said, huh?" She jabbed a well-chewed fingernail in Iris's direction. "Kip Cross and only Kip Cross murdered Bridget Cross. If the DA doesn't prosecute, it's for one reason only—he'd rather take a dive than risk losing another high-profile case. It's a shame that LA is getting a reputation for being an excellent place for wealthy, powerful men to murder their wives and get away with it. If Kip Cross goes free, it'll have repercussions far beyond the scope of this case. It tells women that they'd better stay with the men who abuse them, because if you leave and the guy comes after you, you can't count on the law to protect you."

"But what if Kip didn't murder his wife? Doesn't their daughter have a right to know the truth?"

"I'm sorry about the child, but it is what it is. Good afternoon." Stubbs got in the car's driver seat and Ortiz climbed in the passenger side.

Iris again started walking up the hill. She reached the grave site, which was on the crest in the shade of a tall oak tree. People were quietly standing waiting for the hearse to arrive followed by the limousines carrying the family. When the cars were spotted leaving the chapel parking lot, everyone watched them slowly wend their way up the hill and park one behind the other by the curb.

Out of one limousine exited Natalie and Joe Tyler, followed by two of their sons and their wives. Out of another came the third son, his wife, and Bridget's grandmother.

The crowd grew hushed as Kip Cross exited the last limousine, accompanied by two police officers.

T. Duke said, "Good Lord have mercy."

Today moaned, "Ooh la la. Kip Cross the man."

Toni gasped, "I don't believe it. How *dare* he!"

Iris turned to see Summer Fontaine on Kip's arm, wearing a short, tight, low-cut, black dress that provided a tantalizing view of her gravity-defying breasts.

Photographers called, "Summer! Over here! Summer!"

Kip refused to be photographed and pulled the side of his jacket up to cover his face. Summer wiped a tear from her cheek with a black-gloved hand and gazed at the cameras. Her expression was mournful, but her eyes glittered.

Chapter 14

"It was cut up to here, down to there, and her tits were somewhere out in Orange County. It was *un*-freaking-believable."

Iris and Liz stepped closer to the counter as the line at Jammin' Juice moved through.

"She's certainly enjoying her fifteen minutes of fame," Liz commented. Her short and tight white suit was decorated with silver grommets and appliqués that would have been fitting for Elvis at Vegas. "I tape some of the talk shows and soaps so I can watch them when I get home, and Summer Fontaine is *every*where. This week alone she was on *Sally Jessy Raphael* and *Geraldo.*"

"What does she talk about?"

"Nothing! I think people just want to look at her. She loves talking about all the plastic surgery she's had to make her look more like Pamela Lee. Then the before and after shots go up and . . ." Liz shivered.

Iris studied the extensive menu behind the counter of the colorfully appointed shop that was in the lobby of McKinney Alitzer's office building. "What to have? Peach Pleasure or Citrus Ecstasy. *Hmmm*. The Powersurge looks good."

Behind the counter, a young man wearing a cotton handkerchief tied pirate-style around his head and assorted rings and studs through his eyebrow, cheek, and circling each ear fired off customer orders to a row of smoothie technicians behind him who were manning an army of blenders.

Liz jutted her hand in front of Iris as if to stop her from stepping in front of a speeding car. "Don't, hon. The Powersurge kept me up all night."

"Anyway, the funeral was awful, for more than just the usual reasons," Iris said. "There was Sam-I-Am having a tête-à-tête with T. Duke, Pandora's people tagging after T. Duke like homesick puppies, Baines glowering at me like he wanted to slit my throat, Summer Fontaine acting like the headliner at some totally nude club, and the police patiently listening to me like I was some kid who'd lost her mommy in the supermarket. At least they said they'd return that file of letters. I think there's a whole dimension to Bridget's murder that the cops are ignoring. I'd love to talk to Alexa Platt's husband, but he won't return my phone calls even though I told his secretary that Alexa and I were friends."

"Ozzie knows him. He can set you up."

"Ozzie?"

"Hon, Jim Platt is Ozzie's client. Besides, Ozzie knows *everyone* in Hollywood. But beware. I've heard Jim Platt is a self-important prick. He went from working behind the counter in a video store to being the hottest director in town and he doesn't wear his fame gracefully."

Liz placed her order. "I'll have a Purple Rain with bee pollen, one hit of oat bran, two of protein powder, a dash of wheat grass, and hold the fro-yo." She turned to Iris. "I'll get Ozzie to set you up with him." She hurriedly turned back to the counterman and blurted, "Are the carrots organic?"

"Of course," he said with the attitude of a top chef being quizzed about the freshness of his fish du jour.

Liz breathed a sigh of relief.

Iris ordered next. "I'll have two parts cranberry juice, one part kiwi, a splash of orange, a few strawberries, a glop of nonfat fro-yo, and a hit of protein powder."

"Which one is that?" Liz asked as she searched for Iris's concoction on the menu.

"I call it the Ice Princess. It's off the menu."

"Oh, Iris. You are *so* LA."

Iris brought the smoothie back to her office, first peering into the cubicle of Rick, the broker whose Slade Slayer game had scared Brianna. Today, his computer monitor sedately displayed stock quotes.

"Hey!" Rick called after her. *"Suckers Finish Last*—how do you win? I've played lots of games and I know all the tricks, but I can't figure this one out. Think you could get Kip Cross to give me a hint?"

"I don't think so. He won't even tell the staff at Pandora."

"The buzz among my friends is that if you can figure out how to win *Suckers Finish Last*, you'll find out who murdered Bridget Cross."

"Does the fact that the game might have been played out in real life make it more interesting?"

"Heck, yeah. My friends are buying it like crazy."

"Do your friends think Kip murdered his wife?"

"Sure. But it only makes playing the final level more tantalizing. It's sort of like, what was in Kip's mind when he was designing this?"

Iris returned to her office, waving at Louise as she passed. She leaned back into her soft leather chair and drew the last of the smoothie through the straw, letting it make a rude noise. Toni had told her that *Suckers Finish Last* was selling beyond their wildest expectations, possibly resulting from the hook with a real-life murder. The thought upset her. Maybe T. Duke was right. Maybe virtual violence had spilled over into the real world.

She lobbed the empty plastic cup into the trash can, picked up the telephone, and dialed the research department.

"Hi, Darcy. Iris Thorne. Look, when you have a second, could you please dig up any information you can on 3-D Dimensions? It's a computer-games company that was started by a guy named Harry Hagopian. I believe it was privately held before being bought out by the Sawyer Company, maybe last year or the year before. Hagopian died last year in a car crash—a solo spinout—on the Fifteen going through the Mojave Desert. See what you can find on that. Also dig up anything you can on a venture capital firm called USA Assets. The firms they invested in, what happened to the firms afterward, the principal players, and so on. Thanks so much."

She disconnected the call and immediately dialed another number. The phone on Louise's desk just outside her door began ringing.

"Hi," Iris said, not identifying herself, knowing the display on Louise's phone would indicate who was calling. "Any progress with the PR firm?"

"You have a meeting with Pat Delaney of Johnson Delaney today at three. I told them you wanted to boost Pandora's image in an effort to interest venture capital firms."

"Right. I need to get Pandora ready for the livestock auction."

"Livestock?"

"Venture capitalists examine companies they're thinking of investing in like they would check the teeth and hide of a steer before they buy. I need a good public relations campaign to salvage Pandora's reputation, get the VCs interested, and also get the market excited. Any enthusiasm I can drum up about Pandora will have a significant impact on the IPO's opening price."

"You're going to follow through with taking Pandora public?"

"That's what Bridget wanted."

"People have suggested that's why Kip murdered her. Kip says that's why T. Duke Sawyer murdered her. Are you certain you want to put yourself in jeopardy like that?"

"I'm not concerned about the best solution for Iris Thorne. I've been entrusted with Brianna Cross's financial well-being. I don't intend to breach that trust and I don't care who knows it."

"You're going to have an opportunity to see how that sits with one of Pandora's other shareholders. I see T. Duke Sawyer in the lobby. He's with a big young man."

"That's his goon, Baines. Louise, take a good look at Baines's lapel pin, if you can. Tell me if it means anything to you."

"Will do. Are you ready for them?"

"I've had my protein-spiked smoothie. I am ready! Bring on the Lone Ranger and Tonto."

While Louise retrieved T. Duke Sawyer and Baines, Iris quickly freshened her lipstick and pulled a brush through her hair, which she immediately regretted. A lot of static electricity was in the air and the brush made her hair pop and wildly fly around. She tried to pat it in place, then quickly affected a calm pose when Louise led T. Duke and Baines into her office.

"So nice to see you under happier circumstances," Iris lied.

T. Duke firmly shook Iris's hand. "Same here."

Baines squeezed her hand so tightly Iris had to stop herself from wincing.

Louise inquired whether anyone would like a beverage. As she did so, she took a close look at Baines's lapel pin. "That's an interesting pin. Is that from some sort of a club or something?"

Why didn't I think of just asking about it? Iris thought to herself.

"Yes, ma'am." Baines didn't elaborate.

Louise looked over the top of her half-glasses at the pin. "One times one?"

Baines corrected her. "One by one."

"What kind of a club has that as a slogan?" Louise asked guilelessly.

"Forgive me, kind lady, for butting in," T. Duke interjected, his beady eyes animated, "but we've got a lot to go over with Miss Thorne before we leave."

Baines almost overwhelmed the Queen Anne chair where he was sitting. His back was ramrod straight, his face expressionless.

T. Duke plucked at the knees of his pants before sitting in the matching chair. "Let's get down to business. As much as I enjoy your company, Iris, business is what we came for." He leaned forward on one elbow and smiled, his gash of a mouth rising higher on one side.

Iris suspected he was trying to look jaunty, but it only made him resemble a rat in Boy Scout's clothing.

"Before we get started, I must say you're looking lovely today."

Iris smiled graciously. "Thank you." To herself she added, *You condescending SOB.*

T. Duke held his spread hands up as if he were beginning a sermon at a pulpit. "So where goes Pandora and where goes Iris Thorne?"

Iris loosely folded her hands on her desk. "Pandora goes public. Iris Thorne takes it there."

T. Duke had begun vigorously shaking his head before Iris had finished her short response. "I don't want to hurt your feelings, but you're a day late and a dollar short on a Pandora IPO. The market for initial public offerings has cooled. That's exactly what I told Bridget Cross last week, poor woman. Plus Pandora's tainted goods now."

"I agree the market's cooled, but it hasn't gone cold. It may be cold for some firms who are overvalued and don't have a track record of profitability, but that's not Pandora's case. *Suckers Finish Last* is outselling even the most optimistic projections. We can learn something from other high-tech IPOs. Yahoo! raised thirty-five million with theirs. InfoSeek raised forty-two million, Lycos pulled in forty-eight million. Pandora may not raise as much as that, but the ducks are still quacking. The wisdom on the street is, when the ducks are quacking, feed them."

T. Duke leaned forward with his elbows on his knees and softened his voice, as if to gently deliver bad news. "You can't ignore the effect of Bridget Cross's murder and Kip Cross's arrest on the market. They were Pandora's guiding lights. Talented people, both. Shame." He shook his head sorrowfully, the fluorescent lights causing his large nose to cast a long shadow onto his upper lip. "Without the Crosses, I don't see Pandora surviving on its own." He frowned sympathetically, as if he hated having to speak so boldly, but his rat's eyes shone.

"Kip hasn't been charged with murder. He may be set free today."

T. Duke exchanged a long glance with Baines, then said quickly, "If he is, there's something seriously wrong with this country. Seriously wrong. But let's set aside Pandora's leadership issues. What about their finances? That's a whole other kettle of fish. Funds were misspent left and right. They increased their overhead before they saw an increase in revenues. Think of the legal fees Kip Cross is going to run up." He grimaced. "It galls me to think that money I invested through USA Assets has gone to pay Kip Cross's legal fees. You're responsible for that, aren't you? You sign the checks now."

Iris figured he expected her to justify her actions or apologize. She just looked at him without emotion and tried to avoid looking at Baines, who was studying her with his blue eyes, as he had been since he arrived.

After a few seconds, when it became clear that Iris wasn't going to respond, T. Duke continued in his folksy twang, "The point I'm trying to make is, Pandora looks like a bad risk to any savvy investor. And perception rules the market."

"I have a plan in place to address that."

"You do?"

She nodded cryptically.

"Well, okay, say you do. Say you manage to make Pandora look sexy to the marketplace. You still have to get an IPO approved by the SEC. Are you certain Pandora is squeaky-clean?" T. Duke sliced his hand through the air as if the issue were black-and-white, on one side or the other. "No questionable activities on the part of its board of directors? I'm not talking about just their activities as concerns Pandora, but outside the firm as well. Your job here, for example. It's an environment that's ripe for fraud."

"There are no fraudulent activities going on in my office," Iris said sharply, offended by the suggestion. "And all Pandora's operations are on the up-and-up."

"I don't mean to offend you, Iris, but you have been involved with some questionable business dealings in the past which may not stand up to scrutiny."

Iris's face grew hot and she knew she was glowing red. "What specifically are you referring to?" He was right. She had been involved in a few situations and with a few people that weren't exactly kosher. Some of these incidents were well-known, some she hoped to take to her grave. Which was he talking about? She wondered just how much someone with T. Duke's resources could find out about a person. A lot, she concluded. The thought that she might be forced to be T. Duke's pawn and forgo her plan for Pandora because of something in her past sickened her.

T. Duke raised a cautioning hand. "Now, I'm the last person to throw stones. Everyone knows my past is far from untainted. I'm simply offering you advice as a friend. Part of my job as an investor in small companies is to make the entrepreneurs stand naked in front of a mirror." He paused and leaned forward, eyes narrowed. "You have to take an honest look at yourself and your firm."

Iris took a deep breath, leaned back in her chair, and crossed her legs. "I guess the question is, if Pandora doesn't go public, where does it go?"

He pointed at her excitedly. "I'm glad you asked me that. My offer is still on the table to buy Pandora outright." He drew a half circle in the air with his hands as he outlined his grand vision, concluding by holding up both rounded palms as if he cradled the world between them. "I see Pandora as a key player in my concept to create a network of companies that will work in concert to create a new digital marketplace, leading the consumer from shopping for a product on TV to a vendor's ad to an on-line store, with the Sawyer Company collecting a fee at every stop." He squirmed in his chair as if it had grown too small to contain him.

"T. Duke, I've expressed my confusion about this before," Iris began. "Due to your recent buying spree, the Sawyer Company is over two billion dollars in debt, more than twice its equity level. If interest rates go up, you come crashing down. Why assume more debt by buying Pandora, a company with numerous problems, many of which you've outlined? It seems like you have bigger fish to fry."

T. Duke responded, "And as I expressed before: synergy."

"You can license software to distribute, you don't need to home-grow it. You're critical of the violent and sexual content in Pandora's games anyway. Why not take over a firm whose vision is more in line with your own? Why did you approach Pandora with investment money in the first place?"

"That's very simple. I'm like Wayne Gretzky. I go where the puck's going to be. When I see a company with promise and that's on the cutting edge, I pounce." He stood and walked to the window, the block heels of his cowboy boots leaving indentations in the carpet. He turned to face her and did not speak. It was her ball.

"I assume your purchase offer of seven dollars a share still stands."

T. Duke looked at her with surprise. "Why, no. How could it, in view of recent events? It's been adjusted accordingly. Five dollars a share."

Iris gaped at him. "Seven was too low. Now it's five?"

"The marketplace is a fickle thing, as I know you're well aware."

Iris abruptly slapped her hand against her desk. "That settles it. I'll let the market decide how much Pandora is worth."

"This may be the best offer you'll get. I may not be able to hold the price at five dollars."

"I'm not giving Pandora away."

"Pandora's management may have something to say about your cavalier decision. They're very keen on my proposition. I guaranteed all of them comparable jobs within the Sawyer Company."

"And they believed you?"

"They're good people," T. Duke said defiantly.

"So were all the others you threw out of jobs in all the other firms you took over and dismantled."

"I resent that comment."

"Duly noted."

"I invited Today, Mick, and Toni to my ranch in Santa Ynez this weekend to discuss Pandora. I'd like to extend the same invitation to you."

"I'll have to check my calendar and get back to you."

"It would be nice if you came. You can bring a friend or significant other, if you like. Today and Mick are bringing their wives."

"It does sound nice. Let me get back to you." The meeting was winding down. She decided to pick on Baines while she had the chance. He was sitting like a stone lion with his hands resting on his knees. "What's your opinion of all this, Baines?"

"My opinion is not relevant, ma'am."

"I see."

T. Duke raised his index finger. "I have a question, Miss Thorne."

"T. Duke, why the formality? Aren't we friends anymore?"

He ignored her comment. "You're a busy woman. I thought you would have jumped at the opportunity to unload your responsibility in Pandora. Why complicate your life with an IPO?"

"Because Bridget Cross trusted me to make the right decisions for her daughter's sake. I want one thing to be perfectly clear. If anyone wants to get their hands on Pandora, they have to get past me."

"So you're letting personal issues cloud your business judgment?"

"And you don't? I can't believe your quest to control Pandora has anything to do with synergies or digital marketplaces or any of that mumbo jumbo. You're involved for a personal reason."

"It's true I want to control Pandora, but I have no dark motives. I'm an investor, Iris. My sole *raison d'être* is to make money." He pronounced the French with a Texan accent. "I believe there's a lot of money to be made with Pandora, and I don't think you're the person who can make it."

She straightened in her chair. "Okay. I'll give you a chance to make some money on Pandora right now. I'll buy out your twenty percent stake at six dollars a share."

He shook his head. "No deal."

"How about eight dollars?"

He again shook his head.

"Eleven? Twelve? C'mon T. Duke, everyone has his price." She picked up a pencil and tapped it against the desk.

"This is a foolish game. Everyone knows Pandora doesn't have money like that."

"I can get the money and you know it. You won't get out of Pandora for any price. Your interest in Pandora is not about money and it never was. Why don't you save me a lot of time and just tell me what it is? I'm going to find out, you know. I'm very tenacious."

"I'm sorry to disappoint you."

"You realize that Kip thinks you're behind Bridget's murder and that you set him up to take the fall for it."

T. Duke laughed and looked at Baines to share the joke. The other man gave in to a small smile. "Baines is a much better shot than whoever it was that brought poor Bridget down. I certainly wouldn't hire anybody who couldn't shoot."

"Whoever shot Bridget may have intentionally made it look like they couldn't shoot. Kip wasn't skilled with guns."

T. Duke was still laughing. He shook his head and wiped a tear from his eye. "You tickle me, Iris. I'm amused by this dark plot you're suggesting. You have quite an imagination."

The three of them looked at Louise, who had urgently stepped into the doorway. "There's just been a news report. Kip Cross was released from prison."

Iris slowly rose from her chair.

"Son of a bitch!" T. Duke spat.

Baines gave T. Duke a troubled look.

"What a relief," Iris said, not feeling completely at ease with the news. "At least Brianna will have her daddy back."

"Apparently, Brianna's recalled memory of seeing the murderer clinched it," Louise said. "She insisted it wasn't her father."

"But the guy was wearing a mask!" T. Duke protested. "How could she tell who it was?"

"The DA said there wasn't enough evidence to convict Kip," Louise said. "It was all circumstantial. And with the child's testimony, forget it."

Iris added, "The last thing the DA wants is to grill a five-year-old on the witness stand when her mother's been murdered. It's bound to backfire."

"And to think my money helped get that scumbag out of jail. What the hell is this country coming to?"

Baines uttered the longest sentence he had since he'd arrived. "How much did the little girl see?"

Chapter 15

Natalie Tyler looked through the peephole and closed her eyes as if horrified by what she saw. She took a moment to compose herself before opening the front door. "Why, Kip!"

"Hi, Natalie." He stood awkwardly on the front porch, then reached to touch her arm, realizing some physical contact was warranted.

"And . . . ah . . . hello, Summer." Natalie uneasily extended her hand to Summer, who was standing next to Kip.

"Hi, Mrs. Tyler." Summer smiled demurely. She was wearing skintight, pencil-leg jeans, a short white sweater, and white lug-soled shoes. Her large breasts raised the hem of the sweater away from her body, baring her midriff.

Natalie uneasily rubbed her hands together. "So, Kip, you're out of jail. Good for you!" She nervously patted his shoulder.

"Yeah." He nodded, scratching his ear. "I'm here to pick up Brianna."

Natalie quickly turned inside the open doorway and shouted, "Joe! Joe, guess who's here!" She smiled tentatively at Kip while she cast anxious glances inside the house. "Were there a lot of reporters waiting for you?" she said as if she hadn't heard his comment about Brianna.

Joe Tyler shuffled to the doorway in worn leather slippers. His plaid shirt was not tucked in, his chinos were wrinkled, and his hair looked as if he'd forgotten to comb it. He raised his chin to peer at Kip through the bottoms of his glasses, as if to get a sharper view. "Oh?" was all he said.

"Good to see you, Joe." Kip extended his hand.

Joe shook it briefly, then released it as if to drop something foul.

Natalie grabbed Joe's beefy arm with both hands. "Honey, Kip wants to pick up Brianna."

"Where is she?" Kip asked, peering inside the house. "Isn't she here?"

"She's taking a nap, Kip," Natalie said. "I don't want to wake her. She's not sleeping too well. She has terrible nightmares."

"We don't think that's such a good idea, Kip," Joe said. "You taking Brianna."

Kip crossed his arms over his chest and blinked at the ground, as if trying to digest the message. Summer grabbed a corner of her silicone-puffed lips between her teeth and looked at Kip with distress. He squinted at the Tylers. "Are you trying to keep me from my daughter?"

Natalie fluttered her hands at him. "No, no, dear. No, that's not it at all. It's been so hard for her, hard for all of us. Certainly you can understand, Kip. We thought she'd be better off here. Just for a few more days until you get settled. I mean, all the reporters and going back to that house—"

"I want to see my daughter," Kip said emphatically, taking a step toward the door.

Joe moved into his path, blocking his way with his big body. "Kip, we don't think that's a good idea. Be reasonable. Just give Brianna a couple of days to get used to the idea. You're taking her back to the house where her mother was murdered, for goodness' sake. Think of the child's welfare for a change."

Kip reared back, as if the words had struck him. "What's that supposed to mean?"

"We don't mean any offense, Kip," Joe continued. "You have to face facts."

"I'm not leaving without my daughter." Kip grabbed the older man and tried to move him out of the way.

Whether it was due to strength or will, Joe Tyler would not be moved. "Kip, calm down!" He held Kip away with his arms.

"Don't hurt him!" Summer yelled.

Natalie scampered away from the men and cowered just inside the door, her trembling hands pressed against her mouth.

Kip backed up and tried to barrel past Joe, who lowered his shoulders like a linebacker. "Get ahold of yourself, man!" When Kip came running at him again, Joe lunged, tackling him and sending them both off the porch and onto the grass.

Natalie left the safety of the house and walked to the edge of the porch. "We buried our daughter yesterday, Kip." Tears streamed down her face. "Have some compassion. You're always so absorbed with yourself. You never think about how your actions affect anybody else. It's always you. You, you, you!"

Joe slowly rose from the grass and dusted himself off. Kip remained where he had fallen and looked startled as he watched Natalie, who was uncharacteristically in a rage.

"You have the gall to bring *her* here." Natalie angrily pointed at Summer. "She's one of the reasons you and Bridget were having problems. Bridget made her move out. Now my daughter's dead and she's still there."

"Someone had to watch the house," Kip protested. "All the reporters and people—"

"See? See how you are? You don't think! And this woman is still going to be Brianna's nanny, am I right?"

"It's better for Brianna to stay with someone she knows." Kip finally got up from the ground. "I can't stay with her. I have to get back to Pandora. I'm losing control over my company."

"Brianna loves me," Summer added in her little-girl voice. "Brianna spent more time with me than she did with Bridget. It was almost like she was my baby."

"I have thought about this. I *have,*" Kip insisted to the appalled Tylers. "It's the most logical solution."

Joe rejoined his wife on the porch. Natalie's tears had dried.

Now she was pure fury. "I've never known a man who could be so brilliant and so *stupid* at the same time. For all the things you're good at that have made you rich, you do not understand people. The simplest things about human relations escape you. People don't work like computers, Kip."

Kip ran both hands across his buzz-cut hair, then crossed his arms over his chest. He furrowed his brow, stared intently at the grass, and began gently pulling the hair of one of his eyebrows between his fingers over and over. Summer approached and raised her hand as if to touch him, hesitated, then dropped it by her side.

Finally, Kip looked up and said, "Okay. Brianna can stay here for a few more days, but that's it. Don't get any ideas about keeping her. I was always a good father. You can't fault me for that. Okay, I've made mistakes—I'm the first to admit it. But I don't think I'm making one now. I don't like the way everyone's treating me."

"You should have thought of that before you . . ." Joe couldn't finish the sentence.

Kip glared at his father-in-law. His chest and arms grew rigid. A deep flush moved up his face. The veins on his neck swelled. He clenched his fists. "I did not murder my wife!" He took a deep breath, as if trying to calm himself, opened his hands, and repeated more plaintively, "I did not murder my wife."

Natalie and Joe clutched each other on the porch as they watched Kip walk away while Summer soothingly rubbed his back and murmured into his ear. They got in Kip's Ferrari and drove off.

Toni and Iris were in Pandora's employee lunchroom. Toni opened the refrigerator door. It was stocked with premium bottled water, fresh fruit, jars of flavored iced teas, and a variety of soft drinks. "These are all free to the employees. And we sell the sandwiches, yogurt, and other stuff"—she indicated two food-vending machines against the wall—"at cost."

A collection of bottled vitamins was sitting on the counter. A Post-It note stuck to one advised, "Don't forget your C. Cold season's here!"

"This is very generous," Iris said.

"It all contributes to making Pandora a nice place to work. Bridget realized how competitive the marketplace is for talented computer programmers, graphic artists, and technical support personnel. A talented system designer from a good school can get a top salary right out of college."

"And stock options."

"Exactly. Pandora's always been able to attract good people. We're consistently on the cutting edge of technology. The Crosses brought a certain, whatchamacallit . . ."

"Cachet?" Iris offered.

"Yeah, cachet to the firm. There are people out there—game fanatics, hackers—who think Kip Cross is a god. Bridget, wisely, tried to exploit the Pandora magic and create a fun, funky, and employee-oriented working environment."

"Smart lady."

"Yes, she was." Toni walked to a bank of coffeemakers including cappuccino machines and milk steamers. Shakers of nutmeg, chocolate, and cinnamon were on the counter. "Here's our gourmet coffee bar. Want a cappuccino?"

"Not now, thanks."

They entered a maze of cubicles inside the modified airplane hangar where the noise was loud and the atmosphere, kinetic. "This is the technical support department. The techs answer phone calls, E-mails, and faxes from users."

The techs, all guys, none of whom looked over the age of twenty, were dressed casually in T-shirts and jeans or knee-length shorts. They sported an assortment of hairstyles ranging from military buzz cuts to straight manes long enough to sit on. Body piercings abounded. Each cubicle was crowded with computers, stereos, compact discs, toys, and athletic equipment. There were also board games with rounds in progress of everything from the familiar—Scrabble and chess—to the obscure—go and shogi.

Iris commented on the abundance of basketballs, footballs, baseballs, bats, and mitts. "Appears to be an athletic group."

"Someone's always got a game going outside on the company basketball court or the open field next to the hangar."

The techs were maniacally doing several things at once: talking on the phone, shouting back and forth, swiveling from keyboard to keyboard, playing several computer games at once, and darting into each other's cubicle to execute moves on the ongoing board games. The hyperactivity was set to a sound track of blaring rock music and the clatter of gunshots, phasers, explosions, and screams.

"Lots of activity." Iris had to almost shout over the racket.

Toni nodded, widening her enthusiastic eyes. She pointed at the raised floor they were walking on. "All the electrical and other cabling runs beneath here." They crossed an open area and reached a set of offices located several yards away from the racket of the technical support department. "That structure houses accounting, payroll, human resources, and stuff like that."

Everywhere Iris looked there were computers. They were as common as paper clips. Each office had at least two. Loose components were gathered like dust balls on stair steps, in corners, and shoved against walls.

They walked up a set of raw wood stairs to a large loft along one side of the hangar that held a series of offices. "The art design staff works here." Toni knocked on a door. When there was no answer, she opened it to an office decorated with dozens of unframed drawings and paintings tacked to the walls. "This is Mick's office. Guess he's not in yet."

Iris looked at her watch. "It's one in the afternoon. When does he usually get in?"

"We crunched so hard on getting *Suckers Finish Last* out the door, pulling twelve- and sixteen-hour days, that everyone's kind of taking a break."

"Does anyone have set office hours?"

"Tech support does, because they have to be available to answer client questions, but other than that . . ." Toni shrugged. "Doesn't matter when you come in or leave, as long as the work gets done."

Toni closed the door and they continued walking down the unfinished wood catwalk. "Here's where all the system designers, miscellaneous programmers, and software testers work." She knocked on another door. "This is Today's office." When there was no response, she tried the doorknob. It was locked. "He always keeps his office locked. Hardly anyone else does."

"Looks kind of vacant up here. I guess everyone's relaxing after getting the last release out, like you said."

Toni lowered her voice. "That's part of the reason, but you should know that everyone's freaked out about Bridget's murder and Kip—you know, being accused and stuff."

"Do the employees think Kip did it?"

Toni sighed and raised her eyebrows. "Yeah. Unfortunately, a lot of them do. Even Today and Mick." She leaned against the catwalk railing and looked out across the hodgepodge assortment of structures.

"What about you?"

Toni picked at a splinter of loose wood. "I suspect it's Kip. It's too bad Brianna saw so little. She can't even tell the police the murderer's height or build or anything."

"But she's convinced it wasn't her father."

"Maybe that's because she doesn't want it to be her father." Toni pulled the splinter free and tossed it over the side. "I wonder if she'll remember more details later."

"She might. I'm worried about her. Knowing Kip, he probably doesn't appreciate the danger Brianna could be in. You know how clueless he can be."

They stood quietly for a long minute. Finally, Toni said, "Are we ever going to find out absolutely who murdered B?"

"We have to," Iris said firmly.

"You don't really think it could have something to do with those people or groups who threatened Pandora?"

"I think we need to consider everything. At least, that's more than the police are doing."

"I think your conspiracy theory is far-fetched, but we can't leave any stone unturned. I want to help."

"Really?" Iris was heartened by the news.

Toni widened her big eyes. "I think we can crack it, Iris, if we work together."

Iris felt energized by Toni's offer. "I know you think it's a crackpot idea, but let's look at those letters the police brought back."

"I put them in the filing cabinet in Bridget's office. Let's go."

Just as Iris and Toni were about to leave, they heard something pound against the inside of Today's office door. They were looking at each other quizzically when the door flew open and Today darted out.

"Son of a bitch!" he cursed, stopping short before he stepped on them. He wore a tie-dyed T-shirt over gray sweatpants that were cut off at the knees. Bright yellow stereo headphones dangled from his neck. "Yikes! I didn't know you were there."

"What's wrong?" Toni asked.

"That guy I just hired?" Today stomped back and forth on the catwalk, agitatedly flinging his hands in the air. "Top system designer. Resigned before he even started. Left me an E-mail, for God's sake. Went to another game company." He snapped his fingers and shook them. *"Hasta la vista,* baby." He stormed past them and started jogging down the stairs. "This place is history." He spastically jerked his fingers and bitterly shook his head as if carrying on an internal conversation.

Iris called after him. "Today, why do you say that? Kip's out of jail. Pandora can move forward."

"Kip's out of jail," Today sneered, looking up at her from the hangar floor ten feet below. "Yeah. That makes me feel real good, working next to Kip Cross now. Somebody give me an ashtray to lick." He again started walking in the direction of the lunchroom.

"Please!" Iris pleaded. "We need to resolve this."

Today reluctantly stopped. "Look, Iris, I understand the spot you're in, but this is the situation. The secret of this place was the magic, the chemistry between us. The spell's broken. It started before Bridget's murder. Kip got the engine for *Suckers* done, but he lost the spark after that. Usually, by now he'd be testing a new engine. He'd be showing us something that would blow all of us out of the room. He would have some new approach that *no one* ever considered."

"Engine?" Iris naively asked.

Today shook his head with his mouth open. "Engine! A graphics engine. You're going to run this company and you don't even know the basics?"

Toni whispered in Iris's ear, "I told you how impatient he is with nontechnical people. Fake it."

"Okay," Iris said. "So you know for a fact that Kip hasn't started work on a new . . . engine."

"Unless he's been working on it in *jail*. If Pandora's going to survive, we've got to get another new game out there—and fast. The word on the street is that we're dead. Yeah, we had a lot of top games in the past, but all this industry cares about is the future."

"You can't start work on a new game until Kip finishes the engine?" Iris ventured, not having a clue what she was talking about.

Today slapped both hands against his face, then dragged them away. "Arrggh!" He turned his back and pointed at Iris without looking at her. "I can't talk to her, Toni. I'm not going to waste my time talking to some nontechnical know-nothing."

Toni explained to Iris, "We could kick around some ideas for a new game, but without knowing the kind of graphics engine Kip's going to come up with, we can't do much. We design the game to fit the capabilities of the engine. Each of Kip's engines has been such a dramatic departure from the one before, we can't anticipate what it's going to be able to do." Toni leaned against the railing. "Today, maybe we could release a second version of *Suckers*."

"Maybe you could kiss my ass." He again looked at Iris. "I have one thing to say and one thing only. Take T. Duke's offer."

Iris was surprised. "You want to work for the Sawyer Company?"

"No!" Today bellowed. "I want to cash out my stock options. I've been waiting five years for my Pandora options to be worth something. T. Duke's offering the best chance for me to get a hunk of dough for the time I invested in Pandora. The Pandora IPO's never gonna come off. This place is going to go down the tubes, you're going to screw up T. Duke's offer, and I'll never see any cash out of this deal."

They turned when the front door opened. Mick Ha came in and walked across the long stretch of floor to where Today was standing. In one hand, he was carrying a tool chest, in the other he held the handle of an art portfolio. "What's up?" he asked in his typically subdued way.

"I was trying to tell Iris how she should take T. Duke's offer," Today said.

Mick looked at Iris on the catwalk. "I agree, Iris. Nothing personal."

Iris looked at Toni. "What do you think?"

"I don't think Pandora's done. I'm looking forward to working together to take Pandora into the future in the way that Bridget envisioned. I'm really surprised at you guys and your attitude. I mean, who's saying Pandora's dead? Our competitors? And Iris is working on that. She's hired a top public relations firm. I'm also surprised by your lack of loyalty to Kip, how you want to dump him when he needs us most."

Iris picked up the ball. "And *I'm* surprised you would believe promises from a man who earned the nickname the Liquidator. You actually think he'll come through with the jobs he promised you?"

Today elaborately raised his hands. "Doesn't matter. I'll stay with him long enough to get the dough and the stock, then I'll bail. Hey, I've got ten headhunters a day calling me."

"And you feel the same way, Mick?" Iris pressed.

Looking at his shoes, he nodded without saying anything.

"Did T. Duke talk specifics with you?" Iris asked. "Did he tell you *exactly* how much he was offering for Pandora?"

Mick and Today exchanged a glance. "No," Mick admitted.

"Let me tell you something you don't know. After Bridget's murder, T. Duke lowered his offer price for Pandora."

"Lowered?" Today asked.

"He says the company is worth less. This is the guy you want to leave Pandora in the lurch for? He's taking money from Brianna Cross. He's profiting from Bridget's murder. Look"—Iris rubbed her forehead as she gathered her thoughts. "Pandora is very much alive. You can honor Bridget's memory by working to preserve it." She clapped her hands. "Are we still a team?"

"Abso-tively!" Toni exclaimed, punctuating it with a hop.

Mick and Today looked at each other. Mick shrugged reluctantly. "Sure." He didn't sound convinced.

Today took his headphones from around his neck and swung them like a lariat. "Jesus—okay—maybe. Kip probably has one more rabbit to pull out of his hat, *I guess*. What the hell."

"Great." Iris wasn't thrilled with their tepid enthusiasm, but it was better than their leaving. "T. Duke said he'd invited you guys up to his ranch. I guess there's no reason to go now, huh?"

"Why not?" Toni protested. "It sounded like fun."

"Yeah," Mick said. "I already told my wife."

"Look, Iris," Today said. "Let's just see how the next few days and weeks go, okay? I'm not going to bail tomorrow, but I want to keep my options open. I don't know how it's going to be, working with Kip. For me, it'll be pretty weird because I think he shot Bridget, right?"

"Speak of the devil . . ." Toni looked toward the front of the building.

Kip and Summer were standing outside the glass door, which he was rattling.

"Guess he doesn't have his keys," Toni said.

One of the techs spotted him and let him in.

Iris decided to set the tone and cheerfully bellowed across the floor, "Hi, Kip! Welcome back!"

"Hi, Kip!" Toni said.

"Hi, Summer!" Iris quickly added.

Kip and Summer walked over to them.

Today didn't say anything, but just hitched his head back as a greeting.

"Hey man," Mick said. "Summer."

Kip surveyed the place as if he was determining whether anything had changed in the few days he'd been gone. "What are you guys up to?" he asked suspiciously.

Iris warmly smiled. "Toni's been filling me in on the day-to-day operations. We were just talking about gearing up for the next Pandora release."

Today flicked his long hair over his shoulders. "You been working on a new engine?"

Kip nodded. "Yeah. I was tossing around some ideas before . . ." He opened his fingers then let his hand drop to his side. "Anyway, I sketched out some algorithms while I was in jail. That's why I came, to get my laptop."

Some of the techs had spotted Summer and were indiscreetly leering at her over the tops of their cubicles.

The atmosphere grew prickly. Iris again tried a dose of good cheer. "Well, it's good to have you back, Kip."

"Looks like everything's rolling along without me," Kip said. "Iris, I see you're getting in position as the new president and CEO."

Iris winced at Kip's words. "That's just temporary, Kip. My plan is to recruit a professional. Hire the best executive we can find."

Kip grinned at her venomously. "C'mon, Iris. You always said you wanted to run your own company one day. This is your big chance. Too bad you had to do it over your dead friend's body."

"Kip," Summer whispered as she put a warning hand on his arm.

"Kip!" Toni objected. "How can you talk to Iris that way? She's been here defending you."

"Thanks, Toni, but I know what this is about," Iris said. "Kip, I didn't ask to be put in charge of Pandora. Frankly, it's the last thing I need right now. I know you're mad at Bridget for doing it, but don't take it out on me."

"I just left my in-laws. They won't let me see my baby. They think I murdered their daughter. Is that what you guys think?" Kip looked at Today, who wouldn't meet his gaze, then at Mick, who looked at the ground. Kip shook his head. "Freaking great."

He turned and started walking toward the staircase that led to the loft on the other side of the hangar, with Summer following. He stopped and looked at Iris. "You're right, Iris," he said quietly. "You're absolutely right. You've supported me from the beginning and I don't have that many friends left. I'm sorry for what I said."

"It's all right, Kip," Iris said. "We're all under a lot of stress."

"I'm just going to get a couple of things. I might work at home for a few days." He jogged up the stairs to the loft.

Iris turned to Toni. "Let's get that file of letters."

Mick started up the stairs to his office. "I'm going to work on some ideas for new monsters."

"I need a dose of French roast, now." Today headed for the lunchroom.

After spending a few minutes in his office, gathering up some books and diskettes, Kip emerged with Summer onto the catwalk.

"Let's go straight home, baby," Summer said. "You've had a long day. You must be pretty horny, huh?"

"I haven't thought about it, actually."

"Maybe I can help you think about it." Summer sidled up close to him.

"Not here!" Kip snapped. He ran down the stairs and quickly crossed the floor to the front door.

Summer struggled to keep up with him.

"Murderer." The word was uttered in a loud stage whisper, obviously intended for Kip to hear, which he did.

He spun to look at the maze of offices, cubicles, lofts, and catwalks. He didn't see anyone.

"What is it?" Summer asked, scanning the expansive hangar.

"Who said that?" Kip demanded. He took a few steps in the direction the voice had come from. *"Who said that?"* When there was no response, he angrily turned and continued to the front door.

"Murderer."

Kip shouted, *"Who said that?"* He ran a few feet into the hangar and looked all around, nodding wildly as if something was now clear. "So that's the game now, huh? That's the game? No problem," he shouted. "I'm good at games."

Chapter 16

When Iris arrived home, she was surprised to see her mother's car parked in front of her house, but then remembered that she had asked Rose if she would wait for the cable guy. She also remembered that she'd intended to bring home takeout for the two of them, which she'd completely forgotten.

She unlocked her front door and was greeted with the aroma of hot food. She closed her eyes to better take in the experience, realizing how hungry she was. Cooking was going on in her house. It seemed somehow appropriate. There should be cooking going on in this house. She thought of the previous Sunday when Garland had barbecued for her and how much fun it had been doing nothing special, just being together.

She walked into the living room, which had been cleared of boxes, making her sparse furniture look all the more paltry. Her mother had apparently been busy. The large TV was against one wall, on top was the cable box, next to it the clicker, and in front of that, her easy chair. It beckoned.

Voices, laughter, and music were coming from the kitchen. It was her mother and who? Her neighbor Marge? Excellent.

Maybe it was the slender beginnings of her mother getting a life. Iris cocked her head at the music. It was rap. Curious selection. She walked into the kitchen.

"Hello, I'm home!" she cheerily announced, happy that someone was waiting for her, even if it was just her mother and neighbor.

"Hi, honey." Rose, holding a wooden spoon with which she had been stirring something red, pranced from the stove over to her and ebulliently hugged her. Iris smelled booze on her breath.

Marge was also in the kitchen. She was nattily dressed in light blue slacks and a white blouse embroidered with bird houses sitting atop vine-twisted posts with little red birds flying about. The blouse was tucked into her slacks, which were belted, displaying her slender figure.

Rose was wearing a magenta jumpsuit that Iris hadn't seen before. Made of a shiny, crinkled fabric, it pulled slightly across her large bottom in the back and across her rounded belly in the front. The top few buttons were unbuttoned, revealing serious cleavage. Iris tried not to stare. She had never seen her mother dressed like that.

"I'm making spaghetti and meatballs, honey. It was your favorite dish when you were little. Remember that, Iris, when I used to make that for you? You used to say it *spisghettis.* It was so cute."

"Hi, Iris." Marge waved, then pressed the whip button on the blender, which was full of a yellowish green concoction and thick with ice. "How was your day?" she shouted over the loud appliance. "We heard on the news that the market was down." She pointed a manicured fingernail in the direction the market had taken and tsk-tsked. "Now, my first husband, Ely, he was the one who liked the stock market. My second husband, Herb, wasn't much for it."

She posed with one finger on the whip button. With her other hand, she carefully traced the wave in her coiffure, ensuring that every hair was in place. From what Iris had seen of Marge, she never had a hair out of place. "His thing was real estate. He said he liked to put his money where he could see it. That was Herb for you. Now my third husband, Dub . . . well, poor

Dub didn't last too long after we got married, and I never found out much about him and money except that he didn't have much of it." She pulled her hand away from her hair and drew a prolonged arc in the air in Rose's direction with her fingertips. They both laughed as if it were the funniest thing they'd ever heard.

Iris decided they were toasted. The evidence was on the kitchen counter—two wide-mouthed, narrow-based margarita goblets, the rims marked with traces of coarse ground salt and lipstick. Lime wedges swam in the remaining froth at the bottom of the glasses.

"My garlic bread!" Rose dashed to the stove, grabbed a pot holder, pulled open the broiler door, and pulled out a cookie sheet covered with blackened slices of French bread. "It's ruined!"

"That's okay, love. We have plenty of makings left." Marge washed the two dirty glasses, produced a third, and drew a lime wedge around the rims. She upended the glasses into a small plate of coarse salt, gently turned them, coating the rims, then poured the margaritas from the blender into the glasses. She decorated each rim with a lime wedge and distributed the cocktails with a flourish.

Marge raised her glass in a toast. "To Iris's new house."

Iris and her mother repeated the toast then took a sip.

"This is wonderful!" Iris exclaimed. She took another sip. It was creamy and limey but not at all tart. She could not detect the tequila and triple sec, although she could already feel the effect of the potent cocktail. "Simply wonderful."

"It's El Cholo's recipe." Marge wiped the counter clean with a damp dishrag. "My first husband and I were very good friends with the owner, and he gave me the recipe *many* years ago. *Long* before you were born."

"Isn't she just great?" Rose enthused. "She saw me waiting for the cable installer and came over. We got to talking, went to have lunch, went shopping . . . Do you like it?" She pirouetted in the jumpsuit.

"Very striking. I'm glad you two hit it off. If you'll forgive me, I'm going to get out of these clothes and make a couple of phone calls. Thanks for making dinner. This is a wonderful surprise." Iris looked at a small television that was sitting on the kitchen counter. It was broadcasting a video of what looked like gang members cruising in low-riders and rapping to a relentless beat. "What in the world are you watching?"

"MTV," Marge said matter-of-factly.

"You have to keep up with trends or else life will just pass you by," Rose added.

"Uh-huh." Iris picked up her briefcase and margarita and turned to leave the room. "I'll see you in a bit."

"You go, girl," Marge said after her.

Iris mused about the scene in the kitchen as she walked down the corridor to the room she used as an office. "Well, you told her to get a life," she reminded herself aloud.

She opened a window, letting in the fresh ocean breeze. The small room had two windows that met at the corner. One faced the small strip of yard that separated her house from Marge's, the other faced the backyard and her ocean view. The sun had dipped in the sky but hadn't yet set. She promised herself that she would watch it set, tonight and every night that she could. She took in the view as she licked the salt from the rim of the margarita glass and followed it with a long sip. The margarita was strong, especially on her empty stomach, and she already had a buzz going.

"Hot hors d'oeuvres!" No sooner had Iris become aware of a hunger pang then Marge knocked on the open door carrying a small plate of cheese quesadilla wedges garnished with dollops of guacamole and salsa.

"Marge, you're a phenomenon. *I* may ask you to marry me."

Marge emitted a tinkling laugh. "Oh, I'm through with *that.* But now your mother . . . *There's* someone we need to work on." She winked at Iris and slipped from the room.

Iris picked up a wedge of grilled tortilla and melted cheese and contemplated the possibility of her mother getting married. She crammed the quesadilla into her mouth and licked her greasy fingers. All of a sudden it seemed as if her work clothes had turned into a hair shirt. She'd had them on since early this morning, barely giving them a second thought other than when she'd made adjustments in the ladies' room mirror. Now everything seemed to bind and grab and had to come off.

She hoisted her briefcase onto the desk and was about to go into her bedroom to change when curiosity got the best of her. She clicked open the brass clasps and took out the assortment of Pandora games Toni had given her and the manila folder of letters. She rifled through the fifty-odd pieces of paper. Some letters were from parents who blamed Pandora for the amount of time their kids wasted playing the firm's games. Most were from teacher organizations, child advocacy groups, religious groups, and others concerned about the violent and sexual content of Pandora's games. The organizations had names like Mothers Against Violence in Media, Citizens for Safe Airwaves, Christian Confederation, and Think About It.

"And I thought letter-writing was a dying art," Iris commented to herself. She shoved another quesadilla wedge into her mouth and accidentally smeared guacamole on a missive from Children in Crisis. She dabbed at it with a napkin. She kicked off her pumps, halfway unzipped her skirt, and sat in her desk chair.

Most of the letters had been written during the previous three years when the issue of excessive sex and violence in movies and television and their effects on children had come to the forefront of public concern. Many made reference to the V-chip technology that parents can use to block out television shows and suggested the implementation of a similar system in computer games.

All the letters had responses from Bridget stapled to them, expressing appreciation for the writer's comments. She described how Pandora was examining ways to label their software to warn parents of potentially objectionable materials and was testing methods of blocking access to specific content. She always thanked the sender for their interest in improving Pandora's games.

A year later, she sent follow-up letters, proudly announcing the steps Pandora had taken to address their concerns. They described how she and other software game producers had voluntarily begun to post labels on game packaging describing the quantity of violence, bad language, and explicitness of sexual content. She told how parents could now take advantage of a new feature that could block objectionable language, violence, and access to certain game levels. She explained that, as a mother herself, she shared many of their concerns and had been at the forefront of action to protect children.

Good for you, Bridget, Iris thought. Police yourself before the government does it for you. Iris knew that TV executives had been under fire for doing nothing to stem profanity, violence, and sexual references in programming and had faced the possibility of a government-imposed rating system. They had avoided this by implementing their own, industry-developed system.

Iris downed the last of the margarita and continued reading. She picked up a letter addressed to Bridget Cross, president and CEO of Pandora Corporation, typed on crisp, white bond stationery. The letterhead, in somber raised, navy blue letters, said, "The Trust Makers." The return address was in Washington, D.C. To the right of the heading was something that resembled a small red, white, and blue American flag, but with one key difference. In the flag's upper left-hand corner, where the stars should have been, was a familiar symbol in white on a blue ground: *1x1*.

Iris switched on her high-intensity desk lamp to get a closer look. It was indeed the same symbol as on Baines's lapel pin. She'd heard the name Trust Makers before but couldn't place it. She read the letter.

Dear Mrs. Cross:

It was with great interest that we reviewed your latest software game, *Slade Slayer 3-D*. While we are impressed with the complex and engrossing computer graphics and the bright spots of humor that the game most certainly provides, we feel the language, violence, and sexual content are unsuitable for children, who comprise the core of your audience.

We are aware of the game's password access feature designed to block the more objectionable content from young eyes. However, the computer-literate fourteen-year-old son of one of our members was able to bypass the password in less than fifteen minutes.

Mrs. Cross, as a mother, I'm certain you are as concerned as we are over the spread of violence, pornography, and profanity throughout all the various forms of today's media. Many studies have shown that repeated exposure to harmful images does, over time, desensitize children, rendering them more likely to imitate the behaviors they see. If the United States is to continue to prosper, we must stop the proliferation of this culture of depravity, which is leading to the systematic destruction of our children.

The ultimate solution to this problem, in our opinion, is for the producers of these objectionable and dangerous materials to cease creating them. This does not imply that we would like to close down your business, Mrs. Cross, but that we would simply like you to take a responsible approach as concerns the content of your games.

A year ago, we notified you that Pandora was placed on the Trust Makers' list of boycotted companies. Unfortunately, the boycott has apparently had no effect. We hope that this letter will be sufficient impetus for you to change Pandora's direction. The Trust Makers is a strong organization, our membership roster grows daily, and we do not intend to back down. The American way of life depends upon it. We have God on our side, Mrs. Cross.

I would be happy to discuss this with you in person. Until then, God bless you and God bless the United States of America.

Darvis Brown
Grand Eagle

"Grand Eagle?" Iris said aloud. "Are they like the Ku Klux Klan or something?"

Bridget's response, stapled to the letter, was short and to the point. It stated that she appreciated the Trust Makers' concern, but they'd have to agree to disagree on this issue.

Iris quickly thumbed the remaining letters in the folder until she found the earlier one from the Trust Makers notifying Bridget that Pandora was being boycotted. Bridget's stock response about how Pandora and other software manufacturers were working on their own blocking technology was attached.

Iris turned on her laptop, fished from her purse the business card Toni had given her, and shot her an E-mail.

"Were you aware of Bridget having any problems with an organization called the Trust Makers? Let's talk tomorrow."

Iris turned at the sound of a knock on her door.

"Dinner's ready," Marge announced, holding a fresh margarita in her hand. "And I just made up a new batch."

Iris was amazed at diminutive Marge's alcohol capacity. The one margarita Iris had downed had made her looped.

"Thought you were going to change out of your work clothes," Marge said. She draped herself against the doorframe with one toe of her high-heeled shoe pointed toward the floor, one hand raised above her head. Posing seemed to come naturally to Marge.

"I got sidetracked." Iris clicked off the desk lamp and stood. "Have you ever heard of an organization called the Trust Makers?"

"Trust Makers . . . Oh, sure. They're that men's organization. You know, trying to restore men to their proper place in the home and society. They have these meetings that fill stadiums—*60 Minutes* did an exposé."

"Oh yeah. And no women are included." Iris rubbed her index finger against her forehead. "That's right. Their spiel is that men have betrayed the role that God has entrusted them to perform in their families, their marriages, and in society in general."

"Be careful." Marge raised a warning finger. "They claim they're not antiwomen. They're *pro*-men."

"Interesting. I guess if it stops some guy from beating up his wife or being an absentee dad, it's a good thing." Iris glanced at the letter. "But it seems as if they've expanded their original mission."

Chapter 17

Kip Cross sat at a table in the family room on the ground floor of his mansion, tapping furiously on a laptop. The French doors lining the outside wall were open, and a breeze, surprisingly cool after the heat of the Santa Anas, rustled the pages of magazines that were strewn on the floor. He was barefoot, bare-chested, and wore knee-length shorts in a yellow and turquoise plaid fabric. Deep furrows lined his high forehead as he worked with total concentration.

Summer Fontaine was reclining on a lounge chair, reading the *National Enquirer.* She was completely nude even though the sun was setting and the air was becoming chilled. She looked at the sky and frowned at the few small clouds that dared to cross it. "Don't tell me it's going to rain," she said in her high, sweet voice.

She set the magazine down, slipped on high-heeled sandals that she fished from underneath the chair, and walked inside the house to where Kip was working. She began to massage his shoulders. Her huge breasts brushed against his back and caressed his neck. "How's it going, baby? You've been working really hard. It's like I hardly exist."

He continued typing. Without looking up, he said, "You shouldn't walk around like that. You know this place is being stalked by photographers. I saw a guy sitting up on the hill."

"So what? People have seen me in the nude before. After all, I posed in *Playboy* last year." She shrugged. "I still can't believe they made that tramp Playmate of the Year instead of me." She slid her arms around him and drew her long fingernails across his bare chest. "You used to like it when I walked around like this."

"Keep in mind that the police are watching me, looking for evidence that I killed my wife."

"But you didn't."

"Whether I did or didn't doesn't matter to them. They're out to get me." He sat back in the chair.

She continued massaging his neck and shoulders.

He seemed to relax under the pressure of her fingers. "Some woman called. Said you'd hired her to baby-sit for Brianna."

"I told you about that. When Brianna comes home from her grandparents, someone has to watch her."

"But you're supposed to be her nanny."

"I'm going to be busy with TV appearances over the next few weeks." Summer wrinkled her delicate forehead. "I'd hoped I'd become more to you than just the nanny." She waited for a response. Kip resumed working.

"Anyway, it'll only be for a few weeks. My schedule clears up after that. Casting directors are telling me I'm overexposed. No one tells Pamela Lee *she's* overexposed." Summer pouted.

"You're not Pamela Lee."

"I could be. All I need is a little more plastic surgery and a TV series." She grew thoughtful. "It's okay that my TV work is slacking off. I need time to work on my book."

"Book? You never told me about a book."

"I meant to. I guess I forgot."

Kip turned from the keyboard. "No way, Summer! No book!"

She stepped back from him. "Why not? I'm not going to say anything bad about you and Bridget. I love you guys."

"No book!" Kip's face grew flushed and the veins in his neck bulged. "I have to draw the line somewhere. You women. Give you an inch . . . You write a book about us and you're out."

She blinked her vacuous eyes. "I'm sorry, Kip. I didn't think you'd be mad. I'll call the publisher tomorrow and tell them I can't do it after all. No problem."

Kip gave her a piercing stare before turning back to the keyboard.

Summer resumed rubbing his shoulders. "Besides, my editor was disappointed that the DA didn't prosecute. She would have sold more books if there had been a trial."

Kip shrugged his shoulders hard, flinging her hands off, then tightly clasped his arms across his chest. "What are you doing in here, anyway? I told you not to bother me while I'm working." He smacked the heel of his hand against his forehead. "It breaks my concentration! Even when I'm sitting here, just staring, do not bother me! Got it?" He glared at the computer monitor.

Summer jammed her hands onto her hips, stood with her legs spread, and pouted. "What's with you lately? You got out of jail, you're back to work. I've stood by you. What other girl would do that? Things aren't that bad."

He looked at her incredulously. "Not that bad?" He raised his chin in the direction of the pool. "My wife was shot to death out there. I can still see her blood on the cement. My in-laws don't want to give me my daughter back. My dog is dead. Everyone is stepping on my dead wife's body to get ahead. And I can't work!" He slammed his hand against the laptop, which hit the wall with a brittle noise.

Without a word, Summer left the room.

Kip stared at the wall and leaned back in his chair, tipping it onto two legs. He folded his arms across his chest, pulled the hair of his left eyebrow between the fingers of his right hand, and rocked the chair. Abruptly, he stood. The chair tumbled to the ground. He began pacing back and forth, still stroking his eyebrow.

Shortly, Summer returned, dressed in a clingy black minidress. "Show me what you're working on, Kippy."

He looked at her as if he didn't take her seriously.

"Please," she insisted. "I want to see." She grew bored when

Kip talked about his work, but she knew getting him to talk about it was a good way to calm him down. He always tried to explain it in layman's terms for her, and she was touched that he seemed to desperately want her to appreciate the majesty of it all. Regardless, it bored her to tears.

Kip stopped pacing as he considered her request. He brightened as he went back to the desk and repositioned the laptop in front of him. As he typed, the anger seeped from him. "Okay, look. See the alien grunt?"

Summer nodded as she watched a creature with a long, spiked tail and wings leap off a building into the street. The creature's growls and snorts came through the computer speakers over the game's heavy metal sound track.

Kip rapidly pressed a key several times, and the nose of the double-barreled shotgun at the base of the screen hitched backward as the gun fired. The alien grunt screamed as pieces of his flesh flew off and blood spurted from his wounds. He collapsed in a heap on the street.

"Now watch this." Kip pressed the keys to make the screen look as if the player were bending over, closer to the creature. "We're still okay here . . . and here . . ." The gory dead alien increased in detail the closer the player got, as would occur in real life. The alien rotated on the screen, as if the player were walking around it. "This is what made *Suckers Finish Last* unique. There's not another game out there where you can move the image up and down and around as elegantly as this." Kip's voice was as fervent as one newly converted. "Instead of the image disintegrating into pixels the closer you get, the detail holds. It's because of my graphics engine. No one else's technology even comes close."

"It's amazing, Kip," Summer agreed.

"But . . ." Kip moved the screen image closer to the alien. "You get too close and . . . whoops! There it goes." The image of the alien deteriorated into colored blocks. He dejectedly leaned back into the chair. "It's still primitive."

"But you said it was the best out there."

"It is. But it's still far from top-shelf virtual reality." Kip stood and started pacing again. "I'm not making progress on taking it to the next step. It's not coming."

"It will."

"I need more processing power. I can make the images beautiful and clear and have them hold together, but I sacrifice game speed. And that's what the Slade Slayer games are about—action. The software technology exists, but the next generation of hardware is at least twelve to eighteen months away."

"What are ya waitin' for?" Slade Slayer's baritone said through the computer speakers. "Let's party!"

"You can't just use your *Suckers* work again?"

Kip shook his head with disdain. "No, no, no! The next engine has to be new, fresh. A complete revolution. A quantum leap beyond anything anyone's seen before. There's only one thing to do. I have to find a software solution that maximizes the existing hardware within its limitations."

Summer attempted to be encouraging. "That sounds like a good plan."

"In theory. But no ideas are coming."

Summer climbed onto a sofa, kicking off her sandals and tucking her feet underneath her. "Something will come. You've just started back to work."

"Maybe I've gone to the well too many times." He clenched his fists in front of him. "I'm blocked."

"It'll come, baby," Summer said soothingly. "Don't worry."

He walked onto the patio and began pacing around the pool, his arms tightly folded across his chest, his eyes on the ground. The sun was setting. The automatic timer had switched on the pool lights and the small spotlights that artfully illuminated the expensive landscaping. Summer followed him.

Kip faced her from across the pool. "It's started and I don't know how or when it's going to stop."

"What's started, Kip?"

"Cause and effect. Action and reaction."

"Are you talking about something like fate, or something? Or bad karma?" Summer frowned. "You never believed in stuff like that before, Kip. You always got mad when I tried to read you your horoscope."

"Not karma. Physics. The chain of events started the first time I cheated on my wife. Once you commit an act contrary to the laws of society, it's easy for people to think you'll do it again, or do something even worse. I did do something worse. I can trace how it unfolded all the way down the line."

Summer sat on a lounge chair and clutched her knees to her chest. "That wasn't your fault. You wouldn't have cheated on Bridget if she'd been a better wife."

"It was no fault of Bridget's. It was completely due to my own ego. I've thought a lot about this. I blame myself for Bridget's murder. I didn't do it, but I set into motion a chain of events that precipitated it. I gave an enemy the opportunity to murder Bridget and blame it on me."

"But you didn't do it, Kip. The police let you go."

"They'll be back. But it doesn't matter what the law thinks. The chain's already been put into motion. People think I murdered my wife. Do you have any idea what it's like to live with that? It screws with your head! I don't know who I am anymore. It's amazing, the things total strangers feel justified in saying to me, the way friends look at me. I've never cared what people thought of me my entire life, but this is different. Wasn't shunning a type of punishment in the Middle Ages? If a person broke a law or violated some tenet of behavior, everyone in the community would ignore the offender, taunt him, turn him into a social outcast. Eventually, he'd go nuts or kill himself or maybe end up doing exactly what he was accused of, like some self-fulfilling prophecy. It would be easier to be the person everyone expects me to be."

"C'mon, Kip. You're getting all depressed."

"It's happening. I can't even do the one thing I'm good at, developing software."

"Hire someone to do it."

"Then what do I do with my life? Administrate? Make sure the bathrooms are clean?" He stared into the pine trees on the J. Paul Getty Museum property that abutted his. "Damn! I love designing software! I'm not ready to give it up!"

He walked around the pool to where she was. "Sometimes I wonder if I'm too old for this profession. If I've lost my edge." He held his hands apart in front of him as if he were holding the fragile thing that had vanished from his life.

Summer reached to put her arms around his neck. "Kip, you're only in your thirties."

"That's old in this business. You get responsibilities, you get distracted. With each thing you move further from the edge. It's like your imagination shrinks. Then there's all this talk about taking Pandora public or selling it. Boards of directors, stockholders, people looking over my shoulder, their hands in my pockets. All I want to do is design systems the way I want to design them. I want to get back to work, bring my daughter home and write programs." His shoulders slumped. "I want things to be the way they were."

Summer pressed his head onto her shoulder. "It'll be okay, baby. I'm here for you."

They stood there for a while, with Summer swaying back and forth, rocking him and stroking his head. Finally, she held him at arm's length from her and tweaked his chin between her thumb and index fingers. "Better now?"

He nodded.

"Let's go inside. It's getting cold." She grabbed his hand and started to lead him into the house.

"I want to stay out here for a little bit. You go ahead."

He watched her leave, then continued pacing around the pool with his hands clutched behind his back. After a few minutes, he walked to the back gate and punched the alarm code into the keypad. A light changed from red to green. He opened the gate, stepped outside, and looked up and down the cement stairway. No one was around. He jogged halfway down the steps, bent double, and squeezed between the steel-tube railings, stepping into the dirt and brush.

A few yards from the steps lay an aluminum storm drain, about a foot in diameter, installed to divert rainwater from his patio to the street below. He straddled the drain, struggling to pull apart two sections that were held together by a sleeve. He pounded the sleeve with his foot, tried to pull the sections apart, then pounded some more. Finally, they separated with a metallic squeal. A rat ran out the newly opened end.

Kip kneeled on the ground and looked inside. He dug his hand in and scooped out a mulch of decaying leaves, dirt, bugs, and rat droppings. He straightened, rubbing the small of his back, mounted the stairs, and returned to the patio. Shortly, he returned, carrying a tool from his pool-equipment shed—a long, white plastic pole with a large hook attached to the end. He fed the hook into the storm drain as far as it would go and pulled out wads of leaves and dirt. After three tries, he fit the pieces of the drain back together, dragged his fingers through the loose dirt, leaves, and pine needles to hide his footprints, and returned to his patio. Once inside, he reset the alarm.

Chapter 18

Iris had worked all day on McKinney Alitzer business. Satisfied that her ducks were again in line, she punched the three-number extension for the research department into her telephone keypad. "Darcy? Iris Thorne. Did you get any information on 3-D Dimensions?"

"I just finished putting together some articles and reports for you. I'll bring them down."

"Could you see if you can find anything on an organization called the Trust Makers?"

"Trust Makers—the controversial men's group?"

"That's the one." Iris thanked her, hung up, and dialed Liz Martini's extension. Her voice mail answered. Iris glanced out her window that overlooked the suite and saw that Liz was not in her office. "You know everyone, Liz. Do you know anyone who's in the Trust Makers? How about someone named Darvis Brown? You're probably in the lunchroom. Ignore this message. I'll see you in there."

Iris carried her coffee mug into the lunchroom where Liz was talking with Kyle Tucker and Amber Ambrose.

"Three thousand buys you a pair," Liz said.

"Three thou?" Kyle said. He was carrying the folded sports section of the newspaper under his arm and a half-eaten apple in his hand. His starched, blue oxford cloth shirt was creased down the back and around the elbows, and his fair hair was slightly askew—a sign that the end of the workday was near. Iris liked this slightly rumpled look on Kyle. Of course, she thought he was cute in any way, shape, or form. And he could sell too.

"But he'll give you a discount on six or more." Liz was wearing a bright orange, dropped-waist dress in thick polyester double knit. Her sharp pelvic bones protruded against the fabric, her breast implants the only thing saving her skinny figure from being completely shapeless.

Iris thought Liz was too thin, but wouldn't say anything about it to her. She had commented on it, once upon a time, and had endured Liz's outraged objections, during which the other woman angrily slapped and grabbed at invisible flab on her behind and belly. Iris decided it was like trying to convince an alcoholic in denial that she was drinking too much.

Liz began fussing with the collar of Iris's suit jacket. "Darling, *wear* the clothes. Don't let the clothes wear you."

Iris endured Liz's attention as Liz continued talking about Lord only knew what. "So guess who the owner's the spitting image of? Brad Pitt."

"Well, then, *I'm* sold," Kyle said before he left the room.

Amber caught Iris's eye and gave her a tiny smirk, telegraphing that she thought Liz was nuts. Amber was wearing one of the conservative coatdresses she favored. This one was forest green, a color that she wore frequently and that complemented her auburn hair and green eyes. She was barely five foot three inches tall, and the coatdresses and stocky-heeled shoes she also liked added mass and height to her diminutive figure.

That was part of the power game—displacing physical space, looking like a force to be reckoned with, exuding an aura of energy, strength, and perceived danger.

Iris was lucky in that respect. She was tall and slender and conveyed high energy. She could look most people directly in the eye and down on many of them. And she was blonde and pretty and the world was kinder to pretty women. She didn't care if her looks had helped her in some small way to get ahead. She'd had darn few lucky breaks in life and it didn't bother her at all to take advantage of them. If asked about it, she'd respond, "The harder I work, the luckier I get."

Iris knew Amber's smirk was an attempt to diminish Liz. Amber was jealous of Liz and Iris's friendship and saved a unique venom for female coworkers who were more successful than her. Iris had long been familiar with this brand of cannibalism. She ignored her.

Liz addressed the issue straight on. "Amber, you're looking at me like I'm a lunatic or something."

Iris smiled to herself. Liz did not suffer fools.

"We do think you're nuts, Lizzy," Iris piped in. "But it's one of the things we love most about you."

Amber blushed and stammered, "No, I . . . I'm just confused. I don't see the profit margin."

"Amber." Liz sidled over and grabbed Amber's upper arm. Amber automatically took a step away, not enjoying this physical contact. Liz was almost certainly aware of that but continued regardless. She lowered her voice, which usually meant she was about to discuss something to do with money. Her hushed tones made one feel as if she were about to reveal insider information or international secrets that she had held on to waiting for the right person to share them with. It was a definite attention-getter.

"Listen. Ostrich ranching is the fastest-growing agribusiness in the U.S. Ninety-eight percent fat free, they take less grain and water to raise than cattle, and they taste *fab*ulous." She gave Amber a searching look as if to make sure the other woman appreciated the gravity of what she was saying. She then pulled Amber even closer.

Iris silently laughed at Amber's rising discomfort, which was apparent on her face.

"I know the right people. You can make lots of"—Liz now whispered in a reverential tone into Amber's ear—"money."

Amber managed to disengage herself from Liz's clutches and scurried from the room. "I'll give that some consideration, Liz. Love to talk to you about it at length later."

"Humph," Liz sniffed once she and Iris were alone. "No return on ostriches? I think not."

The lunchroom door opened and Louise stuck in her head. She peered at Iris and Liz over the top of her half-glasses in a manner that, in another time in Iris's life, would have sent her scurrying to hide contraband under the bed and boys in the closet.

"Sam Eastman's here," was all Louise said.

Iris rolled her eyes.

"And he's not alone," Louise added.

"Is he with a tall, dark, handsome stranger?" Liz enthusiastically asked.

Louise squinted at Liz. "How did you know?"

Liz clapped her hands. "Goody! I love it!"

"Love what?" Iris asked.

"That's what my telephone psychic from the Psychic Buddies told me just the other day. A tall, dark, handsome young man was going to become part of my work environment. This must be the day."

"Is this a positive thing, or what?" Iris asked cautiously.

Liz mysteriously slit her eyes. "She said it was complex. Then she said it would be three dollars and ninety-five cents per minute for the next five minutes and I hung up. Ozzie has a fit when I spend too much money on those telephone talk-lines."

"Let's go see what the stars have wrought." Iris followed Louise out of the lunchroom and through the sales department. She turned to Liz, who was following close behind her. "Are you going to come all the way into my office?"

Liz cocked her head at the notion that there might be someplace else she should be. "C'mon, Iris! I have to see. I'll come in to borrow something."

Iris conceded. "But just a quick look, okay?" She entered her office with her hand already outstretched. "Sam, good to see you!"

Sam Eastman rose from the couch and eagerly grasped Iris's hand with both of his. It was an unusually warm gesture for him and it immediately put Iris on guard. "Iris! How are you?"

"Just great, Sam. You remember Liz Martini."

Both Iris and Liz grew distracted when the man who had been gazing out the window turned around. He was just as Liz had predicted: tall, dark, and handsome. His features were chiseled, with a high forehead, seductively intense, deep-set, dark brown eyes, and thick hair that he wore cut short, combed forward from the crown and straight down at the sides. His only jewelry was a gold Rolex watch. His suit was understated and looked expensive, as did his shoes. His crisp, white cotton shirt outlined a V-shaped upper body. He appeared to be in his late twenties.

Sam strolled across Iris's office to greet Liz with a bounce in his step that was decidedly cocky. "Our broker to the stars. You're practically a legend in this town," he enthused as he pumped Liz's hand.

Liz tore herself away from staring at the stranger to respond to Sam. "Oww! How old that makes me feel!"

Still grinning, Sam waved at her as if she were quite the jokester. He was wearing his brown suit. He had five different suits—one for each workday. All of them were at least ten years old.

Iris grabbed a copy of *Wired* magazine from her desk, one of the many high tech publications she'd loaded up on since her increased involvement with Pandora. Also on her desk was a manila folder labeled 3-D DIMENSIONS that Darcy from research must have put there. "Liz, here's the magazine you wanted."

Liz reluctantly took it. "Thanks." She openly eyed the new man in a way that made Iris cringe but that didn't seem to bother him. He gave Liz a small, crooked smile and an appraising up-and-down look in return. He then did the same to Iris, and she blushed in spite of herself. He had the confidence of a man who was fully aware of the effect he had on women, and the effect was not lost on Iris.

There was an awkward moment when the two women, Sam, and the stranger stood looking from one to the next. The younger man appeared to be haughtily amused by it.

Since no one else seemed willing, Iris took charge of the situation. "And who have you brought with you, Sam?"

"Oh, yes!" He rubbed his hands together. "I'm pleased to introduce you to Evan Finn. Evan, this is Iris Thorne, our branch manager, and Liz Martini."

Evan firmly shook hands with Liz, then Iris, bowing slightly. "I'm very pleased to meet you, Ms. Martini. And I've heard a lot about you, Ms. Thorne." He slowly released Iris's hand, drawing his fingers across hers.

Her palm tingled. "Please call me Iris."

He cocked his head a little in her direction and lowered his eyelids as if to say, "Your wish is my command."

"And we came today to bring you some terrific news . . . in confidence." Sam glanced at Liz.

"Oh! Of course." Liz waved the magazine at Iris. "Looking forward to reading that article. Good to see you, Sam. Nice to have met you, Evan." She finally left, and Sam closed the door.

Sam again rapidly rubbed his hands together in what seemed to Iris a false gesture of excitement. "Iris, I've just hired Evan Finn as a new broker."

"Great," Iris said. "In which office?"

Sam's smile expanded. "Here. Your office."

"*My* office?"

"Yes." He nodded spastically as he continued maniacally grinning. "Congratulations."

"Why don't we all have a seat?" Iris sat in her leather chair, which stood slightly higher than the others in the room, allowing her to sit raised above everyone else.

Evan spoke. "I want to say that I'm delighted with the opportunity and so pleased to be working with you."

"Who . . . ah . . ." Iris was discombobulated by Sam's announcement. "Evan, you've worked as a broker before?"

"He has a tremendous track record," Sam interjected before Evan could speak.

Evan answered for himself. "I spent five years with Huxley Investments out of Nashville."

Iris searched to place the name.

"You probably wouldn't have heard of them." Evan casually stretched out his legs and crossed them at the ankles. "They're a small firm whose clients are a select group of high-net-worth individuals."

She nodded, not liking his response. "And before that?"

"I was at Harvard. After graduation, I bummed around Europe for a year, then went to work. Decided I wanted to move out West. Yale Huxley, the managing partner of Huxley Investments, was a casual acquaintance of Sam's." Evan nodded in

Sam's direction. "Sam interviewed me and made me an offer I couldn't refuse. Sam's had nothing but the highest praise for you. When he told me how he'd just promoted this hot new branch manager who was setting the city on fire, I knew this was the place for me."

"That's very flattering." Now Iris was certain that something was up. She plastered a complaisant smile on her face as she waited for more to be revealed. She sensed there was much more.

Sam raised his hands as if to ward off an impending blow. "Look, Iris, I should have called you, I know. But Ron Aldrich over at Pierce Fenner Smith had already made Evan an offer. I know you and he have kind of been on the outs ever since you hired Liz away from him, and he was hot to keep Evan out of your hands. Evan was just about to accept the offer so I had to act without delay and nab him while I had the chance."

"Sam offered you a good signing bonus?" Iris asked.

Evan smiled broadly. "Excellent."

Iris said, "Maybe you'd like to have a tour of the office. I'll have my assistant, Louise, show you around." She picked up the telephone receiver, punched in three buttons, then murmured almost inaudibly into it. Within seconds, Louise was rapping on the closed door. She scooped up Evan and escorted him into the suite.

Iris closed the door behind them. Sam seemed nervous but continued to act inappropriately jovial. She didn't mince words. "Sam, what's up?"

"Up?" He jumped from the chair as if the word were a command. "Nothing's up. Frankly, I'm a little surprised at your attitude, Iris. I'm only trying to help you out. Your goal is to build a champion sales force here, and Evan's the cream of the crop." He dismissively waved a hand. "I know I should have consulted you first, but there was simply no time. Besides, this is a team effort, Iris. We're all in this together. I know you like being the lone wolf, but you have to trust your fellow team members to do the right thing."

He put one hand into his pocket and gestured with the other. "I fully realize this is unusual, and I know you have the final say on hiring decisions in your office. But I remind you that recruiting always was my strength. I had a hand in hiring you, after all."

Iris set her elbows on the desk, rested her head against her clasped hands, and watched Sam without comment.

"Evan's a top-notch guy, Iris. You'll thank me for this. But if you want to think about it for a few days, you have every right to make that decision. Just be aware that he may not be available after you make up your mind."

Don't bullshit a bullshitter, Iris thought to herself. She was familiar with this sales pitch. She'd used it herself a thousand times. "How much was Evan's signing bonus?"

"Five thousand dollars."

"Five thousand? That's not an offer that can't be refused. That's a token. Heavy hitters can command signing bonuses in the high five figures."

"It wasn't just money that sold Evan, it was the opportunity to work with you. I'll admit I was out of line by not consulting you first."

To Iris, Sam's contrition seemed as thin as his worn suit pants. "I assume he took his client book with him from the other firm?"

"Absolutely. He's ready to hit the ground running."

She swiveled her desk chair and looked out the window. Dark clouds moved across the sky. Rain was predicted to arrive in the next few days. Clouds are rumored to have silver linings. She wondered if there was one here. Sam wanted Evan for some unknown reason. The LA office's success or failure directly reflected upon Sam, so presumably he wouldn't do anything that would damage his own standing in the firm. If she acquiesced, maybe it would finally defrost relations between her and her boss. It was possible that everything Sam said about Evan was true. She again swiveled her chair to face him. "Sure. Let's bring him on."

Sam seemed almost relieved. "You've made the right decision Iris. You'll see." He again rubbed his hands as if they were two twigs he was using to make a fire. "This is going to be great."

Sam retrieved Evan. Iris welcomed him aboard.

"Is tomorrow too soon to start, Evan?" Sam asked.

"Look forward to it."

Iris said, "I have very few office rules. I expect you to be here during market hours—six-thirty to one. Most of the sales staff stay much later, doing research, calling clients, but that's up to you. And I expect you to meet your quota."

"Easy enough." Evan smiled at her, and it was all Iris could do to stop herself from bashfully looking away.

"There are two empty cubicles. You can have your pick."

"I noticed an office that looked empty. I'd like to have that."

"Offices are perks given to the higher-producing brokers. If your sales production reaches that level, I'd be happy to give you an office and the title that goes with it." Iris found his request a bit cocky, but she wasn't too surprised by it. She expected salespeople to be pushy.

Sam said, "If the office is empty, Iris, I don't see why Evan couldn't have it."

Evan watched Iris with interest as he waited for her response.

She held firm. "That wouldn't be fair to the other brokers who are working hard to try and earn an office." She extended her hand to Evan before anyone could say anything else. "Congratulations."

After more pleasantries all around, Evan and Sam left. Liz almost immediately appeared in Iris's doorway. "He looks just like Tom Cruise! Who *is* our tall, dark, and handsome?"

"The newest addition to our sales team." Iris then relayed her conversation with Sam and Evan.

"Very irregular," Liz commented.

"I know." Iris raised her eyebrows. "But what's the worst that can happen? If he can't sell, I'll fire him."

Chapter 19

"Ms. Thorne?" asked the Latina maid wearing a crisp light-pink dress who answered the door. "Stay here," she harshly ordered. Iris obeyed and remained standing in the foyer while the maid walked on thick-soled shoes down the hallway and turned through a side door. Her dark braid, long enough for her to sit on, swung as she walked.

Iris casually roamed through the two-story-tall foyer of the brand-spanking-new house that had been constructed to resemble a French château. She tapped a fingernail against what appeared to be gray stone that formed an arch over a doorway. It returned a hollow sound. She did the same thing to the door, a massive block of carved wood. It was hollow as well. The whole place was as substantial as a movie set.

The huge house was located in Calabasas, a thirty-mile trek northwest on the 101 from downtown Los Angeles. Calabasas prided itself on its western heritage and had a couple of good cantinas that drew lively crowds on Saturday nights. Over the past fifteen years, LA's urban sprawl had gradually reached out here.

In addition to the Southwestern-inspired tract homes and

mission-styled strip malls endemic to LA's newer suburban neighborhoods, a curious thing had happened in Calabasas. Nouveaux millionaires fleeing LA and anything that touched it began building fairy-tale mansions in the hills. Where once there were dirt, hills, and an occasional horse, now there were dirt, mansions, an army of sports utility vehicles, and an occasional horse. The homes were mostly owned by people in the business. There were many businesses in LA, but when people referred to *the* business, they were talking about movies and TV.

The maid returned. "Come." Her command of English didn't appear to encompass the subtleties of politeness. Iris followed her down the domed hallway inlaid with faux stone and out a door at the back that led to a lush garden. A marble fountain—or what looked like marble—in the middle of the garden babbled pleasantly. Extensive sprinklers aggressively hissed water in a struggle repeated across Southern California as residents fought daily battles in the war to turn a desert into a verdant landscape.

"I'll be out on the six-o'clock." Jim Platt was pacing around the fountain as he talked into a cellular phone. He wore faded, button-front Levi's jeans, a white, knit, collared shirt with the Polo logo on the breast, and worn leather Top-Siders without socks. His hair was wavy, thick and as unruly as a young boy's. He'd just turned twenty-seven and was one of the hottest directors in town based upon an oeuvre of two stylistically unique, ultraviolent films. He glanced at Iris, frowned, and continued pacing and talking. "He's driving. You know he refuses to fly. That was before he became a star. Now he won't fly. Ciao."

He clicked off the phone, set it on a stone bench next to the fountain, and again looked at Iris as he might at a trail of ants who'd invaded his Froot Loops. She was glad she wasn't there to ask him for a job. She suspected he'd forgotten she'd called earlier about coming over.

"I'm Iris Thorne. I called—"

He stopped her with a wave of his hand. "Yeah, yeah, yeah. Look, I don't have any information." He spoke in staccato bursts. "The police have been over and over this. Alexa didn't have any enemies. You should have known that. You said you were friends with her. She hadn't been receiving threats." He raised his hands, shoulders, and eyebrows at her. "Okay?"

"What's your theory about what happened?"

"My theory about what happened," he repeated dully. "Okay," he said as if he'd decided to humor her. "After she left Bridget and Brianna, some unknown creep, some stranger danger, pulled her back into the park, smashed her head with a rock, and she fell into the ravine. The only person the police know for sure was around was this groundskeeper guy, but there's no evidence linking him—or anyone else—to the murder."

"Apparently, there wasn't a struggle. If there had been, trace evidence would have been transferred to Alexa. It's as if she was killed by someone she knew, someone she felt comfortable turning her back on."

Platt shook his fist. "If only she'd scratched him or pulled his hair or *something*. I get pissed at Alexa when I think about it. I'm like, 'Come on, Lexi! Be a wild woman. I know you can do it.' " He shoved his hands into his pockets and stared into the fountain. The bluster momentarily left and Iris sensed that Platt was deep in mourning. After a while, he said, "What she and I had, most people never touch, you know?"

Iris sat on a stone bench. "I'm very sorry."

Platt again twisted his upper lip into what appeared to be a well-practiced disdainful look. "Yeah, whatever."

Iris was surprised at how quickly his attitude had changed. She suspected the vulnerable side she'd glimpsed was kept tightly under wraps. "My understanding is that Alexa left Pandora on good terms."

"They loved her." He cocked an eyebrow. "She hated to go and they hated to lose her. She said that Kip could be a pain in the ass, but, you know, he's a genius and all that. She thought that Bridget had made him. Taken Kip's raw talent and molded it, so to speak. Alexa always liked being around brilliant people. Being challenged in that way." He shrugged self-importantly. "Anyway, the police have already milked the Kip Cross connection."

"Do you know whether Kip and Alexa had an affair?"

He looked affronted as if the mere thought were outrageous. "Of course not! She thought he was an asshole."

Iris silently reflected on the irony of his comment.

He impatiently glanced at his watch. "Look, I'm realistic about this. I think there's a good chance we'll never know what happened to Alexa. Sorry about Bridget, but—" Platt again openly looked at his watch.

"I think there's an angle the police haven't looked at."

Platt began quickly pacing back and forth, four steps in each direction. "What angle?" He rubbed his almost hairless chin.

"I believe there's a connection between your wife's murder and Bridget Cross's. I'd hoped we could sort of . . . brainstorm."

He stopped pacing. "I don't have time to *brain . . . storm.*" He sarcastically elongated the word.

"Don't you want to find out who murdered your wife?"

Platt raised one side of his upper lip. "Of course I do. What kind of man do you think I am?"

"A smart man. A man who can put together ideas and make connections that everyone else has missed." She stoked the fires of his apparently boundless ego. It might not help, but it sure wouldn't hurt. "I have a theory that Alexa's and Bridget's murders are somehow related to the businesses they're in."

Platt cocked his head at her as if he found this interesting. "How so?"

"Both Bridget and Alexa were in the business of depicting violence. Some would argue, glamorizing it."

Platt bristled. "It's a chicken-and-egg thing. The violence came first. Artists simply reflect what's going on in their world."

"And what's going on is a source of concern for a lot of people. Open any newspaper and you can read about outrage over sex and violence in movies and TV and the misogynistic and antipolice lyrics in gangsta rap records. People are upset over the availability of pornography and hate literature on the Internet, how one can meet pedophiles or find formulas to make bombs."

Platt grabbed his index finger with his other hand. "First, no one has proven that a normal kid, after seeing something of a sexual or violent nature on TV or in a movie, is then more likely to go out and imitate it. The hair-trigger whackos who are out there are probably going to do what they're going to do anyway, whether they've looked at pornography or a violent TV show first or not." He grabbed his middle finger. "Second, isn't it the parents' job to monitor what their kids are doing? Hell, now they've got the V-chip to help them. Movies have been rated for years. They've got blocking software on the Internet—Net Nanny, Cybersitter—there's a bunch of them. So what's the big deal?"

Iris eagerly nodded. "The problem is, any young hacker worth his salt can get around blocking software or password access. If a V-chip is installed on one home's TV, odds are there's another house in the neighborhood that doesn't have it. And in terms of the movie-rating system, I went into R-rated movies when I was younger than sixteen and I'm sure you did too."

"What's your point—censorship? Freedom of expression is our constitutional right, at least it was the last time I checked."

"There are people out there who don't think it's enough for the entertainment industry to monitor itself or to provide tools to block the transmission of materials they deem objectionable. To them, the mere existence of these materials indicates a level of depravity and societal decline that cannot be tolerated. Pandora's name frequently comes up in these discussions—as does yours."

Platt finally stopped pacing and sat on a stone bench facing Iris. He thoughtfully rubbed his chin. "I see where you're going, but it doesn't follow. Why Alexa and Bridget and not me and Kip, or all four of us?"

"Don't forget that Kip is convinced he was framed. If it had stuck, Pandora would have been sunk for sure. In your case, perhaps the thinking was you'd likely tone down your work after suffering the effects of violence in your own family."

"Shouldn't Alexa's and Bridget's murders have been preceded by some sort of threat?"

Iris shook her head. "Too overt. Wouldn't it be more effective to infiltrate the offending organizations and exert pressure to cease and desist from the inside? Or better yet, take them over and dismantle them?"

"Go on."

"You've had people invest in your movies."

"Of course. Even low-budget films can cost a couple of million. *Dimwit,* my first film, was made on a shoestring. I maxed out my credit cards and hit up all my friends and relatives. The second one, the one that made it big, *Retrograde in Havana,* had a handful of investors: a doctor, a couple of attorneys, some business guys from Taiwan and Hong Kong. I'd have to ask my producer about the specifics. The film I'm working on now and the one that's in development are both financed by the studio. They might have gotten outside money, I don't know. It's going to be a major motion picture." He paused, letting the words hang in the air. "We're still deciding which chick we want to play the girlfriend, but I've already got several big names attached to it."

Iris raised her eyebrows and tweaked the corners of her mouth down to indicate she was impressed. "You ever take any money from T. Duke Sawyer or an outfit called USA Assets?"

"T. Duke Sawyer . . . the name sounds familiar. I'll have to get back to you on that. He invested in Pandora?"

"Yes. And in another computer-games company, 3-D Dimensions. It was owned by a guy named Harry Hagopian—a computer programmer and game geek. He designed this game called *Fate—*"

"Sure, I've heard of it."

"—that took off like wildfire. It was an ultraviolent action game that had a major influence on Kip Cross when he designed the first Slade Slayer game. Anyway, Harry became rich. T. Duke came knocking. They had a few rounds of negotiations. My research assistant at the office contacted a programmer who worked on *Fate.* He said that Harry was basically jerking T. Duke around, that he didn't have any interest in selling the company. Lo and behold, poor Harry dies in a solo spinout one dark night on the Fifteen in the Mojave Desert just outside Baker, California."

Platt finished the story. "And the heirs sell the company to T. Duke."

"You got it."

He grinned. "Next, you're going to tell me that T. Duke made an offer on Pandora which the Crosses turned down. But anyone who knows anything about Kip Cross is aware that he would never sell. He couldn't work for anybody else."

"But he might *have* to sell, if he were defending a murder rap."

Platt looked at her with delight. "The plot thickens. Wouldn't it have been easier to just kill both Crosses?"

"Too hard to explain. It was well-known that Kip and Bridget were having problems."

"Alexa told me something about that."

Iris crossed her legs. "Disgruntled husbands kill their wives all the time, no news there. T. Duke figured it was enough to get Bridget out of the way. She was the one who built Pandora and was its guiding force. He knew without her strong hand, Kip would falter, as he has. But whoever murdered Bridget and set up Kip didn't realize that the police wouldn't press charges against him."

"The murder frame-up was imperfect."

"Apparently. They also didn't realize that Bridget wasn't leaving her sixty percent ownership of Pandora to her husband. She left it in trust to her daughter and named me the administrator of the trust."

"You?" Platt said with amusement. "Are you afraid?"

"I was born and raised in LA. I'm always afraid."

He chuckled. "What's the connection between T. Duke and the antiviolence mongers?"

"I think he's a member of the Trust Makers, but I haven't confirmed it."

Platt bobbed his head. "Heard about them. Got it."

"In any of your movies, was anyone ever bludgeoned to death with a rock, the same way that Alexa was murdered?"

"Actually, yeah. I did that in my second film. Gave me the creeps when I realized it. But I've had characters shot, beheaded, stabbed, garroted, run over by cars . . ." He searched his mind for more. "Thrown from a window." He frowned. "I haven't had anybody drowned or hanged." He scratched his chin as if making a mental note, then looked again at Iris. "In Bridget's murder, there was the slingshot, which directly tied in with Kip's work."

"And the fact that the murderer was wearing a Slade Slayer mask."

"Interesting." He again stared into the fountain. "Supposedly, now I'm going to be so horrified by the fact that my wife fell victim to the same type of violence I depict in my films that I'll turn over a new leaf and start making touchy-feely flicks starring Emma Thompson. And that investors will start tightening the purse strings to make sure it happens."

"I admit it's far-fetched."

"It's a lot simpler to accuse Kip Cross."

"That's what the police think, too."

"So, what's the problem?"

"Kip Cross didn't murder his wife."

"You're positive?"

Her faith in Kip's innocence had dimmed, but Platt didn't need to know that. After all, she was in the middle of a public relations campaign to rebuild Pandora's image. "Absolutely."

Platt raised his eyebrows with surprise.

She continued, "In Pandora's files there are letters from individuals and organizations protesting the violent and sexual content of the Slade Slayer games. Do you know whether you've received letters like that?"

"All the time. I'm always pissing somebody off." He grinned again. It pleased him to be a bad boy.

"I'm particularly interested in any letters from the Trust Makers."

"I'm going on location for three months in South Dakota, I'll have someone look through the files. The studio handles all the correspondence."

Iris fished a business card from her purse and handed it to him.

Platt slipped the card into the back pocket of his jeans.

Iris stood and draped the strap of her purse over her shoulder. "Thanks. Like I said, it's a long shot."

"If it in any way helps to find Alexa's murderer, I'm happy to do it. It's a good story, in any event." Platt started walking toward the house. Iris followed.

They went through the house to the front door. He opened it for her. "Ozzie Levinson told me his wife, Liz, works for you."

"Yes, she does. I have to thank Ozzie for arranging this meeting."

"My finances are a mess. I've got money rolling in, rolling out, who knows where it goes? Is Liz really as good as people say?"

"The best. You have my business card. Give us a call."

"I'll do that."

"Thanks for seeing me. You have a very lovely home."

He rapped his knuckles against the faux stone arch. "Fiberglass," he said proudly. "Molded in a single piece. You'd be nuts to install real stone in LA. Besides, why bother with real when fake looks as good and is more practical? It's not going to crush you in a quake."

Chapter 20

Kip Cross attracted scant attention when he parked his butter yellow Ferrari next to the curb in front of Blue's. Employees and regulars of the venerable La Cienega Boulevard hot dog stand, established in 1942 by Ben Blue, were used to seeing just about everything and everyone. Expensive automobiles were of minor interest, especially this close to Beverly Hills.

Kip walked up to the counter. Behind it were vats of boiling hot dogs, steaming sauerkraut, and a thick, lumpy, brownish red concoction swirled with grease known as Blue's chili. French fries and onion rings churned as they boiled in oil. Dozens of soft hot dog buns were piled in a steamer. Two television sets were suspended above each side of the L-shaped counter.

The women who worked the counter had a well-known and even beloved reputation for abrasiveness. Three were working today. One was a stout blonde, the other two were thin brunettes; all of them appeared to be in their twenties, and they were all chewing gum. They wore blue, button-front dresses that were amply splattered with grease and little folded hats attached to their pinned-up hair. One of them nudged her partner in the ribs as Kip approached.

A man standing at the counter shoving a chili dog into his mouth initially ignored Kip until he noticed Kip's flip-flops. He then took a step away as if by reflex.

"One chili kraut dog with cheese and extra onions, onion rings, and a large Coke," Kip said to the big blonde.

She didn't move to fill his order and gave him a long up-and-down look as she snapped her gum. The other two women looked apprehensively from the blonde to Kip and back.

"Something wrong?" Kip asked.

"Onion rings!" the woman shouted over her shoulder. She grabbed a bun, piled the ingredients Kip requested into it, wrapped it in a piece of wax paper, and shoved it toward him across the counter. It would have slipped off the other side if Kip hadn't caught it.

One of the brunettes carelessly plopped a greasy wax paper sack of onion rings next to the dog, spilling several rings onto the dirty counter. The third set the Coke down.

Kip angrily eyed them.

They returned his stare, snapping their gum and ignoring the other customers who had queued up behind him.

He was about to comment on their rudeness, but he didn't want to draw attention to himself. He calmed himself by recalling other visits to Blue's before Bridget's murder when the help was surly. They'd treated him this way millions of times before. Their attitude today had nothing to do with their thinking he was a murderer, he reassured himself. He was overreacting.

Out of the corner of his eye, Kip spotted people waiting behind him, talking quietly among themselves. He couldn't hear what they were saying, but he heard them murmuring. What else could they be talking about except him? What else could be keeping them so entertained? He quickly spun around. He'd confront them. If they had anything to say, they could say it right to his face. A woman who had been discussing menu selections with her husband jumped back, startled, when Kip abruptly turned. Two guys didn't pay any attention to Kip and continued pointing at the menu and talking. A man directly behind Kip gave him a fatigued look and hitched his head in the direction of the counter, indicating Kip had business there.

"What?" Kip said, returning his attention to the big blonde.

"Four eighty-nine!" she said, scowling. "You deaf or something?"

"Oh." He retrieved his nylon wallet from the back pocket of his worn Levi's jeans, pulled open the Velcro-lined flap, and handed the woman some bills. He gathered his food and walked with it to the picnic tables and benches gathered beneath an aluminum awning at the side and rear of the establishment.

"Wife-killer."

Kip twisted his neck and glared at the blonde. "What did you say?"

"Your change!" she shouted.

"Keep it."

"Big spender."

There were no empty tables. He headed toward a spot at the end of a table where two men were already sitting, dumped his food on top, and slid onto the bench. He saw the two men looking at him and stared back until they looked away. He unwrapped his chili kraut dog and took a big bite. A glop of chili dripped from his mouth onto the table. The two men began gathering their remaining food. Kip figured they were finished but saw them move to another table a few feet away. One of the men said something to the others sitting there. Slowly, everyone turned to peer at him like one might stare with curiosity and horror at a traffic accident.

Kip knew he was not imagining this. "I didn't do it," he tried to explain. "I loved my wife."

They seemed stunned that he had spoken to them. No one responded. They began whispering among themselves. People at other tables were now shooting glances at Kip.

Kip resolutely ate his food, mopping up every last glob of chili and sauerkraut with his onion rings. When he had finished, he gathered the soiled wax paper, napkins, and empty drink container, dropped them into a garbage bin, and slowly walked out. He passed a man on the sidewalk who was admiring his Ferrari.

"Nice steel," the man commented.

"Thanks." Kip smiled, grateful for the small kindness.

The man went on, "It's true what they say about the golden rule. He who has the gold makes the rules."

Kip climbed into the Ferrari. The top was down and he turned and squinted at the man to indicate he didn't get his point.

"Rich man's justice."

Kip cranked the Ferrari's engine and burned rubber as he tore from the curb.

Kip pulled, then banged, on Pandora's thick glass door. "Why is this freaking door locked?" he yelled. He answered his own question. "Because of the people who want to see me dead." He sighed and fumbled in his pants pocket for his keys, then jumped when startled by someone who approached him from behind. "What do you want?"

The man looked to be in his early twenties. He was tall and lanky. His limbs dangled loosely from his joint sockets. His straight, dark brown hair reached the middle of his back. The sun had bleached the top layer a reddish hue. His skin was a warm, dark color, deeply tanned on top of already dark skin. His eyes were slightly almond-shaped and small for his face. His nose was squat, his face long, his forehead prominent, and his jaw square. "It's really you, man!" He shook his head as if to dislodge something. "It's the Kipmeister!"

"Who the hell are you?"

The young man wore a tie-dyed T-shirt, printed with an image of the Grateful Dead's top-hatted skeleton holding a long-stemmed rose, over baggy, rumpled black cotton twill shorts. On his feet were huge white basketball sneakers and ankle-high white socks. Between the tops of his socks and the hem of his pants his brown legs, covered with coarse black hair, were visible. One strap of a blue nylon backpack was slung over his shoulder. "Banzai."

"Bonsai? Like the miniature tree?"

"No! Banzai, like the war cry—*banzai!*" He menacingly raised his fist.

"Are you here to harass me or something?"

"Harass you? I'm a mega-fan. You're a god, man. You're my hero."

"I am?" Kip brightened.

"You're the Kipmeister!" He playfully punched Kip in the arm.

Kip looked the kid over and decided he probably was just a game geek and not an assassin. "Hey, I'm sorry, man. It's just that people are looking at me like I have blood on my hands or something."

Banzai swatted at his hair. "I can't believe I'm here. This is so hot. I sent you E-mail, man, when you were in jail. Did you get it?"

Kip smiled tentatively. "Ah, yeah." He started to unlock the door. "You want to come inside?"

"That would be *sooo* great, man! I would love it!"

"You have a last name?"

"Jefferson."

"Banzai Jefferson. Sounds like a character in one of my games." Kip pulled open the door.

"Yeah, I know. My mom's Japanese-American and she's into the culture thing. She thought Banzai was a powerful name. My dad's African-American. People are always looking at me and going, 'What *are* you, anyway?' I say I'm the multicultural man. I'm the future." He laughed and followed Kip into the hangar, slowly walking across the floor as if he were in a daze. "Dude, this place is greater even than on TV. It's . . . majestic." He shook his head with his mouth gaping as if speech eluded him.

Kip surveyed his empire and nodded. "I like it."

Banzai pointed at Kip, his mouth still gaping. "I want to work for you, man. I want to soak in your brilliance."

"Do you do any coding?"

"Yeah." Banzai blinked at him as if the answer were obvious. "Heck, yeah."

Kip nodded. "Come up."

They walked across the floor and up the wooden stairs to the catwalk. On the catwalk traversing the loft on the opposite side of the hangar, Banzai spotted Today going into his office carrying a styrofoam container of one of his many daily cups of coffee. "Today Rhea!" he shouted. "You the man!"

Today squinted across the hangar, then ducked into his office and returned with a megaphone. "Do I know you?"

"He's a fan," Kip shouted. "I'm showing him around."

"Name's Banzai!"

"Banzai?" Today repeated. "Look, Kip, when are we going to meet on the new game?"

"I'm working on the engine now."

Today's amplified voice carried throughout the hangar. "Why don't you show me what you have? I can at least start sketching out some ideas."

"Give me a few days, man. I've got a lot of things on my mind."

Today didn't respond but went into his office, closing the door behind him.

Kip scowled across the expanse at the closed door.

"All this genius." Banzai wove his head as he surveyed the hangar. "It's good. It's all good."

"This is my office."

On one side of the large room were four long tables lined end to end, cluttered with computer equipment. The wood-plank floor under the tables was covered with thick plastic on top of which were two rolling chairs. Two more chairs were in the middle of the room, apparently resting where they had rolled after having been shoved. A wood desk, piled high with books, magazines, and a single framed photograph of Bridget and Brianna occupied the opposite side of the room. Along that wall a string of large white boards was hung. Many of the boards bore scribblings in different colors of dry-erase ink.

Kip nervously stepped toward the door when he saw that Banzai had slipped his backpack off his shoulder and was digging inside it.

Banzai pulled out his hand, holding a large stack of diskettes bound with rubber bands. He was beaming, his broad smile white against his dark skin as he clutched the diskettes between both hands. "It's a game, man." He humbly held the diskettes toward Kip.

Kip, feeling foolish at his thought that the kid might be pulling a gun on him, took the diskettes. "What do you call it?"

Banzai took two steps back as if preparing to make a jump. "*Accelerator.*"

Kip looked at the diskettes.

"I know the name's hokey, but—"

"No, not at all. I think it's good. Let's see it."

Banzai exhaled fiercely, moaning slightly as he did so, as if he was in ecstasy. "I've been living for this moment. The Slade Slayer games were my inspiration. You broke so many barriers. You took computer gaming into the next dimension. *Suckers Finish Last* is just . . ." He exhaled hard again.

Kip pulled off the rubber bands and sorted through the innocuous black diskettes. They made a slight clicking noise in his palm. Each had a handwritten adhesive label numbering it. "Let's see what you've got." He walked to one of the long tables and pressed the switch on top of a power strip, turning on a computer. He rolled a chair over and indicated that Banzai should do the same.

Kip put the first diskette into the drive. "Install?"

"Yeah."

Kip loaded all the diskettes.

"To run it, enter A, C, C, E, L," Banzai said. "I haven't added sound yet." His knobby knees protruded from underneath his long shorts.

Kip typed in the command. Shortly, an image came on the screen of the steering wheel and front end of a long, shiny black car, presented from the point of view of the driver. A country road meandered in front of the car. "Arrow keys, control, space bar, the usual?"

Banzai's eyes were riveted on the screen. "Yeah."

Kip pressed the arrow keys to maneuver the car down the road, avoiding obstacles, killing enemies, going through dark tunnels and mazes. He didn't say anything. The work was competent, even clever at points, but it wasn't extraordinary. The influence of the Slade Slayer games was obvious.

Banzai divined his thoughts. "It starts a little slow." He jerked along with the screen image and anxiously shot glances at Kip as he impassively worked the keyboard.

On the screen, a group of men clad in green Army fatigues leapt from behind a clump of trees and started shooting at the car.

Banzai was on the edge of his seat. "Get 'em!"

Kip was late firing his weapon and didn't seem to care.

The car, its tires shot out, flipped end over end and sailed off the side of a cliff, expelling the driver. The image turned topsy-turvy as the driver fell, legs and hands spinning, his body occasionally colliding into the cliff. The driver's hands clutched passing shrubs, pulling them free. The image did not disintegrate as the point of view neared the cliff or as the scene spun wildly. Everything held. Kip was getting motion sick. It was wonderful.

Banzai detected Kip's heightened interest and grinned. "I worked forever on that algorithm."

Kip shook his head to try to clear the vertigo, then watched as far beneath the driver, the car hit the ground and exploded into leaping flames. The driver headed right into the flames and wreckage. He pressed the arrow keys to no avail. As the flames touched the driver, his flesh began to burn and melt. The image froze.

Kip sat staring at the screen, his hands on the keyboard.

"That's the end of that segment," Banzai said. "There's a parachute and oxygen shield on the road that you can pick up. Can I?"

Kip moved the chair out of the way and turned the keyboard over to Banzai, who demonstrated the game's finer features, as proud as a new father showing off baby pictures. "If you activate the oxygen shield you can survive the fire, see?" He looked at Kip for approval.

Kip silently watched, his crossed arms over his chest, rocking slightly back and forth as he stroked his eyebrow. He commented circumspectly, "It's not bad. You've got some good ideas."

"Really? You think so?" Banzai nervously looped a lock of his long hair behind his ear. "A friend of mine helped with the graphics, but the coding is basically mine. Let me show you the side road. Took me forever."

"It's got possibilities. Like you said, it's kind of rough." Kip continued to slowly rock back and forth. "The sequence when the car was going down the cliff, how did you do that?"

Banzai opened his tiny eyes wide. "You want to see the source code?"

Kip stopped rocking. "You have it with you?"

"Yeah, man!" Banzai dug inside his backpack and pulled out several bundles of rubber-banded diskettes. "I carry it around with me. I don't want my roommates getting any ideas about ripping me off. Especially my algorithm for the cliff dive. That's my signature piece. But I'll show it to you, man. I'd be honored to show it to you." He breathlessly exited the game and started copying up the diskettes.

"How old are you?"

"Twenty-one."

"You go to school?"

"I kind of took a leave of absence. That's what I told my parents, anyway. I really sort of dropped out. I need the space to do my own stuff. I told my parents I'm going back." He shrugged as if it wasn't likely. "Hey, Jobs and Gates dropped out of college." He smiled broadly at Kip. "And so did you."

Lines of code filled the screen, spinning past in a blur as Banzai scrolled through them. Reaching the section he wanted to show Kip, he began clicking through it line by line, describing how he'd designed the sequence of the car and driver crashing and burning.

Kip intently studied the screen, periodically frowning, raising his eyebrows, and nodding. One section he found particularly interesting. He scooted closer.

Banzai babbled on, "This is so great. I'm so honored that you'd even look at my work. So, you think I could come work here?"

Kip held up his hand, indicating he wanted silence, and continued studying the screen.

Banzai didn't get the message. "So, man, you think, like, I could work for you?"

Kip still studied the screen.

"I could start out testing software or something. I don't expect to start at the top. Dude, what do you think?"

Kip leaned back from the screen and looked at Banzai as if he'd forgotten he was there. "Oh, yeah. Uh, let me . . . let me think about it, okay?" He deleted the files from his hard disk, gathered Banzai's diskettes, and handed them to him.

"You don't have to delete it, man. Show it to Today Rhea or something. It's sort of like my résumé."

"I don't want it hanging around."

"You're so right, man. Like my old man says, it's a dog-eat-dog world."

"It sure as hell is."

Banzai tightly clutched the diskettes. "So, Kip, what do you say?" He paused, then went on, "About a job?"

"I'll call you, okay?" Kip stood.

"Great. I am *so* stoked." Banzai stood and awkwardly held out his palm. "Even if nothing comes of this, you've totally made my day."

Kip shook his hand. "I'll show you out."

Banzai put up both hands. "No, man. I can find my way. I don't want to bother you anymore. I've taken enough of your time." He put the diskettes into his backpack and slipped one of the straps over his shoulder. At the door to Kip's office, he jutted one thumb into the air. "Keep the faith, man. We're behind you."

Kip smiled. "Thanks."

Banzai left the office, giving Kip another thumbs-up through the window before walking out of view. The tall kid was wearing sneakers, but his footsteps were still loud on the wood catwalk.

Before Banzai's footsteps had faded, Kip had started coding.

Chapter 21

"The G-string goes *over* the garter belt."

"Over?"

"Think about it."

Iris did. "Okay."

"Get it?"

"I got it."

Liz picked up a bottle of low-cal salad dressing and pulsed the pump top, spraying it on her salad. "What else did he send you from Victoria's Secret?" She stabbed her fork into a clear plastic clamshell container, then shoveled a mountain of greens into her mouth.

"All sorts of things. The box was crammed full of wonderful lacy nothings."

"He's courting you, lady." Liz gazed dreamily out the window. "How romantic."

Iris's container of salad was on her desk. She drank a swig of diet peach Snapple from the bottle. "Definitely."

Liz picked a radish from her salad and gingerly bit it in half, retracting her lips to avoid smudging her lipstick. "This market! Down again—eighty points." She crunched the remaining radish half and shook her head with dismay. "I'm fighting clients all day long, advising them not to sell at the same time I'm grabbing as much McDonald's, GM, and IBM as I can get."

"Doesn't bode well for my IPO." Iris swirled a carrot stick through the gooey dressing that had coagulated at the bottom of the container.

"What's up with that, anyway?"

"I'm having a cocktail party for some venture capital groups tonight at the Edward Club." Iris peered out the door into the suite. "Garland used his membership to arrange for the room. I need to get funds into Pandora and fast. It's hemorrhaging money."

"What's the party for? A sniff test?"

Iris nodded. "But three of the VC firms I invited canceled, giving flimsy excuses."

Liz craned her neck, trying to see what Iris was looking at. Evan Finn was hanging his suit jacket in his cubicle.

"Top Gun is back from lunch," Iris said, returning her attention to her salad. "His two-hour lunch."

Liz shook her head. "That man is constantly and flagrantly violating your rule about being in the office during market hours." She bit into a celery stick. "Pretty cocky for a guy that's only been on the job three days."

"And he always puts on his jacket before he leaves. What's that about? Tells me he's not just going to the rest room."

"He is a smoker," Liz commented. "He carries a pack of cigarettes in his shirt pocket, and I've seen him with a very nice Dunhill lighter. Think he has a drug problem?"

"He doesn't look or act like it, but I've been fooled before. Something about this stinks." Iris attacked the dressing at the bottom of her salad with a sesame seed breadstick. "I mean, Sam Eastman doing anything to help me? What was I thinking?"

"Sam boxed you into a corner. Besides, you said that Louise verified everything in Evan's résumé. The man is P-oh-P."

"Perfect on paper. Garland says he casually knows Yale Huxley, the managing partner of Huxley Investments where Evan worked for the past five years. He's going to call Huxley and see if he can get any off-the-record skinny on Evan. Louise did find something odd with Evan's degree. He graduated from Harvard six years ago, summa cum laude, but the alumni office's records show that he passed away last year."

"Hmmm. What about his licenses?"

"His series seven checked out, but I've heard of brokers who pay people to take the test for them."

"He definitely has money. I know an expensive suit when I see one." Liz closed the clamshell lid on her empty salad container and threw it in the trash. "And he drives a brand-new Range Rover."

"How do you know that?"

"I happened to get out of the elevator on the same parking level as he did and made an excuse to follow him."

"I know the building he lives in—a tony condominium tower on Wilshire in West LA. I once had a client who lived there. Definitely high rent." Iris downed the last of the Snapple and threw the garbage from her lunch into the trash on top of Liz's.

Liz pulled a small mirrored case from her jacket pocket and repaired her lipstick. "Has he made any sales?"

Iris retrieved a tube of lipstick from her desk and smoothed on color between sentences. "Nothing to write home about. He's on the phone a lot, but he's not setting the place on fire. Certainly not earning enough to support his lifestyle. He was supposed to have brought a full client book with him."

Liz peered into the tiny mirror on her lipstick case and shoved her thick, dark curls with her hand. "What kind of signing bonus did he get, if I can ask?"

"Five thousand dollars."

Liz frowned as if she hadn't heard correctly. "That's *nothing.* An average bonus is twenty grand."

"It's not a sum that will throw up flags anywhere. Evan talked as if Sam had given him the moon." Iris crossed her legs, dug one heel of her pump into the carpet, and swiveled her chair back and forth. "Sam said Ron Aldrich at Pierce Fenner Smith made Evan an offer. I wish I could find out if that were true."

"I'll have lunch with Ron and do some detective work," Liz offered. "He's still hoping there's a chance I'll come back to work for him, so he's been very nice to me."

"Ron Aldrich and Sam Eastman are as thick as thieves. It's

not a stretch to think that Ron would back up Sam's story, whether it was true or not." Iris's chair squealed as she turned it.

"What does Garland think about Sam hiring Evan almost without your approval?"

"He says he's never seen anything like it. There's another thing that's odd. Sam's made himself scarce since Evan was hired. Usually, I can hardly turn around without stepping on the guy. It's almost like he's trying to disassociate himself from me."

Louise poked her head through Iris's doorway. "Excuse me for interrupting, but Redwood Equities canceled for your cocktail party tonight."

"Not another one!" Iris said with dismay. "Venture capitalists should be flocking to invest in Pandora. Kip Cross's a free man and back to work, and I'm seeing favorable PR about Pandora everywhere, thanks to the public relations firm I hired. It's all good! So what's spooking the investors?"

She answered her own question. "T. Duke couldn't have *that* much influence. We're talking venture capitalists. We're talking money and the potential to *make* money."

"T. Duke casts a long shadow," Liz said.

Iris became glum. "Venture capitalists not wanting to have anything to do with Pandora. Threatening letters from semi-secret organizations. A corporate raider who's determined to acquire a small computer-games company. Mysterious brokers showing up at my office. What's next?"

"Don't let your mind go off the deep end, Iris. Sam probably hired Evan for the exact reasons he said. Evan Finn is no monster. He's very handsome, polished, and charming."

"That he is. That and what else?"

At three, Iris left the office to check on preparations for her cocktail party. Just as she pushed open the suite's glass doors, she spotted Evan getting into the elevator.

"Hold the elevator, please!" she shouted as she quickly walked toward it. He either ignored her or didn't hear her because she had to thrust her hand between the closing doors. They again flew open.

"Hi, Evan," she said pleasantly, despite the fact he hadn't held the door for her.

He smiled with his lips closed and slightly tilted his head in her direction in the obsequious gesture he'd used the day they'd met.

She touched the heat sensitive button for the lobby and noticed that the one for the ninth floor was illuminated. She searched her mind, trying to remember the offices that were located on the ninth floor. She recalled there were a couple of attorneys and a dentist. Maybe he had an appointment to take care of some personal business.

When the elevator doors opened on the ninth floor, Evan moved his feet as if he were going to exit, then hesitated.

"Isn't this your floor?"

"Oh, right." His surprise seemed feigned.

"See you tomorrow."

He got out. "See you."

The doors closed and the elevator descended. On impulse, Iris madly began patting the heat-sensitive buttons. The elevator finally stopped on the seventh floor. She got out, walked to the stairwell at the end of the corridor, and climbed back up to the ninth floor. On the landing, she carefully turned the doorknob, pulled the door open, and looked out. There was no sign of Evan.

She stealthily entered the corridor, walked toward the elevators, and peeked around the corner. Still no sign of him. Feeling foolish, she was about to press the elevator call button when she heard his voice.

She tiptoed over to the opposite corner of the elevator housing, flattened herself against the wall, and sneaked a quick glance down the corridor. There was Evan, speaking into his cellular telephone.

"Zentron is a great stock and it's a good buy right now," he was confidently saying. "I've put a lot of my clients into it. Any stock is going to be riskier than a treasury bill or a money market account. You have to evaluate your aversion to risk."

It was a standard sales pitch. She knew the stock he was recommending and considered it a good pick. So why was he doing a deal in the ninth-floor hallway?

"You've made the right decision," Evan said. "Make out a check for ten thousand dollars to Canterbury Investments. No, not to McKinney Alitzer. This is my private investment company. I charge lower fees than the big firms. I can certainly set you up with an account at McKinney if you want, but you'll pay higher fees and the service won't be any different. Yes, that's right—Canterbury Investments. I'll talk to you soon. Good—"

Iris sprinted past the elevators, down the corridor, threw open the stairwell doors, and didn't stop running until she reached the lobby.

Chapter 22

Brianna Cross sat at a table next to the pool at the Cross mansion, not far from where her mother had died, singing to herself as she drew with crayons on a pad of paper. She was dressed in a fuzzy pink pullover sweater and blue jeans decorated with colorful appliqués of flowers and butterflies. Her long, dark hair was pulled away from her face and tied with a big pink bow.

"Are you cold, Brianna?" Summer Fontaine asked.

The little girl, engrossed in her work, didn't respond.

Summer was stretched out on a lounge chair, wearing jeans and a pullover identical to Brianna's. She looked up at the dark clouds that were moving across the sky. "I think it's going to rain. I hate when it's not sunny. It gives me the blues," she pouted. She looked at Brianna. "You want to come inside and see what's on TV?"

"No," Brianna flatly responded.

"Are you glad to be home?"

"Yes."

"Did you have fun at your grandma and grandpa's?"

"Yes."

"Do you love me?"

Brianna paused in her work, delicately sorted through the crayons strewn across the table, selected a new color, and continued drawing.

"Brianna!" Summer stood and glared at the child. Summer's full lips were painted in two shades of pink—dark rose around the rim filled in with frosted pearl. "Don't you love me?"

The girl hunkered down closer to her drawing and ignored Summer.

Outraged, Summer thrust her hands on her hips and looked through the French doors into the family room where Kip Cross was intently working. Summer stomped to the house, pulled open a door, rattling the glass panes, stepped inside, and roughly pulled it closed behind her.

Kip had stopped typing and was sitting facing the laptop computer with his hands clasped in his lap, his upper body slightly rocking back and forth. The monitor's screen saver clicked on and colorful tropical fish began swimming across the screen.

Summer watched his back, her hands still on her hips, and angrily tapped her tanned foot. She was wearing hot-pink strappy sandals. Her toenails sported pink polish. A thin gold ring circled her second toe.

Kip continued rocking, not seeming to see the tropical fish that swam across his field of vision. He spoke without turning his head. "Do not bother me. I am working."

"Working? You're staring!"

He pounded his forehead with his index finger. "I'm thinking! I know it's a difficult concept for you, but give it a try."

"Bastard!" She walked up the three steps that led from the family room to the arched corridor, the soles of her stiff sandals loud on the tile floor.

Still not looking at her, Kip said, "And I don't like you tarting up my daughter like that."

Summer spun around, causing her long blonde hair to fly over her shoulder. "Tarted up? We're wearing matching outfits. It's cute."

"Summer, you put makeup on her yesterday. She's not your toy, she's not your daughter."

Summer's fair complexion grew blotchy and her eyes filled

with tears. "I don't know what I am around here anymore. All you do is work. Brianna acts like she doesn't love me anymore. She's hardly said two words to me since the Tylers brought her home yesterday."

"You're the nanny, Summer. Your job is to take care of Brianna, not the other way around."

"Is that so? She's not the only thing I take care of around here. I took care of a little something last night, didn't I?"

Kip shot a glance out the French doors at his daughter. She was still engrossed in drawing.

Summer cried, "It's like you're mad at me lately. What did I do?"

"To begin with, you took down all the pictures of Bridget in the house."

"I didn't think it was healthy for Brianna."

"You don't want her to remember what her mother looked like?"

"All right. I'll put them back."

"Did you tell that publisher that you're not writing that book?"

"Ye-es."

Kip didn't respond and continued looking straight ahead.

"I just thought it was a good way to make some money. I know things are tight right now."

"Don't be so concerned about my finances, okay?"

"I'm trying to do the right thing, Kip." Tears spilled from Summer's eyes. "I thought things would be different between us."

"Brianna and I need a little time to adjust. Is that too much to ask?"

Summer wiped her face with the back of her hand. "You want me to live here like your girlfriend and not date anyone else, but then you tell me, 'All you are is the nanny.' What am I supposed to do? I have feelings too, you know."

Kip rubbed his face with his hands. He stood and started walking across the room.

She thought he was approaching her. She pranced down the steps but stopped, dejected, when he headed for the French doors. "I'm going to fix my face," she said hopefully.

He ignored her and went outside.

Brianna had got up from the patio table and was walking along the edge of the pool, looking at the sky. Kip swooped her up in his arms and twirled around with her. She giggled as she looked at the spinning clouds. He nuzzled her neck and squeezed her tightly.

"I missed you," he murmured.

"Hold me up higher, Daddy." She grunted and stretched her small arms toward the sky.

Kip obliged. "Why do you want to be so high?"

"I want to touch Mommy in heaven." She arched her back and grasped at the air. "That's where Grandma says she is. She's there, isn't she, Daddy?"

Kip looked up at the densely clouded, gray sky. He didn't believe in God or heaven or hell. But he looked at his daughter, happy with the thought that her mother was everywhere and always with her, and he didn't want to rob her of that small sense of security. "Yes, sweetheart. She's there."

The phone rang.

"Summer!" Kip called. "Answer the phone!"

"It's still ringing, Daddy."

Kip set his daughter down and ran to grab the portable phone from the small table next to the lounge chair.

"Hello?"

There was no answer, but the caller didn't hang up.

"Hello?" Kip said more loudly.

Summer stood on the threshold of one of the French doors.

Kip angrily clicked the phone off and looked at her.

"Probably some crank," she said, shrugging.

"It's the third time today and I had the number changed two days ago."

"I already know it by heart," Brianna said from the patio table where she was again drawing.

"Already?" Kip smiled at his daughter. "You're a smart girl, Brianna."

"It's not hard to find out an unlisted phone number," Summer said.

"I haven't heard you get any crank calls," Kip said to her. "Why is that?"

"I don't know." Summer had taken off the pink sweater that

matched Brianna's and now wore a white, long-sleeved top of stretch velour.

"Maybe it's because your boyfriend hangs up when I answer."

Summer dramatically frowned. "Boyfriend?"

Kip laughed. "No wonder you can't get any acting work if that's the best you can do." His smile turned sour. "Liar."

"I'm not lying."

He walked toward her, his body stiff and his arms tight by his sides. "Whatever you do, don't make the mistake of playing me for a fool."

She protectively crossed her arms over her chest as he approached. "I'm telling you the truth, Kip."

He stopped a few inches from her face and angled toward her, his posture still rigid. His face was now bright red. "Don't lie to me!"

She flinched as he raised his hand above her head, still clutching her shoulders with her crisscrossed hands. "Kip—don't!"

He picked a leaf from her hair and looked at her with amusement. "What? Did you think I was going to hit you or something?"

She rubbed her arms and bleated, "No."

"You're afraid of me." He seemed to consider the notion.

"Don't be silly, Kip." She took a step away from him.

"You are. You're afraid of me."

"I'm done!" Brianna shouted as she waved the sheet of paper.

Grateful for the excuse to flee Kip, Summer walked to Brianna and took the drawing from her. She gasped. Kip quickly grabbed it from Summer's hands.

Brianna explained her work. "That's Mommy and that's Slade Slayer. He hurt Mommy."

Kip studied the five-year-old's rendering of her mother wearing a bathing suit, lying on the ground in a pool of blood. Standing above her was a person dressed in black holding a crude gun drawn with silver crayon. The figure had short, yellow hair and a white gash to portray Slade Slayer's snarl.

"My God." Summer pressed her fingertips against her mouth.

"That's Stetson." Brianna pointed at a grayish black blob streaked with red next to a large aqua square—the swimming pool. "I don't think I did him too good."

Kip seemed mesmerized as he studied the drawing.

"Brianna, did you draw pictures like that at your grandma's house?" Summer asked.

She nodded.

Kip tore the thick paper in half.

Summer and Brianna both looked at him, stunned.

He tore it again and again into smaller and smaller pieces.

"Daddy!" Brianna protested. "My picture!"

"Kip!" Summer exclaimed. "Let her draw! It's healthy. She has all that stuff bottled up."

Brianna's mouth opened wide and her face grew red. At first, no sound came out. Then she emitted a long wail and the tears began to flow.

Kip angrily crammed the pieces of paper into his jeans pockets. "I don't see how that could possibly be healthy."

Brianna continued to wail.

"You're as bad as my in-laws," Kip said. "All your psychobabble. I'm not having it. I know what's best for my daughter." He reached for Brianna, but she ran from him and into Summer's arms.

Kip stormed into the house.

Summer stroked the sobbing girl's hair. "It's okay, baby. It's okay."

Chapter 23

"What are you doing to me, T. Duke?"

"Why, Iris, I can't fathom what in the world you mean."

"Most of the venture capitalists I invited to my meet and greet canceled. The ones who didn't treated me like I had an infectious disease." Iris smiled at Louise, who'd brought her a fresh and unsolicited mug of coffee. "When I issued the invitations, they were very enthusiastic. What changed?" She sipped the steaming black coffee.

"If you called for my opinion, I have one. Of course" —he chuckled—"I usually do. Two words: Kip Cross. When you set up the meeting, he was in jail. Now he's out. The VCs don't want to make a murderer who's escaped justice rich."

"Maybe that's part of the reason, but some of these guys would sell their mother's liver to the highest bidder."

"Let's consider another angle. Assume no one believes Kip Cross is a murderer. Was he at your meeting?"

"No."

"Was I?"

"No."

"How about Today or Mick or Toni?"

Iris became defensive. "I know it's important to impress VCs with the cohesiveness and shared vision among a start-up's management, but this was just a preliminary sniff test."

"Iris, I don't need to tell you that these are busy people. You know you have to put on your best dog and pony show because you may not get another chance. I propose that you didn't include the other Pandora principals because you didn't want to reveal the divisiveness that exists within the ranks."

Iris glared at her coffee. He was right and she hated him. "But that shouldn't have anything to do with the VCs' faith in the future of Pandora."

T. Duke scolded, "Iris, Iris, Iris."

She silently stewed.

"I've been around the venture capital world a long time. Let me give you a tip. *Everything* counts."

She was out of her league and she knew it. The sad thing was, she could learn a lot sitting at T. Duke's knee, if she didn't hate him so much. She stood, began pacing behind her desk, and came clean. "You're right, T. Duke. I tried to pull a fast one on the VCs, but I think the real reason they chilled on Pandora has little to do with the firm's potential."

"Oh no?"

"*You* kept them away."

"Go on. I'm dying to hear what you've come up with now."

"You don't want Pandora to get outside money. You want Pandora for yourself and everyone knows it. I don't know if you threatened the VCs—"

He gleefully laughed.

"—or they simply don't want to get on your bad side." She lunged for the phone, which she'd almost pulled off the desk while she was pacing.

T. Duke continued laughing. "Iris, you tickle me."

As he laughed, Iris blushed. She was grateful he couldn't see her.

"Lord, if I only had that kind of influence. I wouldn't have been indicted, that's for darn sure. There's one thing and one thing only that motivates investors, whether it's grandma trying to secure her golden years or a venture capitalist trying to turn arbitrage profits. Money. There's nothing that's going to stand in an investor's way if he smells money. And you know this, Iris, probably better than I do. Detach your emotions and look at the situation coolly. There are no dark motivations behind my involvement with Pandora. I'm about as simple a guy as you'll find. I'm in this to make money. Frankly, Iris, the more Pandora flounders, the less it's going to be worth. I know you want to do right by that little girl. Take a tip and accept my offer of five dollars a share. Tell you what, I'll go to five-fifteen, for the sake of the child."

"Things aren't as black-and-white as you pretend, T. Duke."

"Help me understand these complications that apparently elude me."

"Why don't you start by telling me what happened to Harry Hagopian?"

"Harry Hagopian?" T. Duke paused as if giving the dead a moment of silence. "Poor Harry. They say his car crash was really a suicide."

"He didn't want to sell to you, now he's dead. Bridget didn't want to sell to you, now she's dead. Now you and I are on the wrong side of the fence. Is there an accident in my future?"

"Iris, I'm going to overlook your rude suggestion. I know I don't have to remind you that your primary obligation concerning Pandora is preserving the shareholders' investment. Bridget Cross was a smart lady. Her strategy for Pandora was a good one and she might have been able to pull it off. But that was then. Pandora's fortunes have changed. I admire your loyalty to Bridget's dream. However, consider that you may be wrong. Consider how you would feel if, instead of earning Brianna Cross's trust five dollars and fifteen cents a share, you end up with nothing. Consider that, Iris, then let's talk again."

T. Duke placed the telephone into its cradle on his expansive black marble desk. He looked at Baines, who was standing next to the closed door that led to the outer office.

"Shall I bring her back in?" Baines asked.

T. Duke nodded. He looked out the window across the low industrial buildings, citrus groves, and fields of Somis.

Baines returned with Toni Burton.

T. Duke stood when she entered. "Ms. Burton, I apologize

for interrupting our conversation. I was so delighted by your unexpected visit. Let's sit over here on the couch."

Toni sat on one end of the leather couch and entwined her legs, crossing them and hooking the foot of the top around the ankle of the bottom. She was conservatively dressed in a gray, chalk-striped slack suit worn with a white mock-turtleneck sweater. She bubbled, "I'm thrilled you took the time to talk to me. You must be *so* busy." Her eyes were drawn wide enough to make the white visible around the blue.

"I'm never too busy to talk to you."

"Like I was saying, I'm in a good position to influence Iris. Don't get me wrong! I *adore* her. Just think the *world* of her, but she should accept your offer." Toni quickly raised her index finger. "But not for the reasons you probably think."

T. Duke had a pleasant smile on his lips, as he always did regardless of his underlying emotions. He nodded, encouraging her to go on, his small, dark eyes twinkling.

Toni needed no encouragement. "You know that Today Rhea and Mick Ha also want Iris to sell, but they're only in it for the money." She raised both hands. "Not that there's anything wrong with that."

T. Duke raised his eyebrows. His heavily pomaded, thin hair moved back and forth with the motion of his scalp. "And what motivates *you* to want to sell?"

Toni uncrossed her legs and planted both feet firmly on the floor. She pursed her Kewpie doll lips as if she hated what she was about to say, but had a duty to say it. She spoke slowly and deliberately. "It's time someone did something about the degeneration of the ethics in this country. I understand and agree with your mission and would like to help in any way I can."

T. Duke exchanged a look with Baines, who had resumed his post in the doorway.

Before T. Duke could comment, Toni added, "Your mission's no secret to me. I saw the letter to Bridget from Darvis Brown, Grand Eagle of the Trust Makers. Then I noticed Baines's lapel pin. You're members, aren't you? Both of you. I'll bet the principals of USA Assets are Trust Makers also. That's what USA Assets is all about, isn't it? When companies who promulgate sex and violence won't restrain themselves, you buy into them and try to change them from the inside." She closed her eyes. "It's so simple and so brilliant."

Neither T. Duke or Baines said anything, but both of them attentively watched Toni.

"You're probably wondering why I stayed with Pandora as long as I have if I find their games offensive." Toni nervously chewed on a polished but bitten-down fingernail. "I am a Christian woman and I have to confess that my conscience began to bother me more and more during my years at Pandora. Lord knows, I was in a bad spot and needed a job when I began working there. I just went along to go along, you know. Five years ago, the games weren't nearly as realistic as they are today. As the graphics became more lifelike and as more explicit sexual themes were added, I mentioned my concerns to Bridget and Kip. You can imagine Kip's response."

T. Duke smiled wryly.

"Bridget was more receptive but basically said they have to give the public what they want. I kept my mouth shut and I'm sorry I did. But my moment to take a stand has now come." Toni primly clasped her hands in her lap and batted her eyes at T. Duke.

T. Duke cleared his throat and spoke in a soothing tone. "Well, young lady, any assistance you can give in convincing Iris Thorne to sell Pandora to the Sawyer Company would be most appreciated. You have my personal guarantee that your efforts will be amply rewarded. Please feel free to stop by or call me anytime." With both hands on his knees, T. Duke pushed himself up from the couch.

Toni hesitantly stood, as if disappointed the meeting was so quickly over. "You're saying I'm right—that you want to take over Pandora for ethical, not financial reasons?"

T. Duke stepped from behind the coffee table and held his arm out to indicate he wanted her to follow. Baines opened the door into the outer office and stood waiting for Toni to leave. Sitting on a couch there was a tall, slender woman with straight red hair, wearing a short skirt that was hiked well up her thighs. She wore very high heels. She stifled a yawn behind her hand.

Toni clutched T. Duke's arm and squeezed it. Even in his raised-heel cowboy boots, he was only slightly taller than she was. "Please, T. Duke, it would give me such comfort if I knew that you and other powerful men are actively working to save the country. Tell me I'm right."

T. Duke patted her hand. "Keep up the good work."

As Baines escorted Toni out, she saw the redhead follow T. Duke into his office. Baines led Toni to the front door of the building past the cluttered display cases and antique cars. On the way down, she tried engaging him in conversation, without success, but continued happily prattling on about this and that without his participation. He held the large, bulletproof glass door open for her.

"Thanks for escorting me, Baines." She looked up at him, her eyes traveling the expanse of his body. She had to tilt her head back to look into his eyes.

"No problem."

She grinned at him, revealing both rows of small white teeth, and tittered, ending with a squeal of delight. "Are you *always* so serious?"

"Serious, ma'am?"

She thought she detected a minute softening of his icy blue eyes. She tickled his waist through his starched shirt with her index finger. "Yes, *serious.*"

He jerked away, the corners of his mouth twitching.

"Ticklish, huh?" She reached for him again and he grabbed her wrist a bit roughly, letting the door close.

She audibly inhaled. "So *that's* how you like to play, huh?"

Still holding her wrist, he looked down at her and she up at him. Neither of them spoke. Finally, he let her go and again pressed the door open.

She pushed out her lower lip in disappointment. "I guess you have to get back to work, huh?"

"Yes, ma'am." He mouthed the words but the stoicism was absent.

She sauntered out the door, letting her fingers trail across his chest. Outside, she looked back over her shoulder at him. "See you around?"

"Yes, ma'am."

Through the open door of her office, Iris saw Evan Finn return from his umpteenth break that day, but she wasn't concerned with him at the moment. She was wondering whether she was out of her mind. Maybe T. Duke Sawyer was just a businessman trying to make a buck.

T. Duke was right about one thing, damn him. She was not looking at Pandora's circumstances from a detached, unemotional perspective. Pandora needed a cash infusion and soon. Even though *Suckers Finish Last* was selling beyond everyone's expectations, it wasn't enough. Bridget had invested too much in transforming that airplane hangar into kitschy offices. It would have been much cheaper to rent office space somewhere. There were an excessive number of people on the payroll, plus Kip had squandered megabucks on enhancing his lifestyle.

Iris had another problem. She could not run Pandora and McKinney Alitzer's LA branch at the same time. There were only so many Iris hours in the day. She was certain Bridget never intended the administration of Brianna's trust to drag down Iris's life. What was Pandora anyway but just an investment? If the firm was as T. Duke described, an underperforming dog with slim prospects, she should unload it while she could still get a good price for it. That's what she'd advise her own clients. Kip would just have to deal with her decision. His losing control over Pandora was his own fault, anyway. If he'd been more responsible, Bridget would have left the management of the company to him.

So if there was no dark plot involving T. Duke, who murdered Bridget? It was still possible it was T. Duke. But, again forcing herself to look at things unemotionally, Iris had to admit she had begun to more strongly suspect Kip. Why hadn't he been acting like a grieving husband or trying to find Bridget's murderer? The answer to that was a no-brainer.

Louise buzzed her. "Summer Fontaine is here to see you."

"Really? I don't have an appointment with her, do I?"

"She said she just stopped by."

"Please send her down."

Iris stood and quickly retucked her blouse into her skirt as she peeked out the window that overlooked the suite, watching for Summer's arrival. Even though the market was busy again that day, everyone momentarily stopped what they were doing to watch Summer pass.

Louise walked ahead of her down the corridor. Summer was wearing a clingy, long-sleeved, pearl pink sweater dress with a low scoop neckline.

Iris admired the woman's consistency. She had never seen her without her hair and makeup elaborately done. Her every outfit, be it kick-around sloppies for home or funeral attire, seemed selected for ultimate bimbo appeal. When the Crosses had originally hired Summer, she was merely cute. She had since transformed into a bombshell. Who knew?

Kyle Tucker and Sean Bliss found excuses to loiter near the watercooler.

Evan Finn was more bold. He stood inside his cubicle and extended his hand to Summer as she passed. "Summer Fontaine. I'm a big fan."

"*Are* you?" She beamed, clutching his fingertips. "How nice."

"I'm Evan Finn." He kissed the back of her hand. "Very pleased to meet you."

No-nonsense Louise discreetly led Summer by the arm away from Evan, who appraised the rear view. His eyes indicated he wasn't disappointed. Summer turned and gave him one last smile, coyly looking up at him through her eyelashes before entering Iris's office.

"Hi Iris," she breathed like a graduate of the Marilyn Monroe school of speech. "Oooh. This is nice."

"Thank you. Have a seat."

Summer sat in one of the chairs facing Iris's desk, crossing her legs in the clingy dress.

Iris saw Kyle, Sean, and now Warren too hanging around outside her door. She ignored the men's downcast faces as she closed it. When she turned to walk back to her desk, she noticed that Summer's cheek was bruised.

Summer drew her fingers through her hair, pulling the long strands over to cover the dark area that she couldn't completely disguise with makeup. "Thanks for taking the time . . . " Her voice broke before she could finish.

Iris pulled a tissue from a box she kept in a drawer and handed it to her.

"I'm sorry," Summer said, carefully patting the tissue against the corners of her eyes. "I told myself I wasn't going to get upset, but . . ."

"It's all right," Iris said soothingly, noticing that Summer even cried cute. Unlike herself, Summer's face didn't turn beet red and swell like a pimple, mucus didn't run in an endless stream from her nose, and her makeup remained in place instead of migrating all over her face. She was easy to hate, and Iris would have if she hadn't sensed the woman's sincere distress. "What's wrong?"

Summer examined the makeup that had come off on the tissue. "Kip and I had a fight. I don't even know how it started. I was mad because all he does is sit at that computer all day."

"Working?" Iris asked hopefully.

"I guess so. Anyway, he started complaining about the way I dress Brianna and . . ." Summer relayed every detail of the incident, tears streaming from her eyes, which were astonishingly emerald green. She was wearing colored contact lenses.

Iris supplied her with a mound of tissues, all the time wondering, *Where's the beef?*

"Oh, Iris. It was awful." Summer twisted a damp tissue between her hands. "I don't know how that sweet little thing could draw something like that."

"Like what?" Iris thought she'd been paying attention, but something had apparently slipped past her.

"The picture. Brianna starts waving this picture and going, 'Daddy, look!' It wasn't the best picture. She's only five. But it was all there. Slade Slayer holding a gun, Stetson lying by the pool, and"—she began sobbing—"her mom."

"Would you like a glass of water?"

Summer shook her head. "Anyway, Kip went bat shit. He grabbed the paper from her, tore it into a million pieces, and shoved them into his pocket. Brianna was screaming and crying. It was awful. I told him he should let her draw. She's probably working it out that way, but Kip wouldn't hear of it."

Summer spoke in a whisper. "I'm starting to get afraid of him, Iris. He's been talking crazy. He's accusing me of seeing other men and he goes on and on about all this weird stuff. About how Bridget's murder was cause and effect or something. How he might as well act like a murderer since that's what people think of him." She inhaled tremulously. "I think the things people say to him—how they call him murderer and wife-killer and stuff—are really doing a number on his head."

She placed her fingertips against her cleavage. "I never believed Kip murdered Bridget. I swear to God, I didn't. But Iris, the way he's been acting . . ."

"Did he hit you?"

Summer gingerly touched the bruise on her cheek. "You can still see it?"

"When?"

She shook her head as if the memory were too painful to recall. "Last night. Brianna was in bed, thank God. I told the police. I thought they should know in case something . . ." Her voice trailed off. "Can *you* talk to Kip? I don't know what to do. I've never seen him acting like this. I'm worried about Brianna."

"Sure."

"I don't think he'd do anything to Brianna, but I can't figure out why he was so upset over her drawing. I think she should draw. We need to find out exactly what she saw. She said she drew pictures like that when she was staying with Bridget's parents."

"She did?"

"I wonder if Natalie has them."

Iris didn't comment but resolved to get to the Tylers before Summer did.

Summer finished drying her eyes and dropped the soiled tissues in a wad on top of Iris's desk. "Thanks, Iris. I always thought you were a really good person. I just had to tell someone what's going on in that house. I wish I had a friend like you."

"Thanks. That's very kind." Iris considered Summer's comment. She didn't recall ever seeing the other woman with or mentioning any girlfriends. The same went for family. She hadn't thought about Summer much at all until Bridget's murder. Now she realized she knew hardly anything about her.

She walked Summer to the front doors of the suite and left her waiting for the elevator. Just as Iris came back into the sales department, Evan was again leaving. She casually followed him and reached the lobby in time to see him get on the elevator with Summer.

Chapter 24

Traffic on the westbound 10 was almost at a standstill. Iris switched from her light-jazz FM station and began pounding the preset buttons on the AM band, surfing her favorite news and talk stations. Before long, she found a traffic report, just about the same time that one of the large, illuminated FREEWAY CONDITION signs loomed into view. One word said it all: ACCIDENT. By the time she'd inched forward another quarter of a mile, she'd determined the exact location, number of cars involved, and the magnitude of the injuries sustained, but it didn't matter. The accident could have been anything from a minor fender bender to a multicar pile-up. Hypersensitive LA drivers treated them all the same. Traffic stopped.

A big raindrop plopped onto her windshield. It was quickly followed by a second. Iris peered through the windshield and looked at the threatening sky with disdain.

"That's exactly what this situation needs right now," she sarcastically said aloud. "A little rain."

In LA, a light drizzle might as well be a blizzard in terms of the effect on traffic. Los Angelenos can work through almost any horror, but a disruption in their daily commute sends them awry. Poor little flowers.

Iris evaluated alternate routes in her head. Each one she considered seemed like a lot of trouble. The freeway, although slow right now, took a straight, sure path to her destination. She stayed put and pulled out her cellular phone. She called Natalie Tyler, Bridget's mother, and told her about Summer Fontaine's visit.

"Brianna did draw pictures of . . . what happened," Natalie confessed. "Please don't tell Kip, but I called a child psychologist about it. She wanted me to bring Brianna in, but I was afraid. Kip had made it clear that he didn't want Brianna seeing any head doctors, and I didn't want him to keep our granddaughter from us if we defied his wishes."

"What did the shrink say?"

"That anything Brianna does to help her work out what she saw that night is good. Anything—talking, playacting, drawing."

"Do you still have the drawings?"

"I wanted to throw them out, but something told me I shouldn't, that they were important."

"Do they . . . show anything?"

"Nothing that can identify the murderer. She's got this figure in black from head to toe with a Slade Slayer head. The drawings are nothing but stick people and blobs of color. You have to know what to look for to figure it out."

"I'd love to see them." Iris mentally went over her schedule and found no time to drop by the Tylers. "Could you please FedEx them to me?" She gave Natalie the necessary information.

Iris finally saw a flare on the road in the middle of lane one. A few yards beyond the flare, another was placed even further into the lane, squeezing traffic from four lanes into three. Drivers cooperatively knitted together the lanes of traffic in a "you go, I go" pattern. Iris merged.

Iris thought she'd try an idea on Bridget's mother to see how it played. "Mrs. Tyler, what if I can't fulfill Bridget's vision for Pandora?"

"What do you mean?"

"What if I can't take it public and build it into a computer entertainment giant? What if circumstances have changed such that now the best decision would be to sell Pandora to T. Duke Sawyer? Would Bridget think I'd failed her?"

"No, honey. Of course not. You did the best you could. That's all Bridget expected. Under the circumstances, she would have come to the same decision."

They ended the telephone call and the accident finally came into view. There were California Highway Patrol cars, khaki-clad officers, dazed civilians, a red-and-white paramedics van, and three damaged cars: a Jeep Cherokee, a Honda Passport, and a Dodge Intrepid. It looked as if the Intrepid had lost.

A CHP officer stood at the edge of the mess, scowling as he angrily swooped his arm, trying to move the lookie-loos past. Iris was not dissuaded. She'd waited just as long as everyone else. She took a good long look before driving on.

Iris left the Triumph parked in her driveway, the garage still too crowded with boxes to accommodate it. She had been so looking forward to moving into her new house, and now she felt that she was using it as a place to flop. She hadn't even capitalized on a consumer-durables shopping spree. Her favorite chichi boutique was having a sale and she hadn't had time to check it out. She hadn't talked to Garland in three days. All they'd done was exchange phone messages. What a way to build a relationship. What was she thinking, falling in love with someone who lived on the East Coast? She couldn't find anyone in LA?

Oh woe is me, she told herself. *Oh woe. I'm just a bird in a gilded cage.*

In her bedroom, she stripped off her work clothes, throwing her panty hose into an ever-growing pile. She put on worn sweatpants that had shrunk several inches in length, a soft, plaid flannel shirt, and tired Vans slip-on tennis shoes with cracked, peeling rubber soles.

In the kitchen, she shoved the take-out sushi and cellophane bag of prepared salad she'd bought for dinner into the refrigerator and poured a glass of chardonnay. In her backyard, she relaxed into her Adirondack chair and looked at the ocean and sky that the sunset had tinged with pink. It was chilly. Looked as if winter had finally came to Southern California.

She briskly rubbed her arms. She hated being cold. An LA native, she probably hated being cold more than anything. More even than being hungry. After all, she'd spent a large portion of her life voluntarily starving herself. More even than physical pain, she hated being cold.

She set her wineglass on the redwood deck and started to go in the house to put on something warmer, then heard some indiscernible wailing followed by laughter. Soon after, there was music with a Latin rhythm and a full brass section. It was coming from Marge's patio.

Iris crept to the thick hedge that obscured the chain link fence separating her yard from Marge's and peeked through the dense foliage. She was startled to see her mother wearing colorful crepe-paper flowers in her hair, an elastic-neck peasant blouse embroidered with bright designs around the yoke, and a fringed scarf tied around her hips. She was wantonly dancing, shimmying her shoulders and snapping her fingers with both arms held in front of her. Her partner was an older man wearing a broad-brimmed, black sombrero decorated with silver sequins.

"Olé!" Marge shouted as she clapped along with the music. *"Arriba!"*

"Yi, yiyiyi!" yelled a short, second man with thick, white hair who was shaking a martini shaker in time with the music.

Iris stared at the scene. Men, music, martinis, *and* her mother? What the hell was going on?

Marge spotted Iris. "Hi, cutie! C'mon over and join the party!" Marge pointed to indicate Iris's mother's partner. "This is Mel."

Mel took off his sombrero and bowed with it, revealing his completely bald pate.

Next, Marge introduced the silver-haired devil. "This is Frosty. We just got back from Olvera Street. Don't you just *love* Olvera Street? It's the oldest street in Los Angeles, you know. I adore the way they honor the city's Mexican heritage there."

"Mom!" Iris cried. "What are you doing?"

"I think the mambo," Mel explained.

"Just having a little fun," Rose said, out of breath. "You told me I should get out more, and you were right."

The four of them tried to no avail to get Iris to come over. She had been happily sulking, thank you very much, before they had interrupted her. And this new aspect of her mother was a bit more than her frayed nerves could handle at the moment.

She downed the last of her wine and retreated into the house, which the thermostat indicated was a frigid sixty-six degrees. She cranked on the heat to raise the temperature to a habitable seventy-two.

Sitting at her dining room table, she shoved a wedge of maguro into her mouth and contemplated this turn of events. Sure, she had told her mother to get a life, but this wasn't what she'd had in mind. She'd envisioned a few nice, older ladies for her to play bridge with. She had certainly never expected her mother to start having more of a life than she was. Iris grabbed a handful of dry salad from the cellophane bag, shoved it into her mouth, and chewed gloomily.

She licked wasabi and sticky rice from her fingers, opened her laptop computer, and turned it on. It made scratching noises as it booted. She loaded *Suckers Finish Last* and resumed playing where she had left off, in the middle of the second level. Not a power player, she hadn't gotten very far.

She'd successfully grabbed the Teflon suit, used it to swim across the river of green slime, and killed three of four rottweilers and most of the Morph Drones before she'd picked up a box that she thought would contain ammo. Big mistake. It was full of snakes that jumped on Slade Slayer, who went down screaming in agony.

"Damn."

She restarted the game three more times and died three more times before she finally turned off the computer. Two hours had melted away. She knew she was avoiding telling Kip she'd decided to accept T. Duke's offer. She'd been avoiding it ever since she got home. She should have driven straight to his house.

She changed into jeans that were more presentable than her sloppy sweat pants, tucked in her flannel shirt, and dug through her piles and boxes of clothes until she finally located her heavy wool Irish fisherman's sweater.

She got into the Triumph. She was only going two steep blocks to Kip Cross's house, but it was getting dark and she was already spooked. She turned the key in the ignition. It emitted a sharp click. She tried again and it clicked again. The starter had been behaving beautifully for the past few days, but now seemed to be on the fritz again. She tried a few more times before the engine turned over. As she backed out, she noticed that in the short time the TR had been parked, it had already deposited a glutinous glob of oil on her clean driveway.

"Baby, please don't do this to Momma," Iris pleaded.

Iris rang Kip's doorbell and rang again. She tried the door. It was locked. His Ferrari was parked in the driveway. She didn't see Bridget's Volvo, which Summer had been driving around—when she couldn't get her hands on the Ferrari—but it could have been parked in the garage.

She walked to the side of the house and down the cement steps that ran next to the property, thinking she'd try the patio gate. She was surprised to find it ajar. She slowly pulled it open, afraid of what she might find, and darted her head inside. There wasn't anything or anyone there. She was about to enter the patio and try the French doors when she saw something move in the brush next to the cement stairway, midway to the street below.

She crept down a few steps and saw someone straddling the storm drain that led from Kip's backyard. She moved a few steps closer. In the dim light, she made out a flip-flop-clad foot.

"Kip?" Iris was clearly visible in the light coming from the open back gate.

He dropped the storm drain that he had been holding between his legs. "Oh, hi."

She walked down to him. "What are you doing?"

"Rats. I think there's a rats' nest in here."

She looked around for implements of rat destruction but found none. She also found it curious that he was bare-handed and almost bare-footed. It wasn't the clothing she would wear to go rat-hunting, but Kip was never known for being practical.

He seemed to sense her question. "I was just checking it out." He stepped over the drain and between the railings onto the stairs next to her. "So, ah . . . you stopped by."

"Yeah." On the ground next to the drain, she spotted a long, white plastic pole with a hook on the end. "Summer and Brianna aren't here?"

He carelessly raised a shoulder. "Shopping or something." He saw that she had noticed the pole and started walking back up the steps, away from the drain. "You want to come inside? You want a drink or something?" He was not much of a host and his efforts seemed forced.

"What's that? That pole?"

Kip peered into the darkness as if he couldn't make out what she was referring to. "Oh, that. That looks like . . . Yeah. We use that to drag stuff out of the pool. I think Brianna must have brought it down there." He walked back down the steps, slipped between the railings, and picked up the hook.

"Summer came to see me today."

He faced her, holding the hook like a staff. "Why?"

"She told me about Brianna and the pictures. She told me you hit her."

His knuckles grew white where he grasped the pole. "She told me she slipped on the area rug and smacked her cheek on the tile steps in the foyer. Now she's going around telling people I hit her? I guess this is her way of getting back at me for telling her to do her job and to stop making money off Bridget's murder." He twisted the pole, grinding the end into the dirt. "It's happening. See? See how it's happening?"

"What's happening?"

Kip fed the hook between the railings before crawling through himself. "The boss monster has made his move."

"You think the boss monster is out to get you."

"Yes."

"He killed Bridget?"

"Yes. Murdered Bridget and tried to frame me. But it's going to be okay. He can't play the game without revealing some of his strategy." Kip pinched his thumb and index fingers together and held them up. "I need a little more information. Just a little more."

Iris recalled what Summer had told her about Kip acting crazy.

Kip continued, his voice excited, his eyes bright, "But he

screwed up. That's good. He revealed his weakness, just like I revealed mine. There's still a lot of play left."

"Is the boss monster a person?"

"You think I'm mad, don't you?"

"Not mad, Kip, but . . . you have to admit your theory's a bit unusual."

"Yeah. Right. No matter."

It was now pitch-black outside. A raindrop plopped on her head. No way was she going to talk to him about T. Duke's offer here. Instead she was going to flee home and double-check that all her doors and windows were locked. "Kip, I'm freezing. I'll call you tomorrow, okay?" She started jogging up the stairs.

"I know you've been talking to T. Duke."

She stopped dead and turned around. "Of course I've been talking to T. Duke." She wouldn't ask how he knew. She didn't want him to think she cared that much. T. Duke probably called Kip himself to taunt him.

"Rumor is, you're close to taking his offer. You're close to selling Pandora out from underneath my feet." A cold breeze blew and Kip squinted his deep-set eyes, making them small, glimmering slits.

Her only response was to take another step away from him.

"Do me a favor?" He was speaking in an emotionless monotone that was exceedingly controlled. She'd heard him use that tone of voice shortly before he'd gone ballistic. "Don't do anything until you see my new graphics engine. It'll prove that I'm stronger than ever."

"Okay, Kip. Sure. I'm looking forward to it. You've been working hard, huh?" She forced a smile.

He leaned against the pole with both hands as if he might fall without it. "Everyone who thinks they've got me beat is going to be in for a big surprise. *Everyone.*"

She held her hand out palm up. "Looks like it's going to pour! I'll call you." She jogged up the steps, barely making it to her car before the clouds opened.

Chapter 25

"Have you heard of a firm called Canterbury Investments?" Iris sat on the corner of her desk, hoping her posture seemed casual and nonchalant. She actually wanted to get as close to Sam Eastman as possible to see if he flinched, batted an eyelash, or otherwise gave anything away.

He did. His eyes quickly shot to the corner of the room before he recovered and informally crossed his legs. "No, no, can't say that I have. What is it? New player in town?"

Iris frowned, indicating that it was nothing. Less than nothing. "Just something I heard . . . around. I don't even remember where."

The wind blew rain against the window and whistled through a small gap where two large panes were joined. The junction had most likely been thrown askew by a temblor somewhere down the line. Iris was wearing her suit jacket but she still shivered. She returned to her desk chair.

"So how's Evan doing?" Sam asked.

Iris thought it odd for him to mention Evan on the heels of her bringing up Canterbury Investments. "Mediocre at best."

Sam looked concerned. "That surprises me. Course, you

haven't given him much of a chance, Iris. He's only been here about a week."

"Do you know that his résumé doesn't jive?"

"You mean you can't verify it?" Sam asked in a way that suggested he was surprised she'd tried.

"Yes, I can."

Sam's shoulders relaxed as if he was relieved.

"But when Louise calls Huxley Investments and asks for information on Evan Finn, she's never put through to their Human Resources Department. She's always sent directly to Yale Huxley."

"But that's good. That shows how important Evan was to the firm."

"Sam, it's weird. A routine question regarding a former employee's employment dates should not be routed to the managing partner of the firm." The wind whistled and Iris shivered on cue. "There's another thing. Harvard's records indicate that Evan Finn died last year."

"It's a simple mistake."

"Is it?"

"Iris," Sam chided. "You've been reading too many mystery novels."

"I don't like mystery novels. I don't like mysteries at all. I like everything laid out, crystal clear, easily understood."

Sam smiled indulgently at her. "I don't believe that, Iris."

His condescending tone frosted her to no end. "Tell me why Evan's here, Sam."

"You hired him."

"You twisted my arm."

"Nonsense. You had the last word. You made a point of telling me that."

"Okay. Now I'm about to fire him."

"Don't do that." Sam quickly uncrossed his legs, as if jolted. He held his open hands beseechingly toward her. "Try him just a little longer. He's a good kid. Give him a chance. A month."

"Garland Hughes tells me that Yale Huxley and T. Duke Sawyer are cronies from way back. What's going on, Sam?"

Just mentioning Garland, Sam's former boss, made him bristle. "I don't know what that has to do with anything. Lots of men like Huxley and Sawyer run in the same circles, belong to the same clubs."

"I'll find out why Evan's here, you know."

Sam grew huffy. "Evan's going to do a lot of good for this office, Iris. You have to trust my experience on this. I've been in this business a lot longer than you have." He looked at his watch. "Gotta go. Keep me posted. Remember, I have my branch managers' conference call at ten o'clock tomorrow morning. Speak with you then."

He opened the door and bustled out, stopping to give Evan a quick pat on the back and exchange a few words.

Louise walked into Iris's office with a Federal Express envelope from Natalie Tyler.

Iris, still steaming after her conversation with Sam, angrily pulled the tab, slicing open the top of the letter-size cardboard container.

"Get anything out of Sam?" Louise asked.

Iris shook her head.

"Why don't you just fire Evan?" Louise said in a low voice designed to carry less than six inches, an inflection well-practiced by anyone who worked in a crowded office.

Iris responded in the same tone of voice. "I will. But first, I want to find out why he's here. If I fire him, I'll lose the opportunity to gather evidence. I need solid proof that Sam is up to something." She pulled several folded sheets of heavy drawing paper from the envelope and opened them.

Louise gasped. "My God! Did little Brianna draw those?"

Iris speechlessly looked through the pictures, putting one behind the next. There were five, all variations on the same subject. Three of them showed Slade Slayer shooting at a prone and bloody Bridget. Two showed Slade Slayer bending over Bridget with a slingshot in his hand. All of them showed a tiny figure in the corner cowering behind the French doors. Stetson, the German shepherd, was in three drawings.

Iris felt empty. She hadn't forgotten that Brianna had been an eyewitness, but on some level, she wanted to forget. The drawings brought it all back.

"There's an amazing amount of detail for a five-year-old," Louise commented.

"Even down to Stetson's collar and the infamous flip-flops. It's logical that she would have seen the murderer's shoes since she was probably crouched in a corner."

"Are you going to give the drawings to the police?"

Iris tilted her head. "I hadn't thought of that. Their investigation has been so one-dimensional, I've discounted them." She looked over the drawings again. "Doesn't seem to be anything here that gives any indication who the murderer might be. Maybe if Brianna drew more, she'd remember more details. Or maybe this is all there is."

"Is Kip encouraging her?"

Iris didn't want to tell Louise the truth, knowing how incriminating it sounded. She lied. "I don't know."

Her phone rang and Louise reached to pick it up. "Iris Thorne's office." She turned to Iris. "Toni Burton is here."

"Good. Could you please bring her down?" Iris gathered the drawings and turned them facedown on her desk.

Iris stood in her doorway and watched Toni follow Louise through the sales department, almost running poor Louise down. Even at a distance, Toni looked effervescent. She was smiling at everyone, playfully mugging if someone's glance lingered, her bonhomie compelling them to smile back. It didn't seem completely natural and Iris didn't know why Toni did it. She hadn't quite noodled Toni out. But she was grateful for one thing—she would be in a world of muck trying to decipher Pandora without Toni. She had found her to be a bright and capable ally.

Toni spotted Evan Finn. The girl had a good eye for beefcake. She pulled down her lower lip, revealing both rows of gleaming teeth, creating a Goldie Hawn effect, and mouthed, "Hi," as she passed. She raised her shoulders when she spotted Iris, as if seeing her new boss made her tingle. "Hi, Iris!"

"Hi, Toni. Come in."

Toni stepped inside Iris's office and gave an openmouthed appraisal of the decor. "Oh, *Iris*. Oh! This is *gor*-geous! Of course, I knew you would decorate like this. This is so elegant. It shows such panache." Toni surveyed the view from the corner windows and shook her head with awe. "There's a whole world out there, isn't there?"

Iris noticed that Amber Ambrose had found an excuse to linger at Louise's desk, just outside Iris's door. Iris didn't need the fact that she was conducting Pandora business on McKinney Alitzer time to get back to Sam Eastman. She walked to her door, smiled amiably at Amber, then closed it.

Sitting in her chair, Iris told Toni, "I love your suit. The color's great on you."

Toni flitted to one of the chairs facing Iris's desk, where she perched on the edge. She pinched her jacket lapels. "Do you really think so? I've been upgrading my wardrobe. Have you noticed?"

"I have."

"Don't get me wrong!" Toni put up a warning hand. "I *love* the trendy stuff. Everything that's fun and hot, all the new colors and hemlines, each season, I've gotta have it. But it's true, what they say, about how clothes make the person. Take *you,* for example. You manage all these people. You can't come in looking like you just fell off the set of *Friends* for goodness' sake."

"The Summer Fontaine look."

"Ugh!" Toni made a face. "Isn't she disgusting?"

"She's . . . unique." Iris folded her hands in front of her on her desk. "So what happened that you couldn't tell me about over the phone?"

"I can't *believe* I did this!" Toni fluttered her hands, quickly recovered, then soberly regarded Iris. "I met with T. Duke."

Iris didn't like hearing this. "Really?"

"I told him I wanted to talk face-to-face about his offer to buy Pandora. And that Today, Mick, and I all want you to take the offer and that I was in a position to influence you and would help him in any way I could. But I said that unlike Today and Mick, I'm not in it for the money."

Toni quickly glanced to each side as if to see whether someone was eavesdropping, although no one could be because the door was closed. "I told him I figured out his true mission in relation to Pandora and that I agree wholeheartedly."

"You agree?"

"Abso-tively posi-lutely! I only said it because I wanted him to tell me about the Trust Makers and the conspiracy."

"You now think that Bridget's murder was part of a conspiracy."

"Yes!"

"The other day you told me you thought my conspiracy theory was far-fetched. What made you change your mind?"

"When I got to thinking about all the things you pointed out that don't add up, I *had* to come to the conclusion that Kip didn't do it. When you consider Alexa Platt . . ." Toni's eyes were wide with excitement. "Everything you were saying about the conspiracy started to make a whole lot of sense."

"Huh. I'd just talked myself out of it."

Toni looked shocked. "Iris, *no!* Your theory's *brilliant!* You're so clever. As clever as T. Duke—and that's the key thing."

Now Iris didn't know what to think.

"I thought really hard about it and I said, 'You've got to do this, Toni. You've got to do this for Bridget and Brianna.' First thing the next morning, I called T. Duke."

"So what else happened when you were at T. Duke's?"

"I asked if he and Baines were members of the Trust Makers and suggested that the principals of USA Assets were also."

"And?"

"He didn't deny it."

"But he didn't admit it."

"Did you expect him to?"

Iris considered that and shook her head.

Toni excitedly waved her hands. "Listen to what I did next." She leaned forward and whispered, "I went out with *Baines.*"

Iris raised her eyebrows.

"When I was at T. Duke's, I kind of gave Baines the eye and he kind of gave me the eye. I called him later and asked him if he wanted to have a drink, and he said *yes!*"

"I'm impressed," Iris said truthfully.

Toni grinned. "I thought I'd loosen him up with a few drinks, you know. Problem is, he doesn't drink. He's *so* straight. But he likes sex!" She squealed with delight.

"Toni, you didn't have to go to extremes."

"We-ell, it wasn't exactly *torture,* if you know what I mean. What a bod! But he's way too conservative for me. You know me, I like the bad boys. I initiated a little pillow talk and he went on and on about the Trust Makers. He is so into the whole thing. The big meetings, the singing, the praying, the crying." She rolled her eyes.

"What about T. Duke?"

"Didn't talk about T. Duke. Wouldn't talk about T. Duke."

"Loyal."

"To a fault. Bu-ut"—Toni playfully wrinkled her nose—"he told me who the USA Assets investors are."

Iris was now all ears.

Toni rummaged through her purse, shuffling through handfuls of folded and bent papers. She handed a rolled-up length of toilet paper to Iris. "It's kind of scribbled. After Baines told me, I made an excuse to go to the bathroom. All I had to write with was my lipstick."

Iris unscrolled the paper on her desk. She could barely make out the writing. "Darvis Brown, Clinton Cormier, Yale Huxley, and T. Duke Sawyer." She read the list again.

"Darvis Brown is also the Grand Eagle of the Trust Makers." Toni sat erect and shoved her hands underneath her thighs. "You remember, he sent a letter criticizing Pandora. There's your connection between the Trust Makers and USA Assets."

Iris focused on Yale Huxley's name. He was the managing partner of Huxley Investments, the firm where Evan Finn had supposedly worked before moving to California. Garland had already told her that Yale Huxley knew T. Duke. She hadn't heard of Clinton Cormier and wondered if Garland had.

Iris leaned back in her chair and massaged her forehead with one hand. "I'm confused. Yesterday, T. Duke made a compelling argument that his only interest in Pandora was to make money. I decided it was foolish not to take his offer."

Toni gaped at Iris. "Even after what Jim Platt said?"

"You heard from Jim Platt?"

"He didn't call you? He said he lost the card you gave him and knew you were involved with Pandora and tried to reach you there. They put the call through to me. He found out that USA Assets *did* invest in his second movie."

"They did," Iris said quietly.

"It's all falling into place, Iris. Bridget Cross is murdered, Kip Cross is framed for it. Alexa Platt is murdered. Harry Hagopian dies in a solo spinout. Each individual is involved in producing entertainment media with a high violent and sexual content. All of them had a financial connection to T. Duke Sawyer and USA Assets. USA Assets has a connection to the Trust Makers, an ultra-right-wing group." Toni flung herself back into the chair and folded her arms across her chest with finality.

Iris stood and looked out the window behind her desk at the rain sweeping across the sky. She twirled a lock of her hair. After a while, she faced Toni. "Consider the possibility that you and I have overactive imaginations. Sometimes a cigar is just a cigar."

"Iris! *Hello!* The clue phone is ringing and you're not picking up!"

There was sharp knocking on Iris's door, obviously administered by someone who didn't care that Iris was otherwise engaged. Iris strode across the room and angrily opened the door to find Liz standing there, her fist still raised in the air.

Liz surged ahead without uttering a greeting. "The market finally closed up today, just five points, but it's the first time it's been up in three weeks. We're all going for drinks. C'mon, Iris." It was an order, not an invitation.

"Liz Martini, this is Toni Burton. Toni's my lifeline at Pandora."

Toni stood and shook Liz's hand.

"Pleased to meet you," Liz said. "So get your purse."

Kyle Tucker appeared in the doorway behind Liz. "It's cigar night at Julie's! Drinks are half-price. And for ladies, cigars are half-price. Now that's an offer I know a cigar lover like you won't be able to refuse, Iris," he teased.

"Half-price cigars for ladies?" Iris retorted. "How sexist! I demand to pay full price for my cigars."

"Come on downstairs and we'll talk to Julie personally. Then we'll go over to the car wash and demand they discontinue half-price washes to ladies on Wednesday afternoons." He glanced at Toni.

Toni had already spotted him.

"Bring your friend."

"I'd love to," Toni said.

Iris leaned forward to see Evan's cubicle. "Kyle, invite everyone. It'll be on me. We deserve a break." She opened the top drawer of her corner filing cabinet, reached inside her wallet, and took out her newly issued corporate gold card. She flicked the stiff plastic. "About time I took this baby for a ride." She slammed the file cabinet drawer closed.

"Even the mystery man?" Kyle jerked his head in the direction of Evan's cubicle. "He'll hardly give anyone here the time of day. It's like his poo-poo don't stink or something."

"Everyone," Iris affirmed. "Consider it a team-building exercise."

"Yes, ma'am." Kyle saluted Iris and sprinted off to do his assigned job.

"Is the mystery man you were talking about that hunk sitting out there?" Toni asked.

Liz was nosily scanning the items on Iris's desk. "Top Gun, as we affectionately call him."

"His name's Evan Finn," Iris said. "He's only been on the job about a week and he's very private."

"He's dreamy," Toni swooned. "He looks like someone famous but I can't think of who it is."

"Tom Cruise." Liz picked up Brianna's drawings and stared aghast at the first one. She rolled it back to look at the second, clucking with dismay.

"What?" Toni looked over Liz's shoulder. "Uh!" she gasped. "Brianna drew those?"

Iris raised an eyebrow in confirmation.

"She remembers," Toni said as she watched Liz flip through the stack. "She remembers everything. God help that poor child."

Chapter 26

By the time Iris, Liz, and Toni were ready to leave for Julie's, everyone else in the office had already left. Everyone except Evan Finn.

Iris put on her suit jacket as she walked down the corridor, slipping her credit card into a pocket. Toni was close on her heels.

Liz leaned against Evan's cubicle with one hand on the five-foot-high wall and the other petulantly dug into her hip. "Says he's got too many things to do," she said as Iris approached.

"Unacceptable," Iris said sternly. She noticed Evan's briefcase sitting open on his desk and tried not to seem too interested in it. Her eyes were drawn to it in spite of herself. "You're going to turn down an invitation for drinks with three attractive women, one of whom is paying?" She pulled out the gold card and waved it in front of him.

Evan smiled. His mouth pulled slightly higher to one side, deepening his dimple there and giving him a rakish air. Iris thought she heard a tiny swoon emitted by Toni, who was standing close beside her. Evan's charms weren't lost on Iris either, but she tried to maintain a cool and professional aura. It was either that or disintegrate into schoolgirlish giggling.

"I suppose I should spend some time getting to know my boss a little better," he said. "And my coworkers."

Iris felt her cheeks coloring. Liz provided a needed distraction by clamping her manicured fingers on Evan's shoulder and playfully shaking it. "That's right. There's a time for work and a time for play. We frown on workaholics around here, don't we, Iris?"

Iris blew up her cheeks as if she were choking on something.

"Don't we, Iris?" Liz persisted.

"Absolutely."

"Sold," Evan said as he stood and took his jacket from a hanger that swung from a hook attached to the back of his cubicle. "But I didn't have a chance, did I?"

"Evan, this is Toni Burton."

Evan shook the hand that Toni only too happily offered.

With Evan momentarily distracted, Iris stared more pointedly into Evan's briefcase. After snooping as much as she dared, she noticed that Liz was looking at her. Liz winked and Iris wondered if she'd figured out what was on her mind. Iris's cheeks colored again with the thought. Then she realized it was her guilty conscience getting the better of her. Liz couldn't possibly know what she was thinking. Liz was just winking to be friendly. She was always winking at people. She approached life as if it were one big party and she were the life of it.

"So what do you guys think of this cigar craze?" Toni asked.

"It's just *awful,*" Liz proclaimed in her typically dramatic way. "We certainly don't need to encourage people in such a filthy habit."

Evan slipped on his jacket and Iris saw the Armani label.

"Personally, I'm glad to see it," Evan said. "I've always enjoyed a good cigar. Until now, people looked at you like you were a leper if you lit up."

He wasn't shy about expressing his opinion, even if it was unpopular. Iris liked that.

"I think it's fun!" Toni piped in, not wanting to be left out.

Iris saw Evan put his hand on the top of his open briefcase and start to press it closed and, presumably, locked.

"Oh, leave it!" she said to him. "I'm just going down for a few minutes myself. I have a ton of work to do."

Evan hesitated, but before he could put up a struggle, Liz had crooked her arm through his and was sweeping him down the corridor. "Come on, mystery man. Leave your work behind."

Toni rushed to snag Evan's other arm. Iris walked behind them.

"Mystery man?" Evan said. "Is that what you think of me?"

"That's what we think of you," Liz confirmed. "Is that the image you wanted to create?"

"Of course not," Evan protested. "My life's an open book and pretty uninteresting."

"Hmmm," Liz said skeptically.

"Hmmm?" Evan repeated. "What does *hmmm* mean?"

"It means I think you protest too much."

At the elevator, Iris pressed the call button.

"How about you, Iris?" Evan asked, changing the subject. "You smoke cigars?"

"Oh, yeah. The day's not right unless I get my stogie in."

Evan narrowed his eyes and peered at Iris, as if trying to visualize something. "A cigarillo. Yes, definitely. Be a nice counterpoint to your girl-next-door looks." His dimple deepened when he smiled at her.

You devil you, Iris thought. *Flirting with your boss? You're certainly a bold SOB.* She let his comment and his gaze drop as she turned to walk into the elevator. It was empty. She pressed the button for the lobby.

"What about me, Evan? What sort of cigar would go with my all-American, girl-next-door looks?" Liz said with a twinkle in her eye as she moved to the back of the elevator. With her thatch of dark, tangled curls, fashion-forward clothes, dramatic makeup, and big boobs on her tall, pencil-thin frame, Liz was anything but girl-next-door looking and she knew it. Her self-deprecating wit was one of the things that Iris especially loved about her.

"For you, I think an eight-inch, thickly wrapped Havana."

"Don't they come any longer than that?" Toni asked, sounding disappointed. "Can't a girl at least get twelve inches?"

The three of them laughed. Iris would have too, but suddenly remembered that she was the boss. "Whoa, guys! This conversation's getting a little suggestive for the workplace." Almost to herself she said, "It can be boring to be the boss."

The elevator stopped several times to pick up passengers, who observed elevator etiquette and quietly stood facing the front with their arms straight down at their sides. Iris's group talked raucously behind them.

"Oh, Iris," Liz scolded with her hands on her narrow hips. "Your mind immediately goes straight to the gutter."

Toni added, "You were just telling me that sometimes a cigar is just a cigar."

Iris folded her arms across her chest and leaned against the corner of the elevator. "Hmmm."

"Now she's saying it, too," Evan said. "What does *hmmm* mean?"

"She likes to do that sometimes. Stand off to the side and quietly observe people." Liz cupped her hand against her mouth and in a loud stage whisper said, "You may not know this, but around the office, Miss Thorne is known as the Ice Princess."

Evan looked at Iris as if he were seeing her for the first time. "Uh-huh?"

Toni came to Iris's defense. "C'mon, you guys. Iris isn't icy and she certainly doesn't act like a princess."

"I would consider that nickname a compliment," Evan said. "She sort of coolly sits back and appraises a situation. It means she's thoughtful and deliberate and not a woman of brash action. I can definitely see it."

Iris raised an eyebrow at him.

"Iris, brash?" Liz said. "Ha! Why, you'd never even think to use those two words in the same sentence." She gave Iris a playful shove. It was an inside joke. Over the years, Liz had seen Iris brashly throw herself headfirst into a variety of situations, only pausing to consider the consequences after it was too late.

Evan again sized up Iris with his sable-colored eyes. No doubt about it, she decided, he was flirting with her. He definitely had that je ne sais quoi. Sex appeal. Animal magnetism. Whatever one wanted to call it, Evan Finn had it in spades and he knew it. He knew he could push the envelope with women and they'd let him. Lord, yes, would they. There was something about this man that was sending her radar on overload. He was dangerous.

He was trouble. And he worked for her. She defiantly met his bold stare.

Finally, Iris said, "How long are you guys going to stand there and talk about me in the third person like I'm not even here?"

"As long as you let us." Liz laughed gaily.

The elevator reached the lobby and everyone spilled out. The lobby was darker than usual, the rain preventing the sunlight from filtering through the skylights installed three stories up. They rounded a corner and were met with laughter and animated talking. It was on the early side of happy hour, which was almost always two hours long, but the crowd and the cigar smoke had already poured into the lobby.

Evan gallantly pushed his way through, cutting a path for the ladies. Toni was close behind, resting her hand on his back, presumably not to lose him in the crowd. The McKinney Alitzer group, who had taken over one end of the large, oval bar, let out a hurrah at the sight of their missing compatriots. They were especially glad to see Iris. They had taken full advantage of her largesse and had ordered ample hors d'oeuvres, premium booze, and good cigars. They'd promised the establishment that a credit card was due to arrive.

Iris presented her credit card to the bartender. "Could you please run a tab for the McKinney Alitzer group? And I'll have a glass of the house chard."

Liz pressed in front of Iris, who was cramming a piece of oily focaccia into her mouth. "The house cab, please."

"What would you like?" Evan asked Toni.

"Diet Coke."

"That it shall be." He leaned over the crowd and shouted to the bartender. "A diet Coke and what kind of Scotch do you have?"

"Glen Fiddich and Glenlivet."

"I'll have Glen Fiddich, straight up."

Amber Ambrose was posed on a barstool with her legs crossed, holding court. "There's plenty of money to be made in a bear market. The stocks of security firms haven't stopped skyrocketing since the crash of TWA Flight 800 and the bombing at the Atlanta Olympics." She took a sip of her mineral water with lime.

Evan passed Toni her diet Coke.

Toni tapped her glass against his. "Here's looking at you."

"And at you." He smiled back.

"Where are you from?" she asked.

"I was raised in California."

Toni smiled flirtatiously at him, but he seemed more interested in Amber's conversation.

"Amber's made a fortune capitalizing on life's dark side," Kyle explained to Toni and Evan. His long lips twitched with amusement. "She was one of the first to leap on companies specializing in hospice care."

Amber defended herself. "With the aging of the population and no cure for AIDS in sight, hospices are only going to get bigger. You should have got in on Compcare's IPO when I told you about it. From an opening price of eleven dollars, it's been holding steady around forty-five, even in this market."

Kyle continued, clearly enjoying rattling Amber's cage, "Now Amber's hawking the stock of a firm who opened a chain of shops that sell spy equipment—listening devices, stun guns, invisible ink, bulletproof clothing—I don't know what all."

"I'm just leaping on a trend," Amber responded. "The point I was trying to make was that there's plenty of money to be made in a bear market."

"I agree with that," Evan interjected.

Everyone seemed surprised that he had joined in.

"Lately, the bear market doomsayers are enjoying talking about how overvalued blue chips are now and how a similar situation existed in '73 when the market peaked at a thousand fifty-one. By December of '74, the Dow had plunged to five hundred seventy-seven, a forty-five percent drop. It took almost *ten years* for the index to get back to its 1973 peak."

A pall fell over the group. The brokers silently stared into their drinks. Few were old enough to remember the last great bear. Most had entered the profession during the nineties bull market in which all boats floated. The seasoned veterans who had survived shared war stories.

"The blue chips turned into blue gyps," one man said.

Another shook his head. "Between '73 and '84, stocks were

cold. People were putting their money into oil partnerships and real estate, for Christ's sake."

"Everything you bought just sat there and looked at ya."

Evan sipped his Scotch and set the glass back on the bar. "But Amber's right—there *is* money to be made in a bear market. During every year since '75, the Nasdaq composite rose. The smaller companies were able to react much faster to changing economic conditions. Even blue chips did well if they sold for a low price-to-earnings ratio." He picked up his glass again.

Iris was impressed as she listened to Evan. He knew his stuff.

Toni seemed awestruck.

"We have to work smarter," Amber said. "The key is to diversify your stock holdings: big and small, growth and value, and don't forget the foreign issues."

Iris picked up her almost full wineglass from the bar. "Foreign markets frequently move in the opposite—" She quickly turned and bumped into Evan, spilling both his drink and her own on him. "I'm so sorry!"

Toni immediately procured a napkin and started dabbing Evan's suit.

Iris set her wineglass on the bar, plucked Evan's glass from his hand, and told the bartender, "Another Scotch, please," as she grabbed the napkins he offered. She joined Toni in patting napkins against the spilled booze on Evan's suit, at the same time managing to conceal Evan's empty glass in a napkin and handing it to Liz, who was standing next to her. "Hold this," she whispered.

"Ladies, c'mon," Evan protested. "I like all the attention, but this is nothing."

Iris gave Toni a quick shove. "Why don't you go over by the rest rooms where there's more light?"

Toni didn't need any encouragement. She grabbed Evan's hand and led him away from the crowd.

Iris turned to Liz. "Keep the party going. I'll be back in a minute." Iris took the glass from Liz and slipped it inside her jacket, holding it underneath her armpit.

"What are you up to?"

"I'll be back in a few. If anyone asks, tell them I had to make a phone call."

* * *

Iris cautiously walked through the sales department. Apparently, everyone who hadn't gone to Julie's had left for home. She deposited Evan's glass, still wrapped in the napkin, in her briefcase.

Wasting no time, she went to Evan's cubicle. Before she touched anything in his briefcase, she formed a mental picture of its position so she'd be able to return it to the exact location. She started rummaging. Her initial examination yielded nothing out of the ordinary: today's *Wall Street Journal,* a rubber-banded stack of personal bills, a *Business Week,* and a thick list of names and telephone numbers. From a pocket in the top, she pulled a manila folder full of sheets of light blue paper in a heavy bond. She rifled them with her thumb. The Canterbury Investments stationery letterhead was imprinted in raised navy blue letters and gave a West Los Angeles street address.

She jumped when she thought she heard the front door open, almost dropping the stack of papers. The stationery was printed with statements of account activity, not unlike those issued by McKinney Alitzer or any other financial services firm. They tracked buys, sells, dividends, and changes in market value of individual investors' portfolios for the previous month.

Iris selected one that showed a fair amount of activity and took it to the photocopy machine on the other side of the suite near the lunchroom. She'd made her copy and was on her way to put the original back when she heard the soft whine of the suite's glass front door opening. She turned to make sure and saw Evan walking toward her.

She continued past Evan's desk and proceeded to her office, folding the statement and photocopy into small squares as she walked.

"Hey!" Evan called out to her. "Thought you were making a phone call downstairs."

She shoved the papers into her jacket pocket. "It was too noisy."

He walked over to her. "I wanted to thank you for inviting me to have a drink with you guys."

"I'm sorry I spilled it on you."

"Don't worry about that. I'm glad you talked me into coming."

She jammed her thumb into her pocket, forcing down a blue edge of paper that was still visible. "It was my pleasure. Welcome aboard."

"What luck I've had lately. One minute, I'm new to LA without a job, and the next thing I know, Sam Eastman's offering me a big signing bonus."

"Five thousand dollars, right?" Iris wanted to make sure she was clear on what Evan considered big.

"Five thousand?" Evan made a face. "Try fifty thousand."

Iris gaped at him then quickly recovered. "Fifty?"

"You didn't know?"

"No, no, of course I . . . ah . . . You must have been pleased to find out you're worth that much in the marketplace."

"Heck, yeah. I know I have tremendous potential, but I'm new in the industry and don't have much of a track record yet so I was surprised that you and Sam thought I was worth that much."

"Fifty is good dough." She casually leaned against a sales assistant's desk. "How did you get hooked up with Sam Eastman?"

"Yale Huxley at the firm where I used to work gave Sam a call." He eyed her boldly. "I get the impression you weren't aware that Sam was recruiting me."

Iris tried to meet his stare as she had in the elevator, but couldn't make it stick. Her gaze darted away. She couldn't tell him the truth, that against her better judgment she'd caved in to Sam's wishes thinking she'd score a political gain. "Of course I was."

His brown eyes still rested on her. "Okay."

She could tell he didn't believe her. She was a lousy liar.

"You run a nice office." He walked to his cubicle.

She hopped after him, hearing him snap the brass fasteners on his briefcase closed just as she reached his desk. "Aren't you going back down to join the party?"

"I've got too many things to do. I'll see you tomorrow." He grabbed the handle of the smooth, black leather briefcase, swung it off the desk, and walked down the corridor, turning to wave as he disappeared into the reception area.

She shouted, "See you tomorrow."

After she heard the heavy glass door swing open on its creaky hinge then close again, she pulled the Canterbury Investments statement from her pocket.

Kip Cross sat behind a heavy wood desk in a cozy room of his house that Bridget had used as her office. Thick, exposed beams cut across the low ceiling. A large stone fireplace extended the entire length of the room. The furniture was overstuffed and comfortable. The turquoise blue shutters that decorated the windows of every room of the house were closed here. The rain pounded against them. It had been raining all day with no end in sight.

The only light in the room was given by the eucalyptus logs burning in the fireplace and the computer monitor on the desk. Kip hadn't touched the keyboard for many minutes and a screen-saver program displayed colorful, exploding fireworks. He stared at the screen without seeing it, his right hand massaging his left eyebrow, his upper body rocking, the rhythm as steady as a metronome.

He suddenly looked at the ceiling as if he'd only then become aware of the pounding rain. He scanned the ceiling, listening, as if the rain were speaking to him. He slowly rose from the chair, unlocked the iron bolt lock on the thick door, and walked into the arched main corridor of the house. It was dimly illuminated by electric candle sconces set along the wall. He crossed the tiled foyer, went down the three steps that led to the family room, his rubber flip-flops squeaking slightly against the tiles, opened one of the French doors that led to the patio, and walked into the rain as if it weren't there. His jeans and T-shirt quickly became soaked.

In the poolhouse, he removed the long, hooked pole from the wall. At the patio gate, he entered the code to deactivate the alarm and stepped outside onto the cement staircase. The rain was pounding so hard, the narrow, gray stairs were almost invisible. There was no moon or other natural or artificial light to guide him, but he had been up and down those stairs so many times that he didn't need light.

He hopped down sixteen steps, the rainwater swirling around his ankles, until he reached the fifty-fourth step up from Capri

Road. There he wriggled between the steel railings. The blanket of dead leaves and pine needles had been washed away, leaving slick mud behind. His flip-flops created a suction with the mud, almost causing him to pitch face forward as he struggled to walk. He finally pulled the rubber shoes from his feet and stretched to set them on the stairs, where they were quickly washed away by the rushing water.

Grasping the mud with his toes and using the pole end of the pool hook as a cane to avoid slipping, he walked to the storm drain, struggling to remain upright on the steep slope. He set the pool hook on the ground next to the drain, quickly grabbing it again before the light plastic was swept down the hill. He awkwardly tucked the pole under his arm and straddled the drain. He pulled the drain sections apart without too much difficulty as the rain had worked fine sand underneath the sleeve that held them together. Water rushed from the drain's open end. He slipped onto his knees. He got up, fed the hook inside the drain and pulled it out, finding nothing. It had been washed clean. He angrily kicked the drain with his bare foot, almost losing his balance.

Leaning on the pool hook with one hand and trailing his other against the stair railing for balance, he inched his way down the muddy hillside. The open end of the drain jutted over the edge of a retaining wall four feet above the street. He climbed over the wall and jumped down to the street below. His arms and legs were covered in mud. He looked to the left and right. It was the wee hours of the morning and the houses along the street were dark. No one was around.

He fed the pole into the open end of the drain, fished around, and pulled it out—coming up with nothing but wet debris. He was standing in a pile of wet leaves, pine needles, and mud that had washed from the drain. He dragged the hook around in it, finally hitting something solid. He dug his hands in the muck and pulled out a handgun.

Chapter 27

It was still raining when Iris opened her front door to retrieve her newspaper. She looked at the rain and her flooded lawn and flowerbeds and at the Triumph parked in the driveway. She had never replaced the badly corroded rubber seals around the frame that held the ragtop in place. The car was bound to be damp inside. She worried about this and about the other job she should have done before the rains came—shoring up her backyard. It wasn't supposed to be raining like this. It was supposed to be a dry winter.

Mulling over these and a million other things to do, she started to dash from the house to get the paper, but stopped when she almost stumbled over a box on the front porch. About a foot square, it was wrapped in glossy pale pink paper and had a large white bow on top. There were no stamps or address. It had to have been hand-delivered during the night. She looked without touching it and noticed that the box's bottom and lid were wrapped separately, with the ribbon tied just around the lid, like a television show gift that can be opened without any of the wrappings torn, leaving the package looking pretty.

She cautiously stepped around it, visions of the Unabomber

dancing in her head. She toyed with the idea of calling the police, but decided it was probably a housewarming gift from Liz. It looked like something Liz would do, dropping off an elaborately wrapped gift on her way home from some gala.

Still, she went back inside the house and retrieved a broom. Holding the front door partially closed as a shield, she hooked the broom handle underneath the lid, counted to three, and flipped it off. She screamed and slammed the door as something exploded into the air. Within seconds, her phone rang.

"Iris, love!" Marge cried. "Are you all right? Did I hear you scream?"

Iris was panting. "Just a second." She peeked through her living room blinds at the front porch and laughed with relief. "It's nothing. Someone's playing a joke. There was a package left on my front porch full of those exploding snakes. Thanks for calling. I'm fine."

Iris went back outside and looked at the long snakes of accordioned yellow, blue, and red tissue paper that now covered the front porch and were growing soggy. One had a small, folded piece of white paper attached to it. The note had apparently weighted down this snake, as the end still dangled inside in the box. She leaned over and picked up the note from the end that lay on the porch. The typed message said, *Wrong move! Mind your own business or your next move might be your last.*

She heard a sound that she at first thought was rain flowing through the gutter leading from the roof. Then she realized it was coming from somewhere much closer at hand. She peeked inside the box. A snake, not of tissue paper, was coiled there, shaking its rattle.

"It could have been any one of a number of people who think I'm too involved in their business: T. Duke Saywer, Summer Fontaine, Evan Finn, the managers at Pandora who want me to sell to T. Duke . . ." Iris looked into her mug of coffee and trailed off. "Or Kip Cross."

Detective Tiffany Stubbs was taking notes on a small, spiral-bound pad. "This is the first time since Bridget Cross's murder that anyone has threatened you?"

Iris nodded. "I wish I knew where that rattlesnake went. I don't want to meet it again in one of my closets."

"Too bad the animal control people couldn't find it. Like the guy said, it'll probably find itself a nice home in the brush around here." Stubbs flipped the notebook closed and slipped it and her pen into her purse.

"Lovely."

Stubbs pinched her fingernails against the edge of the threatening note, picked it up, and dropped it inside a brown paper bag. "Looks like it was produced on a laser or ink-jet printer. Virtually impossible to track to an individual machine. I miss the days of the manual typewriter. But we can test the note and the box for fingerprints."

She started to get up and Iris put her hand out as if to prevent her. "Look, Detective, I'm positive this Evan Finn guy has some connection to T. Duke Sawyer."

Stubbs stood in spite of Iris's admonition and slipped the strap of her handbag over her shoulder, as if she wasn't particularly interested in what Iris had to say about Finn. "Ms. Thorne, I'm sorry about any difficult situations you have at your office. I know how trying things like that can be, but I don't see any connection between this Evan Finn and the Bridget Cross and Alexa Platt murders."

"But he might have a *huge* connection!"

Stubbs pursed her lips. She was getting annoyed.

Iris went on, "I have a cocktail glass with Finn's fingerprints. Please—"

Stubbs put her hand up, cutting Iris off. "I'm sorry, but I'm working on six murders right now. I don't have time for this."

Iris stood also. She had quickly changed from her nightclothes into jeans and a sweater before Stubbs arrived. "Maybe you have time for this. Brianna Cross has been drawing pictures of what she saw the night of the murder." Iris had Stubbs's attention now. "I have them."

"And you didn't immediately turn them over to us?"

"I only got them yesterday. I didn't have to tell you about them at all."

"Fair enough. Give me the glass with the fingerprints."

"Thanks," Iris said with relief. She left the room and returned with Brianna's drawings and the cocktail glass that she'd sealed into a Ziploc bag.

Stubbs eagerly looked through the drawings. "I'm going to petition the court to have Brianna interviewed by a psychologist whether Kip approves of it or not."

"He's still your main suspect?"

Stubbs dropped the glass into her large purse. "Ms. Thorne, he's our only suspect."

"Poor Iris!" Toni commiserated. "Who would do such a terrible thing to you?"

"Seems like someone's playing *Suckers Finish Last* for real."

They were sitting in Toni's office at Pandora.

"The vipers' nest is in the second level," Toni said. "Whoever's behind this is very clever, I have to hand him that."

"And very sick."

"Maybe."

"How's the temperature around here?" Iris asked.

Toni rolled her eyes. "Mick and Today are mad at Kip, mad at you, they're just tweaked in general. They don't think you know what you're doing and feel like no one's running the company. I told them to show a little compassion. I reminded them that if it wasn't for Kip, there would be no Pandora. He still has contributions to make to the firm. He's almost finished a new graphics accelerator engine, and from what he says, it's brilliant."

Toni pulled her legs underneath her to sit cross-legged on the rolling desk chair. She was wearing a long purple sweater, black leggings, and lace-up boots. "And I told them to give you a break. You didn't ask for Pandora—it fell into your lap. I told them I've been helping you as much as I can, and I'm happy to do it."

"I appreciate it, Toni. I don't know what I'd do without you."

"I was kind of hoping to become indispensable."

Iris sensed more was coming, having long suspected there was a method to Toni's madness.

Seeming to recognize her demeanor was less than professional, Toni put her feet on the floor, sat up straight, and looked at Iris with a sober expression. "I know you're recruiting someone to run Pandora. Give me a chance, Iris."

Iris let her go on.

"I don't pretend for a minute that I could immediately step into Bridget's shoes, but with a little time, I know I could. I know the players, I know the culture. You might find someone with more experience, but I know how *this* company works and what makes it work."

As dippy as Toni frequently appeared, right now she was coming off as controlled, clear, and assertive.

Toni went for the close. "What do you say?"

"You make some good points, Toni. You've given me a lot to think about, and I will think about it."

Toni looked at Iris as if she was expecting more. When nothing more was forthcoming, she said, "That's all I hoped for. Thanks." After a few prickly seconds, she changed the subject. "Guess who I went out with last night?"

"Baines?"

"Evan Finn!"

Iris wasn't completely surprised. Toni seemed to have a problem with looking for love in all the wrong places.

Toni's professional demeanor disappeared and she giggled again. "Thanks *so* much for inviting me to have drinks with you guys. I'm *so* happy I met Evan. He's *wonder*ful!" she gushed. "We're going out again tonight."

Iris was less enthusiastic. "You didn't ask my opinion, but I'd go slowly with him. Frankly, I'm not too sure about him at all."

"What do you mean?" Toni asked, her eyes impossibly naive.

"I don't think he's everything he pretends to be. I don't want you to get hurt."

Toni bristled. "Easy for you to say, Iris. You already have a man."

Iris let the subject drop. It was clear that advising Toni to examine her taste in men was as pointless as telling Liz to eat more. Iris looked at her watch. "It's showtime."

They left Toni's office and traveled down the catwalk to the computer lab. Kip, Today, and Mick were already there, sitting in front of an extralarge computer monitor, engrossed in what was displayed there. Summer was there also, standing behind them, appearing interested in the goings-on but easily distracted when Toni and Iris came in. The men seemed unaware of them.

Summer smiled at Iris and then at Toni, who gave her a cool look in response. Summer petulantly shrugged a shoulder and dimmed her eyes at her.

"It's neat, Kip," Mick enthused. "Really cool."

"The UI is a little dicey," Today said.

"It's a rough prototype," Kip responded. "I took some of our existing graphics and adapted it just to give you an idea of how the engine works."

"UI?" Iris whispered to Toni.

"User interface," Toni whispered back.

"You haven't seen the best part yet. Watch this." Kip moved the screen image so it looked as if the player were approaching a precipice. The player then went over the edge, free-falling through the air. The screen image tumbled and turned, shifting between sky and landscape as the ground grew closer.

"Wow!" Mick exclaimed.

"Now *that's* new!" Today said appreciatively.

"Just terrific," Iris added.

Toni put her hand against her forehead. "That can really make you motion sick."

The screen image moved still closer to the ground. Then there was impact.

"Whoa!" Today shouted as he thrust both hands into the air. "Un-fucking-believable, man! How the hell did you do that?"

"It's high image resolution and speed," Mick said. "I've never seen anything like it."

"Show it again," Toni said.

Kip diffidently turned back to the keyboard. "Okay."

Summer looked at her watch. "Kip, don't forget you promised to take Brianna to that birthday party in Glendale. You need to pick her up by two."

"I know." Kip restarted the falling sequence. "I discovered a new way of caching that increases the graphics response on the currently available hardware. It was one of those things that was almost too obvious."

"My algorithm!"

No one had seen Banzai come into the room. When he

crossed the floor, everyone instinctively stepped out of the way, clearing a path to Kip.

Kip turned from the computer and asked no one in particular, "How did he get in here?"

"Who are you, man?" Today asked.

"He's a nut," Kip said. "He's been calling me and hanging around the house." He glared at Banzai. "You'd better get out of here, before I call the cops."

Banzai pointed at the computer screen. "You stole my algorithm. I showed it to you so you'd give me a job here. And you stole it!"

"Me—steal from you?" Kip looked at Banzai derisively. "Your stuff had some possibilities, that's all. Don't flatter yourself."

Everyone looked from Kip to Banzai. Toni walked to a phone, dialed a number, and spoke quietly into it.

"I know my work!" Banzai pointed at the monitor. "That's my work!"

"No, that's *my* work. You and I happened to have a similar idea, that's all." Kip's face was growing red. "Happens all the time."

Banzai grabbed handfuls of his hair, stumbled across the floor, and screamed, "Liar!"

"Dude, calm down." Today held his hands out pacifyingly.

"You're getting scary, man," Kip said. His forehead was beaded with perspiration. "You'd better get out of here before there's trouble."

"I idolized you."

A security guard arrived and grabbed Banzai, who pulled free. The guard again grabbed Banzai, twisting the young man's arm behind him, and started dragging him toward the door.

Banzai yelled, "Kip Cross is a has-been! Get out before he rips you off and takes credit for your work!" His cries echoed in the cavernous hangar until he was outside the building.

Chapter 28

Holding her trench coat over her head, Iris dashed from her driveway through the rain to her front door. Dripping wet, she unlocked the door, stepped inside, and eagerly bolted it behind her. She was finally safe. The rain, traffic, mud, snakes, and attitudes were outside and she was inside. Although she wasn't too certain about the snake.

She slipped off her soaked, well-worn pumps that she had selected that day because they were already beat-up and left them next to the door. Her stockings were soaked through and she left wet footprints on the hardwood floor when she walked into her bedroom. She stripped off her clothes and put on her thick terry cloth bathrobe. In the bathroom, she examined her rain-soaked suit and hung it on the shower rod where it hadn't a prayer of drying in the damp air. She flipped on the heater built into the wall. The wires soon glowed red. She turned her back and stood close to the heat until her legs grew prickly, then she sat on the tile floor in front of it. She was just starting to feel delightfully hot when the phone rang. She had no intention of answering it but flew to grab it when she heard Garland's voice on the answering machine.

"Garland, I'm so glad it's you. I've had such a terrible day."

"You poor little pumpkin, you," he cooed. "Tell me all about it."

She did—not leaving out a single comma, raised eyebrow, or raindrop—and he listened without interrupting. After listening in turn to the events of his day, she broached the issue of Pandora, T. Duke Sawyer, and USA Assets. "Do you know Clinton Cormier?"

"Old Clint! Sure. He works for one of the old-line investment banks in Manhattan."

"What about Darvis Brown?"

"I don't know him, but I know people who do. These guys are investors in USA Assets?"

"According to Baines. He says the group has four investors: Darvis Brown, Clinton Cormier, Yale Huxley, and T. Duke Sawyer."

"All prominent businessmen," Garland said. "Why would they want to keep their affiliation with a venture capital enterprise secret?"

"I can't imagine why either, unless they're involved in something they don't want to broadcast. I know for a fact Darvis Brown is a prominent member of the Trust Makers. Is Clinton Cormier a Trust Makers kind of guy?"

"He doesn't seem like he'd be involved in something like that, but who knows? I've been meaning to call Clint for the longest time to have lunch anyway. I'll call him, see what I can find out for you. I'll put some feelers out on the other guys, too."

"Thanks. What about Canterbury Investments? Ever hear of them?"

"Nope, but I'll ask around. Anything else I can do to be of service?"

"Well, there is one small thing, but you're not here."

"My goodness, pumpkin."

After Iris ended her call with Garland, she warmed up a can of low-calorie, low-salt soup in the microwave. It was so bland, she added salt to it. It was still bland, so she cut up a hot dog and added a dash of Tabasco. After simmering for a few minutes, it was downright palatable.

She flopped in her easy chair in front of the television, deciding she would do nothing but channel surf, read the newspaper, and look at some fashion magazines she'd just bought. Maybe she'd forget about the newspaper and just read the fashion magazines. Maybe she'd forget the magazines and just channel surf. She clicked through the channels, landing on one of several that broadcast in Spanish. It was a game show. The grand prize was $1,000 U.S., they made clear, and a new Honda Accord. The global village is here.

Before long, it became apparent she was too restless to relax. Even the "Agony" column in *Cosmopolitan* couldn't hold her interest. She went into her office and looked at the Canterbury Investments statement she'd stolen from Evan Finn's briefcase.

The statement was made out to a man named Otis Zajac, who lived in Meridian, Mississippi, and it detailed the account's activity. Mr. Zajac held shares in several blue-chip stocks and had a smattering of smaller high-tech issues. Last month, he purchased 7.645 shares of a pharmaceutical company that Iris herself would not have recommended because the firm had recently been sued in a large product-liability case.

The Canterbury Investments letterhead included a toll-free phone number. She picked up the telephone receiver, then put it back in its cradle, remembering that telephone statements for toll-free numbers list the calling party's number. She didn't want Evan to find out she was on to Canterbury Investments.

She picked up the phone again and called directory assistance to get the area code for Meridian, Mississippi. She then called directory assistance servicing that area. Soon, she had Otis Zajac's home number. A young-sounding woman answered.

"Is Mr. Zajac in?"

"Who's calling?"

"This is Miss ah . . ." Iris looked around for something to give her an idea. "Smith." She shrugged to herself. What the heck, it had been a long day. She wasn't feeling creative. "Miss Smith with Canterbury Investments. I'm doing a client satisfaction survey. Is Otis Zajac in?"

"Dad! Lady on the phone wants to talk to ya!" she shouted. "I'm his daughter," she explained.

"Do you know whether Mr. Zajac is happy with the service he's been receiving from Canterbury?"

"I believe so." She drawled her words in a way that made Iris feel hyped-up and impatient. "I try to watch over how he spends his money, but you know how independent old folks can be. I'd never heard of Canterbury Investments and told Dad to be careful. This guy called Dad out of the blue. Next thing I know, Dad's sending money to a total stranger. I told Dad I saw a show about con artists like that on TV, but you can't get him to listen once he gets his mind set. That was a couple of years ago. Guess everything's on the up-and-up. Gets these little dividend checks every so often. Here he is." She turned away from the phone. "She wants to talk to you about that Canterbury Investments."

"Hello? Yes. Good firm, Canterbury." His voice had the rough edge of old age. "That Evan Finn is an excellent stock picker. I've recommended him to several of my friends."

"Mr. Finn called you over the phone and asked you to send him money to invest, is that correct?"

"That's how she happened. He first called about three years ago."

"And you're happy with your return on your investment?"

"Ecstatic. Does my heart good to prove my daughter wrong. She and her husband think I don't have any brains left, that I can't think for myself anymore. But I've still got a few tricks up my sleeve. My investments increased thirty-seven percent last year. Thirty-seven percent!"

"Did you ask to see any references or check on Mr. Finn's broker's license before you sent him money?"

"I asked him. Of course I asked him. I wasn't born yesterday, you know. And I know there's lots of trash out there just waiting to rip off the old folks. He tells me he's employed with this big firm out in Nashville, Huxley Investments, and he's just doing this on the side to make a little extra money. He charges lower commissions than a big firm. He told me to feel free to check up on him, but don't mention Canterbury Investments because it could get him in trouble. Moonlighting, you know. I thought to myself, this sounds like a nice ambitious young man."

"Did you call Huxley Investments?"

"No, ma'am. Went on my gut instinct. I'm eighty-four years old. I wouldn't have made it this far if I hadn't trusted my instincts."

"Did you ever try to cash out any of your investments?"

"Very recently I did. I got a little spooked by this bear market everyone's starting to talk about and told Evan I think it's time to clear out of town. He said no. There's still lots of money to be made. He said he's so certain that he'll pay me five hundred bucks to ride it out."

Iris thanked him for his time and hung up. Zajac fit the profile of a target for financial con artists. The elderly who are lured into bogus investment schemes are not frail and feebleminded but tend to be fiercely independent.

Evan's scam was now clear to her. Clients write checks to Canterbury Investments, thinking they're sending money to a management firm that is going to invest it for them. Evan simply cashes their checks but covers his tracks by preparing official-looking statements of activity. He even periodically pays out dividends. If a client insists on cashing out, which Evan would actively discourage, he pays the client with funds from other clients. It was nothing more than a Ponzi scheme.

Sam Eastman was probably planning to blow the whistle on Evan after Evan got good and settled in her office. Even if Iris claimed to know nothing about the scam, her reputation would be tarnished, making it easy for Sam to remove her as branch manager. How did Sam find Evan and pay him $50,000? Louise had done some checking and found out the bonus was not paid by McKinney Alitzer. There was only one answer: T. Duke Sawyer. Question was, how did T. Duke find Evan?

Iris looked at the clock. It was 9:10 P.M., past her bedtime if she was going to get enough sleep before her alarm went off at 4:45 A.M. She needed more proof of Evan's scam. One statement from one client wasn't enough. The statement could disappear and the client could be bought off.

Canterbury Investments was located in a small business park in an industrial area of West LA. The office was situated in what appeared to be one of the less desirable, probably cheaper spots in a back corner near the trash bins. Iris was planning on just checking out the address to see if it really existed, but she couldn't resist peeking through the office's single window. There was a crack in the drapes but it was dark inside. She tried the doorknob. It was locked.

She was jiggling the doorknob for good measure when a security guard approached from behind, startling her. She had always been leery of rent-a-cops and felt none too safe in this remote, dark corner far from the street. She played it cool.

"Hi! I'm so glad you're here. I can't believe how stupid I am. My husband's going to *kill* me. He's packing to take the red-eye to New York tonight and he sent me to get something from his office, but I forgot the keys. If he doesn't have this folder for his meeting tomorrow, he's going to blow the deal he's been working on and I'm going to lose the new coat I wanted. Could you, *please?*" She pressed her hands together as if she was begging. She was.

He was young and had the inflated upper body of someone who lifts weights. She wondered what twisted personality flaw had prevented him from getting into the police or sheriff's department. "Well," he hemmed and hawed. "I'm not supposed to do anything like that."

"I know, and the last thing I want is to get you in trouble . . ." She gestured toward herself with both hands and broadly smiled. "Do I look like a thief?"

He chuckled. "Nah, I don't suppose you do." He pulled out a ring of keys attached to a retractable cable that was hooked on to his belt, sorted through them, and fitted one into the lock. "There you go."

"Thanks so much. I won't be a minute and I promise I'll lock up when I leave." She stepped into the office and slid her hand up and down the wall, desperately searching for the light switch. She finally found it and closed the door behind her. There was a chain lock inside the door. She fastened it, giving herself a false sense of security, knowing the guard would be able to bust it open with one butt of his overdeveloped shoulder.

She looked down and saw she was standing on mail strewn beneath the mail slot in the door. She quickly stepped off it, but the soles of her wet tennis shoes had left marks on some of the envelopes. She picked them up, dried them on her jeans, unable to completely remove the marks, and dropped them again.

The office held a minimum of modest furniture. There was a steel-sided desk, a worn, wheeled desk chair, two four-drawer filing cabinets, and a photocopy machine. She opened the top drawer of the desk and found a checkbook. In it were stubs made out for rent, utilities, pest control, and other routine bills. At the end of each month, a bunch of checks were made out for client dividends. Occasionally there was one labeled "account closed." In another drawer she found a handful of angry letters from clients. Many indicated they had instructed Evan to cash out their accounts but were still waiting for their money.

On a corner of a desk was the thick manila folder full of blue statements that Iris had found in Evan's briefcase. Since the office had no computer equipment, she suspected Evan hired a service to do the data entry and print the statements.

She switched on the photocopy machine and waited impatiently while it took a seemingly interminable amount of time to warm up. Finally, it indicated it was ready. It was an inexpensive desktop model without an automatic feeder, so she had to photocopy the statements one at a time. The light inside the machine slowly moved up and back down each sheet. She took a sample of about twenty statements, not daring to take the time to copy them all.

After she was finished, she put everything back where she had found it, at least where she thought she had found it. In her haste, she hadn't been as careful as she should have been. She grabbed her photocopies, turned off the lights, and went out the door.

She had almost locked the door behind her when she gasped, darted back inside, and shut off the photocopy machine. She was already in the Triumph when she spotted the guard. She cranked the ignition key, praying silently that the starter wouldn't act up. It didn't.

"Baby, I have to go."

"Nooo," Toni moaned. "Can't you spend the night?"

Evan got out of bed and started putting on his clothes. "I

have to be at work at the crack of dawn. I'd hate to wake you up on account of me. Plus I have a couple of errands to run before I go home."

"This late at night?"

"Busy, busy." He shrugged.

He left Toni's apartment and drove to the Canterbury Investments office. Inside the office, he turned on the lights and reached down to gather his mail. As he was picking it up, he noticed a few envelopes had footprints on them. He didn't think anything of it and continued gathering them into a pile. He tapped the edges of the assorted envelopes together against the desk, pulled a rubber band from his top desk drawer, and stretched it around the stack.

He'd switched off the lights and was outside with his hand on the doorknob when he spotted a piece of mail that had slid against the wall. He went back inside and bent over to pick it up, resting his hand on top of the photocopy machine for balance. It was warm.

He was locking the door when the security guard came by.

"Say," Evan said, "did you let anyone in here tonight?"

"Yeah, your wife. Hope it was okay."

Evan's expression didn't change. "Tall, good-looking, in her thirties?"

"Yeah. There's no problem, is there?"

"That's her. Do you know when she left?"

"Couldn't have been more than a few minutes ago."

Iris drove home. She had just turned into her driveway when she heard sirens coming up the street behind her. She watched as an LAPD black-and-white and a plain sedan, both with their sirens and lights going, sped past, made the sharp turn on Capri Court, then switchbacked onto Capri Road. They stopped at what appeared to be the bottom of the steps that led to the Cross house. Iris could see the flashing lights through the trees.

Ignoring the pouring rain, she ran up the eighty steps that connected her street, Casa Marina Drive, with Capri Road, jumping over the overgrown vines, weeds, and broken steps. At Capri Road, the police were cordoning off an area with yellow plastic ribbon. A few neighbors had wandered out from their homes to see what was going on. They were peering at the bottom of the steps. She crept closer, pushing her way through the small crowd. Banzai's head was twisted backward on his neck. A thin line of blood trailed from his mouth, across his cheek, and onto the cement steps.

Detectives Tiffany Stubbs and Jess Ortiz were asking if anyone in the crowd knew the dead man.

"I do," Iris said. She looked toward the mansion at the top of the hill.

Chapter 29

Detectives Stubbs and Ortiz rang the doorbell at the Cross house. The big house did not have a porch to shield them from the pouring rain. They stood with their shoulders hunkered, their hands deep inside the pockets of their slickers.

Stubbs's hat had a broad brim, but the edges of her hair were soaked anyway, the thick, dark strands lying lank against her collar. "This is the moment I've been waiting for," she muttered. "Too bad another body had to drop before we could get that SOB."

Ortiz wore a crushable hat, in the same fabric as his slicker, pulled down tight on his almost bald head. "Wonder how long that kid had been laying there before the homeless guy found him."

Stubbs picked up the door's heavy brass knocker and pounded it loudly several times. "Iris Thorne said Banzai Jefferson was escorted out of the Pandora offices around one-fifteen. It's about a forty-five minute drive in the best conditions from the west side to here. Say it took him an hour. That would place the time of death between two-fifteen and when we found him." She again loudly pounded the knocker.

A light went on at the far end of the house.

"Seems incredible that the kid could have laid there in the middle of the day without anyone seeing him," Ortiz said.

"It poured rain all day. No one's walking around. The moms around here have their kids overinvolved in activities. Probably hardly anyone is home until it's almost dark." Stubbs looked at a beat-up Volkswagen Rabbit parked near Kip's house. "Wonder if that's the kid's car."

Kip Cross opened the door. He was wearing a quilted, red satin bathrobe with deep cuffs and a monogram on the breast. His expression indicated that the detectives were the last people he wanted to see.

The officers didn't need to introduce themselves. Stubbs said, "Mr. Cross, can we come inside and ask you a few questions?"

"What's this about?"

"Sir, can we come inside?" Stubbs again asked.

Without a word, Kip turned and walked into the house. He crossed the tiled foyer and padded in his bare feet down the three tile steps into the family room.

The detectives followed, closing the door behind them. Rain dripped from their clothing onto the floor.

Kip didn't seem to care. He didn't extend an offer for them to remove their raingear or sit down. He undid the sash of his robe, opened it, and readjusted it, pulling it tightly around himself before tying the sash again. He was nude under the robe and wasn't modest about displaying it. He flicked his hands out, gesturing for the detectives to begin.

Stubbs started. "Do you know a man named Banzai Jefferson?"

"Slightly."

The detectives were closely watching him, trying to determine whether he knew the reason for this midnight visit. "We just found him dead at the bottom of the staircase next to your house."

Kip stared at the ground with his hands on his hips as if trying to process what he'd just heard.

Stubbs and Ortiz exchanged a glance. Stubbs arched one of her eyebrows. The rain pounded against the roof and windows.

Kip impatiently ran his hand over his bristly hair. "What happened?"

"Mr. Jefferson either fell or was pushed," Stubbs said. "It appears his neck is broken."

Ortiz unsnapped his slicker, reached inside his jacket pocket, and took out a spiral-bound notebook that had a pen stuck through the wires. He began making notes.

"When?" Kip asked.

"A homeless man found him about an hour ago. We understand he was at your office between about one to one-fifteen this afternoon."

Kip said nothing.

Stubbs continued, "We also understand that during this time there was an altercation between you and Mr. Jefferson."

"Who told you this?"

"Iris Thorne."

Kip fumed.

"She said Mr. Jefferson accused you of stealing something from him. Some computer program."

"His algorithm—a section of software code. I didn't steal anything from him." Kip walked backward a few feet and dropped into a large leather chair. He didn't invite the detectives to sit. He folded his arms across his chest and began stroking his eyebrow, staring at a point a few feet ahead.

Stubbs seemed pleased with Kip's apparent distress. "Can you tell us your whereabouts after you left Pandora this afternoon?"

Kip continued staring, answering the detective without looking up. "I was in a meeting at Pandora until one-thirty, then I left and came home to pick up my daughter to take her to a birthday party in Glendale."

"When did you leave for the party?" Stubbs asked.

"Two o'clock."

"When did you arrive?"

"Four." Kip put his elbows on his knees and rested his head between his hands.

"It took you two hours to get to Glendale in the middle of the day? Even in this weather it shouldn't take more than an hour."

Kip pulled his hands from his face. "There was traffic! It was pouring rain. There was an accident. This is LA, remember?"

Stubbs casually put her hands behind her back, her slicker rustling as the nylon rubbed together. "Anyone see you leave the house?"

Kip thought for a minute. "Summer, my daughter's nanny."

Stubbs, amused by how Kip had described Summer when everyone knew she was more than just the nanny, smirked slightly at Ortiz, who didn't respond.

"Summer came home from shopping when Brianna and I were leaving," Kip said.

"And you arrived at the birthday party at four."

"I just told you that. Call and ask them."

"Afterward, you brought your daughter straight home."

Kip bolted from the chair. "Oh, I get it. I get it now. You think *I* murdered that kid. I'm calling my attorney. Shit, Kip. You never learn, do you? Fucking cops."

"We'll wait while you call your attorney."

"I did not kill Banzai!" he shouted. "I left my office, came home, and drove my daughter to a birthday party. Then we came home, had dinner, and were here all night. No one came by. The last time I saw Banzai was at Pandora this afternoon."

Summer came into the room. She was wearing an embroidered kimono of white silk. The clingy fabric accentuated her nipples, a detail that did not get past Ortiz.

Her partner's interest seemed to irritate Stubbs.

"What's going on?" Summer asked in her little girl's voice.

"They found that kid, Banzai, dead at the bottom of the steps," Kip explained.

The skin on Summer's forehead folded slightly. "What happened?"

"He either fell or was pushed, according to the cops," Kip said. "They think I had something to do with it. Tell them how you saw me leaving for the birthday party with Brianna."

Brianna appeared at the top of the tile steps in a flannel nightgown, clutching a worn teddy bear.

Summer rushed toward her. "Sweetie, go back to bed."

"What do they want?" she asked, recognizing the detectives.

"Don't worry." Summer pushed the girl's tangled hair from her face. "Everything's okay."

"Can I have some milk?"

"Go ahead, sweetie," Summer said. "Go in the kitchen, have your milk, and go to bed."

When Brianna had left, Summer continued, "I came home from shopping just as Kip and Brianna were leaving. It was three o'clock."

"Three o'clock," Stubbs repeated.

"Three?" Kip bellowed. "It was not three o'clock, you fucking idiot!" He opened and closed his fists and took a step toward Summer. She took a step back. The detectives looked ready to separate them.

"It was two! Two, two, two! Pea brain!"

Summer stammered, "Uh . . . That's right, that's right. It was two o'clock. Kip's right."

"Don't open that idiot mouth of yours again until my attorney gets here. I'm going to call him right now." Kip stormed from the room.

Summer seemed stunned and kept repeating, "It was two. He's right. I don't know what I was thinking."

Ortiz put his notebook away. "Don't worry about it."

"Mind if I look around?" Stubbs asked.

Summer shrugged. "I don't care. I can't speak for Kip."

Stubbs walked up the tile steps and down the corridor in the same direction Brianna had gone.

Summer began to quietly weep.

Ortiz shifted uneasily from foot to foot. Then he followed Stubbs.

"U, V, W, X, Y, and Z. Now I know my ABCs. Tell me what you think of me." Brianna was sitting on a stool at a bar that ran along one side of the kitchen, dunking graham crackers into a glass of milk that had a layer of brown sludge at the bottom. She held a cracker in the milk too long and it broke in half inside the glass. She was trying to fish it out with her fingers when Stubbs came in. "Do you carry a gun?"

"Yes."

"Have you ever shot anybody?"

Ortiz walked into the kitchen.

"No, no. Fortunately I've never had to use my gun," Stubbs said.

Brianna gave up on the soggy cracker and immersed a fresh one into the milk.

Stubbs walked closer to the girl. "Brianna, can you tell time?"

"Tiffany," Ortiz warned.

"Of course," Brianna said brightly. "I know how to tell time, and I know all my ABCs, and I can print them all too, in big and little letters."

"That's excellent!"

"I know how to use the computer too."

"Very good. Look, do you remember today when you went to the birthday party?"

"It was Joshua's party. Caitlin won at pin the tail on the donkey, but I saw her peek. That's not fair, is it? I told my daddy and he said that life's not fair."

"Sometimes it's not. Do you know what time it was when you left to go to the party?"

"What the hell do you think you're doing?" Kip grabbed Brianna and swept her from the stool into his arms. She began to wail. "Trying to get information out of my daughter. You're on thin ice."

"Not as thin as what you're skating on, Mr. Cross." Stubbs walked from the room with Ortiz following. "We'll be in touch."

Sam Eastman answered his door wearing his pajamas and robe. He'd looked through the peephole before opening up, so he already knew who was calling. "What do you want? Do you know what time it is?"

"You set me up." Evan Finn was standing underneath the front porch roof. The rain was still coming down.

"What the hell are you talking about?"

"You know damned well what I'm talking about!" Evan shouted.

Across the street, a dog with a deep voice started to bark. Another one elsewhere in the neighborhood chimed in.

An upstairs window slid open and a woman looked through the screen. "Sam? What's going on out there?"

"Nothing, Janice. Go back to bed. I'll be up in a minute." He turned to Evan. "Wait a second." He disappeared briefly inside the house, then pushed past him. "Come on." He cut across the rain-saturated front yard. As he was walking, he pointed a clicker at the garage door and it automatically opened. He squeezed past the two cars parked there until he reached a high, long worktable. Tools were hung from a Peg-Board nailed against the wall above it.

Evan surveyed Sam's empire. "Nice house, two cars—kids have good bicycles. Nice comfortable life. I bet you want to keep it."

"Tell me what you want before I call the police."

"I was suspicious when you offered me fifty grand to join McKinney. You didn't even start at a lower figure. Even if I really had worked at Huxley Investments, I didn't have the credentials to merit that kind of dough." Evan strolled past the worktable, picking up and examining tools.

"What do you mean, if you'd really worked at Huxley?"

"Don't tell me you believed everything in my résumé. How much did he tell you about me?"

"Who?"

Evan smiled. "Don't bullshit me, Sam." He picked up a power drill, plugged in the cord, and pulsed the starter lever.

Sam cringed at the noise.

Evan haphazardly drilled a hole into the worktable. "I knew the deal was too sweet. I should have listened to my instincts. But hope springs eternal. I thought he'd finally come around, decided to cut me some slack for once in his life. Use his connections to set me up with blue-blood references. Even a Harvard degree. Imagine that! Me, the family screwup, a Harvard grad. All I had to do was stay away. Sounds easy, huh? Just stay the hell away."

Evan brushed sawdust from the hole he'd drilled and examined his work. "I thought, California's a big state. Apparently it's not big enough for the two of us, though. Funny thing about families. They might be the most messed up people you've ever seen in your life, but you still want the bond."

It was cold in the damp garage, but Sam wiped perspiration from his forehead with the cuff of his robe.

Evan set the drill down. Sam quietly exhaled with relief.

"That brings us to Iris. She didn't want to hire me. She didn't know the first thing about me. It didn't take her long to figure out there's some ulterior motive for my being there—and there is, isn't there? It's too bad. She's a nice person and she works hard."

Sam looked pale under the garage's fluorescent lights. "Evan, it's late. Let's talk tomorrow."

"Stop playing stupid with me! What did he promise you? Money, a job, women, drugs?"

Sam swallowed hard, sensing the jig was up. "Money."

"Money. But the money was just frosting, wasn't it? The real pull was the possibility of bringing Iris down. I know all about your little feud with her. It's a big topic at the office. Or maybe you thought it was hot to hobnob with the rich and powerful. You're not alone." Evan shook his head with amazement. "He's clever, I'll hand him that. He wants Iris in a vise so she'll cave in and sell Pandora to him for a song. You want her ruined. He wants me gone. Very efficient use of manpower. T. Duke Sawyer knows how to maximize his resources."

"Who *are* you?"

"He didn't tell you?" Evan considered that possibility. "Probably not. He works on a need-to-know basis. I'm the prodigal son who's come home. Coming home wasn't part of the deal, see? Now he has to exact retribution. I knew he'd do something, but I had no idea I'd play right into his hand."

"You're his son? And he's setting you up like this?"

"Who did you think I was?"

"I don't know. Some thug he hired. You sure don't look like you're related to T. Duke."

"I was adopted. So were my two sisters. Story is, the old lady couldn't have kids. I always wondered whether it was him, shooting blanks."

"If I'd had any idea of what I was getting into—"

"You would have turned him down? I doubt that. He's played you like a harp, my friend. He knows you better than you know yourself. How else do you think he's built an empire?"

"Why would he do this to his own son?"

"The whole thing is very T. Duke. Let's just say there are some long-standing issues between Daddy and me. But he made one mistake, he underestimated Iris Thorne. She figured out the game before he could make his move. Problem is, now she knows about Canterbury Investments. She's photocopied my records."

"I can't help you with any trouble you get into. That's the price you pay for being involved in securities fraud."

Evan grabbed Sam by the lapels of his robe and shoved him against a car. "You *can* help me and you *will* help me."

Sam stammered, "Now . . . now, let's not get angry. Let's calm down."

Evan released Sam and rubbed his hands as if they tingled with the imagined sensation of squeezing Sam's neck between them.

Sam nervously rearranged his garments. "Why don't you just quit McKinney Alitzer? You can run this so-called business anywhere."

"You're right. I can run the business anywhere. I started it when I was in jail. But I don't want to quit McKinney. I like working there. I have legitimate business cards, a phone line, health insurance, a little work space all my own. I even went out for drinks with my coworkers. We talked about business. It was fun. I like it. I'm not giving it up."

"But now that Iris knows about your scam, there's nothing I can do to keep her from firing you and having you investigated."

"Yes, there is. And you'll do whatever I ask if you want to keep this nice life of yours intact."

"But you claim to admire Iris. Why would you want to get her in trouble? As for me, I'll give the money back to your father and call the whole thing off. I'll give it to you, if you want. I'll even help you find another job. We'll let bygones be bygones."

Evan laughed at Sam's serious expression. "This isn't about you or Iris. This is about me getting what I want and keeping my father from getting what *he* wants. If a couple of innocent people get hurt as a result, that's the way the ball bounces. My father's spent a lifetime destroying people's lives and profiting from it. I learned a few things from him. I'm more his son than he would like to admit." Evan pulled over a tall stool from underneath the worktable. "Have a seat and we'll talk."

Chapter 30

"How much?"

"Four seventy-five a share."

Iris couldn't help but laugh and did. "T. Duke, last week you offered five dollars. Then you raised it to five-fifteen, for Brianna's sake. Gee, I guess you're really concerned about the little girl."

"This is about business, Iris. Not about sentimentality. Kip Cross's been linked to another murder since my last offer."

"Accidental death."

"Whatever. Pandora's value is diminishing by the day. Four seventy-five is a fair offer. You say you're concerned about making the best deal for Brianna Cross. You should have made that deal two offers ago. Stop being emotional and start being realistic."

"All right, as soon as you stop using dirty tricks to tarnish my reputation and stall a Pandora IPO."

T. Duke played dumb. "Tarnish your reputation?"

"I know all about Canterbury Investments. A chain of deceit is only as strong as its weakest link. What made you think that Sam Eastman could pull off something like that?"

"Sam Eastman? Canterbury what?"

"Oh, puh-leese."

"Iris, it's unsportsmanlike to make accusations without backing them up."

"Unsportsmanlike? T. Duke, I'll talk to you later." She hung up and stared at the now placid torture device known as the telephone. Conduit of countless horrors.

Liz came into her office. "No Top Gun today?" She wore a white wool knit suit with a zip-front jacket.

"Hasn't even called," Iris said. "Maybe he's doing me a favor and falling on his sword."

"I had lunch with Ron Aldrich yesterday, my old boss over at Pierce Fenner Smith. He didn't remember even interviewing Evan much less making him a job offer."

"Doesn't surprise me."

"Why?"

Iris briskly shook her head. "Can't talk now."

"Why not?" Liz peered out Iris's door and down the corridor. "Uh-oh. Here comes Sam-I-Am and he looks all aflutter."

"Good." Iris brightened. "Just the man I wanted to see."

"Really?" Liz gave Iris a probing look. "What's going on?"

"I'll tell you later."

Liz hoisted a buttock onto the corner of Iris's desk. "Tell me now."

"*Liz,*" Iris pleaded.

Liz raised her hands, conceding defeat. "Okay, okay. I'm gone." She met Sam as she was leaving. "Morning, Sam."

"Morning, Liz." He entered Iris's office. "Good morning, Iris," he said, beaming.

"Morning, Sam." He was jolly. Something was up. "To what do I owe the pleasure of this early-morning visit?"

"Oh"—Sam shrugged and looked aimlessly around Iris's office—"just thought I'd check in and see how you're doing. Things are going well, I hope?"

"Generally well, but I do have one problem, Sam."

"Oh?" He smoothed his tie.

"It concerns Evan Finn."

"I noticed Evan wasn't at his desk. Where is he?"

"I don't know. Look, Sam—"

He snapped his fingers, cutting her off. "Before I forget, I need information on the branch's participation in the direct deposit program."

She looked at him quizzically.

"You know, where the payroll department shoots your paychecks right into the bank."

"I know what it is. What about it?"

"The home office wants to make sure all the employees are participating." He walked back and forth in Iris's office as he talked, anxiously glancing into the bull pen each time he passed the door. "It saves the firm a lot of money. There was a memo encouraging compliance. Didn't you see it?"

"I didn't see any communication on that." Iris raised her hand to indicate Louise's alcove next to her office. "Louise can get you whatever you need."

"Ah!" he exclaimed as if Iris had made a brilliant suggestion. "Louise, of course. I'll touch base with her."

He fled Iris's office, giving her the impression that he was trying to avoid talking to her. Through the window that overlooked the suite, Iris saw Louise walk away carrying a manila file folder. Sam bounced from one foot to the next as he waited. Shortly, Louise returned carrying some photocopies, which she handed to Sam. He looked at them, folded the stack into thirds, slipped them into his jacket pocket, and poked his head inside Iris's office. "I've gotta run. Bye."

"Sam!" Iris got up from her desk and followed him into the suite, reaching to touch his arm. He looked down at her hand as if it had mud on it.

"I need to talk to you about something very important. Please." She turned and started walking toward her office.

Sam reluctantly trailed after her.

"I'm going to fire Evan Finn the minute he sets foot in the door," she announced.

"What?"

"He's perpetrating fraud. He's taking money from clients but he's not buying the securities."

"Why would you think that?"

"I have good reasons. That's all I can tell you right now."

"That's ridiculous! Evan's an established broker with a good reputation. Why would he steal from clients?"

"God only knows. You mean you never had any idea that Evan might be involved in something like this?"

"Of course not! Furthermore I don't believe it and I don't want to hear any more about it unless you have firm proof. Making accusations like that is a good way to get yourself and the firm sued. Evan's a good broker from where I sit."

"His sales figures are mediocre at best. Even if Evan wasn't stealing, I'd rather have an ambitious newcomer sitting at that cubicle than a guy who's six years out of college and still doesn't take his job seriously."

Sam sternly responded, "I'd advise you to leave well enough alone, Iris."

His tone surprised her. She didn't know what to say, so she said nothing.

Sam seemed to realize that his comment was a bit strong. "What I meant is, give him a few more weeks. He'll turn around. Just give me that, please."

She walked to her desk and started gathering papers. They didn't need to be gathered, but it made her look purposeful. "I've made my decision."

"You can't fire Evan on the basis of a suspicion. You have to have cause!"

"He's been with us less than a month. I don't need cause."

"You can't fire him."

"I can and I will." Her eyes burned into his.

"Please, Iris. Do me this favor. Just a few weeks."

"A few weeks? Is that the amount of time you need to start an SEC investigation on my office? Is that the time frame you agreed to with T. Duke Sawyer? Or are you involved in Evan's scam too?"

The intercom on Iris's phone cut in. It was Louise. "Evan's arrived."

"Have him come down here, please."

Sam pulled at his tie, which seemed to have grown tight, and anxiously looked out the window, turning his back to the door.

Evan came in and stood in front of Iris's desk without saying anything. He looked at Sam's back, then again at Iris.

"Leave it open," Iris said to Louise, who had started to close the door behind her.

Sam turned, acting startled to see Evan. "Good morning, Evan."

Evan didn't respond, but his dark eyes grew darker. Sam pressed his lips into a thin line.

"Evan," Iris began, "I'm sorry but I have to let you go."

Evan asked Sam, "She's firing me?" A look of rage crossed his face as he stepped farther into the room.

Sam drifted against the wall toward the corner, wedging himself between the window and credenza, as far from Evan's menacing approach as he could get. "Evan, I—"

"Where do you think you're going?" Evan moved to block Iris's escape through the open door.

"Louise!" she yelped as he put his hand on her shoulder, forcing her against the filing cabinet. Still holding her, he reached behind, closed the door, and flipped the lock.

Iris craned her neck to look out the inside window and saw Louise urgently yammering into the telephone. Someone started pounding on the door. She heard Kyle Tucker and Liz yelling.

Sam continued to cower in the corner. "Evan, don't do something you'll regret."

"Stay there!" Evan ordered Iris. He grabbed one of her chairs and wedged it underneath the doorknob.

When his back was turned, she snatched her brass letter opener from her desk and held it behind her back.

Evan pressed his body against hers. She felt his hot breath on her face. She tried to shove him off, which only made him lean harder against her. She could barely breathe.

"Sweet Iris," he whispered. He brushed his lips against hers.

Someone outside was fumbling with keys in the door. It gave, but the chair wouldn't allow the door to be opened.

The commotion did nothing to dissuade Evan. "If you fire me, I'll have you arrested for breaking and entering."

Iris neither confirmed nor denied his accusation. Behind her back, she tightened her grasp on the letter opener.

"What have you got back there?" He slid his arm around her back, closed his hand on top of hers and pulled it from behind her, her resistance slowing him only slightly. "You want to play rough, huh?"

"Evan!" Sam shouted. He made a show of taking a firm step, but didn't take another.

The noise outside grew louder. Someone was now ramming the door.

Evan bent Iris's arm, still holding the letter opener, turning it toward her. She tried to force him away but felt the point jammed against her belly. They looked into each other's eyes. She saw his change; they grew cold. She now believed him to be capable of anything. She tried with all her might to push his hand and the letter opener away. He grinned. The more she struggled, the more he seemed to enjoy it.

"You want to fight me, huh?" he taunted.

"Maybe." She narrowed her eyes.

He licked his lips and pressed his body more closely against her.

"Evan!" Sam impotently shouted.

Iris had forgotten he was there. She stared at Evan. He was the only thing on her mind.

He parted his lips and pressed them against hers.

She returned the kiss, feeling his energy transform into sexual desire. Then she jammed her knee into his groin.

He went down. She stepped over his coiled body and kicked the chair from underneath the doorknob. Two security guards rushed in and dragged Evan, still bent over, from her office.

The employees who had gathered outside were all talking at once.

"Thank God you're all right!" Sam exclaimed as he ran from his corner.

"Oh my God, Iris." Tears streamed down Liz's face. "What *happened?*"

Iris was dazed. "I fired him."

"Way to go, Iris!" Kyle yelped. Someone else followed with a whoop, and soon everyone was clapping and cheering.

Employees traded their views of Evan. "What an A-hole!" "Rude." "Arrogant." "Glad he's gone."

Iris grinned, wiping nervous tears from her eyes. Suddenly feeling shaky and unsteady, she leaned against the doorframe.

"I felt so helpless to do anything," Sam sheepishly explained.

Iris couldn't resist a final shot. "I guess Evan just gave me cause to fire him, didn't he, Sam?"

"Still no sign of Finn," Detective Tiffany Stubbs said to Iris after checking in with her precinct office. "Those guards were stupid not to have handcuffed him. Stay inside, keep everything locked, and don't let anyone in."

Iris nodded.

"Mind if I warm up my coffee?" Stubbs asked.

"Please, help yourself."

"How about you?"

"I'm fine, thanks."

Stubbs walked to the coffeemaker on the counter in Iris's kitchen, filled the mug, and poured in the nondairy creamer and sugar substitute that Iris kept in the house for guests.

Iris read aloud from the file that Stubbs had brought her. "Evan Finn is really Randall Sawyer, T. Duke Sawyer's only son. He spent five years in a Nevada jail for manslaughter. He confessed to throwing a prostitute off a seventeenth-floor balcony of a Las Vegas hotel. When asked why he did it, he said he was drunk and high and something she said made him mad. Over she went. There were no witnesses, although T. Duke was in an adjoining room of the suite. The charge was reduced from second-degree murder to manslaughter, probably because of T. Duke's influence. Before that, Randall had a couple of arrests for driving under the influence and possession of drugs. Went to high school in Europe."

Stubbs sat across from Iris. "Father probably sent him there, thinking he'd remove him from his environment and give him a fresh start."

"He didn't graduate from high school. Must have learned about the stock market on his own. He's a bright guy, that's for sure," Iris commented. "Just whacked-out."

"Dangerous combination."

"Ironically, he's probably not that different from his old man." Iris pointed to something on one of the sheets. "In prison, Evan recanted his confession. Claimed his father was responsible for the murder. Said he was the one in the adjoining room, not T. Duke, and that T. Duke hatched a scheme for Evan, the ne'er-do-well with a lot less to lose, to take the rap. Said his father had promised he'd pull strings to get Evan a short sentence."

"But five years is not a short sentence for manslaughter," Stubbs said. "I'm unfamiliar with Nevada, but in California, someone could be out of jail in eighteen months."

"Sounds like Evan pinned the murder on his father to get back at him for not doing more to keep him out of jail. That must have ticked off T. Duke, but he still pretended to take the high road, setting Evan up as an established businessman after his release. The Pandora situation falls into my lap. T. Duke sees a way to use Evan to neutralize me and get revenge on his son. One question remains: Who threw Rita Free out of that hotel window?"

"Based upon your adventure with Evan today, I'd put my money on him. How did you find out about his Canterbury Investments scheme, anyway?"

Iris felt her cheeks coloring and nervously shuffled the papers in the file folder. "Eavesdropped. Looked at stuff he left on his desk." She didn't tell Stubbs she broke into Evan's office. She picked up her mug and went to fill it with more coffee. It occurred to her she should hide the photocopies of the Canterbury Investments statements—the only physical evidence of her break-in. Perhaps she should burn them.

She leaned against the kitchen counter. "Detective Stubbs, even you have to admit there's more to Bridget Cross's murder than a disgruntled husband taking vengeance on his wife. If T. Duke Sawyer is capable of destroying his own son's life, what would he do to a businesswoman who . . ." She trailed off as an idea occurred to her. "Maybe Evan was the shooter."

Stubbs stood and slipped the manila folder into a black vinyl portfolio. "Is this latest theory a new spin on the one about the Trust Makers fringe group taking over companies to put them out of business, killing the principals if they have to—or is this a new hypothesis altogether? We get more bang for our buck with the conspiracy theory—Alexa Platt's and Bridget Cross's murders solved and Harry Hagopian's car crash explained. If it was a case of pure greed on T. Duke's part, we only solve

Bridget's murder. And in neither case do we explain what happened to Banzai Jefferson. There's no evidence, just a lot of talk, to implicate anyone except Kip Cross."

"But there's not enough evidence to implicate Kip, either."

"I have bloody footprints and a man with gunshot residue on his hands. Don't forget, I do have a witness. I showed Brianna's drawings to a child psychologist, who thinks she could easily remember more details with time and guidance. In another day or two, I should have the request approved to have Brianna interviewed over her father's objections."

Stubbs walked to the front door with Iris following. "I figure time is on our side. Once things quiet down for Kip and he's settled back into his day-to-day life, his conscience will begin to prey on him. Your mind can do funny things to you in the wee hours of the morning."

All the coffee Iris had drunk so late in the evening had made her wired. It was unusual for her to feel so alert so late in the evening. She knew she'd pay for it later.

She went into her home office and got the photocopies of the Canterbury Investments statements from the top drawer of the desk. She weighed the idea of burning them versus putting them in her safe-deposit box. She didn't know how the situation with Evan would end up, but if it became a case of his word versus hers, it would be useful for her to have documentation. She took the photocopies to her bedroom closet and stashed them underneath the mountain of dirty panty hose in there. Now she had a reason to put off doing her hand laundry another night.

Back in her office again, she turned on her laptop computer to pick up her E-mail. She leaned back in her chair, chewed her thumb, and idly watched the monitor as the system loaded. The screen displayed something she'd never seen before.

A shadowy staircase appeared. A woman, viewed from the back, was ascending it. She looked like Cherry Divine from the final level of *Suckers*. The woman turned to look behind. She had Iris's face.

The woman continued walking, approaching a dark castle at the top of the steps. As she reached the front door, it burst open, revealing Slade Slayer. "Hello, Iris," he said in his familiar baritone, his trademark sneer on his face. With both hands, he pushed her down the steps. She tumbled all the way to the bottom, screaming, finally coming to rest with her head twisted backward on her neck.

Slade Slayer remained at the top of the stairs. He pointed to the real Iris and said, "Behave, or you're next."

Chapter 31

"Toni! Somebody put something weird on my computer!" Over the phone, Iris heard a rustling noise that led her to believe Toni wasn't vertical and wasn't alone. "Is this a bad time?"

"No, no. Go. What happened?"

"I turned on my laptop and it played this sequence that looked like it was from *Suckers*. But it was Cherry Divine with my face. Slade pushes her—or me—down the stairs and says, 'Behave, or you're next.' It executes each time I boot the computer."

"Oh my God."

"It had to have been done by someone from Pandora, doesn't it?"

"Not necessarily. The Slade Slayer specs are available on the Internet. Anyone with some programming skills and access to your laptop could have done it. Can you bring it to Pandora tomorrow?"

"Sure . . ." Iris heard more rustling on the other end of the line.

"Just a sec." It sounded as if Toni had put her hand over the receiver. After several long seconds, she came back. Her voice was tense. "I'll come over now."

"Now?" Iris looked at her watch. It was 8 P.M. "Is there someone with you?"

The other woman's voice grew more pinched. "No . . . no one."

"I thought I heard you talking to somebody."

"Uh-unh, no. So, can I come over, please?"

Iris was perplexed by the sudden urgency in Toni's voice. She shrugged it off to another bout of Toni's endless man problems. "Okay, I'll see you in a few minutes. And I have something to tell you about Evan."

Forty-five minutes later, the doorbell rang. Iris looked out the peephole and saw Toni standing on the front porch. Iris unlocked the door. Toni quickly came inside, grabbed the edge of the door, and tried to slam it closed. Only then did Iris see that Toni had been crying. Iris didn't have time to ask questions. Evan easily pushed the door open.

"Move back." Evan waved the handgun he was holding at the two women.

"I'm sorry, Iris," Toni wailed, her eyes filling. "He made me! He was at my apartment when you called." She pouted at Evan. "I don't get you."

Evan looked around the spartan living room. "I would have thought you'd have more furniture than this."

"I just moved in."

"Sit here." He indicated the easy chair.

Iris sat.

"Toni, sit on the floor next to her."

Toni dropped to her knees and sat cross-legged on the floor. She quietly sobbed, wiping her eyes and nose with the backs of both hands.

"I'm coming back to work for McKinney Alitzer tomorrow morning," Evan stated.

Iris raised her eyebrows. "Are you?"

"You'll tell everyone we had a misunderstanding and you've hired me back."

Iris relaxed into the chair and crossed her legs, feeling oddly calm. "Why would I tell them that?"

"Because you have no choice in the matter."

"And why is that?"

"Because I've set it up to make it look like you're getting a cut of the Canterbury Investments money."

"But I haven't taken any money from you."

"Have you verified your checking account balance today?"

Iris remembered the direct-deposit information that Sam Eastman was so eager to get his hands on. The list Louise gave him included the banks and account numbers of the participating employees.

"Go ahead," Evan said. "Call your bank."

She pointed to her purse, which was sitting on a chair in the dining room, adjacent to the living room. He waved her on with the gun. She walked to pick up her purse. He grabbed it from her hands on the way back, dug around inside, and handed it back to her. She returned to the chair and took out her electronic phone book and her checkbook, found the bank's twenty-four-hour account-balance line, and picked up the cordless phone that stood on an overturned crate that served as an end table. After punching many numbers onto the telephone keypad, the automated voice read out her balance. It was $20,000 more than it should have been. She hung up and blankly stared at Evan.

He looked at her smugly. "A Canterbury Investments check made out to you with your forged endorsement was deposited in your account today. You may decide to never touch the money. You may try to return it to me. It doesn't matter. That check went into your account and you can't undo the audit trail. Just hire me back and let me go about my business and no one will be the wiser. You can even keep the twenty grand. Consider it good-faith money. Otherwise, I'll make sure you go down with me."

Iris twirled a lock of her hair and said nothing.

"Evan," Toni implored, still crying, "don't be like this."

"What's Sam Eastman's angle?" Iris asked, trying to keep her voice strong and sure. "Is he in on Canterbury Investments, getting a cut?"

Evan shook his head. "Sam Eastman's no friend of yours or mine, Iris. He knew about Canterbury Investments all along. Sam set you up for a fall all right, but he's not the genius behind this."

"T. Duke Sawyer," Iris said. "I know all about you and your father, Evan."

Toni's jaw dropped. She looked at Evan as if seeing him for the first time.

Evan gave Iris an appreciative look. "Not much gets past you. I like that."

Iris again crossed her legs, trying to adopt a casual air. "Who really threw the prostitute off the Las Vegas hotel balcony?"

Toni's mouth gaped even wider.

"My father. I was in the other room of the suite, passed out. He was having a party with an expensive call girl. That's one of his hobbies, you know. Professional snatch."

Iris recalled the woman who had made a suggestive gesture at Baines the first time she visited T. Duke at his Somis office.

"Why bother with an amateur when you can get a pro, he says. Rumor is, my mother hasn't come near him in years. The old man likes having plenty of beautiful women around. That's the only reason he included me in his escapades—to make him look good. At the same time he used me, he hated me for it. That's why the bitch ended up on the ground. The way the story goes, the old man was drunk and couldn't perform. That alone was bad enough, but this girl made some comment about how she didn't want him to waste his money. She offered to do me. Then she made a fatal mistake. She told him she'd do me for free."

Evan's story sounded a bit pat to Iris, especially after she'd witnessed his violent side firsthand. But since he seemed of a mind to talk, she thought she'd milk it with the hope that a few grains of truth would tumble out. "Do you know if T. Duke is involved with a group called the Trust Makers or if he's worked to keep sex or violence out of the entertainment media?"

Evan laughed. "Are you kidding? My father works for the benefit of one charity—himself."

Toni suggested, "But it sounds like you haven't had much contact with him over the past few years. He might have had a change of heart."

"Yeah, right."

"Why is he so obsessed with controlling Pandora?" Iris demanded.

"It's a game, Iris. When you're as rich as he is, it's not about money anymore. It's about winning."

His comment surprised Iris. "But T. Duke's living on credit. The Sawyer Company's hocked to the hilt."

Evan laughed again. "He bleeds every company he gets his hands on. He's got dough, art, and antiques stashed all over the world. Pandora is sport for him. A way to pass the days."

"Tell me this. You're a good broker. You're smart. You know the business. Why don't you go legitimate?"

"There's nothing I would like more than to be a regular citizen."

"So be one."

"Give me a break. No legit firm would hire me."

"You don't have to work for a big firm. You could build a business, like you have with Canterbury. Charge a percentage for your advice and get a licensed broker to do the trades."

"Can't make any real dough like that."

"Okay," Iris said unconvincingly. She wasn't going to press the issue since he was the one with the gun. The guy obviously enjoyed being a criminal, in spite of what he said.

Evan seemed intent on making his case. He punctuated his words with the gun. "I've never murdered anybody. I've never stolen anybody's money. When a client wants out of Canterbury, I give them their money back."

Iris couldn't stop herself. "Better hope the market doesn't take a dive and everybody wants their money at the same time."

He looked at her evenly and for a long time. Iris silently beat herself up for having such a big mouth. Finally, he said, "You're cute, you know that?"

She smiled thinly. It was better than being dead.

"Look"—he glanced at his watch—"I'll see you tomorrow morning, say, nine o'clock? That'll give you time to tell everyone about our disagreement and how it's been resolved. And I'm not sitting in one of those cubicles in the bull pen. I'm taking a window office."

"Okay."

"And you'll tell the police that incident in the office was a simple misunderstanding?"

"Fine."

He seemed pleased that she was so compliant. "You and I are now partners. You let me go about my business and I'll let you go about yours. Remember, just because we have a mutual enemy doesn't make us buddies. You screw me over, you're going down too."

"Understood."

"One more thing. I want the photocopies you made of the Canterbury Investments statements."

"I don't have them." Iris forced herself to steadily look him in the eyes. "I burned them."

"I don't think so." Evan jerked the gun up and down in Toni's direction, indicating he wanted her to stand. Once she did, he put his arm around her, kissed her cheek, then held the gun to her head. To Iris he said, "Make it snappy, or you're going to have to recruit a new marketing manager for Pandora."

Iris leaped from the chair and disappeared down the hallway.

"Evan," Toni pleaded, "how can you do this to me? I thought we had something special."

"We did, for the ten minutes it took."

Iris returned with the photocopies. Evan released Toni, who was again crying. He folded the wad of papers in half, stuffed them inside his jacket, and walked backward toward the door. When he had the door open, he finally put the gun away. "Iris, don't underestimate my father. You'd better watch your back." He stepped outside and closed the door behind him.

Iris and Toni looked at the closed door.

Toni cried, "I thought I meant something to him. All the time, he was just using me." Her head bobbed back on her neck and she wailed to the ceiling.

Iris still looked at the door, stunned. "My career is over. Everything I've worked and sweated blood for all these years."

"I wasn't anything but a quick screw for him." Toni smacked her hand against her thigh. "I built up this big thing and it was all in my head."

Iris drifted across the room, as if dazed. "Why did this happen to me? All I wanted was to do right by Bridget and Brianna. What did I do to deserve Evan Sawyer in my life?"

"What's wrong with *me?*" Toni slapped her head hard with her open hand. "Why do I always get involved with these men who just *use* me? I believed all of Kip's pretty pictures about us. Now Evan. I'm not even talking about all the others." She again slapped her head hard. "Toni, you're such a loser!"

Iris paced through the room, rubbing her hands over her face. "What am I going to do? I'm screwed no matter what."

Iris and Toni both stopped stewing in their private hells and looked at each other from across the room. They met in the middle and gave each other a hug.

"I'm sorry about Evan, Toni."

"You tried to tell me about him. I'm sorry about the fix you're in. What are you going to do?"

"I don't know."

Kip was sitting in Bridget's office, working at the computer by the light of the wood-burning fireplace. He leaned back from the keyboard, looked into the dying flames, got up, and put on another log from the stack in the brass carrier next to the hearth. He rolled it into place with a poker, then watched it slowly catch flame. He frowned at the sound of rapid footsteps down the corridor. There was no mistaking the creak of the heavy front door opening and clicking closed.

Kip quickly padded from the room in his flip-flops and went out the front door in time to see a flash of blonde dart around the corner of the house and down the stairs. He peeked down the dark staircase and was just able to make out Summer bounding down them. He kicked off his flip-flops, so as to not make any noise, and jogged after her.

When he reached the street below, Capri Road, he saw Summer in a passionate embrace with a tall, handsome man next to a dark green Range Rover.

"Evan, baby," she purred.

"Let's go." They hopped inside and took off.

Chapter 32

Louise arrived at the office and poked her head through Iris's doorway before reaching her own desk. "You're here bright and early."

"Early, anyway." Iris was at her desk, staring into a cup of black coffee as if it were a crystal ball.

"Everything okay?"

"Everything's rotten, to tell the truth."

Louise's face grew concerned. She came inside Iris's office. "What's wrong?"

Iris knew she had to get her out ASAP. It was all Iris could do to hold herself together as it was. A sympathetic look from a kind person would tip her over the edge and make her lose her composure. Just when she needed all her wits, they were failing her. She stared hard into the coffee. Regaining a brittle calm, she looked up at her assistant. "I have an announcement to make when everyone comes in that I think you'll find interesting. Once I do, Louise, please don't question my decision. I have my reasons."

Louise, looking more concerned than ever, nodded and made her way to her desk.

Iris watched the minutes tick past on the clock on the corner of her desk. When it was 6:20 A.M., ten minutes before the market opened in New York, Iris walked to the front of the sales department, turned, and faced the bull pen. "Can I have everyone's attention? Please, guys. Up here!" She clapped her hands.

"Hey, the boss is going to make a speech!" Sean Bliss said.

"Hail our fearless leader!" Warren Gray yelled.

Kyle Tucker lobbed a Nerf ball that he had been hiding in the crook of his arm at her head. She ducked before it hit her and laughed good-naturedly.

Someone else picked it up and threw it at her again.

She caught it in the air and threw it back.

Liz Martini left her office and sat on the corner of her sales assistant's desk.

Amber Ambrose leaned against her doorframe.

Sam Eastman walked into the department and looked baffled at the gathering.

Iris began. "Good morning, Sam. Glad you could join us. Just wanted to share a few thoughts with everyone before we start the day. The market's been nervous lately, to say the least. I think you've all done a terrific job of keeping your clients calm, not panic selling, making reasoned decisions, and taking advantage of the bargains."

There were hurrahs and pats on the back.

"I also wanted to say how I've appreciated the way you've all supported me since my promotion to branch manager." Uh-oh. She'd stepped into emotional quicksand. Her voice had cracked. She quickly looked around and was relieved to see that almost no one had noticed. The guys were still pushing and jiving. Amber was too self-absorbed to have noticed. Louise, of course, already knew that something was up. The waver in Iris's voice had tipped Liz off, who now frowned with concern. Iris avoided her gaze.

Kyle started applauding and soon everyone joined in, including Sam Eastman, who anemically clapped. There were whoops and hollers.

Iris would have disintegrated into tears then and there, but the thought of the real purpose of her calling the assembly sobered her.

The group grew restless, thinking she was about finished. "One last thing. Evan Finn will be rejoining our team today."

She could have heard a pin drop. Everyone looked from one to the next with expressions ranging from disbelief to horror. Everyone, that is, except Sam Eastman, who looked visibly relieved.

Seeing how disconcerted everyone was by her announcement, Iris decided to offer no explanation. She knew the one she'd cooked up was lame anyway and wouldn't have satisfied anybody. She thrust her fist in the air—*"Carpe diem!"*—and walked back to her office. Out of the corner of her eye, she saw Liz making a beeline toward her. Iris stopped her by turning to Sam and saying, "I'm so glad you were able to change your schedule to stop by."

"Anything for you, Iris."

Inside her office, Sam eagerly rubbed his hands together and prowled around, as if too nervous to sit. "I was so pleased to see that you changed your opinion about Evan. We had that little . . . incident, but when you think about it, no harm was done."

Iris quietly closed the door and leaned coquettishly against it with her hands in her jacket pockets. "Let's be frank. Evan's behavior was a bit out there. I'm going to have a heck of a time explaining why I took him back."

"Yeah, I guess it was." Sam shook his head with amusement as if Evan were an irrepressible six-year-old scamp, a lovable troublemaker. His good humor dimmed slightly as reality nudged in. "Why did you decide to rehire Evan?"

Iris amiably shrugged. "He made me an offer I couldn't refuse."

They both gaily laughed.

"He can be persuasive, can't he?" Sam enthused.

"Hey, if you can't beat 'em, join 'em, huh? I wasn't too enthusiastic at first, but he sweetened the deal for me. Several grand, tax free . . . I have a lot of expenses now."

"I can imagine. I was really surprised when you bought that house. Casa Marina, of all places." Sam settled into Iris's couch and expansively extended his arms across the cushion backs. "It was way over your head, in my humble opinion."

Iris's eyes dimmed slightly. For many years, she had made twice as much in commissions as he had earned in salary—a fact that Sam had apparently conveniently blocked. It was okay. She had him where she wanted him—relaxed and sharing secrets. Just like two old friends. "I wish I'd asked your opinion before I jumped."

She walked to her western-facing window and leaned against the credenza, closer to where he was sitting. "Just between you and me, I think this scheme is brilliant. I want you to know, I'm not taking this at all personally. Business is business."

"I'm glad, Iris. I didn't mean it personally. I only had yours and the firm's best interests at heart. I'll pull strings to ensure you come out of this unscathed." He casually crossed his legs, as if he'd spent the better part of his life pulling strings for friends. "Of course, it will be apparent to everyone that your skills are not suited to running a branch office. You have to admit, Iris, that you haven't been happy as branch manager."

She smiled tightly with her lips closed and didn't respond. "I want to reiterate that the scheme is brilliant. You gathered ammunition to get me out of the branch manager position and a way to make money on the side. Just how much did T. Duke pay you?"

Sam winced. "I shouldn't say."

"C'mon, Sam. I'm dying to know. Brag a little."

Sam sucked his bottom lip, as if fighting to hold the words in. "Well, I don't want to get into specifics. Let's just say it was in the six figures."

Iris appreciatively raised her eyebrows.

"In the middle six," he volunteered.

"Indeed." Iris nodded. "It must make you feel great to play with a heavy hitter like T. Duke. You told me early on how much you admired him. I imagine he approached you?"

Sam beamed. "Actually, *I* approached him. I knew he was trying to buy Pandora and didn't want you to take it public because the odds were he'd end up having to pay more for it in that case. I told him I had a personal interest in effecting some changes in this branch office and would help him out any way I could. A few days later, he put me in touch with Evan Finn."

Iris shook her head with disbelief. "Brilliant. Terrific. Did you know Evan is his son?"

"I didn't at the time, but Evan later told me."

"Does T. Duke know about this recent turn of events?"

Sam's face darkened. "Oh no. Uh-uh. That's why I was so glad you rehired Evan. He told me to make absolutely certain that you didn't find out what was going on. That was his one requirement. Now everything can continue as planned, without T. Duke being any the wiser."

Iris pursed her lips and looked troubled. "That's a bit of a pickle for you, Sam. T. Duke knows I know all about Evan, Canterbury Investments, and your involvement in the whole thing."

Sam uncrossed his legs and leaned forward on the couch. "How?"

"I guess I told him," she said guilelessly.

"Oh no." Sam stared at the carpet as if a series of unpleasant possibilities were being played out in his mind.

"Boy, if T. Duke was willing to set up his own son," Iris breathed, "it's scary to think what he might do to a total stranger."

"But I fulfilled T. Duke's bargain. I never told Evan or you about the scheme." Sam's voice was tinged with panic. "It wasn't my fault you found out on your own. T. Duke has no reason to be mad at me."

"One wouldn't think so." Iris became thoughtful. "But the guy does seem to have a code of ethics that harkens back to the Wild West."

Sam grew more agitated.

Iris did her best to feed it. "Since it's all out in the open, he doesn't have any further use for you."

"What do you mean?"

"You're extraneous."

"But . . . but I'm not," Sam stammered. "I still have to call New York and tell them about all the dirty stuff going on in your branch office."

"That's right. When are you going to do that?"

"I have to wait for instructions from T. Duke."

"I see. In the meantime, I guess I'll go about my business like normal." Iris walked to the door and put her hand on the doorknob.

Sam got the cue that the meeting was over. He stood. "You're being surprisingly calm about this whole thing. I never expected that."

Iris shrugged. "Well, I am a professional, Sam."

"T. Duke knows, huh?" Sam asked, hoping he'd heard wrong.

Iris nodded and opened the door.

Without another word, Sam left.

Iris closed the door behind him. She pulled a tiny tape recorder from her jacket pocket, rewound a few seconds, and played it to make sure she had got their conversation. She had.

"Amber Ambrose and her spy shops," she said aloud to herself. "I'm going to have to buy some of that stock myself."

Evan Finn walked through the large, high-ceilinged room of the exclusive club, his footsteps silent on the thick oriental carpet. Bulky leather club chairs were arranged in small groupings, each with a coffee table, end table, and lamp. A fire snapped in a bricked fireplace on one wall. Along another wall were several A-shaped newspaper stands with papers from around the world hanging from round dowels. It was late afternoon, not quite cocktail hour, and the room was almost empty. An elderly man wearing a cardigan sweater with the elbows completely worn through dozed in one of the chairs. Drool seeped from the corner of his mouth.

A dark-suited, middle-aged Latino, balancing on one hand a tray that held a brandy snifter of amber liquid, walked to a chair on the far side of the room. The chair faced the window. A man's head was barely visible above the back. The waiter picked up an empty snifter from a small round end table and left the fresh one.

"Anything else, sir?"

T. Duke Sawyer shook his head, picked up the snifter, resting it between two fingers, and rolled the cognac around the glass.

"I'll take one of those."

Both the waiter and T. Duke were surprised by the intrusion.

"Certainly, sir," the waiter politely responded.

Evan sat in a chair across from his father. "There's some old guy over there who looks like a homeless man asleep with drool running down his chin. Thought this was supposed to be a high-class, members-only joint."

"That old guy, as you refer to him, was once the CEO of two of the largest airlines in the world. He's earned the right to wear his old sweater and drool, if that's what he chooses." T. Duke held the snifter to his nose and inhaled the cognac's aroma before taking a sip. "You have little grounds to criticize. Rate you're going, you won't make it to age thirty-five."

"If you had your choice, I'd spend the years left to me in jail."

"Laws are to be enforced, not broken, in spite of what you might think."

"T. Duke the Liquidator should know all about that, huh?"

The waiter returned with another snifter of cognac. While he was setting a coaster on the end table, Evan swept the glass from his tray. The waiter's expression didn't change as he quietly turned and left.

Evan didn't savor the cognac's aroma or color before taking a long drink, consuming half of it. "I was discharged from my responsibilities at McKinney Alitzer yesterday."

T. Duke crookedly smiled. "She fired you, did she?"

"Yes, but what a difference a day makes. She hired me back this morning."

"Why?"

"Let's just say I was persuasive." Evan took a package of imported cigarettes and his monogrammed Dunhill lighter from his inside jacket pocket. He put a cigarette between his lips, lit it, and inhaled deeply. "I even got a window office from her. You should have seen the expressions on my coworkers' faces when I moved into that office." He smiled at the recollection.

"You boxed her in. That strategy will come back to bite you."

"You ought to know, Dad." Evan slid a heavy, cut crystal ashtray on the coffee table closer to him and tapped his cigarette into it. "I admire the way you found out about Canterbury Investments and then devised a scheme to use my little business for your own ends. Have to hand it to you. You've always got an angle. The great T. Duke Sawyer."

"What's your point, Evan? I know you didn't come here for some father-son bonding."

"I think I've found a way to turn this all back around to my advantage. I've got my own angle to work." Evan downed the rest of the brandy and waved at the waiter, who was now patiently standing in a corner of the room. The waiter nodded, then disappeared through a rear door.

Evan continued, "You were stupid to make it so obvious that you're out to destroy someone who you're having a business dispute with. That someone turns up dead, could put you in a real sticky situation."

T. Duke responded, "I'm engaged in many business disputes. Which are you referring to?"

"Two people come immediately to mind. Kip Cross and Iris Thorne. Unlike you to wear your heart on your sleeve like that, my father."

"You're threatening to murder Iris or Kip—or both—and frame me for it?"

"It's poetic justice, isn't it? It's what Kip Cross says you did to him."

"You don't have the balls to do something like that."

The waiter returned with a fresh cognac. This time, Evan let him set it on the end table before picking it up. "I don't, huh?"

"You've got a wild card. Iris Thorne." T. Duke rested the ankle of one leg on the knee of the other. His feet were shod in black, ostrich-skin boots that had very high heels. "She's big on doing the right thing. She might get to you before you get to her, even if it means bringing heat on herself."

"I've got her right where I want her. She can't do a damn thing to me. All I have to do is pick the time and place." Evan twirled the cognac. "And the method."

"That Sam Eastman blew it, didn't he?"

"It doesn't matter who blew what," Evan replied coolly. "The deed is done."

"Why didn't you just go away and stay away?"

"I'm like you in that respect, I suppose. I hate people telling me what I can and cannot do. I've waited a long time for this moment. I found out that you did get my charge reduced to manslaughter, but that you asked the judge to lay on the years. So typical of you. Every favor has strings attached. Now it's payback time."

Chapter 33

Kip was sitting in Bridget's office without the lights on. It was early evening but very dark due to the heavy sky and pounding rain. The colorful images displayed on the computer screen in front of Kip cast a dim light. He sat quietly, his hands folded in his lap.

The front door opened and closed. Kip didn't move.

"Kip! I'm home, sweetheart!" Summer cheerily announced. "Where are you?" Carrying several bags from her favorite exclusive boutiques, she walked down the corridor, passing the office door.

Kip called out to her. "Summer."

There was the crisp rustling of paper as Summer turned and walked back. "Why are you always sitting in the dark lately?" She flipped on the switch for the overhead light. "You're going to ruin your eyes . . ." She saw the handgun in the middle of Kip's desk.

"I cleaned it up. Went outside and fired it. Just once. Didn't want to alarm the neighbors. Still works, even after all this rain." Kip smiled. "There's something so wonderfully simple about mechanical appliances."

"Is that the gun you told the police was stolen?"

Kip slowly nodded.

"The one they think was used to kill Bridget?"

"The one that *was* used to kill Bridget. It had washed down the storm drain all the way to the street."

"Storm drain?"

"The boss monster won the first level. He killed Bridget. He intended for the police to find the gun, but I hid it before they had the chance. That was one for me. A case of dumb luck, but I was smart enough to capitalize on it. I won the second level. Now Banzai is dead. That's one for him. But again, an imperfect strategy. The police haven't been able to pin that on me. The boss monster's getting closer. He's tightening the noose: I can feel it. It's my move now. And I finally have my strategy in place. Took me a while, but then it fell open right in front of me."

"Kip, why don't you come to bed and get some sleep? I know you've got a lot on your mind, honey, but—"

"Why did you lie to the police about what time I left to take Brianna to the party? Because of your lie, I have an hour of my day that's not accounted for. An hour in which Banzai could have followed me home, we could have argued, and I could have pushed him down the stairs. Why?"

Summer's silicone-enhanced bottom lip quivered. "I didn't lie. I swear I thought it was three o'clock. I didn't pay that much attention to the time. I told the police I made a mistake."

"After the damage was done. Good tactic."

"Don't look at me like that. I'm not plotting against you."

"Soon the monster will make his ultimate move." Kip knowingly lowered his eyelids. "But I have a strategy. I have a strategy."

"I'm not out to get you, Kip!" Tears spilled from Summer's eyes. "I love you."

Kip opened a desk drawer and pulled out several pads of yellow paper bound together with rubber bands. He tossed them on the desk. Summer gaped at them.

"Love me? Not according to this. Says here, you admire my genius and at times felt fond of me but you never loved me. Sometimes you even felt sorry for me." He rested both hands on top of the bundle.

She limply shrugged.

"I told you. No fooling around on me and no writing tell-all books."

Summer dropped the shopping bags and covered her face with her hands. "I did it for you," she sobbed. "I wanted to set the record straight about you. I know you didn't murder Bridget. I said that in there. When I told the publisher that you didn't want me to write the book, they wanted their advance money back. But I'd spent it. I have to give them the book now."

"Burn it."

"What?"

He opened a drawer, took out a box of matches, and tossed it across the desk at her. "Nothing's ever enough for you, is it? You always have to have more. Your breasts were fine but you had to have them enlarged. Your lips were fine but you had to make them fuller. It's not enough that you get to live in my house, you want to be in my bed. Then when my wife is gone, it's not enough that you get to be the mistress of the house, you want to earn money off it. Is that why you pushed Banzai down the steps? Your TV work was drying up and you needed another controversy to boost your public image?"

Summer hiccuped and made small squeaking noises as she sobbed.

"Go on," he said, gesturing toward the fireplace.

"Kip, please." She crept to the desk and picked up the matches with trembling hands. "It took me so long." She fumbled as she tried to pick up the stack of yellow pads.

He impassively watched her.

Clutching the pads to her chest, she walked to the fireplace, grabbed the brass handle on the rounded fire screen, and pulled it away from the opening. She threw the pads on top of the partially burnt logs and ashes in the grate, took out a match, and struck it. Her hands were trembling so badly, she didn't make good contact. She tried again. A flame hissed from the match. She held it against a corner of the stack until it lit, then tossed the match on top.

Both she and Kip silently watched as the flames took hold.

When she finally turned to face him, her tears had dried and her face was hard. "I'm not sorry about how I made money off Bridget and you, telling people how it was to live here. She deserved it. She treated me like dirt, then threw me out on the street. Her getting murdered was the best thing that happened to me. I'm not going to deny it. I'm glad it happened."

"You have ten minutes to pack your things and get out."

There was a high-pitched scream that startled both of them. Kip bolted from the desk chair, shoved Summer out of the way, and ran into the hall. "Brianna!"

The screams continued.

Summer was close behind Kip as he ran into the family room and saw Brianna with her face pressed against one of the glass-paned doors. Kip flew out the door and into the darkness. On the patio was someone in a long black raincoat and a black hat. Something silver flashed in his hand.

From the open doorway, Brianna continued to scream hysterically at the intruder, her eyes transfixed by the shiny object.

"I'm with your security company," the man explained to Kip, putting the flashlight into a pocket of his raincoat. "I was patrolling the area and I saw the back gate open. I'm sorry I scared her so bad."

"It's okay," Summer said. "It wasn't your fault."

Kip dropped to his knees and began shaking Brianna, who was still hysterical. "Who do you see, baby? Who do you see?"

Summer tried to pull Kip away from Brianna. "Leave her alone!"

Kip shrugged Summer off. "Tell me, who is it?"

"Can't you see she's upset? You want to terrorize me, fine. But leave her alone!"

"I'm on my cellular phone. The air must be dirty around here," Toni said. "Look, Iris. I found out there's a Trust Makers meeting this weekend. I think we should go. We could disguise ourselves as men to get in."

"Toni, I don't think there's anything to our theory," Iris said. "I got a call from Garland today. He had lunch with Clinton Cormier, who's one of the USA Assets investors. Cormier laughed when Garland told him about T. Duke's secrecy regarding USA Assets. He says T. Duke is just screwing with the Crosses. T. Duke thought Kip and Bridget were uppity know-it-alls who got rich quick and was jerking their chains by withholding information. When I entered the Pandora picture, T. Duke didn't see any reason to stop his fun. Garland says he's confident Cormier is being candid with him."

"I don't believe it, Iris." Toni was agitated. "We have evidence linking all these deaths to USA Assets. C'mon!"

"Based upon what I've learned about T. Duke in the past few days, I don't for a moment believe he's found religion and turned over a new leaf. But if you think there's something to be gained by going to a Trust Makers meeting, why don't you go ahead and infiltrate it by yourself? Although I can't see you disguised as a man!" Iris chuckled.

"Just you wait, Iris. I'll get in there, and I'll come back with all the proof necessary to have T. Duke arrested for the murders of Bridget Cross and Alexa Platt." While she talked to Iris, Toni did not remove her eyes from the front door or garage of the tall condominium complex half a block down from where she was parked on Wilshire Boulevard. It was dark outside but the facade of the exclusive building was well-lit.

"Okay," Iris said, surprised by Toni's agitation over the issue. "Good luck—and let me know what you find out."

Toni disconnected the call and set the phone on the passenger seat of her Toyota Camry. She continued watching but didn't have to wait much longer. The gate over the building's underground garage rolled open and Evan Finn exited, driving his green Range Rover, and turned right onto Wilshire Boulevard. Toni started the Camry and followed him.

Evan carried Summer's two hastily packed suitcases down the path that traversed the old hotel's broad lawn. She walked ahead of him, her wet blonde hair flattened against her head and down her back. Her pink knit dress, which left little to the imagination when dry, now held no secrets at all when drenched through. She located the bungalow, in a corner on a knoll above Sunset Boulevard.

The Château Bordeaux Hotel, built in the 1920s on several acres of rolling lawns above the section of the boulevard known as the Sunset Strip, had once upon a time been a renowned hideaway for the rich and famous. It was now in need of some TLC, but the slightly derelict air was one of the attributes the hotel's loyal patrons liked best.

Most of the rooms were located in the three-story main structure, but a handful of bungalows—some with notorious reputations for the celebrity deaths and other scandals that had occurred in them over the years—were scattered among the once well-tended gardens.

Summer unlocked the door of Bungalow 5 and quickly appraised her new surroundings, inspecting the sitting room, tiny kitchen, bathroom, and separate bedroom.

Evan sat in a wingbacked chair by the window; he lit a cigarette and set the package and lighter on an end table. "So Kip flipped out, huh?"

Summer left the bathroom rubbing a thick towel over her wet hair. She sat on a matching chair across the room from Evan, picked up the receiver of an old rotary telephone on an adjacent end table, and began dialing.

"Who are you calling?" Evan asked.

"I have to do something about Brianna." She waited for her call to be answered. "Iris? Hi, it's Summer Fontaine. I'm sorry to bother you like this, but Kip threw me out of the house." She rolled her eyes as she listened to Iris's response. "Look, I'm not calling about me. I'm worried about Brianna. Kip's acting strange. He's sitting in Bridget's office in the house, in the dark, with a gun."

She paused. "He says it's the gun used to kill Bridget. He says he took it from the storm drain where he hid it after Bridget's murder. If that doesn't tell you who killed Bridget, I don't know what does."

She listened again. "I don't care what you think about me, but you've got to get Brianna out of that house. I'm staying at the Château Bordeaux in Bungalow Five, on the corner closest to Sunset. Please call. Thanks."

Summer hung up and was startled when she looked out the window over which sheer drapes were drawn.

"What's wrong?" Evan asked.

"I thought I saw someone looking in."

Evan got up and pulled the drapes open. "There's no one there."

She tightly closed her eyes, as if to block out an image. "I'm getting as bad as Kip, seeing boss monsters everywhere."

Chapter 34

Iris pulled the Triumph out of her office-tower garage, clicked on the windshield wipers, and waited for a break in the traffic so she could turn right onto Flower Street. She had noticed another car, a dark blue Lincoln Continental with tinted windows, fall in behind her as she made the myriad twists and turns required to exit the garage, including dodging the guy with the dustpan, but she didn't think anything of it. It was a big building and people were always coming and going.

She got on the southbound Harbor Freeway, then changed to the westbound 10. She drove all the way to west Los Angeles, fifteen miles, with the Lincoln staying a polite distance behind. She exited on Overland and pulled into a 7-Eleven's parking lot. The Lincoln parked a short distance away.

Iris pulled her electronic phone directory from her briefcase, looked up the numbers she had on file for T. Duke, and dialed one on her cellular phone. She stepped outside with the phone to her ear, popped open her automatic umbrella, and walked up behind the Lincoln. Through the tinted glass, she could see the driver's profile.

He answered the ringing car phone. "Baines."

"Why are you following me?"

He whipped his head around and saw that the Triumph was empty.

"Baines, over here."

He spun his head the other direction and saw Iris standing in front of the car.

"Call T. Duke, like a good bruiser, and tell him I want to talk to him."

He hesitated.

"*Now,* please." Iris disconnected the call, pressed the antenna down, and slipped the cellular phone into her skirt pocket.

The Lincoln's tinted window slowly slid down. Baines handed Iris his phone.

"Why are you having me followed, T. Duke?"

"You're in danger," T. Duke responded. "I told Baines to watch out for you."

"I'm flattered about your concern for my welfare. Who am I in danger from—you?"

"My son has hatched a scheme to kill you and Kip Cross and make it look like I'm responsible."

"Interesting. He told me to watch my back around *you.*"

"Don't trust him, Iris."

"I'll tell you what I'm going to trust. My own instincts. By the way, I reject your offer of four seventy-five a share for Pandora. I wouldn't sell to you if you were the last buyer on earth. Have a nice day." She handed the phone back to Baines and pointed at the Aryan giant. "Scat."

Iris stood on the porch of the Cross house, hunkered under her umbrella in the pouring rain, and rang the doorbell for many long minutes. When she received no response, she started banging the solid brass knocker. After there was still no response, she tried the door. It was unlocked. She pushed it open and stuck her head inside the darkened house.

"Kip?" she said tentatively. She didn't hear anything but the pounding rain.

She closed her umbrella and stepped inside the door, dropping the umbrella into a nearby stand. "Kip? You home?"

She straightened her suit jacket, which she had not removed

while driving because it was cold in the Triumph, and dusted raindrops from her skirt as she looked around. She couldn't see much in the small foyer. Reaching for a light switch on the wall, she toggled it with no response. It then occurred to her that the streetlights in the neighborhood were also off. The storm had knocked the power out.

She ran from the house and back to the Triumph. Once she was safe inside her car, she was tempted to crank the engine to beat a retreat, but didn't give in. She fished a flashlight from the glove compartment and banged on it when it wouldn't light.

"Dollar ninety-nine special," she muttered.

The cheap instrument finally emitted a thin beam. She walked back to the house where the door stood ajar, as if beckoning her. A rambling old mansion, a madman, no electricity, and no weapon. It was the makings of a grade B horror flick. She would have fled in a nanosecond if it weren't for Brianna. She took a deep breath, steeling herself.

"Kip?" she called again from inside the foyer. She turned left and walked through the living room, dining room, and then entered the kitchen, continually banging her hand against the flashlight, which kept cutting out. The kitchen was empty. A set of cook's knives of all sizes were affixed to a magnetized strip on the wall. She selected an eight-inch kitchen knife, then shoved a less conspicuous paring knife into her skirt pocket, hoping, even under the circumstances, that it didn't cut the fabric.

From the kitchen, she walked into the family room. Outside, she could see the dark pool and patio area, which appeared to be empty. Distant fingers of lightning crackled, not giving much light. A clap of thunder sent her heart into her throat.

She went back up the three tiled steps to the foyer, then turned down the dark corridor where the bedrooms and Bridget's office were located. She passed the office, took a quick look inside, then continued on. Something wasn't right. She stopped and looked again.

"Come in, Iris," Kip said from where he sat behind the desk.

Holding the knife behind her back, she swung the flashlight beam around the room.

"No lights!" he ordered.

As if on command, the flashlight cut out on its own.

"He works in darkness. He won't come if the lights are on."

"Who?"

"Who do you think? Sit down."

A crackle of lightning briefly cast a halo around Kip's head. Iris saw the handgun on the desk in front of him. She tentatively sat in a chair near the desk, first turning it so she could quickly exit if she had to, and tucked the knife under her thigh.

"Iris, do you think if a person commits a crime, once that moral boundary is crossed, there's no going back? Is that person now likely to commit more crimes and more serious crimes? Is crime so seductive that, once you've tasted it, you're doomed?" He spoke in a quiet voice that was a bit hoarse, as if she were the only person he'd spoken to all day.

"I don't know, Kip. I haven't really thought about that."

"I have. I used to think criminals were low-life scumbags. Those guys who were in jail with me, I thought I was superior to them. But now I understand them. Living outside the law *is* seductive. You get a feeling of control. There's a jolt from taking what you want for no other reason than you want it. It's better than sex."

"Have you committed a crime?"

"Would you think differently of me if I had? Would you be afraid of me?"

She felt his eyes on her without seeing them.

"Yes, you would. You're afraid of me now. I can sense your fear. It's exciting in a way. I made a fortune trying to give people that feeling while they were sitting safely at their home computers, but it's a pale imitation of the real thing. Life's strange, isn't it? It frequently exceeds anything I could ever imagine."

Iris leaned toward him. "Let's get out of here, Kip."

Kip shook his head. "I can't. I have to stay right here. It's part of my strategy."

"Where's Brianna?"

"She's in a safe place. I've seen to that. This is the only way I can trap him. That's the secret key at the highest level of *Suckers Finish Last,* you know. Levels one through nine require the player to use aggressive action, speed, agility, wits, and big weapons. But then the player reaches the tenth level and the strategy changes completely. Players call Pandora's tech support lines in droves, tearing their hair out because they've tried and tried again and failed each time to win the final level. They accuse me of making the game impossible to win, but it's not true. See, the key to winning the final level is sitting quietly and waiting. The boss monster will eventually seek the player out, and the player will be ready. I must sit here and wait in the dark. I have the advantage. The boss monster is getting closer."

"Who is the boss monster?"

"You think I'm crazy, don't you?"

"No. No, Kip. I don't think you're crazy."

Kip rapidly inhaled and exhaled, silently laughing. "You always were a lousy liar, Iris. It's a trait I found rather endearing."

"Where did you get that gun?"

"This is the gun that was used to shoot Bridget and my dog. I found it the night of Bridget's murder. When I jogged home, it was sitting right there on the fifty-fourth step up from Capri Road. Then I saw the bloody footprints go off into the brush and dirt. I heard the police sirens and the commotion and I knew immediately what had happened. For a while I had felt something was at play, something had started. I just didn't know what it was yet. But now it's clear. The boss monster had made his move, killing one enemy and setting things up to punish his other enemy for life. He'd stolen my gun, disguised himself as the wild creation of my darkest thoughts, killed my wife and dog, left my footprints and left my gun, still smoking, for the police to find. But I found it first. His strategy was imperfect."

"You picked up the gun. That's how you got gunshot residue on your palm."

"And I climbed into the brush, in the opposite direction of the bloody footprints, to the storm drain Bridget and I installed. I pulled it apart, threw in the gun as far as I could, put the drain back together, took a branch, and wiped out my footprints, then ran up the stairs to enter the patio of death."

"You have to turn the gun over to the police. Don't you want them to find Bridget's murderer?"

"They think they already have. You know they don't want to hear anything that questions their view of reality. I've said too much already. I'm caving in to my emotions. I can't make the same mistakes he made."

"Let me take Brianna home with me."

"No."

"Certainly she doesn't have a role in this thing."

"But she does. A very important role. His strategy was foiled in large part because of her. I've become a secondary target."

"Kip! How long are you going to . . . play this game?"

"Until it's over. We've got plenty of earthquake supplies. I had them put away for four people. We're only two now. If we eat modestly, we can make it stretch for weeks."

"Earthquake supplies?" A bead of perspiration formed between Iris's shoulder blades and made its way down her back. "Aren't you afraid the boss monster might harm Brianna?"

"Not if I intercept him first. This is going to be played out one way or another. You don't seem to understand that."

Iris stood, taking the knife with her.

Kip didn't get up. "Iris, she's not yours to take."

"I refuse to let her be used as bait, Kip." Iris banged the flashlight against the back of the chair until it lit.

Kip stood behind the desk. "Iris, I'm warning you."

She shone the beam into Kip's face. He moaned and covered his eyes. She flew to the doorway, closed the door behind her, and pulled a low bench that was against one wall in front of it. She broke into a run down the corridor, looking in the numerous rooms for the child and not finding her. "Brianna!"

Kip opened the door and felt with his hand the bench that Iris had shoved in front. He could easily have moved it out of the way, but didn't. "Leave her alone!" he yelled.

Iris reached Brianna's room near the end of the hall. She frantically searched it with the flashlight but didn't see the child. "Brianna!" She heard something in the closet, fell upon the door, and opened it. There the little girl was, sitting on the floor with flashlights all around, playing with her dolls.

"Don't take my daughter, Iris!"

Iris exhaled with relief. "Hi, Brianna."

She seemed dazed. "Aunt Iris?"

"Yes, sweetheart. It's Aunt Iris. You're going to stay with me for a little while. Okay?"

Brianna got to her feet. "Who's going to take care of my daddy?"

"I'll check on him to make sure he's okay."

Holding Brianna in one hand and the flashlight and knife in the other, Iris walked into the corridor. The bench in front of the office door had not been moved. They hurried past the office. Iris saw Kip standing motionless in the doorway.

"Iris, please," he said.

She jogged the rest of the way, moving as fast as Brianna could go. She left her umbrella in the stand and loaded Brianna into the Triumph. Thankfully, the starter worked on the first try.

Chapter 35

"She looks so much like Bridget," Rose commented.

"Poor thing must have been exhausted," Iris said. "She's still asleep. It was so weird. It was like Kip couldn't leave that room."

"He probably wanted you to take Brianna," Marge said. "That's why he didn't stop you."

The women moved from the doorway of Iris's home office where Brianna was sleeping on a pullout couch and walked into the kitchen.

"I have some *darling* little great-nieces. Maybe they can come and play with her today while you're at work," Marge suggested.

"Iris, you did the right thing," Rose said, guessing what was on her daughter's mind. "From what you said, it sounds like Kip *has* lost his mind. That poor child has been through enough."

Iris sighed deeply. "I don't even know what the right thing is anymore. Could Kip have me arrested for kidnapping? I'd better call Brianna's grandparents and let them know where she is."

As Iris was dialing the Tylers' number, Rose peered inside the refrigerator. "No wonder you look like skin and bones. There's no food in this house."

Iris dug her thumb into the loose waistband of her skirt. "I've lost weight. I'd been so busy, I hadn't noticed. Cool." She looked out the large picture window at the rain that was still steadily falling as it had all night. "Hi," she said into the telephone. "This is Iris Thorne. Who's this? . . . You're one of Bridget's brothers, aren't you? I'm sorry to be calling so early. Is Natalie around? . . . No, no, there's no need to contact them. Let them enjoy their time away. Everything's fine. I just wanted to let them know that Brianna's staying with me for a few days. My number should be in Natalie's book. . . . Okay. G'bye."

"Where does Brianna go to school, Iris?" Marge asked.

"School?" Iris said. "I forgot about school."

"She can miss one day," Rose said.

Iris looked at her watch. "I'd better make an appearance at the carnival of horrors. I've got my own boss monster to deal with. See you later."

Iris walked into McKinney Alitzer's sales department with her head held high, her footsteps firm and certain, and a pleasant smile pasted on her face. She was late arriving and the department was in full swing with everyone pitching product as if their lives depended on it. They did.

She saw Evan Finn on the phone in his new office and had to count to ten to calm down. *Your hours are numbered, pal,* she silently reassured herself. *Kip Cross isn't the only one with a strategy.*

"Morning, Louise," she said to her assistant, who looked at her over the top of her half-glasses. That gesture always made Iris feel like a recalcitrant schoolgirl. "How's the temperature?"

"I think everyone's trying to pretend that Evan doesn't exist. Half a dozen people have asked me what in the world is going on."

"And you tell them?"

"Nothing's going on."

Iris nodded with satisfaction and went inside her office. She was putting her things away when Louise came in.

"Jim Patel of Tech Associates called and canceled his lunch date with you today."

"Another venture capitalist who won't come near me. He's not getting off the hook that easily."

"You have his number?"

"Indeed I do." Iris sat in her leather chair, picked up a manila file folder from the corner of her desk, opened it, and dialed the number scribbled on the inside front cover. After plowing past a receptionist and stepping on a secretary, she reached Patel.

"Hi, Jim. Iris Thorne. Sorry to hear about our lunch date today. I'd like to reschedule. Let's set something up for when you return. . . . Uh-huh. Sure. Jim, let's be frank. Do you not want to meet with me because you have doubts about Pandora's prospects? . . . Who told you that Kip Cross's holed up in his house acting like a lunatic? . . . Well, the grapevine is passing misinformation. Kip Cross is holed up in his house, all right, but it's because he's hard at work on Pandora's next release. When the new game is out and it leaves everything else in the technological dust, you'll regret not having jumped in early." They ended the call with obligatory and false pleasantries.

Iris was still steaming when Louise came in with a mug of black coffee.

"Kip Cross is losing his mind and the word is already out."

"T. Duke Sawyer?" Louise ventured.

"Maybe. Or it's someone at Pandora. Each time T. Duke lowers the price, the employees lose money. I wouldn't put it past them to try and sabotage me."

"Even Toni Burton?"

"No, she's for going public. She's already made a play for me to name her president of Pandora. She wouldn't have that kind of clout if Pandora was absorbed by the Sawyer Company." Iris leaned to one side and looked out her door, catching a glimpse of Evan's office. "Speaking of Sawyers, what's Top Gun been up to?"

"Quietly working in his new, private office. Iris, I have to let you know that you lost face around here by hiring Evan back and giving him special perks."

"Thanks for your candor, Louise, but I'd figured as much." Iris took a sip of coffee, then stood and fumbled inside her jacket pocket. "I'd best wish him a cheery good morning."

Evan was on the phone, his chair swiveled to face his office window, his back to the door. When she knocked on the doorjamb, he turned and seemed pleasantly surprised to see her. He regally waved her inside.

She closed the door behind her and gave a quick twist to the rod of the miniblinds over the window that faced the suite, closing them. She sat stiffly in a chair facing his desk.

A cigarette burned in an ashtray in front of Evan. There was a no-smoking policy in the building. She figured no one had got up the courage to confront Evan about it.

"Sounds good," he said into the phone. He took a drag on the cigarette and rakishly winked at her.

Can it, A-hole, she said to herself. *It's lost on me.*

When he tapped his cigarette over the ashtray, Iris noticed his knuckles were bruised.

"Iris!" he enthused as he hung up the phone. "To what do I owe this pleasure?" He clearly thought she was working for him.

"I've been thinking a lot about you, Evan," she confessed.

"Have you?" He took another drag on his cigarette and slowly let the smoke trail from between his sensuously parted lips.

She surveyed the surroundings. "Looks like you've got it all now. Window office, title, paycheck . . . just like a real citizen."

Grinning, he pressed out the cigarette in the ashtray. "It all started here."

"Next you'll be paying taxes, voting, curbing your dog . . . ," she recited sarcastically.

"Yeah, that's right."

"My ass. You never were and never will be anything more than a freak"—she paused—"with good taste in clothes."

It wasn't hard to tell that he didn't like her comment. His eyes grew cold the same way they had the day he'd assaulted her in her office. "Freak?" He raised his eyebrows. "Speak for yourself. I've been watching you. I know how you live. You're the fucking freak."

Iris knew she was in deep, but she had no intention of stopping. She was taking a sadistic pleasure from prodding him, having been on the other end of that stick one too many times lately. She casually examined her fingernails. "Tell me, Evan. That prostitute in Vegas, Rita Free . . . Did you throw her over the balcony in one clean thrust or did she struggle?"

He stared hard at her. "You got some mouth on you, you know that?"

"How did it sound when she hit the ground?"

"You tell me. Sounds like you know all about it."

She gave herself an impromptu manicure as she talked. "Did it excite you?"

"You're asking for it, Iris."

She feigned disappointment. *"C'mon,* Evan! I've never talked to a real murderer before. Well, no one who I knew for sure . . ."

"I'll give it to you, Iris. You know I will."

"Is this the way Rita Free talked to you before you killed her? How about Bridget? You probably didn't give poor Bridget a chance to talk."

He bolted from the chair and circled the desk. She stumbled getting up, knocking her chair over as she backed up against the wall. He had almost reached her when he stopped in his tracks and slowly stepped back.

The .22 she held was aimed straight at his heart. "Put your things in your briefcase and get the hell out."

"You'd never shoot me."

"Maybe I wouldn't. But I've been doing a lot of crazy things lately. Are you willing to take that chance?"

They stared at each other for several long seconds. Finally, Evan returned to the desk, threw his belongings into his briefcase, snapped it closed, opened the door, and walked out.

Iris tentatively stepped into the doorway where she could see Evan quickly moving through the suite and into the lobby. After he was gone, she slipped the gun back into her pocket, righted the chair she'd knocked over, collapsed into it, and pressed her hand against her pounding heart. She was still sitting that way when Liz came in.

"There you are!" Liz looked around. "Where's Top Gun?"

"Off in the wild, blue yonder, I guess." Iris nervously smoothed her hair, then pulled the gun from her pocket. "I want to give this back to you."

"But you just borrowed it yesterday. I thought you wanted to try it out at the gun range to see if you'd like one for yourself. Keep it awhile. I've got three bigger ones at home. Hell, the one I keep in my glove compartment is bigger than that bitsy thing."

Iris again held the gun toward Liz. "I've changed my mind. Don't want a gun. Don't like guns. I'd have to get a permit to carry one anyway."

"Permit schmermit," Liz said disdainfully as she took the weapon from Iris. Liz checked to see if it was loaded. It was. "Know what my cop clients tell me: better to be judged by twelve than carried by eight." She slipped it into her jacket pocket.

"I've found you." Louise breathlessly appeared in the doorway. "Sam Eastman's wife just called. Sam's in the hospital. He's been beaten."

At the hospital, Janice Eastman got up from the chair next to Sam's bed and met Iris outside the door, but not before Iris caught a glimpse of her boss. His face was swollen almost beyond recognition.

"Janice, what happened?"

"Sam figures the guy snuck into the garage when he was pulling the car in last night. When he got out, the guy slugged him in the head from behind, then beat him." She covered her face with her hands. "He kicked him when he was on the ground. What kind of monster would do something like that?"

"Did Sam see who it was?"

She shook her head. "He was tall, male, wearing a ski mask." She gazed into Sam's room. "The doctors say he'll be fine. He wants to talk to you."

Iris walked into the room, trying to look natural and not horrified by Sam's appearance. He probably didn't know how bad he looked. She rested her fingers lightly on his arm.

He looked at her through thin slits in his swollen eyes. "I'm sorry, Iris. I told myself I did it for the money. Lying here, I've had time to think about it. It wasn't about money. I was jealous of you."

Iris didn't say anything. She didn't like or respect the man, but it pained her to see anyone in the shape he was in, and the bold honesty of his confession brought a tear to her eye. "Who did it, Sam? Evan?"

"I don't know. Last night, T. Duke called me, wanting the money back he'd paid me. Told me the deal was that Evan would stay in the firm until the SEC got wind of it and started investigating. I told him I had fulfilled my part of the bargain. I wasn't going to give the money back. Could have been Baines, for all I know."

"I think it was Evan, Sam. The knuckles on his right hand were bruised today. It was revenge for setting him up."

"Is he at the office?" Sam asked.

"He's gone. For now, at least."

Chapter 36

It had rained hard for many days and nights without reprieve. The long-overdue rain that had initially been welcome, cleansing, and refreshing now felt oppressive and claustrophobic. California didn't do much weather. But when she did, she did it to death.

Iris felt a moment of panic when she walked into her house and found it empty and eerily quiet except for the relentless rain. Then she remembered that Marge was going to have her great-nieces come over to play with Brianna.

Iris knocked on Marge's door and was greeted with squeals of laughter, high-pitched screaming, the aroma of food cooking, and two frazzled older women.

"They've been having a *ball,*" Marge said, resting her fingertips on Iris's arm. "And so have *we.*"

"We bought her some of the cutest clothes," Rose said. "Just a few things. How long are you going to keep her?"

"Her grandparents will be back tomorrow. I think it's best to take her over there." Iris dialed a number on Marge's telephone. "I should call Kip. Could you get Brianna, please? She probably wants to talk to her daddy."

Iris listened to Kip's phone ring and ring. "C'mon, Kip." After many rings, the answering machine picked up. She was chilled to hear Bridget's voice still on it.

"This is the Cross residence. Please leave a message for Bridget, Kip, or Brianna at the tone. Have a great day!"

Iris was so stunned, she forgot to speak. "Kip? Kip, pick up. I know you're there."

He finally came on the line. "Bring my daughter home."

"Kip, she's fine here. She's playing with some little friends, having fun and laughing. You have to agree that this is better for her than being cooped up in that house."

"She needs to come home."

"Here she is, Kip. You'll see she's fine."

Brianna bounded into the room, her hair, which Rose and Marge had arranged with ribbons and barrettes, flying behind her. It was the first time since Bridget's death that Iris had seen the child so carefree. "Daddy! I went shopping with Marge and Rose, and they bought me the Barbie doll I wanted, and now I'm playing with Alissa and Kayla." Brianna held the receiver with both hands, intently listening. "But I like staying with Aunt Iris and Rose and Marge."

Marge handed Iris some crayon drawings that Brianna had drawn.

Brianna jammed the phone in Iris's direction. "He wants to talk to you." Brianna was out of the room in half a second.

"Kip, can't you see that she's better off here for now?"

"Bring her home, Iris."

"Why?"

"I told you why."

"She's safe here. I'm taking her to the Tylers' tomorrow. You have my phone number." Iris hung up, shaking her head.

"He wants her to come home?" Rose asked. "And what—sit there in that house like a prisoner or worse? What's wrong with that man?"

Iris looked at Brianna's drawings.

"I've got a roast in the oven," Marge said. "You're staying for dinner, of course."

"Thanks, Marge. I'd love to." Iris frowned at the drawings. They were variations on the same theme of Brianna's other efforts. Two showed Slade Slayer standing over the bodies of Bridget and Stetson, holding a gun. A tiny figure lurked in the background. One was of the turquoise and white Cross house. Someone with a fuzz of gray hair, probably Kip, was peeking out a window with bars over it, like a jail. Behind another barred window was the tiny figure with dark hair that Brianna drew to symbolize herself. A gigantic Slade Slayer loomed next to the house. The drawings were crude, appropriate for a five-year-old's skill level, but the inherent messages were clear.

"Doesn't take much to interpret this one," Iris commented.

"They're kind of creepy, aren't they?" Rose said, looking over Iris's shoulder.

Iris looked more closely at one of the drawings of the crime scene. "It's interesting. These recent works are more detailed than the ones Brianna drew when she was at her grandmother's. Look here. Slade Slayer's hands have five little lines for fingers. On the early ones, she drew flesh-colored blobs for hands."

"And the fingers are black."

"You think the murderer's a colored man?" Rose asked.

"But the feet aren't black." Iris pointed there. The feet were nothing more than L-shapes with five little lines at the end of each *L* to indicate toes. A black line was drawn underneath each foot with a loop drawn over the first toe, in a crude rendering of a flip-flop sandal. "She used the flesh-colored crayon."

"The murderer was wearing black gloves," Rose exclaimed.

"Why don't we ask Brianna if that's what she meant," Marge suggested.

"I don't know if we should," Iris said. "She seems to be engaged in some free-flowing subconscious thing. I don't want to hamper it by drawing attention to it."

Marge folded her bony fingers around Iris's arm and led her toward the kitchen. "Why don't the adults have an aperitif?"

"Great idea," Rose said.

As they walked past the living room windows, Iris noticed a green Range Rover pull up in front of her house next door. "Oh, no."

"Who's that?" Rose looked out the window. "A friend of yours?"

"Hardly." Iris expected to see Evan, but Summer Fontaine

got out of the Range Rover's driver's door and started walking to Iris's front door.

Iris walked onto Marge's porch and called, "Summer! I'm over here."

Summer was wearing trousers with suspenders over a skin-tight, black turtleneck sweater, the high collar making her breasts prominent. She waved at Iris and walked down the sidewalk and up Marge's front path.

"Hi," she breathed. "Aren't you sick of this rain?"

Iris was in no mood for small talk. "Isn't that Evan's car?"

"He's letting me borrow it."

Iris searched her mind for a way that Evan might have come into contact with Summer. Then she remembered the day Summer had come to McKinney Alitzer and Evan had followed her out of the suite and into the elevator. Iris felt sorry for Toni. She not only fell for a louse but was thrown over for a bimbo. A double whammy. "So you and Evan are . . . ," she started, even though she thought she already knew the score.

"He's been helping me since Kip threw me out."

It was wet and cold outside. Any civilized person would have invited Summer inside, but Iris felt like being a bitch.

"Look, Iris. I know you don't like me, but I just had to make sure Brianna's all right."

Iris noticed her mother and Marge peeking at them through the dining room drapes.

"She's fine. I picked her up from Kip's last night. Thanks for letting me know about the situation there." Iris recalled that Summer had considered the child's well-being and she warmed to her slightly. "Do you want to come inside?"

"Is Brianna here? Can I see her for just a minute?" Summer wiped her feet on the mat and stepped inside.

Marge, ever the gracious hostess, came to welcome her and offer something hot to drink.

"No, thank you," Summer answered. "I just want to see Brianna and I'll go. I miss her. I raised her since she was a baby, you know. I was with her more than Bridget was."

Iris defended her friend. "You know that's not true. Bridget was a wonderful mother."

"Everyone talks about poor Bridget. What a tragedy. But I've suffered too. You don't know what it was like to work for that woman."

"Summer, I'm surprised Bridget put up with you as long as she did. When she fired you, you quickly found a way to get back in the house, didn't you?"

Summer drew her eyebrows together in an overwrought look of confusion. "What are you saying?"

Iris was about to show Summer the door when Brianna ran out and flung herself onto her. "Summer!"

Summer dropped to her knees and enveloped the child between her arms. "I missed you so much, baby." Tears ran down her cheeks. "Are you having fun?"

Iris scowled as she watched their interchange.

Brianna abruptly ran from the room, yelling, "I made you something! I'll go get it."

Summer, still kneeling on the ground, looked up at Iris. "My life's been turned upside down too." She rapidly blinked, squeezing large tears from her eyes.

Iris was unmoved.

Brianna ran back into the room, clutching a sheet of paper. "I drew a picture of you, Summer."

The drawing appeared to be the patio of the Cross house. A large, light blue rectangle, drawn with no sense of perspective, represented the pool. Inverted *Ls* around it looked like the patio furniture. On one, a figure with long blonde hair, wearing a hot-pink, two-piece bathing suit reclined. One spindly, starfish-like hand was raised in a wave. A crude table stood next to the lounge chair. On it was a glass of something brown with a straw in it and a little pink square next to it.

"That's your diet Coke," Brianna explained. "And that's your nail polish. See?" She pointed to the figure's fingertips, which were each topped with a pink blob.

Summer grabbed the child hard and sobbed, "Thank you, baby." She let her go, then took the picture. "I'll keep it always." She stood and stroked Brianna's hair.

Marge's great-nieces began yelling for their new friend from the back of the house.

"Gotta go!" Brianna importantly announced, and sped off.

Summer was wiping her face with her hand when Rose appeared with a tissue. Iris could always count on her mother to have a supply of tissues, no matter what the circumstances.

"Thanks." Summer delicately dabbed the tissue against her face. "Well, I'd better go. Can I come see her again?"

Iris nodded, even though she was jealous of Summer and Brianna's close bond. "Sure. You're still at that hotel. The Château . . ."

"Bordeaux. Bungalow Five." Summer sniffed and smiled, putting on a brave face behind her tears.

Iris felt a flicker of sympathy for the woman, even though she still wanted to slap her silly.

Summer raced back to the Range Rover in the rain, like a featured performer in a chipper diet-soda commercial. Iris watched Summer's bouncy buttocks recede and considered her dislike of bimbos. It was almost an instinctive thing, like a snake and a mongoose or a Crip and a Blood. But she was now beginning to wonder whether Summer wasn't being dumb like a fox.

It took Iris a few minutes to realize she had awakened for a reason, that it was more than her subconscious churning too loudly that had made her open her eyes and blink at the darkness. It was hard to separate other noises from the rain, but something about the sound of her front door opening was like no other. She heard it on a visceral rather than aural level.

She threw off the goose-down comforter and layers of blankets and struggled to untwist herself from her long flannel nightgown before she managed to set her bare foot on the floor. She pulled open the bedroom door, which she had left ajar, and walked down the hallway, passing the room that Brianna was sleeping in on her right. She would have peeked in there but something else caught her attention. Moonlit rain was pounding on the porch outside the open front door. A small semicircle had been cut from the adjacent window.

She ran to Brianna's room and switched on the light. Her bed was empty. Iris climbed on top of it, looking around and underneath, whimpering, her heart pounding, hoping that the child was hiding somewhere, knowing her hope was irrational but hoping anyway. She flung off the covers, finding a doll and stuffed dog but no Brianna. Crayons were scattered on the mattress, as if Brianna had been drawing when she dropped off to sleep. The pad of drawing paper had worked to the end of the bed. Iris grabbed it. On it was another portrait of Slade Slayer in black with crudely drawn sneer and gun. The figure was wearing flip-flops, like in her other drawings, but in this rendering, each of the spindly toes was topped with a blob of hot pink.

Chapter 37

Iris stumbled into some clothes, her mind and mouth going a mile a minute, with nothing lucid resulting.

"Why didn't I get an alarm? I have to call Kip. What if he didn't take her? I have to get her back before he finds out. My God! Why didn't I install better locks? I should call the police. They won't believe me, they never believe me. They'll take forever to get here and by then . . . Oh my God!"

She threw on a raincoat, pulled a baseball cap on her head, and waded to the Triumph. A river of water coursed down the hill. She cranked the engine and was soon off. The intersection of Casa Marina Drive and the Pacific Coast Highway was flooded, submerging the low Triumph to its floorboards. She ran the traffic light at the bottom of the hill, not daring to risk having the car short out and become trapped in the swirling water. There wasn't much traffic to worry about. A person had to be nuts to be outside.

There was no easy way to get where she was going. The freeways in the rain could frequently be more treacherous than the surface streets, developing vast lakes many yards in diameter and as deep as a foot in low spots. She took Sunset Boulevard, where the two lanes closest to the center were the only ones navigable. Some of the intersections were flooded, and she forced herself to slow to a crawl going through them to avoid hydroplaning. She cooed to the Triumph, "C'mon, baby, c'mon. Do it for Momma," which valiantly kept running even though its guts had been partially submerged.

The low, wide car held the curves as Sunset twisted and turned through Pacific Palisades, Brentwood, Westwood, and Beverly Hills. At the Sunset Strip, the boulevard straightened. The marquee lights of the clubs and restaurants were dark. It was then that Iris noticed everything was dark. The electricity was out.

She parked on the street near the gardens and bungalows of the Château Bordeaux. Taking her cheap flashlight from the glove compartment, she pounded on it. It lit, darkened, then lit again. She climbed the grassy knoll, the flashlight barely illuminating a few feet ahead of her, the rain saturating her hair through the baseball cap, and headed for the bungalow farthest from the others. When she got close enough, she could see a brass 5 on the closed door. She knocked, and the unlatched door creaked open.

"Hello? Summer? Brianna?"

She smelled cigarette smoke as she leaned over the threshold without entering the room. She shone the flashlight around. On a table next to an easy chair near the door was a full ashtray and a cigarette lighter that looked like Evan Finn's. She felt the flashlight batteries clunk to the end of the base, breaking the connection and cutting the beam.

"Crap!"

She madly shook the flashlight to no avail, then pushed the door all the way open, letting in the scant light available from the night sky. She made out the silhouette of someone sitting in a chair against the wall across the room.

"Summer?"

Iris futilely pounded the flashlight as she crept closer to the motionless figure. Suddenly, the electricity sputtered on, powering the lamps in the room, throwing it into a bright light. Summer was wearing a flimsy pink nightgown and a bullet hole between her sculptured eyebrows.

The door to the small kitchen creaked open an inch, and Iris was confronted with the platinum crew cut and porcelain sneer of Slade Slayer. As the lights dimmed and again went out, Iris saw the flash from the gun before she heard it. She ran.

When she was halfway across the lawn, she turned to see Slade Slayer, dressed in black, taking aim. She flung herself onto the ground, and the bullet hit the soggy grass in front of her. She clambered up and kept low as she lurched across the grass, finally reaching the Triumph. She smoothly got her keys from her pocket and into the ignition without a second lost and cranked the key for all it was worth. The starter clicked. She tried again. It clicked again.

"Son of a bitch!"

Slade Slayer was almost upon her. She gave the ignition one last try, then fled the car and ran down the sidewalk. Another bullet sailed past, again missing her. She was terrified to look back but had to see how close the monster was. She did. It was close.

A car heading in the opposite direction on Sunset Boulevard slowed as it neared Iris. It skidded as it made a U-turn on the vacant street, hopped the curb, and came to a stop almost in front of her. It was a green Range Rover. The passenger door flew open. Evan leaned across the seat and yelled, "Get in!"

Iris looked at him, then at Slade Slayer, who was again taking aim, and climbed inside just as a bullet hit the open passenger door. Before she could close it, Evan peeled away from the curb, the tires skidding on the wet street. Iris madly grabbed at the open door, trying to snag it without falling from the car. Then Evan took a curve hard and the door slammed closed on its own, propelling her into him.

Iris didn't breathe a sigh of relief.

"Don't look at me like that," he snapped. "I didn't kill her. I went out to pick up some food, came back, and that's how I found her."

"Where's Brianna?"

"Isn't she with you?" Evan sounded genuinely surprised.

"You and Summer didn't kidnap her?"

"No!"

"Take me to a police station."

Evan didn't respond and kept driving, too fast on the rain-slick streets.

"Why were you driving by just now?" Iris asked.

"I told you—I went out to get cigarettes. I saw Summer dead and split. My car was parked in back. I swung around the front, that's all."

"You said you went out to get food."

"Cigarettes. I went to get cigarettes."

He had turned off Sunset into the hills above Hollywood. On the other side of the hills were sparsely populated canyons. A favorite dumping ground for bodies.

"Where are we going?" she demanded.

He didn't say anything or look at her. But she detected a satisfied curl around the edges of his lips.

"They're going to think you murdered Summer, you know," she attempted. "You did prison time for manslaughter. You left the scene of this murder. What else would the cops think?" She looked around, trying to figure out where they were. "I hope you know that I wasn't really going to shoot you this morning," she tittered nervously.

Evan didn't respond but reached inside a pocket on the driver's door and pulled out a fresh package of cigarettes. He opened them, steering the car with his forearms, put one between his lips, then started patting his front pockets.

"You left your lighter in Summer's bungalow. I saw it right there near the door."

"Shit!" he cursed.

Iris could tell his mind was racing. She helped it along. "Did you sleep in that room?"

"No."

"Did you have sex?"

"Yesterday, but the maid changed the sheets since then."

"There's still probably trace evidence around. Course, your lighter is a bit more than a trace, especially if your fingerprints are on it. And the cigarette butts—bound to have your DNA on them. Oh, boy. Even worse." Iris became overtly thoughtful. "If I were you, I wouldn't be so flip about leaving stuff like that at the scene of a murder."

"You think the cops are there yet?"

"I doubt it. In this rain and darkness, I'd be surprised if anyone heard or saw anything that would merit calling the police."

Evan stopped the car in the middle of a narrow street, turned around, and started back.

Iris barely breathed, afraid she'd exhale a sigh of relief if she did. She forced herself not to fidget. Finally, the Château Bordeaux was in sight.

"You're in luck, Evan. Doesn't look like there are any—" As he was slowing down to park, Iris jumped out of the still-moving Range Rover and fell into the street. Evan screeched to a stop a few yards ahead, threw the car into reverse and headed for her. She hopped inside the Triumph and locked the door. The keys were in the ignition where she'd left them. She cranked it.

"C'mon, baby."

It clicked. She tried again and again and it clicked. Evan was out of the Range Rover and next to the Triumph. He pulled on the locked door. When it wouldn't give, he pounded his fist on the ragtop.

She continued trying to get the engine to turn over as Evan opened a pocketknife. He slit a gash in the car's top, reached in with both hands, and grabbed her. She held on to the steering wheel with her left hand and cranked the ignition key with her right. Just as she was about to lose her grip and go sailing out the top of the car, the engine turned over. He still had ahold of her. She struggled to reach the gearshift. Her fingertips grazed the plastic knob, her foot barely depressing the clutch pedal. He pulled her hard and her foot slipped from the clutch, popping it. The car stalled but not before it lurched forward, making him slip on the street and lose his grip on her. He started to pull himself up, clinging to the door handle. She turned the ignition key. It again clicked without firing. She tried again. The engine turned over. She threw it into first gear and tore down the boulevard, knocking Evan into the street.

Iris swung the Triumph around the dead-end street in front of the Cross house, positioning it for a quick getaway. She left the lights on and the engine running. The electricity was out here too, and she'd lost her crummy flashlight somewhere at the Château Bordeaux. Lightning flashed high in the sky, followed by a clap of thunder.

She opened the front door, which Kip never seemed to lock anymore, and left it open.

"Brianna?"

She felt her way down the corridor and into Bridget's office. "Kip?"

She squinted into the darkness, to which her eyes were now adjusted. The office was empty. She heard Brianna scream.

She ran down the corridor into the family room. Through the French doors, next to the pool, she saw Kip standing in front of Brianna, shielding her from Slade Slayer, who was holding them both at gunpoint. Now that Iris got a good look at the size of the person wearing the mask, she was confident she knew who it was.

Iris picked up a telephone from the coffee table. The line was dead. The storm had knocked the phones out. She remembered the gun Kip had in his office and wondered whether it was still there and if she had time to get it. Something in Kip's posture grew more frantic, and something in the monster's became restless and edgy. Iris decided she'd run out of time.

She ran to the French doors, raised both fists, and started pounding on the glass. "Hey! I'm over here! Yoo-hoo! Come and get me!"

When Slade Slayer turned to look, Kip lunged for the creature's ankles. Iris flew from the house and scooped the terrified child into her arms. Just as she reached the back gate, she heard a gunshot and a sharp cry. She covered Brianna's eyes and turned to see Kip falling backward into the pool.

Iris ran out the gate and down the stairs as fast as she could, carrying Brianna. She wasn't aware of the child's weight. She wasn't aware of anything except the need to get away. Reaching the bottom of the stairs, she ran across Capri Road. She took a quick look behind her and saw that Slade Slayer was close. Iris ran into the abandoned house.

The front door swung open from a single hinge. The foyer was cluttered with trash, broken masonry, the remnants of a dead campfire, and piles of clothing. The walls were covered with spray-painted graffiti. Iris peeked behind the dangling front door, then squeezed herself and Brianna into that space.

"Don't be scared," she told the child, telling herself at the same time. "We'll hide until it's safe. Shhh." She wrapped her arms tightly around Brianna.

Iris clutched her tighter as they heard footsteps pass on the warped and pitted hardwood floor. The footsteps receded, then returned. Iris was relieved when she heard their pursuer ascend the staircase. The second she heard footsteps on the floor above, she and Brianna would slip unseen out the front door.

Iris felt something brush against her jeans leg. She thought it was Brianna's foot, but looked down and saw a large rat sniffing around their legs. She looked away, gritting her teeth, hoping that Brianna didn't see the rat. It didn't work. The child screamed.

Iris picked Brianna up underneath her arms and swung her from behind the door onto the cracked front porch. "Run down the stairs to Aunt Marge's and pound on the door."

Brianna looked at her with a mixture of confusion and fear. She took a hesitant step, then turned back. "I don't want to leave you!"

Iris pointed in the direction of the stairs. "I'll be fine. Go!"

Brianna looked as if she was about to burst into tears, but she turned and ran. Iris went back into the house as the figure of Slade Slayer appeared at the top of the stairs. Iris darted into the rubbish-strewn living room, which looked ghostly in the light filtering through the large broken windows, leaped onto one of the window frames, and was about to lower herself onto the hill below when the whole house shuddered. She lost her balance and fell into the mud.

She was struggling to pull her arms from her long, mud-soaked raincoat when she saw Slade Slayer in the window above her. She freed herself from the coat but couldn't get out of the way before her would-be killer jumped. The rain-soaked earth shifted again. They both slid down the hill in the mud, helpless to halt their descent. When they stopped, the masked figure was climbing to its knees, aiming a gun at her. Iris sprang forward. They struggled for the weapon. There was a terrifying noise above them as the house moved. Then they were in motion again, tumbling down the hill of mud.

Iris toppled head over heels, futilely grabbing at passing bushes, some of which were sliding along with her. Slade Slayer had gone down headfirst, losing the gun. When the slide stopped, Iris's head was partially submerged in mud. Grunting, choking, she pulled free. Looking up, she saw the exposed foundation of the house above. The huge structure creaked ominously.

Iris screamed as the figure of Slade Slayer loomed above her, black-gloved hands reaching to wrap themselves around her throat and push her head down into the soft, suffocating mud.

Iris grabbed the face above her with both hands, jamming her thumbs through the mask's eyeholes. Slade Slayer emitted a guttural moan but still did not release her. Mud seeped into Iris's mouth, but she maintained her grip. Finally, the monster let go. Iris spit mud as she tried to sit up but couldn't. The suction-like mud held her fast.

The house creaked loudly.

The monster was crouched low, keening as it rubbed its eyes with one hand and steadied itself with the other against the mud, as if dazed. Iris had almost pulled herself free when Slade Slayer screamed with fury and again fell upon her. Iris blindly clutched at the ground. Her hand grazed something hard. She tightened her fingers around a chunk of concrete, said a prayer, then slammed it with all her might against Slade Slayer's head.

The masked creature fell backward. Iris leaned over and continued to strike . . . until with a cry of horror, she let the concrete fall from her hand. Hurriedly, she hooked her fingers beneath the edge of the killer's torn mask and laboriously pulled it off, revealing the bloody, unconscious face of Toni Burton.

"Oh, my God!" Iris cried. "What have I done?"

On her knees, Iris grabbed Toni by the collar and began dragging her over the rumbling, shifting ground toward the stairs, sobbing with the effort. She slipped against the slick mud but reached the railing, grabbing it and hauling herself onto the staircase. Gasping, spitting out mud, she slipped one arm underneath Toni's and was hoisting her onto the steps when the house, and the hillside beneath it, gave way.

Iris clutched both the railing and Toni with all her might. The cement staircase rattled and swayed as if it was going to be pulled down. She clung harder. Then it stopped. She opened her eyes and saw a crater where the house once stood.

"Don't move! Put your hands up!" Detective Stubbs was poised on the steps above her. She was armed.

"It's me," Iris said in a weak voice that surprised her. "It's Iris."

Stubbs ran down to her. "You're covered in mud. I didn't know it was you."

They both struggled to pull Toni onto the steps.

Iris sat up and looked at the woman's seemingly lifeless body with horror. "She tried to smother me. I hit her. I hit her hard. I . . ."

Stubbs took Toni's pulse. "She's alive."

Iris imploringly raised her hands. "I couldn't stop."

"You saved her life. You both could have been buried in that slide."

Iris crouched against the stairs and surveyed the scene of devastation with a sense of dark relief.

Chapter 38

Unseen by Iris, a hand slipped around the doorframe of her office and turned off the lights. She looked up from her work, momentarily thinking the rain had knocked out the electricity again, but remembered that the storm had passed through. The sky was clear.

"Happy anniversary to you!"

Louise came in carrying a whipped-cream-topped pie with a single lit candle on top. Liz Martini, Kyle Tucker, Amber Ambrose, Warren Gray, Sean Bliss, and all the rest were singing as they crammed into Iris's office.

"Happy anniversary to you!"

Sam Eastman came in last, still wearing bruises and bandages but walking under his own power.

"Happy six-month anniversary as branch manager, dear Iris. Happy anniversary to you."

Everyone clapped and cheered.

Iris smiled at the group. "Wow! Thanks. I guess it has been six months. Went by in the blink of an eye." She looked at the pie. "Mmmm . . . this looks good. What kind is it?"

Louise handed her a pie cutter. She was holding a stack of paper plates and a box of plastic forks.

"It's a special recipe, just for you, Iris," Liz said, smirking.

Iris stood and cut into the pie. "Does it have an Oreo crust or something?"

"Something," Liz said.

When Iris saw Liz and a few of the others exchange glances, she knew something was up. She finished cutting a piece, lifted it out, and frowned at the heavy, dark brown filling. The group started snickering.

"What *is* this?"

"We figured you hadn't eaten any for a week and were probably having withdrawals," Kyle said.

Iris poked at the filling. "It's *mud!*"

The snickers turned into belly laughs.

"Not funny," Iris said, trying to look stern and hurt, but losing to laughter. "Very unfunny. I'm still washing mud out of my hair."

Liz came around Iris's desk and hugged her. "I confess. It was my idea."

"You!" Iris shoved the pie toward Liz's face, getting whipped cream on her chin. "Some friend you turned out to be!" she said without meaning it. They struggled with the pie, which ended up face-down on top of the reports Iris had been reviewing, reducing everyone to tears.

Louise came to the rescue and scooped up the mess from Iris's desk. "The real cake is in the lunchroom." She handed the plates and forks to Liz. "Why don't you take these in there while I take care of this?"

Iris walked to the lunchroom next to Sam. "Looks like you're feeling a lot better."

"I am, thanks. There's still no sign of Evan Finn. The police have a warrant out for him, but I think he's long gone."

"He'll probably turn up somewhere with a new name. Start up Canterbury Investments again."

Sam and Iris lingered outside the lunchroom, out of earshot of the group. Sam said, "The police searched that office in the business park, looking for records, but he'd already cleaned it out. They wanted to warn the people he'd conned not to do business with him anymore. I guess those poor folks will just continue getting ripped off." He looked at Iris a bit sheepishly. "This whole thing has been a wake-up call for me, Iris."

Iris leaned close to him and said in a low voice, "Other than me, no one here knows Evan's true story except Louise and Liz. You could put bamboo splinters underneath their fingernails and they still wouldn't tell. Everyone thinks Evan was mad about being fired and he beat you up." She shook her head. "It's really a shame. Smart, good-looking guy, screwed up like that."

"Guess he's just a bad seed," Sam added.

"Let's get some cake."

Liz handed Iris a big corner piece with lots of frosting and a rose, which she dug into with relish.

"Look who's here!"

Iris heard Louise's voice above the crowd, which parted to let Kip Cross, his arm in a sling, and Brianna pass. Brianna was trying to lead a recalcitrant German shepherd puppy by a leash.

Liz winced at the dog. "Isn't that the cutest thing you've ever seen?"

Brianna bent over and picked up the puppy around its middle. The dog slipped through her grasp so that she was clinging to it underneath its forelegs. The dog didn't seem to mind. He happily nipped at Brianna's fingers. "It's Stetson the second."

Brianna set the dog back down, and everyone in the room had to play with it.

"You look good, Kip," Iris said.

"Feel good. Brianna and I leave tomorrow to go to Hawaii for three weeks."

"That's wonderful," Iris said. "You deserve a long vacation."

Rick, the computer-games enthusiast, edged close to Kip. "I downloaded the working copy of Pandora's new game last night from the Internet."

"You already threw it up there?" Iris asked Kip.

"Just the first level. It's only a prototype, but we wanted to start some buzz."

"Man, it's *awesome!*" Rick enthused. "It blows everything else I've ever seen out of the water. Who would of thought you'd outdo *Suckers.*" He raised his fist. "Banzai!"

Kip grinned. *"Banzai."*

"Banzai?" Iris repeated.

"That's what we decided to name the new game," Kip explained. "It's the least I could do for the kid."

Iris licked frosting from her fingers and studied Kip, wondering if this was an admission that he'd stolen Banzai's algorithm. Deciding to ask him about it in private, she changed the subject. "T. Duke's set up a meeting with McKinney Alitzer's investment banking division and some attorneys today at his office. The additional cash he's pledged to invest will keep the company going."

"I was just over at Pandora," Kip said. "T. Duke's got bean counters taking inventory of the rubber bands, for chrissakes. I met the guy that you and T. Duke brought in to run the place." He shrugged. "He seems okay."

"You like him? You think he's good?" Iris asked hopefully. She didn't need Kip's approval on her decisions regarding Pandora, but preferred to have his support. They were going to be in business together for a long time, and she prayed it wouldn't be an endless battle.

Kip gave her a wry look, as if guessing what was on her mind. "Face it, Iris. I'm not going to like anybody who tries to tell me what to do."

Iris dismally pressed her cake frosting into mush with her fork.

"Don't worry," Kip continued. "I've accepted that the best route for Pandora is to go public. But I still can't bring myself to trust T. Duke."

"To be frank, Kip, I don't trust him, either. His transformation from trying to destroy Pandora to working to position it for an IPO has been a bit remarkable." Iris watched Liz and Brianna playing with the puppy. "But, like he's claimed all along, he's in this to make money. Pandora's in the news again, but this time the press is good. T. Duke claims he's riding the wave into a big payout."

"Pandora has shown it's still on the cutting edge of game technology," Kip added sadly, "thanks in part to my friend, Banzai."

Iris threw away the decimated remains of her cake. "Let's talk in my office. Liz, would you mind keeping Brianna occupied for a few minutes?"

Liz looked up at Iris from where she was crouched on the ground. "Occupied? I'm taking her and the puppy home with me."

Once Kip and Iris were sitting side by side on the couch in her office, she asked the question that had been nagging her. "I'm going to be blunt. Did you steal Banzai's algorithm?"

"I had a feeling you were going to ask me that." Kip crossed his arms and began stroking his eyebrow. "Guess it depends on how you define *steal.* Did I copy it, byte by byte? No. Did I use his approach? Yes. Would I have stumbled on his solution on my own? Maybe. Perhaps the most honest thing to say is that he inspired me to look in a new direction. I'm grateful to him. He bought Pandora time, let us build a new game much faster than we would have otherwise. I'm sorry I treated him so poorly. All he wanted was a job, but I had my head too far up my ass to give him the time of day. If I had, he wouldn't have come into the office like he did, giving Toni more ammunition to use against me." He dropped his hands in his lap and stared at his upturned palms.

"Kip," Iris said quietly, "you can't blame yourself for Banzai's death."

"I know, but I didn't need to be such a prick, either. There are many people I should have treated better, Iris." He shot a glance at her. "Including you."

It was sort of an apology. Iris didn't expect anything more contrite from Kip. She was surprised when he went on.

"I feel especially bad about breaking into your house that night and taking Brianna." He exhaled heavily. "I've got a lot of apologizing to do to my daughter. I wonder if she'll ever forgive me for the way I've behaved this past year."

Iris touched his hand. "She will in time, and if, going forward, you're steady and true and . . . behave yourself. I think it's a great idea, you taking Brianna to Hawaii for three weeks."

"She and I both need some time away. There've been so many things happening so quickly. It hasn't sunk in yet." Kip grew somber. "What it means to . . ." His voice trailed off and he pressed his hands against his eyes. "What it means to live without her." A sob broke free. "How am I going to go on, Iris? I don't know how I'm going to . . ."

His expression of grief brought tears to Iris's eyes. In all the years she'd known Kip, this was the first time she'd seen him cry. She snagged a box of tissues from her desk. "I know, Kip. I've been wondering that myself. What will all of us do without her? There's been so many times I've wanted to call her, ask her . . ."

Kip quickly pulled out a few tissues, wiped his face, then shoved them between the cushions as if to hide them. "But I have to go on. I have to raise our daughter the way Bridget would have. I have to . . ." He paused and laughed ruefully. "I have to stop being such an asshole."

Iris chuckled also at the bald truth. She put his hand between both of hers and squeezed it. "I guess we could all learn from our mistakes and move forward. It was a nutty time. We were all acting crazy." She thought of how close she'd come to seriously injuring Toni. "You were right about one thing: you were doing battle with the boss monster."

Kip's demeanor grew stern. "And Toni's still playing a game. I hear she's trying to cop an insanity plea." He shook his head. "Insane, my ass. She knew exactly what she was doing. She had each step planned. When I ended the affair because Bridget found out, Toni shrugged it off. Very flip. 'Fun while it lasted,' and all that. 'Just a fling.' It *was* a fling, for me. Apparently, it was much more than that for her. Much more than she let on."

"This trail of nightmares was about nothing more than a scorned woman seeking revenge," Iris said. "I knew that conspiracy theory about the Trust Makers and USA Assets was harebrained when I pitched it. But when Toni latched on to it and made such a convincing case, I began to think it was crazy enough to be true. She twisted the facts to suit her. Like her conversation with Jim Platt. He did call Pandora trying to contact me and did talk to her, but he told her he had found no connection between the financing of his films and USA Assets or the Trust Makers."

"When I was released from jail, Toni had to come up with another scenario that diverted suspicion away from her." Kip stared at the carpet. "It conveniently explained both Bridget's and Alexa Platt's murders."

"Bridget, Alexa, Banzai, and Summer. Four murders committed by a woman desperate to be taken seriously."

"And Toni won't confess to a single one," Kip added.

"Fortunately, in Toni's apartment, the police found black sweats that match the fibers found on the bushes near the steps. No bloody flip-flops, but they found a drop of dried blood on her living room carpet. The police are testing the DNA now. It's bound to be Bridget's blood. The police have verified that Toni was at the movies the night of Bridget's murder, like she claimed, but the alibi's flimsy. That old movie theater has a back exit."

Outside her office door, Iris saw Brianna, Liz, and the puppy gleefully playing with a ball of paper. She continued the grisly inventory of crimes. "The police will be able to prove that the bullets the masked person shot at me at Summer's bungalow match the gun that Toni had on the hillside—assuming they find it underneath the mud."

"Poor Summer. She was a bit dimwitted but she didn't deserve that. Honey, be careful with the puppy," Kip warned Brianna. "A witness has come forward who saw Banzai and Toni near the staircase around the time of Banzai's murder."

"That was a bit of luck. There's evidence tying Toni to all the murders—"

Kip finished the sentence. "Except Alexa Platt's."

"That's the piece I don't understand. I guess Toni could have followed Bridget to the park. Maybe Toni lured Alexa back into the woods after Bridget left. Maybe something Alexa said made Toni mad. Alexa wasn't one for subtlety. Maybe Toni spilled her plans for you and Bridget, then realized what she had done." Iris sighed. "But it's still goosey. You'd think with the deck stacked against Toni the way it is, she'd just confess to everything."

"She's still playing the game, Iris. She will never confess." Kip looked at his watch and stood. "We'd better go."

Iris stood as well. "You have a house sitter while you're in Hawaii?"

Kip couldn't help but laugh at Iris's piercing expression. "Yes, I do. A retired couple, you'll be pleased to know. I'd appreciate it if you'd check in on them."

* * *

Baines unlocked San Somis's thick glass front door and stepped back to let Iris in. "Miss Thorne."

"Baines."

They wordlessly walked across the ground floor between the antique automobiles and entered the elevator. At the top, Baines stepped aside to let Iris out first. He opened the door to the outer office, then the door to T. Duke's office, and finally the conference room door. Inside that oval room, a group of men were gathered at one end of the large table. They were laughing jovially and did not notice when Iris came in.

"Here's another one for you," T. Duke said. "What do women and condoms have in common?" He crookedly smiled before delivering the punch line. "They both spend more time in your wallet than on your dick."

The room erupted with laughter. T. Duke slapped his thigh, turned on his heel, and spotted Iris. "Uh-oh. I had no idea a lady was in the room." He walked toward her with his hand outstretched. "Please forgive the ribald humor."

He grabbed her arm and led her into the room with his other hand on her back. "Gentlemen, here's the lady of the day! For those of you who haven't yet had the pleasure, I'm most pleased to introduce you to Iris Thorne. I'll bet you never saw more grit in a prettier package."

He turned to Iris. "That incident in the mud with the house . . ." He guffawed and slapped his thigh again. "Just slays me every time I think of it. Let me introduce you. You already know Pandora's own Today Rhea and Mick Ha."

Iris waved at Today and Mick, who were sitting in front of a keyboard and computer monitor at the end of the table.

T. Duke introduced everyone else. There were handshakes and pleasantries.

"Today's been showing us Pandora's next release, *Banzai,* and we're all impressed. Word in the marketplace is good. We anticipate *Banzai* breaking all records, continuing Pandora's winning streak. These men here are convinced that an IPO will make Pandora's stockholders very wealthy."

"Music to my ears."

"Guys, make room for the lady." T. Duke maneuvered Iris through the group. Someone got up to give her the chair next to Today, closest to the monitor. Normally, the chivalry would have irked her, but today, she was enjoying it.

As T. Duke pulled out the chair for her, he whispered in her ear, "Don't worry, Iris. Getting into business with me is like lying down with an old dog, but I'll make sure you don't wake up with fleas."

"Okay, this is the deal," Today said. "With this engine, we get crystal-clear graphics without taking a speed hit." His fingers ran across the keyboard. "Ignore this. It's that loop. Crap! I thought I'd fixed that."

"Lather, rinse, repeat," Mick said, citing the instructions for an infinite loop found on any bottle of shampoo.

As Today demonstrated the new game, Iris let her eyes drift to the trompe l'oeil painting on the ceiling. A cloud still remained over Evan's face.

Epilogue

Iris parked the Triumph in the sand-and-packed-dirt parking lot of Coldwater Canyon Park next to a Jaguar convertible. She got out of the car, turned her face toward the sun, and deeply breathed the rain-washed air. She fingered the gash Evan had cut in the Triumph's ragtop and made a promise to the car that had been with her through so much. "Tomorrow, you're going for a complete checkup at the mechanic's, then I'll have you detailed inside and out."

She put on her sunglasses and turned, meeting the gaze of a khaki-uniformed groundskeeper who was standing a few yards away holding a rake. She knew immediately that he was the man Bridget had described. He gave Iris the creeps too. It was nothing she could put her finger on, which made the feeling all the more compelling. Alexa Platt's face popped into her head and Iris shivered. *If only there was proof,* she said to herself.

Instead of slinking away, she was assertive. "Hi! How are ya? Beautiful day, isn't it?"

He mumbled something or nothing in response and disappeared behind a toolshed.

Iris anxiously looked around, checking her watch a few times.

"Darn him." She grew edgy waiting and quickly walked into the canyon while the groundskeeper was still out of view. Along the way, she picked up a heavy stick and used it as a staff. It was the middle of a Friday afternoon. Birds sang. A light breeze rustled the leaves and tree branches. She relaxed slightly, deeply inhaling and exhaling, as if filling her lungs with fresh air would wash away everything that had happened.

She glanced behind her before rounding another bend. She was still alone. Shortly she reached a large pine tree growing in a deep ravine; its branches extended almost across the path. Behind the tree, she spotted a pair of tennis shoes and jeans-clad legs. She scampered down the steep hillside, using the stick to keep from sliding. As she rounded the tree, she saw Jim Platt sitting with his back against the trunk, holding a pine branch, slowly turning it in front of his eyes. "I thought I might find you here," she said to him.

Platt continued turning the branch and spoke without looking at her. "There are still raindrops on the needles. Look at how the light reflects off the water."

Iris crouched next to him, not wanting to sit on the damp ground. She picked up a twig and drew an aimless pattern in the dirt. "I was surprised when you suggested meeting at the park."

"It was time. I'm glad I came. I thought it would be ugly, but it actually gives me a sense of closure. It's peaceful. I can see why Alexa loved it." He set the branch on the ground. "Even though we may never find out what happened to her."

"Toni might confess in time."

"Does it matter? The woman's bound to spend the rest of her life in jail, even if she isn't sent there for my wife's murder."

"I still wonder about that groundskeeper. Did you see him?"

"Yeah."

Iris drew concentric circles in the dirt and sighed with despair. "It makes me so mad. Someone has to be held accountable."

Platt got up and brushed the wet leaves and pine needles from his pants. "Alexa's still gone. Nothing will bring her back."

Iris stood as well, painfully, still suffering the effects of her mud fight with Toni.

Platt looked at his watch. "I don't have time for lunch. I've got to catch a plane. Apologize to your friend for me."

Iris walked with him down the path toward the park entrance. He extended his hand. She took it. He was much changed from the first time she'd met him.

"Take care." Platt got into the Jaguar Alexa had been driving the day she was murdered and drove off.

Iris leaned against the Triumph. The groundskeeper had resumed raking a short distance away and occasionally cast glances at her. She was glad when a nondescript white sedan pulled into the lot. Garland had barely got out of the rental car when she flung herself on him, her knees around his waist. He spun her around. She shrieked with abandon.

When he stopped, he noticed she had tears in her eyes. "What's wrong?" he asked, alarmed.

"Nothing." She smiled. She wiped the tears and they were gone. "I'm just glad to see you."

He hugged her tightly. "Wasn't Alexa's husband meeting us here?"

"He had to leave."

"You want to take a walk before we have lunch?"

She nodded and put her arm around his waist. "Hopefully, by the time I get home, they will have bulldozed the mud from the street in front of my house."

"That mudslide stopped just in time."

"I think I've used up a couple of my nine lives."

"Save at least one for me."

She squeezed him more tightly as they walked with their arms around each other.

"I can't get over this weather," Garland said. "It was snowing in New York. I think I could get used to living in California."

"Really?"

He shrugged. "Once both the kids are in college."

"Oh," she breathed, almost with relief. "That's at least two years away, huh?"

He seemed bewildered. "I thought you wanted us to be together . . . don't you?"

"I *do,*" she insisted. "It's exactly what I wanted."

"And that's the problem, right?" He tickled her.

"Well," she yelped, suspecting he was starting to know her too well. "I'm kind of enjoying things the way they are."

"I'll admit this long-distance relationship has been romantic, sexy, passionate . . ." He nuzzled her neck and she giggled. "But it's not real life."

"I know." She smiled crookedly. "Isn't it wonderful?"

